M
Christilian Christilian, J. D.
Scarlet women

	DATE DUE		

MYNDERSE LIBRARY

Seneca Falls, N.Y.

Scarlet Women

ScarletWomen

a novel by

J.D. Christilian

DONALD I. FINE BOOKS

New York

DONALD I. FINE BOOKS
Published by the Penguin Group
Penguin Books USA Inc., 375 Hudson Street,
New York, New York 10014, U.S.A.
Penguin Books Ltd, 27 Wrights Lane,
London W8 5TZ, England
Penguin Books Australia Ltd, Ringwood,
Victoria, Australia
Penguin Books Canada Ltd, 10 Alcorn Avenue,
Toronto, Ontario, Canada M4V 3B2
Penguin Books (N.Z.) Ltd, 182–190 Wairau Road,
Auckland 10, New Zealand

Penguin Books Ltd, Registered Offices:
Harmondsworth, Middlesex, England

Published in 1996 by Donald I. Fine Books
an imprint of Penguin Books USA Inc.

ISBN 1-55611-475-3

Printed in the United States of America

Some conflicting opinions expressed during America's Victorian period, in the second half of the nineteenth century, concerning its troubling "Woman Question":

"Let no woman deceive herself. The wages of sin is death."

—JAMES D. McCABE

"I have an inalienable, constitutional, and natural right to love whom I may, to love as long or short a period as I can, to change the love story every day if I please, and neither you nor any law you can frame have the right to interfere."

—VICTORIA WOODHULL

"At present man, in his affection for and kindness toward the weaker sex, is disposed to accord her any number of privileges. Beyond that there seems to him to be something which is unnatural in permitting her to share the turmoil, the excitement, the risks of competition."

—THE NEW YORK *HERALD*

"A woman's sphere seems to me just what she can fill, and I don't see why Charlotte Corday had not as good a right to a dagger as Brutus, although I have no doubt she may have been missed in the kitchen."

—ELLEN STURGES HOOPER

One

The day had been abnormally hot for early winter, with the sun blazing from a cloudless sky. It had melted patches of snow in the city's cobbled, congested streets, leaving muddy pools for the horse-drawn traffic to splash through, dirtying the trousers and pavement-sweeping skirts of pedestrians. It had also heated the waters surrounding the City of New York—which in late 1871 was still confined to Manhattan and a few much smaller islands near it.

After the sun set, however, the air temperature dropped sharply, and mist began rising from the surface of the warmed rivers and bay. By eight that night the mist was so thick that vessels entering and leaving the port under sail and steam power—the ocean and river ships, the tugs, barges and canal boats—could no longer see each other's lights at a safe distance.

Adding to the danger was Manhattan's lack of any bridge or tunnel connection to the New Jersey mainland, to Long Island or to the independent City of Brooklyn. All traffic between them moved by water, via twenty-three different ferry routes. On this night all of the ferryboats, carrying passengers, wagons and carriages back and forth, were as near invisible as the other vessels groping blindly past each other. Disasters were averted, narrowly, only by all of this shipping proceeding dead slow and filling the night with clanging bells and blaring foghorns.

The mist shrouding the lights out on the water did the same to the gas lamps along the waterfront. In this dark pea soup they reflected back upon themselves, revealing nothing a few yards away. Even within those few yards, their diffused glare merely created hallucinatory pools of shadow and half-light.

These were the nights that provided optimum working conditions for the myriad gangs of river pirates that infested America's greatest harbor.

New York City was still a bumptious, undersized infant compared to the great European capitals of London and Paris. But in the New World it had become the most important and populous of all cities, bursting its britches with a precocious adolescent's powerhouse energy. The Erie Canal, connecting the Great Lakes to the Hudson River, had made it the natural transfer point for merchandise imported and exported between the Midwest, the Atlantic seaboard and Europe. New York was a city of enormous, ostentatious wealth, cheek-by-jowl with abysmal, degrading poverty. The pirates came out of the latter to plunder the former.

A social worker named Charles Brace had warned the rich of this, when vainly trying to persuade them to invest some of their money in helping the children of the poor: "Why should the street rat, as the police call him—the boy whose home in sweet childhood was a box or a deserted cellar; whose food was crumbs begged or bread stolen; whose influences were kicks, curses and destitution—why should he feel himself under any of the restraints of civilization? Those too negligent to notice them as children will be fully aware of them as men, embittered at the wealth and luxuries they never shared. They will poison society and wrest back, with bloody and criminal hands, what the world was too careless or too selfish to give."

River pirates were some of those street rats, now grown and using nights like this to "wrest back" what they'd never had.

The harbor police were being extra vigilant as they patroled the waterfronts of the East River and the Hudson in their rowboats, their rifles and revolvers ready for swift use. River pirates never gave up without a fight when caught looting a ship or dockside warehouse. They were as heavily armed as the police, and ready to add murder to burglary if trapped. A running gun battle was the norm when pirates tried to escape in their own rowboat and police tried to catch them before they vanished into the dark maze of shipping and piers.

Over the past few years the casualty rate between police and pirates, in dead and wounded, was about even.

Shortly after midnight a patrol boat was prowling in and out among the blurred shapes of the wharves along East Street, near

Corlears Hook. The bow man shone his bull's-eye lantern underneath the piers while the men at the oars and tiller scanned the decks of vessels crowding the docks. The percentage of paddlewheel steamers had increased every year since the Civil War. But sailing ships still predominated: their bowsprits jutting like giant spears halfway over East Street, their masts, spars and rigging forming a leafless forest all along the riverfront. The patrol boat had turned into a narrow water passage between a river steamboat and an old trans-Atlantic square-rigger, when its officers heard a familiar signal. The staccato rapping of a police baton on the paving of a nearby street: a shoreside patrolman calling for assistance.

Within seconds two men from the police boat, Clancy and Riordan, were scrambling up a pier ladder. As they ran across the quay they drew revolvers from their hip pockets and unfastened their long night-sticks, the formidable clubs that the underworld called "locusts."

Guided by the rapping signal, they turned into Broome Street, and from that into Mangin. The glow of a lantern on the cobbles there showed the crouching figure of a Thirteenth Precinct patrolman named Costello, drumming a repetitive pattern with his club. His other hand held a revolver aimed at the side door of a narrow, three-floor warehouse. As soon as he saw Clancy and Riordan, Costello hung his stick back on the belt of his long blue overcoat, picked up the lantern and straightened up with it.

"I been checking the doors around here every night," he told them quickly and quietly, and gestured at the door he was watching. "Somebody's busted the locks on that one. If we're lucky, maybe they're still inside."

Riordan nodded eagerly. "Let's have a look."

Clancy pushed the door open and Costello led the way with his lantern. Wharf rats scurried away from its beam as the three men went through a timber-roofed passage that led them to a small inner courtyard. A wooden crate with French language markings lay on its side there. One corner of it had broken and was leaking fluid onto the old bricks paving the courtyard. Riordan crouched and sniffed.

"Liquor," he whispered.

Two doors led off the courtyard. One hung wide open. They

tried that one first, and found themselves inside a storeroom half-filled with stacks of similar crates. Some of the stacks were much lower than others. Two were partly overturned. By the light of Costello's lantern, they explored between the stacks. The thieves were gone—from this room, at least. But there was another door, partly open, at the far end of the storeroom.

Moving cautiously, the police trio advanced through it and Costello flashed his lantern around the room on the other side. It was a small office. There was a rolltop desk, two chairs and a large safe that was still locked and didn't appear to have been tampered with. They didn't find any of the thieves in there, either.

What they did find, finally, was a woman with a well-rounded figure in a green velvet ballgown that bared her shapely shoulders and arms and that appeared to be new and of excellent quality. She was sprawled face down on the rough floorboards behind the desk. There was an ugly lump on the back of her head. Blood had seeped from it in her tangle of yellow hair. But not enough to account for the dark pool that spread from under her head and torso.

Clancy grimaced and bent to turn her over. The body rolled stiffly, and when she was on her back Riordan turned away and vomited against the side of the safe.

Her eyes were partly open, peering up at them with no expression at all. Not shock, nor fear, nor anger. Nothing. She had the delicately painted face of an upper-class harlot, and the plump upper rounds of her breasts bulged from the gown's low-cut bodice with no lace insert to provide the usual modesty veil. She appeared to be younger than thirty, and she might have been quite pretty in life. But one could no longer be sure of that, because the blood that soaked the front of her gown and torso had also mixed with her makeup to form a hideous mask.

Someone had inserted the point of a knife deep into her throat, below one ear, and ripped it across, keeping it deep, all the way to her other ear.

Two

It was the next afternoon when Vance Barclay Walburton alighted from a hansom cab in front of the massive Egyptian columns that gave the city's main holding prison its popular name: the Tombs.

There were almost four hundred men, women and children in its cells that day, awaiting trials or sentencing. Plus a few awaiting their final walk across the inner courtyard's "Bridge of Sighs" to the gallows. But Walburton, though he was a lawyer, had no business with any of them; he had never been inside the Tombs in his life, and he didn't expect to have any reason to visit it in the future.

The law practice he had inherited from his late father and uncle confined itself to handling estates and investments for some of New York's distinguished families. Walburton himself came of such a family. He was scrupulous about refusing to represent the Johnnies-come-lately who were getting rich via dubious land speculation, railroad company manipulations and corrupt politics. It was true that he did not shrink from representing certain people who had vastly increased their wealth through profiteering during the Civil War—as long as they belonged to New York's old guard. If part of his mind sensed hypocrisy in this, he was not consciously aware of it. He kept that part of his mind under permanent lock and key—and contented himself with the certainty that none of *his* clientele were likely to ever find themselves inside the Tombs.

Walburton had told the cab driver to bring him to this address because it was less embarrassing to him than his actual destination on the other side of Centre Street.

It was for this same reason that he had not come in his own carriage. His coachman might gossip with the other servants. Or his carriage might be recognized by some chance passerby of his own class who would wonder, with raised eyebrow, at his purpose here. One had to be so careful, at all times, to do or say nothing to give his patrician circle reason to question one's adherence to its social, financial and moral taboos.

None of these taboos applied to the lower classes, of course. Those people, lacking breeding, could not be expected to behave properly, and their ways were best ignored. But among their own, New York's uppercrust was more "Victorian" than Victorian London—and proud of it. London might wink at the unsavory goings on of certain rakes among its nobility. New York's cabal of top families never winked.

One's position in society depended on a combination of three essentials: genealogy, money and moral rectitude. Lack of a distinguished background could sometimes be overcome, if you were rich enough, by marrying your children into one of society's established families. Lack of adequate funds might be tolerated in someone descended from one of the older families that had originated society's traditions, if that person had the good taste to be inconspicuous and not flaunt his frayed cuffs. Unseemly behavior, if allowed to surface and attract attention, was social death.

Vance Barclay Walburton's family tree was impressive. His financial inheritance made it obvious that he didn't need the income from his law practice: that it was merely a praiseworthy means of occupying himself at something useful but not too demanding. And no breath of scandal had ever threatened to tarnish his reputation.

Until now.

Walburton waited until the cab's driver cracked his whip over his horse and pulled away, cutting in ahead of two utterly exhausted horses dragging an overloaded streetcar along its tracks. Then he glanced up and down the crowded street, trying to be casual about it, as though he wasn't looking for anything in particular. He was a handsome man of forty-six, dressed with expensive sobriety, his side whiskers neatly trimmed, without the luxuriant fullness favored by some. His silk top-hat rested squarely on his head, without the slightest hint of rakish tilt. Nevertheless, he pretended to straighten it a bit while he made sure there was no one in sight whom he knew. Finally, he looked across the street at his destination.

It took up the ground floor of a dingy three-floor building. A vast sign—HOWE & HUMMEL LAW OFFICES—made sure that nobody charged with a crime could miss it while being conducted into the Tombs.

William Howe and Abe Hummel were not attorneys of Walburton's kind. The nearest approach to respectable persons among their clientele were some newspaper owners and many theater people. Walburton's circle did not consider journalism a respectable profession; and the morals of even the most illustrious opera singers, actors and musicians had to be suspect. One might invite a famous performer to one's home, to amuse one's proper guests, but one never actually associated with them.

The bulk of the Howe & Hummel clients, however, were thieves, murderers, hoodlums, gamblers, prostitutes and other members of the city's teeming underworld. It was the firm's ability to win acquittals for obviously guilty clients that was rapidly making it one of the richer firms in New York. Certainly it was the city's most cynical and disreputable. Much of its success was rumored to be the result of bribing judges and juries. On top of that there was Howe & Hummel's growing practice of blackmail—in the form of threatened breach-of-promise suits by young women against gentlemen who could not afford to have their reputations besmirched.

Everyone knew that many men of the very best families—young or old, married or single—were vulnerable to liaisons with scarlet women. That was to be expected in a society where virtuous women were not supposed to have sexual drive and men regrettably did. As long as these affairs were handled with the utmost discretion, society could pretend not to know. Quite a number of these men had paid Howe & Hummel large amounts to keep their moral lapses from being exposed in open court.

It was a wonder that Howe and Hummel had not already been disbarred for such practices. Vance Walburton could not agree with the distinguished jurist, a candidate for the Supreme Court, who opposed disbarment proceedings because that odious pair "contribute a bit of amusement to our dry calling." Walburton had never met either partner; but he detested what the men stood for.

Walburton resisted an impulse to raise his ebony walking stick and hail another cab to carry him away. He acknowledged himself prone to certain private faults; but cowardice, he hoped, was not one of them. Besides, he could think of nowhere else he could go to for the kind of help he now required. After a last check on the people around him, he started across Centre Street.

Crossing any of the wider streets of New York was not easy when circulation was heavy. There were no enforced traffic laws. You had to be nimble to avoid being run over in the clattering chaos of cabs and private carriages, streetcars and omnibuses, freight wagons and brewery drays. At the same time you had to be alert to avoid stepping into the reeking piles of droppings left by the thousands of horses pulling all these vehicles. But, like all veteran New Yorkers, high and low, Walburton was adept at coping with these tactical hazards. He reached the other side unscathed and with his boots unsullied.

The note he had sent by messenger to Howe, the elder partner, had begged for this meeting to be and remain secret. The cordial message he'd gotten in return had told him how to reach Howe's office without being seen by anyone in the waiting room. Angling away from the entrance under the Howe & Hummel sign, he went around the corner into Leonard Street and rapped his cane against an unmarked door.

Both of the partners had once been pointed out to him at Delmonico's. So he recognized the coatless fellow who opened the door to him as William Howe, and was not startled by the vulgar flamboyance of his appearance.

The man was very large and fat and ablaze with diamonds. Clusters of them dangled from the gold watch-chain across a satin vest of atrocious purple, and adorned the big stickpin jutting from his carmine red silk cravat. His shirt had diamond studs and cufflinks, and three more sparkled on his plump fingers.

Even Howe's face seemed part of the theatricality: a florid, meaty slab sporting three different shades of hair. The bristling hair atop his head was gray, the jutting eyebrows black, and the flaring mustache white. It seemed a face fashioned for scowling. But his smile was warm as he took Walburton's elbow and drew him inside a windowless brick corridor lit only by the small kerosene lamp in Howe's other hand. He shut and locked the door as he said, with apparent sincerity, "Mr. Walburton, this is indeed an honor and a pleasure."

There was a trace of British accent. Reminding Walburton of rumors that Howe had long ago fled England one jump ahead of the police, changing his identity to adopt a new life and career in America.

Brick dust crunched under their boots as Howe led the way. It was a long time since anyone had cleaned this back exit. Howe opened a door at the other end, snuffed the lantern, hung it from a wall hook and ushered Walburton into his office.

Howe & Hummel obviously didn't spend much of its ill-gotten income on trying to impress anyone. Howe's office was furnished with items that appeared to have been bought from second-hand shops. Two desks with mismatched swivel chairs. A pair of visitors' armchairs with faded leather padding. An old armoire. A basic Chatwood office safe. A pot-bellied coal stove that gave off just enough heat to keep out the winter chill. The room was lit by two dusty overhanging gas lamps, the single window having been shuttered against the daylight in deference to Walburton's request for privacy.

Abe Hummel stepped in from an adjoining office as Howe shut the door to the rear corridor. It would have been hard to imagine a greater contrast to Howe than his partner. Hummel was a small man, delicately thin, two decades younger than Howe but almost entirely bald, with a receding chin that accented the thrust of his large nose. Unlike Howe, he wore a frock coat, fashionably tailored in the best of taste and properly buttoned; and it, like his waistcoat and trousers, was a solemn black.

There was nothing solemn, however, about Hummel's eyes. They glittered with humor and curiosity as he and Walburton acknowledged each other with brief nods.

That there was an exceptional mind at work behind those eyes, Walburton did not doubt. It was known throughout the legal profession that Hummel had joined Howe's firm as a lowly errand boy, the son of Jewish immigrants in the slums east of the Bowery. He had become Howe's apprentice in less than one year, and achieved full partnership in three.

Howe gestured to one of the visitor chairs. "Please, sir, make yourself comfortable."

Walburton sat down, stiff-backed, leaning his cane against one of the chair's arms, removing his hat and holding it his knees, resisting an urge to bolt. Howe had settled his bulk into the swivel chair behind one of the desks. Hummel leaned against the other desk and folded his arms across his meager chest. With that nose and his black garb, he reminded Walburton of Poe's Raven, about to croak "Nevermore."

Howe's smile was benign. "Well, Mr. Walburton, how may we be of service to you?"

Walburton hesitated. "It is an exceedingly delicate matter . . ." he began, and then hesitated again, questioning once more the wisdom of confiding in men like these.

Hummel read his hesitation accurately. "You're not at ease with us," he said with restrained courtesy. "Perhaps you have been listening to unpleasant stories circulated by the stuffed shirts of our profession?"

"There *are* certain rumors," Walburton admitted.

Howe managed to look mildly astonished. "Such as?"

Walburton didn't feel this was a time to mention bribery and blackmail. "I have also heard certain reassuring things," he said. "There is, for example, the general belief that matters revealed to you in confidence go no further."

"Well, that's certainly true," Howe said. "But that applies to everyone in our profession. As a fellow lawyer, you know that. None of us could expect to do much business if potential clients were afraid secrets they told us might get bruited about."

Abe Hummel unfolded his skinny arms and clapped his hands together once softly, as though marking an end to preliminary courtesies. "Now then, Mr. Walburton—your delicate problem?"

Three

Vance Walburton was abruptly impatient with himself. Genteel last-moment reticence in the face of a distasteful necessity might not be unbecoming in a well-bred woman. It was for a man who prided himself on his strength of character.

"Late last night," he began in a tone he kept quietly firm, "a woman was found murdered in a warehouse near the East Street docks. The warehouse had been broken into and valuable goods stolen. The police assume that the dead woman was associated with the thieves, went along during the burglary and was killed by one or more of them for some reason unknown. Perhaps simply a drunken quarrel. At any rate, the police contacted me in the hope that I might be able to shed some light on what happened to her. I could not, of course."

"You were associated with this woman?" Howe asked, gently.

"Certainly not. The woman was the sort who is known to the police. A part-time prostitute, apparently. She may have also occasionally been employed as an actress, in a small way."

Walburton refrained from voicing his opinion that most actresses, and certainly all of the minor ones, were not much of a cut above prostitutes. He didn't want to anger Abe Hummel, whose passionate love of the theater and anyone associated with it was well known.

In contradiction to their appearances, it was the flashy Bill Howe who was supposed to be totally devoted to home, wife and children. Little Abe Hummel was the gay bachelor-about-town, out most nights at the theater or opera or some party of stage personalities, and usually accompanied by a bevy of pretty girls who were actresses "in a small way." The sort of girls for whom the Howe &

Hummel firm prepared its charges of "seduction under promise of marriage"—claiming that any well-off man who tampered with the affections of a poor girl at least owed her some monetary compensation as "heart balm."

"According to the police," Walburton continued, "the murdered woman's name was Alice Curry. A name which meant nothing to me. But I agreed to go along and have a look at her corpse. I can assure you, as I did the police, that I have never seen the woman before in my life."

"What led the police to contact you concerning her?" Hummel asked, with those glittering eyes fixed on Walburton's expression.

"The clothes she was wearing. An evening gown and two petticoats that belonged to my wife. Her name, Mrs. Vance Barclay Walburton, was sewed inside them, by the dressmaker who often sews my wife's garments."

"Ah," Hummel said, putting no particular meaning into that single word.

"I told the police that I was not too surprised. That my wife often gives garments to charitable organizations, and that one of those must have passed on the gown and petticoats to this unfortunate female."

Bill Howe had leaned back in his swivel chair, regarding the ceiling. Howe's talents were not confined to being a persuasive bag of courtroom wind: he had an ear for the slightest nuance in the voice of a witness. Returning his gaze to Walburton, he said mildly, "But what you told the police was not exactly true?"

"No," Walburton admitted. He hesitated one last time. This was getting to the hard part. "The truth is, I cannot imagine how that woman happened to be in possession of my wife's clothing."

"What does your wife say about it?"

"I explained to Captain Redpath—the commander of the precinct where the burglary and murder occurred—that my wife is presently touring Europe. That she has never been much of a letter writer, and as I don't know exactly where she might be at this time, there is no way I could contact her about this sordid matter. Even if there were any reason to do so. Captain Redpath agreed with me that there is *no* reason. As far as he is concerned, the fact that my wife contributes garments to charity is explanation enough, and satisfies him that there is no connection of any kind between the dead woman and me or my wife."

Neither Howe nor Hummel said anything to that. They looked at him and waited.

"It is true that I don't know exactly where my wife is," Walburton told them. "But the reason is that she left me more than two months ago. I haven't seen her since."

"Ah," Hummel said again. "There's your delicate problem."

Walburton kept a resolute grip on his expression and tone. "She did sail off to England, and may have gone on to the continent. But about three weeks ago I received a short letter from her saying that she has still not decided whether to return to me, or finally to make a different life for herself. Asking me to allow her more time, and not to look for her. That letter was mailed from this city. So she is back. And I am naturally worried by the fact that the dead woman was found wearing things belonging to her."

Howe said, "You discount entirely the possibility that your wife may have donated those garments to charity?"

"Whatever my wife's failings, she is a thrifty woman. When she tires of a garment she has the material used for some other purpose. The dress this prostitute was wearing was almost new. My wife wore it only once before . . . before our separation."

"What is it you want of us?" Howe asked.

"I want you to find out how this murdered woman came in possession of my wife's clothing. I know you have extensive contacts among the criminal circles in this city, and can make inquiries without attracting public attention to their purpose. I cannot envisage any sort of connection my wife could have with a prostitute and a gang of thieves. But if there is one, it would mean my wife is in trouble and I must find and help her."

"There's probably no connection at all," Hummel said. "The most likely explanation would be that your wife's things were stolen—by this gang of thieves. I suppose you've considered that."

"I have," Walburton said. "And I agree. Almost certainly that is all there is to it. But—I must be *sure* of that."

Howe nodded thoughtfully. "Have you attempted to find your wife before this?"

"No. She asked me not to, and I have respected that. Until now.

Also, how could I make inquiries about her without stirring up embarrassing gossip among our acquaintances?''

"You people are always inviting each other to dinners," Hummel said. "Over the past few months surely some of your friends have noticed your wife wasn't with you any more."

"They know she went off to tour Europe. I have told no one that she is back. I am sure some people suspect that my wife and I have had strains in our relationship. Such as arise between many if not most couples from time to time. Such strains are normal, and are accepted as such. Unless they lead to divorce or some other form of scandal. I must be certain you understand: your investigation must be conducted in such a way that no one I know gets any hint that something is wrong. That means that no one in my circle must be approached. Not even through their domestics."

Neither partner voiced what both thought: that fear of scandal —of the sort that would surface if Walburton's wife *had* gotten herself involved with criminals—was at least part of the reason he was desperate to find her now.

Abe Hummel regarded Walburton with a certain measure of sympathy—as one of those unfortunates trained from birth to fit into an emotionally stunted clan that understood nothing outside its own distorted set of values and vanities. A man for whom "respectability" had become a narcotic as potent as opium, as difficult to break free of, and as prone to pervert one's true nature and relationship with the rest of the world.

Bill Howe saw Walburton more simply: as a client who could pay the firm top dollar to help him avoid being humiliated before his peers. "Why," he asked, "did your wife leave you?"

"As I've told you," Walburton replied stiffly, "there were certain strains between us. Of an intimate nature, which I do not care to discuss."

"If she ran off with another man," Hummel said, "anything you know about him would help in locating her."

"There is no other man." Walburton paused, frowning. "I am quite sure not. I think the problems were entirely in her imagination. An imagination overheated by the sensational trash English novelists—especially the female variety—have been turning out over the past decade. As well as their translations of unhealthy works by decadent French authors."

"It sounds," Howe said, "as if your wife has a taste for the romantic."

"Of the most insidious sort, in books. *Lady Audley's Secret. Great Expectations. The Lady of the Camellias.* That sort of thing. Stimulation for the instincts, rather than the mind. Calculated to inflame female passions and make the responsible conduct of a normal, fastidious family life seem boring by comparison. Unfortunately my wife is vulnerable to such undesirable influences, being subject to nervous weakness of a female nature—"

Walburton stopped himself abruptly. Both partners understood what he was shying from. Menstrual disorders were prevalent among genteel women of that time; but they were the most taboo subject of all. Decent people never mentioned the shameful "curse of Eve"; except perhaps to one's physician, and even then only obliquely.

"I tried to break her of her habit of reading such trash," Walburton finished lamely. "But she would not obey me. My efforts only upset her more."

"Is there anyone you know of," Hummel asked him, "that your wife may have contacted since her return from Europe? A close friend, or a relative?"

"No. I don't believe so. Or I would have heard." Walburton looked away from Hummel to Howe, whose expression he found more sympathetic. "Will you try to find her for me—find out how the murdered woman came in possession of her clothes?"

"Yes, of course. It may require a great deal of effort, though. I'm sure you realize that will have to be reflected in our fees."

Walburton's mouth hardened. "How much?"

"For ourselves, professional courtesy between fellow attorneys dictates that we ask only a token fee. But the man we would use to conduct the actual investigation does not come cheaply. And there are others he will have to bribe, in order to obtain essential information—"

"I believe I have made the point," Walburton cut in, "that I don't want other people learning the reason for this inquiry."

"That would be known only to this one man whom we would use. If you'll reflect for a moment, you will see that without this knowledge he could not accomplish what you want. But he is an unusual person. I can safely say that he is probably the living grave of more secrets than any other citizen of our fair city. You may rest assured, if he has reason to contact you, that nothing you tell him in confidence will reach anyone else—not even Mr. Hummel and myself.''

Walburton considered this and gave a reluctant nod of acceptance. "How much?" he repeated firmly.

"Let's say just two thousand dollars at this point. If more is required later, we will let you know."

Walburton stared at Howe. A factory workman earned between one and two dollars for a full day's work. A "sewing girl" who worked at home got seven cents for each shirt she finished. You could buy a three-pound chicken for fifty cents, hire a full-time cook for eighteen dollars a month and a live-in nursemaid for less. Two thousand dollars was a bit more than a police captain's annual salary; for that amount a family could rent a three-story house in a decent neighborhood—or one of the new luxury apartments on lower Fifth Avenue, complete with three bedrooms, bathroom, butler's pantry, parlor and dining room.

"That is hardly," Walburton said bitingly, "what one would consider a token fee."

Howe's smile was amiable. "Many men of your class import Paris gowns for their wives at prices of close to one thousand dollars apiece. Perhaps you have not—but I assume you could afford to. Am I wrong?"

Walburton exercised restraint. "Very well. Agreed. I will pay you half to begin with. The other half when you can tell me what has happened to my wife."

"We don't work that way, Mr. Walburton. The two thousand up front."

"You don't trust me to pay the second half?"

"It is not a matter of trust," Howe explained calmly. "Suppose you were to die before the second half was due? Of a sudden illness or an unfortunate accident? After we had gone to the trouble and expense of finding out what you wish to know?"

"Can you?" Walburton demanded.

"Probably."

"Very well, then. I am not accustomed to haggling, Mr. Howe. I'll make out the check."

Walburton was reaching for his checkbook when Abe Hummel

spoke up: "We deal only in cash here, Mr. Walburton. No checks, no written contracts. No records for busybodies to pry into."

Walburton looked at Hummel with distaste. "I can't get cash from the bank until tomorrow morning. I assume you will start when I place the money into your hands?"

"No, we'll start now. Immediately." Hummel grinned at him. "You see, we do trust you."

Howe nodded gravely. "Now then, some basic facts. What was your wife's maiden name?"

A bit discomfited by Hummel's grin, Walburton returned his attention to Howe. "Olivia Bixby. Old friends usually call her Livvy."

"A photograph of her would be most helpful."

"I brought one with me." Walburton took it from his pocket and placed it on Howe's desk. It was a cardboard-framed head-and-shoulders portrait, taken in the studio of a professional photographer.

Howe studied it admiringly. "My congratulations, Mr. Walburton," he said, without a hint of irony, "Your wife is a most handsome young woman. When was this taken?"

"Last year."

"Then she won't have changed much in looks. She appears to be in her late twenties?"

"Olivia had her twenty-seventh birthday four months ago."

"How long have you and Mrs. Walburton been married?"

"Eight years."

"So she was nineteen when your marriage took place. Children?"

"No." Walburton forced himself to say the distasteful words: "Olivia was . . . in a family way, once. But she lost the child before it was born. She took it badly."

"Did you?"

Walburton looked startled and offended. "Of course."

Hummel took over from Howe: "Separated from you, your wife must have a source of money to live on. Does she have a bank account in her name, or access to yours?"

"Olivia has a comfortable inheritance, which is managed for her by the same bank that I deal with. But I do *not* want any inquiries being made there. The bank's manager is definitely one

of the people I do not want knowing about this inquiry. Make
certain your man follows my wishes on this.''

"We'll tell him,'' Hummel assured Walburton.

"By the way, what is this man's name? In case he should contact
me.''

"His name is Harp,'' Howe said, and then tried more questions
on Walburton. None resulted in further information that might
be useful to the investigation. It was obvious that Walburton was
holding back embarrassing details that would have been useful;
but neither partner pushed him too hard. It was, after all, his
problem. As long as he paid them for it he had a right to have it
handled any way he wished—even badly.

Howe concluded the meeting and ushered Walburton out the
back way. Hummel marched off to the waiting room to get the rest
of that day's business moving.

The waiting room's bare benches were crowded with the usual
variety.

An assortment of underworld characters made up the largest
number. They ranged from scruffy hoodlums to two elegant gentlemen: one of whom owned the city's most thriving gambling
hell, and the other specializing in planning and directing bank
and jewel robberies.

Most of the non-criminals were also known to Abe Hummel. A
respected business attorney who had come to discuss how much
one of his clients, an equally respected department store owner,
was going to have to pay to get out of a breach-of-promise suit. A
pair of garment manufacturers having trouble with an overgreedy
building inspector. A saintly-looking old woman who owned four
of the city's whorehouses. And a celebrated actress with a livid
bruise on the right side of her face.

Plus half a dozen of the Howe & Hummel odd-job performers.
"Runners'' who hung around waiting to be given any type of work
the firm needed done. Process serving. Scouting around for
young women about to be discarded by rich lovers. Giving whatever testimony was required to shore up a court case.

Hummel stabbed a skinny finger at three of these. A plump,
natty former opera tenor who'd lost his voice when a jealous mis-

tress clubbed him across the throat with her umbrella. A hard-
faced twelve-year-old street kid in patched trousers and a ragged,
buttonless federal army jacket that came down to his ankles: ex-
chief of a young hoodlum gang wiped out by a rival gang in a
territory war. And a shapely little redhead of seventeen with a look
of insolent humor, wearing the cheap dress, coat and ribboned
hat of a typical shopgirl, which she'd been until discovering she
could earn better than a near-starvation wage running sometimes
risky errands or perjuring herself for Howe & Hummel.

"Go find Harp for me and bring him here," Hummel told the
three of them. "Five dollars to the one who digs him up."

As they hurried out to the street, Hummel informed the waiting
attorney that Howe would be with him in a minute—and went to
the bruised actress. "What happened, dear?"

"He finally did it. He *struck* me."

"Wonderful," Hummel said. "Go right out and get that side of
your beautiful face closely photographed, from several angles.
When the pictures are developed bring them to me and we'll
discuss the witnesses to this beastly assault on you."

"Unfortunately," the actress told him, "There were no witnesses."

"There will be," Hummel assured her, and gestured for the big-
time robbery mastermind, who paid the firm an annual retainer,
to follow him into his office.

Outside the building, the trio Hummel had dispatched to hunt
for the man called Harp scattered in three different directions.

The street kid jogged east to find out if Harp was on one of his
prowls through the squalid, crime-festering immigrant slums
around Mulberry Bend—from which, some claimed, Harp had
originated.

The former opera tenor went off in a horsecar to check the
haunts from which Harp picked up odd bits of fact and rumor to
be added to the information lode which was his stock in trade.
First stop: the Slave Market just south of Union Square—a group
of cafes that had gotten that nickname because they were usually
full of out-of-work actors. If none of them had a lead to his quarry,
he would try the back room of an all-night saloon by Printing
House Square, where Harp sometimes joined the nonstop poker
games of reporters from the nearby dailies.

The shapely young redhead boarded an omnibus going to Greenwich Village, where Harp kept bachelor quarters he didn't always occupy, to see if he was sleeping off one of his periodic bouts of serious drinking.

Four

Louise Vedder left home for a secret rendezvous with Harp at about the same time that Abe Hummel sent the three runners off to search for him.

Her house was a pleasant brownstone in modish Murray Hill; with a view through the trees of her rear garden of the steeple of the Church of the Incarnation, J. P. Morgan's favorite place of worship. She rode off in an open victoria phaeton, the very latest fashion in elegant park carriages. Its paintwork had a rich glow: the body cherry red and royal blue, the springs and slim-spoked wheels jet black. Her horses were a magnificent pair of matched grays, with sprigs of holly decorating their polished bridles. Similar sprigs were fastened to the tall hats of her liveried coachman and footman. Though it was colder than the previous day, Louise Vedder was quite snug in a hooded cloak of dark Russian sable that enveloped her down to the ankles of her high-button, cork-soled winter promenade boots. The hood protected and shadowed her enchanting face. Her slim hands, sheathed in kid gloves, were tucked into a muff of Canadian ermine.

Louise Vedder belonged to what journalists called "the Aristocracy of Sin." A kept woman, the mistress of a single rich and generous protector.

Some people lumped women of Louise Vedder's sort together with courtesans. But she had little in common, in looks or background, with even the most prosperous of those ladies of pleasure.

Hers was a slender allure, lacking the buxom and dimpled ripeness that most men preferred. Her extraordinarily expressive eyes, like the rest of her fine-boned face, were enhanced by none of the bold makeup that courtesans used to attract attention to their availability. And where they advertised their conquests by flaunting a major portion of their jewelry on their persons, Louise Vedder seldom went out wearing more than a single strand of pearls and her smallest diamond or emerald brooch.

There was a more essential difference between Louise Vedder and most of the *corps d'elite* of New York's scarlet women. By birth and breeding, she was a lady. It was evident in her manner and speech. Her family had been Louisiana quality. She had been sent to the best schools for girls in France and Germany, returning, at eighteen, with an education superior to that of most of New York's respectable ladies and gentlemen.

Within a month of her return from Europe she had married Simon Beaumont Vedder, a handsome young man of similar background with whom she'd been in love since she was twelve. Within three years she was a widow: her husband killed, like her father and only brother, in the Civil War that also destroyed the incomes of both her family and her dead husband's.

Louise Vedder had not been raised to adapt herself to a life of penury. And there was no respectable means by which she could use her considerable intelligence and energy to improve her financial situation. Women were barred from advancement in business enterprises. The plight of those like Louise—who lacked a working husband, money in the bank or family support—was put bluntly by the postwar journalist Edward Craspey: "There is nothing which pleads so strongly against the flagrant injustice which has closed the doors of productive industry against women, as the fact that when forced to fall back upon their own resources, so many of them have been compelled to choose between prostitution and destitution."

As for the menial jobs open to an impoverished woman, there weren't enough left in the broken South for the men, let alone the women. In the prosperous North the best she could hope for was three dollars and fifty cents a week as a seamstress or laundress, four or five dollars a week as a salesgirl or sixteen a month as a nursemaid.

When the Union army's Brigadier General Uriah Gibbon asked her to return to New York with him as his mistress, and agreed to her terms, she accepted.

Accepting as well, without undue squeamishness, the sexual obligations of the arrangement. She was not a neophyte in the arts of lovemaking. Her husband had seen to that. Simon had been a virile and uninhibited young man; and like most young men of his circle, he had received a thorough sexual education from the most accomplished of the New Orleans *haute bicherie*.

Louise thought often of their last night of love. Before he had marched off so gaily to the war, looking magnificent in his brand new, tailored Confederate lieutenant's uniform. She tried not to think too often about what she had learned of the way he must have died. In that first confrontation, after almost three years of the war, between General Lee's tactical genius and the bludgeoning tenacity of General Grant—now president of a reunited United States.

The horrible Battle of the Wilderness. Like so many on both sides in that battle, Simon hadn't been able to extricate himself from the entangling thickets that all the shooting had set on fire. If he hadn't died first from his wounds, he had burned to death.

Afterward, Louise had been told, it had been impossible to figure out which among the charred skeletons belonged to men who had died for the Confederacy, and which to men who had died for the Union. So her husband's bones were interred in a common pit somewhere together with the bones of men he had killed and been killed by.

And if Simon could share a grave with his former enemies, Louise had decided, she could share a bed with one of them.

Uriah Gibbon had neither military background nor aptitude. He headed a Wall Street bank, and also had controlling interest in a shipbuilding firm that made canal boats. He had become a brigadier general like many had: through political influence. In Uriah's case, his connection with Boss Tweed of New York's Tammany Hall. A connection which Uriah had judiciously severed the previous year, having been alerted ahead of time about the criminal indictments now beginning to disintegrate the power of the Tweed Ring.

During the war Uriah had distinguished himself more as a financial opportunist than as a fighter. After the war, until he had met and fallen in love with Louise, he had been one of the military carpetbaggers stripping the South of what little wealth it had left.

But he had been good with Louise, keeping all of his promises. He had bought her the house in Murray Hill, stocked it with servants and the fine furnishings she selected. And at the start of each year he put into her bank account a sum more than sufficient to maintain herself in style until the next New Year. Because Uriah took his obligations to his wife and children as seriously as he did his business responsibilities, he seldom visited Louise more than once or twice a week. Even then, he was never too sexually demanding. More of the time, during his visits, he liked to spend simply relaxing over dinner, drinks and conversation with an attractive and cultured woman who didn't mind a gentleman smoking a cigar in her presence.

Also, he was lavish with gifts. His latest was the ruby choker that Louise was carrying to her meeting with Harp, wrapped in a silk scarf inside a pocket of her cloak.

Uriah had given it to her several days ago for her birthday. Her thirtieth birthday. Louise had promised herself, from the start, that she would remain no man's kept woman past the age of thirty. Soon she would have to break the news to Uriah, and do her best to make him accept it without too much anguish.

The Murray Hill house and its furnishings were in her own name. They would remain hers; as would her two carriages, her horses and enough clothing to last for many years. The monetary value of the various jewels Uriah had given her ensured that she would be able to live out the rest of her life in comfort, if not in her present luxury.

Some of her savings she intended to invest in a commercial venture of her own: one that, in addition to bringing her a small but steady profit, would make demands on her time, intelligence and vigor. What she had in mind was to open a small shop along the Ladies Mile—the stretch of Broadway between Union Square and Madison Square that drew a steady flow of purse-heavy shoppers. A boutique specializing in laces, ribbons, embroideries, flounces and other dress and home trimmings. Imported goods: that would give her a practical reason for annual trips to Europe to replenish her stock.

She wondered if she would ever marry again.

Taking into account both her character and her past, no part of which she intended to go to the bother of concealing, any future husband would have to be an unusual sort of man.

There were times, lately, when Louise Vedder had found herself speculating about *Harp's* potential as a husband.

Their wildly disparate backgrounds would make it a most unlikely pairing. But not, she thought, an unworkable one.

Unlike her dead husband Simon, Harp was not what one would call a handsome man. There was that hard mouth that didn't become much gentler when he smiled. And the scar that a knife or sword had slashed cross his broad forehead. But Louise found his look compelling, in a dark, rough-hewn way. And there was that voice of his that sent a shiver down her spine.

There were other facets to the man that continued to intrigue her. The combination of sharp intelligence and quiet strength. The way he didn't let a lack of illusions interfere with a healthy appetite for life.

And most of all, the mystery of his feelings toward her.

Louise was quite sure Harp was infatuated with her. Perhaps something stronger and deeper than infatuation. She could sense it behind his too-controlled manner with her. She had registered it in the strange look that had come over his face, very briefly, when they'd first been introduced: at a party Jim Fisk had staged to celebrate becoming owner of the Grand Opera House on West Twenty-third Street.

It had seemed, in that first brief moment, as though Harp had already known and desired her, before they'd met.

But he had never done anything since then, by word or touch, to express that desire—let alone to try to get what he desired. Which made it even more peculiar. Because Harp was not one of those men who grew shy in the presence of the fair sex. Louise doubted that she had ever known a man who was more unaffectedly at ease with women.

As others puzzled by Harp had said: "A queer fellow."

Five

Louise rode up Fifth Avenue past the high-walled reservoir that loomed like a fortress between Fortieth and Forty-second streets, and continued on toward Fifty-ninth Street—which most people regarded as the north end of New York City. Only half of Manhattan's twenty-two square miles had been built on as yet, and almost all of those buildings were south of Fifty-ninth Street. Above that line was spoken of as "out of town."

Central Park began there: a far-reaching marvel of landscaping in which city people could enjoy fresh air and pleasant scenery along miles of carriage roads and bridle and strolling paths. On either side of the long park, to the east and west, there was little except vast areas of largely undeveloped terrain.

City planners and land speculators were sure that situation could not last much longer. Manhattan, being a relatively narrow island originally settled at its southern end, had nowhere to grow with each spurt of population except northward. Early in the century Fourteenth Street had been considered the northern limit of the city. By the beginning of the Civil War it had been expanding across Thirty-fifth Street. Now, with the population nearing the one million mark, and more immigrants pouring in every year, the Fifty-ninth Street line seemed bound to crack. So the urbanists had mapped out grids of city blocks on either side of the park.

As of 1871 their map was still an optimist's daydream. The available acres east and west of the park remained almost entirely unexploited. The only reason most New Yorkers could see for going north of Fifty-ninth Street was to take a pleasure jaunt in the countryside of Central Park.

Louise's victoria phaeton entered the park via the Scholar's

Gate, and followed a curving carriage road leading between bare-branched trees toward the lake. She observed that the small number of other carriages in sight were going to or coming from the same place. In milder weather all of the roads would be crowded with carriages. When there was enough snow there would be sleighing parties out. But today it was just cold enough for the lake to be frozen over, making it a magnet for ice skaters and for people who liked to watch them.

Louise saw a great many of both as she reached the lake. The skaters out on the ice, avoiding the weak spots that were marked by danger signs. The watchers scattered around the terrace and at the boathouse, or using their carriages as observation posts. Louise had her coachman halt near some other carriages. Her footman jumped down and stood ready to hand her out of the carriage whenever she wished.

Harp wasn't in sight yet. Louise stayed where she was, alternately scanning the borders of the lake and watching the crowd out on the ice.

There was a sprinkling of upper-class skaters and many more from the middle classes: couples, pairs of women, beginners being helped along by professional instructors, some lone males showing off their skating skills. The number of working-class adults was, as usual, much smaller: workers were at work by day, or looking for work. But there were a lot of ragamuffin kids, some with handmade wooden skates or sleds, the others seeing how far and fast they could slide on their shoes or the seats of their pants.

Louise noticed several richly dressed courtesans, each skating with an expertise few of the other women could match. A foppishly dressed young man, awkward on his skates, approached one of them, almost toppling over when he skidded to a halt and said something that made her smile. She was gliding around him in teasing, ever-slower circles when Louise saw Harp in the distance.

He was approaching from the other side of the lake: a tall, powerful figure on a strapping, dun-colored horse that he'd probably rented from one of the livery stables along Fifty-ninth Street. Louise had once asked him where he'd learned to be such a good horseback rider, and Harp had told her he'd been with Stuart's cavalry. Since Stuart had been a Confederate officer, and one of the few fairly sure facts everyone knew about Harp was that he'd been in the Union army, it was the kind of lie he expected you to know was a lie.

Louise hadn't been surprised or offended. Ask Harp a personal question and he was likely to give you some fanciful story or change the subject. What little she knew of his past she'd heard from others. And since his response to personal questions from others was no different than with her, she couldn't be sure which stories were true and which were unsubstantiated rumors.

One story was that he'd been among the many homeless and parentless children who roamed the notorious Five Points district down in the lower east side, sleeping in alleys and doorways; and that he'd paid for his food by becoming an expert pickpocket. According to that story, he'd been caught by the authorities and sent to the homes for abandoned children on Randall's Island; had escaped and joined a boys' gang that carried out various forms of thievery when not battling other gangs. That was supposed to explain his wide acquaintance among the city's criminals. They were the grownup survivors of the kids' gangs Harp had stolen and fought with: the ones who hadn't been hanged, killed by rivals or sentenced to life in prison.

Another story had it that some wealthy whorehouse madam had plucked the boy out of his gang, unofficially adopting him and hiring tutors for him. That would explain the considerable book learning that Louise had discovered in Harp. It was said that his growing up in a brothel had formed the basis for the extensive network of prostitutes, from the lowest to the highest, that supplied him with much of the information that he earned his income from.

As for Harp's becoming a Union soldier during the war, Louise had heard that the police had caught him for some crime and he'd been given a choice: ten years in jail or join the army.

Louise had no way of knowing if any of this was true. She only knew what Harp was now: or some part of what he was, anyway. Letting her footman help her out of her carriage, Louise went for a solitary stroll that took her around past the other side of the boathouse, to the outer edge of the terrace near a bridle path. She waited there, watching the skaters again, until Harp reined his horse to a stop on the path near her.

He swung down from the saddle and held onto the reins with

one hand as he doffed his hat, uncovering that long scar. " 'After-noon, Mrs. Vedder," he said as though this were an unexpected meeting. "Out for a breath of winter air?"

Louise kept up the pretense with a small gesture of surprise, for the benefit of anyone who noticed them together. "Why, hello! The air feels as though we may be in for more snow soon, don't you agree?"

"Wouldn't be surprised," Harp said. "But don't take that as a definite forecast. I haven't been able to establish a reliable source among the weather gods yet."

He hadn't put his hat back on. It was a flat-crowned, broad-brimmed hat of the kind you saw on countrymen, but seldom here in the metropolis, where toppers and derbies were the standard headgear. Harp dangled the hat from his hand, letting gusts of cold wind ruffle his dark hair, blowing a thick forelock across his scarred forehead as he stood looking down at her.

He had eyes, Louise thought, that saw his fellow men and women a bit too clearly for comfort. Other people's comfort, or his own.

As though reading her thought, he turned his face from her to take in the skaters. "It looks like fun."

"Have you ever tried it?"

Harp shook his head. "I never learned."

"Would you like me to teach you sometime?" Louise asked. "I'm rather good at it."

"I know you are," he said. And when she looked at him with an inquiring frown: "I saw you out there one day, last winter. Very graceful. Very sure of yourself."

"You just happened to be passing by and noticed me out on the ice, among all the other skaters?"

He gave her that faintly mocking smile she'd become familiar with. "You're a special attraction, you know. Even among so many others. There was a bunch of men standing around gawking at you. I stopped to see what they were so fascinated by."

"But you didn't call me over to say hello."

"No time. I had some business to take care of. And speaking of business . . ." He didn't bother finishing it.

Louise glanced around them, before slipping the scarf-wrapped choker to Harp. It disappeared into a pocket of his overcoat without him looking at it.

Their arrangement was always the same. Each piece of jewelry that Uriah had given Louise, she turned over to Harp. One piece at a time. Harp would take it to a highly skilled gem cutter who would remove the precious stones from their setting and substitute imitation gems that were perfect copies. Knowing people like that, and being able to deal with them, was another part of Harp's trade.

Harp would return the piece of jewelry, with the substitute gems, to Louise before Uriah asked too often why she wasn't wearing it. The genuine stones would be sold by Harp to a buyer for one of the prestige shops, like Tiffany's, who paid a fair price and didn't ask questions. Harp would take ten percent of what he realized for himself, ten percent for the gem cutter, and give Louise the rest. Which she deposited in the savings that were to sustain her after she was on her own.

"I have something else for you," Louise told Harp. "Uriah's bank is going to back Daniel Drew in building a new railroad line from Kingston into the western Catskills. That seems to me a highly valuable thing for someone to know ahead of time."

Harp nodded slowly. "I'll sell the tip to some other railroad king rich enough to pay what it's worth, and glutton enough to eat more. Gould or Huntington, probably."

"Either one could make a killing by squeezing into the project on the ground floor."

Harp's smile bared his teeth a bit. "Or by stealing the whole project out from under Drew."

Like the arrangement with her jewelry, the financial agreement on any business information she gave Harp was always the same. Whatever he sold it for was shared between them equally. It was only recently that Louise had learned that was not his usual arrangement with informants. One of the other women who supplied Harp with leads garnered from their tycoon lovers—or husbands—had told Louise that Harp customarily gave his source twenty to thirty percent. Louise didn't ask him why he went to a fifty-fifty split for her alone. She knew he wouldn't give her a straight answer, so there was no point in asking. It just added to the mystery of what he felt about her.

She looked at him speculatively. "Suppose *I* wanted to get in on the ground floor? With your help. Put some of my own money into the project and reap the profit myself?"

"Not a good idea," Harp told her. "Don't invest your savings in *anything* right now. I think the country's building up to a financial panic. In a year, maybe two at the most."

"That is not what I've been hearing from Uriah and others. Everyone keeps talking about an ever brighter future. Continuing and growing prosperity."

Harp shrugged a shoulder. "That's how it looks on the surface, and what they want to believe. Underneath, I begin to feel stirrings of trouble. Things getting shaky. Men like Gould or Huntington or Vanderbilt are fat enough to lose a few and weather it. You can't."

Louise accepted his judgment without asking for specifics he based it on. None of the advice he'd ever given her had proved wrong so far.

Harp patted the pocket that held the ruby choker. "I'll get this back to you as soon as I can. And the money, for this and the railroad tip."

"I know you will." Louise hesitated. "Perhaps by then we could have dinner together. At my house." She watched him closely as she told him the rest of it: "I am going to break with Uriah."

For an instant the same look she had seen the first time they'd met crossed his face. Then he looked down at his hat, flicking it softly against his thigh. When his eyes came back up to hers, what she'd seen was gone.

"Maybe," he said, in an offhand tone. "We'll think about it. When the time comes."

He put the hat back on his head, tugging it down against the wind, turned from her, toed a boot into the stirrup and swung back up on the dun horse. When he was settled into the saddle he looked down at her for a moment. Then he touched a finger to his hat brim and rode away.

Louise gazed after him for a long time, until he was gone from sight, before walking back to her carriage.

Six

It wasn't until Harp was finishing an early supper at the Suze la Rousse that he learned of the urgent summons from Howe & Hummel, because it took him until after nightfall to set both of the Louise Vedder projects in motion.

After leaving his rented horse at its Fifty-ninth Street stable he walked to the Broadway stagecoach line and squeezed aboard an omnibus for the ten-cent ride down the length of Manhattan, standing room only all the way. This late in the day, with traffic reaching one of its most tangled periods, a hansom cab wasn't likely to make the trip much faster for the much higher price.

There were the usual delaying traffic jams during his ride downtown. One was caused by a street battle between a group of cab drivers and a bunch of freight-wagon drovers. The other by a streetcar horse dying on the tracks while its panicked teammate kicked at anyone trying to do something about it. Dusk was gathering when Harp pulled the strap attached to the bus driver's leg and got off near Wall Street.

The lamplighters were at work, moving from one street lamp to the next with their long wands, as Harp walked up Nassau Street, past the banks and insurance companies, to a block dominated by the jewelry trade.

The cubbyhole workshop of Willem Jacobs was on the top floor of a four-story building honeycombed with other business cells, some of whose transactions were not always accurately described by their signs outside. Jacobs was from Antwerp, a world center for precious stones. The expertise as a gem cutter he had brought to New York attracted plenty of legitimate business his way. But he was ambitious to open a swank jewelry shop on the Ladies Mile, and was not averse to earning extra money towards it from illicit work for someone he could trust.

Harp left the ruby choker with him, confident that Jacobs would do an artistic job of making copies of the rubies and substituting them for the genuine ones. Also, by the time Harp picked them up, Jacobs would have made a close estimate of what he could sell the real rubies for.

As for how much Harp could get for Louise Vedder's tip about Daniel Drew's new railroad line, he intended to leave that to Leland Van Tromp to find out for him.

Leland had worked as a Wall Street broker before the war. Since the war he hadn't worked steadily at anything. Hadn't been able to, after what the war had done to him. Even before then, by his own admission, he had never worked very hard at being a stockbroker. Wall Street had tolerantly overlooked his laziness, because of his name. Leland was a "Knickerbocker," part of that small clan that high society revered as the most exclusive segment of its old guard: the Dutch families that had been the first to settle and prosper in New York—back when it had been called New Amsterdam.

The prosperity of his own family had vanished before Leland got to it. His late father had lost the last of it by the war, through investing it with Jacob Little, "the big bear of Wall Street." Little had lost the Van Tromp money, along with ten million dollars of his own, by betting the wrong way on the same market fluctuation that earned Daniel Drew his first millions.

All that was left was the Van Tromp house on the north side of Washington Square. That had become Leland's only regular source of income. He kept two rooms for his own living quarters, renting the rest of his home to the owner of a company that made the carpets for most of the city's government buildings and for firms doing business with the city. The man's social-climbing wife, son and daughter made the most of the house's prestige location and long association with the Van Tromp name.

In spite of Leland's genteel poverty, his name still caused Manhattan's financial tycoons to give him their time and respect whenever he chose to visit with them. This would not be the first time Harp had made use of those connections.

The early night of winter had settled in, with a thin drizzle falling from a low overcast, when Harp entered the mews behind the Van Tromp home. Leland's two ground-floor rooms were in the back, next to the house's private stable. There was no light inside his windows, and no response when Harp knocked at his door. He left a note in Leland's letter box, asking him to drop by any time that night—at his Greene Street apartment a few blocks away.

Leland was one of the very few who knew about the other place he kept, for times when he didn't want most people to be able to find him.

Harp's block on Greene Street, between Bleecker and Houston, was part of a small low-income Greenwich Village enclave that polite people called the French Quarter and others called Frogtown. His rooms there were on the third floor of an old red-brick house that had a French restaurant on its ground floor and a French bakery in the basement under the stoop. Some people might not have found it pleasant to go to sleep at night with the odors of French cooking wafting up to the apartment and to wake in the morning with the fragrance of fresh-baked breads and pastries. Harp did.

He walked the few blocks from Washington Square intending to change clothes before tackling the night. But when he reached the house the smells from the restaurant—the Suze la Rousse—reached out to him and an abruptly alerted appetite pushed him inside.

He did not resist. Harp had spent his last war year as a prisoner, on intimate terms with relentless hunger. Since then his appetite was like a child spoiled by all the attention focused on it during a long bout of near-fatal illness. When balked, it threw a tantrum and retaliated by reminding Harp too sharply of that bad year.

The front part of the Suze la Rousse was sectioned off as a small odd-goods shop, managed by the owner's daughter. It was filled with unrelated items: European toys and buckets of coal, wooden shoes and copies of the *Courrier des Etas Unis,* America's French language newspaper. A curtained doorway led into the restaurant that took up the rest of the ground floor. Bare sanded floors, small tables covered with blue-and-white-checked oilcloth, a stocky Madame Letessier serving and presiding over the cash drawer while her husband stayed in the kitchen engrossed in the manly art of cooking. And those wonderful smells.

This early, Harp was the first diner. The French immigrants stuck to their old-country habit of dining after eight. The restaurant's good food, low prices and relaxed ambiance were beginning to attract some of the bohemian artists, writers and bums who were settling into the Village; but they wouldn't start drifting in until much later. The only other clients sharing the restaurant with Harp were a pair of Frenchmen nursing their glasses of cheap Bordeaux while they played chess at a corner table.

Back home the two would have been enemies. One was an aristocrat exiled because his family had been on the wrong side when Louis Philippe's government had fallen. The other was an anarchist pamphleteer forced to flee during the recently terminated reign of Napoleon III. In exile they shared threadbare clothes, the gaunt look of restricted diets and their passion for chess.

Harp had played each of them, winning more games than he lost. Leland Van Tromp had taught him the game in Libby Prison, where there'd been little else to distract their minds from their deteriorating hold on life.

He finished off a delicious onion soup, with its thick crust of browned cheese, and was delving into his main course of succulent beef stew before the chess players completed their game and noticed his presence. Both raised questioning eyebrows: did he want to play the winner? Harp shook his head and devoted himself to his meal while they set up their next game. He had eaten his last forkful and was drinking the last of his wine when eleven-year-old Jean-Pierre Carjat came into the restaurant looking for him.

The son of a local shoemaker, the boy was one of the kids who kept an eye on Harp's place while playing in the street. Late at night the prostitutes who worked Greene Street performed the same service. What he paid for the service depended on the value of what they had to tell him.

"There's a girl been up into your house three times," Jean-Pierre told Harp. Unlike his parents, he had New York's version of English down pat. "Last time just now. I snuck up the stairs after her. She's sitting on the floor outside your door."

"What's she look like?"

The boy described Kitty Shay—the saucy young redhead Abe

Hummel had sent off with the two other runners: "Red hair. Pretty. Nice figure. Okay duds but nothing rich. Not a swell. Not a street cruiser either. Just a regular girl . . ."

Harp gave him fifteen cents. "Send her down."

The boy scampered out with the three nickels clutched triumphantly in his grimy little fist.

Harp was sipping a strong black coffee laced with whiskey when Kitty Shay hurried into the restaurant, looking weary but happy, and plumped herself down across the table from him.

"I been searching the whole Village for you for hours. Mr. Hummel wants you. Billy Doyle and Mr. Cavalucci are out looking for you too, so remember I found you first. It means five bucks for me."

Harp didn't ask what Abe Hummel wanted him for. Kitty wouldn't know. Whatever it was, there would be good money in it for him. Howe & Hummel knew his fees and wouldn't send for him unless prepared to pay well.

Nor did he ask where Hummel was likely to be at this hour. Many of the Howe & Hummel clients were disinclined to venture out of their holes in daylight. The law offices stayed open for business well after dark. If Abe Hummel had already left for an early theater or party date, Bill Howe would still be in his office, and would know what Harp was needed for.

"Wait here," he told Kitty. "I'm going up to put on other things before we go."

"Let me go up with you," she said eagerly. "That's a jim-dandy tub you got up there, and I ain't had a real bath in so long I can't remember when."

His bathtub was the standard zinc-lined wooden six-footer. It was no longer a rarity in New York, but over half of the city's dwellings lacked anything like it. Where Kitty lived there was no bathroom. You washed in your room, with a pitcher of water and a tin basin, and the outhouse in the backyard served everyone.

Harp shook his head. "Takes thirty minutes to fill the tub and add hot water from the stove. It's not going to take me more than ten to change and be on my way."

"So let me stay after you go. I trust you to bring me back my five dollars." Kitty's mock-naughty grin showed a missing front tooth resulting from childhood malnutrition. "I can take my time with the bath, get myself all clean and get in your bed to wait for you."

"Behave yourself. You'll wait here."

"Don't be stuffy. I been up in your place before, remember. You even let me stay all night."

"You had a bad fever."

Kitty winked at him. "I think I feel another fever coming on. Not the same kind, maybe, but . . ."

"Have you had supper?"

That diverted her interest immediately. "I ain't eaten a thing since breakfast. I don't even have a dime left on me for—"

Harp called Madame Letessier over. "Serve her whatever she wants. Put it on my bill."

Kitty was already ordering when Harp went out.

The door to his house was next to the Suze la Rousse entrance, but he didn't use it. The kids on the street were usually alert to anything going on, but they could miss something. It wasn't any specific, current danger that made him wary. Just an ongoing survival instinct. You couldn't function in an edge-of-the-law profession of his kind without making enemies. Harp liked to vary his approach to his apartment, especially at night.

He went down the stoop, halfway around the block, into its back alley, and used one of his keys to enter the back door of the house attached to the side of his own. There was a locked storage closet on the third floor. Harp had installed the lock, and only he had the key. Inside the closet there was another locked door. Before opening that one he crouched, pried up a floorboard and straightened up with a revolver in his hand. He stepped through into the back of his bedroom closet and stayed there for a minute, listening. Then he stepped out of the closet and stopped again, sniffing the air while he listened, before moving noiselessly through the rest of his apartment.

When he had made sure he was alone, he struck a match and lit the oil lamp on the front room table. Returning to the bedroom, he lit another that was on the chest of drawers near a small photograph in a silver frame.

The photograph was a tintype. If it hadn't been, it wouldn't have survived all it had been through. Harp had framed it almost two years before he had met the woman in it. The picture was stained in spots, smoky in others. But the face looking at him from it was unmistakable. Especially those remarkable eyes.

He had realized she was the one in his tintype the first second he'd seen Louise Vedder at Jim Fisk's party. Months before she had spoken to him about herself—and about the young husband she remembered so tenderly, who had died in the Battle of the Wilderness.

She had asked him then if his part of the Union forces had been anywhere near that battle.

Harp had lied and told her, "No."

Seven

The light rain had stopped when Harp entered the lower east side. But the moisture had frozen, making the sidewalks slippery in places. Harp was dressed for whatever the cold night had in store. A winter greatcoat, with a large turn-up collar. His hat with its broad, turn-down brim. Thick hobnail boots. He walked toward the Thirteenth Precinct stationhouse, alert to every nuance of the active night life around him.

This was an area where recently arrived Italians and Jews mixed, not always peacefully, with the much larger tribes of Irish and Germans from earlier waves of immigration—and with criminals bred in the neighborhood slums. Old-timers or greenhorns, most of the immigrants were already American citizens, or soon would be. The Tammany Hall political machine had always seen to that. Easing the newcomers' way to citizenship swiftly and for free. Assured that the grateful immigrants would repay the machine by voting whatever way they were told to. It was the people of neighborhoods like this who had kept the Tammany wire-pullers, from Mayor Oakey Hall and political boss Bill Tweed on down, solidly entrenched until now.

In spite of the weather and the hour, there were a great many of these neighborhood people out along Delancey and its cross streets. Shivering peddlers—for whom each penny counted toward bringing their families over before the next Polish or Russian pogrom—presided over pushcarts lit by kerosene lamps and piled with old clothes, kegs of rusty nails, loaves of stale bread: anything that could be bought and sold cheap. Factory and construction workers, women and children from the garment sweatshops, laborers from the docks—all trudging homeward to

cramped tenement flats, or to single, windowless rooms crowded
by entire families, or to sections of dank cellars shared with dozens
of strangers. There was a fruit huckster with an ancient horse and
wagon calling out his wares in Greek. Vagrants begged outside the
many saloons. A decrepit woman and a mangy dog were pulling a
lopsided baby carriage loaded with rags and bottles toward a junkyard.

Harp paid more attention to the other breed of night people he
passed. Streetwalkers who ranged from scrawny girls of eleven to
aging slatterns keeping to shadows and trying to hide ruined faces
under thick layers of paint. Pimps leaning against the lampposts
and telegraph poles. Thugs scouting for anyone who looked as if
he might be worth luring into a dark back alley: preferably an
uptown tourist, down here for a spot of "elephant hunting"—the
current slang for slumming.

Most of the thugs knew Harp for what he was, and would keep
clear of him. As for those who didn't know him, and weren't
warned off by those who did, he was prepared to deal with any
who cared to try him on. The walking stick he carried was of
knobby hickory, thick and heavy. Hobnail boots could be useful
for more than walking. For more serious encounters, his greatcoat
concealed an item he usually brought along on prowls through
areas like this.

He stopped several cruising whores he knew to ask about Alice
Curry. Vance Walburton's stricture against alerting anyone in his
circle to his problem prevented Harp from tracking down his er-
rant wife the most logical way: by questioning everyone she knew
or had known, and checking the places where she'd shopped or
dined regularly. That left delving into the recent life of Alice
Curry, searching for how she had acquired Olivia Walburton's
clothes. That—the moment when the lives of Alice Curry and Mrs.
Walburton had intersected—was what Harp needed as a starter.
Even if the clothes had been stolen, finding out when and where
could put him on Olivia Walburton's present trail.

But none of the whores he talked with had known Alice Curry.
All they could tell him was that she hadn't lived or worked around
here. As for who had burglarized the warehouse, they hadn't a
clue. Harp was pretty sure they told him the truth. They knew he
paid promptly and fairly for inside dope, and kept its source to

himself. He told each of them to keep her ears open and leave a message for him at the Suze la Rousse if she heard anything new.

He already had others checking around for him. Cavalucci, the ex-tenor, was trying the Alice Curry name on actors, theater managers and the dramatic agents around Union Square. Young Billy Doyle was asking about her in the harlot hangouts on both sides of the Bowery. And Harp had an elderly former pimp named Carson doing the same around the more expensive sin center of upper Sixth Avenue known as Satan's Circus.

He had also given Kitty Shay a copy of Olivia Walburton's photograph to show to cab drivers, on the slim chance one might remember having driven her, during the past few weeks, to or from wherever she was staying.

The work of his searchers was handicapped by the fact that none of them knew exactly what he was after. But that couldn't be helped. What he was paying had to compensate for that. Two dollars a day, expense money. Five to ten dollars for anything they learned that he found useful. And a mouth-watering fifty dollars to the one who gave him something that led him directly to his ultimate objective.

Harp figured he could afford to spread a little around from the thousand he'd be collecting: his half of Walburton's payment to Howe & Hummel. Howe had also assured him that if the investigation lasted more than a week, Walburton would be gouged for more.

The precinct station house was on the corner of Delancey and Attorney streets: across from a seedy bowling saloon with an upstairs whorehouse. Nine blocks from the warehouse where Alice Curry had died. Harp went up the steps and was let in by Jack Kelly, the station's elderly night doorman. Kelly had gotten this restful job through his nephew, who was fourth clerk to the superintendent of the Bureau of Street Improvements.

Harp shook his hand and said, "Hello, Jack. Nasty night out."

"Doesn't bother me," Kelly told him. "I stay inside. Where you been, I ain't seen you lately."

"Keeping busy. Anything new on the Alice Curry killing?"

Kelly shrugged. "I wouldn't know—or care. Whores getting themselves killed, that's just in the nature of things. Like leaves falling off trees. You know there'll be new ones coming along, so what's it matter?''

"You've always been a philosopher, Jack. About other people's troubles.''

"Ain't met anybody yet who gives shucks for any troubles 'cept his own,'' Kelly said, and settled back into his entrance armchair as Harp walked on.

The main hall was brightly lit by its gas lamps. Pat Quinn was the sergeant on duty behind the big black-walnut desk. He was listening with poker-faced patience to a haggard young woman in a tattered coat and broken shoes, with a stained bandanna for a head covering and a baby wrapped in wool rags in her arms. Her story was not a rare one. She had no money for a place to spend the night and was afraid if she fell asleep outside, her baby would freeze to death before morning. Without change of expression, Sergeant Quinn picked up one of the speaking tubes and called down to the matron in charge of the female section of the homeless shelter in the cellar.

While they waited a reserve patrolman, dozing in a chair between the sergeant's desk and the telegraph instrument, woke with a snort, noticed Harp and raised a hand in sleepy greeting. Dick Crowley: another Irishman, like Quinn and Kelly—like the bulk of the city's police force, for that matter. It probably made good sense, considering that such a large proportion of the lawbreakers the cops had to deal with at this time were also Irish.

Of the 78,451 men and women arrested in New York City the previous year, 51,126 had been immigrants. Of those, 37,014 were from Ireland. The next highest number on that list was 8,281 from Germany. Those statistics were bound to change drastically with the new waves of immigration arriving from Italy and Greece, Russia and Poland. But as of now the Irish were it: cops and robbers, vagrant beggars and thriving politicians.

Harp watched the matron take the mother and her baby down to the cellar. He knew the young woman wasn't in for a restful night. He'd spent time in the men-and-boys section of various police shelters, before he'd grown old enough to steal for his basic needs. You got a bare plank to sleep on. No mattress, no blanket, no food; locked in with an unwashed crowd groaning and snoring and coughing all around you throughout the night. The best you could say for it was that at least it gave you protection from the elements and heat from the cellar grates.

Sergeant Quinn looked at Harp with an angry grimace. "I wish I could show people like her a little human sympathy, but I let my feelings get loose and I'd drown in my tears. There's just too many of 'em."

"Full house tonight?"

"Not yet. But it will be by midnight, cold as it is out. Even if it don't snow."

Harp nodded at the closed door behind Quinn that led to Captain Redpath's private office and on-duty apartment. "The Thumper in?"

Captain John Redpath had gotten the nickname from telling every new patrolman that the best way to calm a difficult customer was to "thump him wit' your stick—and keep thumpin' till he's reasonable." It was advice that he himself had followed conscientiously during his rise through the ranks.

"No," Quinn said. "He's off to the Tenth Precinct, talking something over with Captain Brennen." Quinn got out a plug of chewing tobacco, bit off a chunk and shot a pointed look at the reserve patrolman half-dozing with his eyes open in the chair near him. "Crowley, go up and get your beauty sleep on your dormitory bunk. I got something private to talk with Harp about."

The sergeant chewed steadily while he watched Crowley drag himself to his feet and up the stairway. Then he gestured Harp to the vacated chair. Harp sat down and turned the chair to face Quinn, who tucked the chewed wad into his left cheek and gave Harp an anxious scowl.

"You hear any inside dope on these grand-jury investigations?"

Quinn's anxiety was part of an increasing nervousness throughout the police force as the grand jury kept grinding away. Investigating, among other matters, how police headquarters could claim that it was impossible to come up with addresses of the city's haunts of vice—and why its much-publicized rogue's gallery turned out to contain fewer than five hundred photographs, all of very minor criminals, with not a single one of any of the big-league lawbreakers.

"What I hear," Harp told Quinn, "is that Mayor Hall and every other bigwig in the Tammany machine are likely to wind up in jail. Including the boss, Bill Tweed himself.''

"I can't believe it'll go that far."

"Believe it," Harp said. "It's this simple. Tammany is Democrat. The state legislature and its grand jury are mostly Republicans. Plus a few reform Democrats who'll go along with them in this case. Every banker in this town is a Republican, too. The grand-jury investigators are asking them if they're carrying accounts for any of Tammany's important names. And if so, how much money's in their accounts—and who made out the checks that put the money there. Do you figure those Republican bankers are going to refuse to open their books because it's unethical?''

Quinn chewed reflectively on his tobacco wad. Finally he shifted it to his right cheek and said, "Well, I'm not gonna worry too much about it. My bank's in Jersey, and anyway I'm too small potatoes for 'em to get around to me. If I was a captain, be different, but I ain't.'' He glanced around to make sure they were still alone, and lowered his voice. "One good side to it for me. If Tammany does go under, I won't have to pay the rest of the installments on what I still owe 'em for promoting me to sergeant.''

"Don't get your hopes up," Harp told him. "Reform movements come and go. And they go faster than they come. The machine goes down, then bounces back up—under new management. Better sock your installments away. The next Tammany boss —my bet's on Dick Crocker—will want the rest of what you owe the machine. Every penny of it.''

"Yeah—you're probably right." Quinn's sigh was rueful and short. He eyed Harp narrowly for a moment. "I once heard somebody say you get your protection from somebody high up in Tammany. Any truth in that?''

"I'm married to Mayor Hall's mother-in-law.''

"Come on—I never asked you about it before because—''

"So don't ask now.''

"Okay, okay—" Quinn turned his head and spat a dark spurt of tobacco juice at his cuspidor. Not a perfect shot. Some of the juice hit the side of the cuspidor and dribbled to the floor. Quinn frowned and turned back to Harp. "So—what brings you over here tonight?''

"The Alice Curry murder. Any progress on it?''

"Not as I know of. I'll tell you one thing, I'm glad I wasn't here when they found her. So I didn't have to look at the corpse. Pretty ugly, they tell me. It was my night off, home with the wife and kids."

Precinct police were on active duty—or at the stationhouse acting as reserves for emergency situations—four continual days and nights at a time. After which they were entitled to a twelve-hour night off. Followed by another four days and nights on duty. Then twelve daytime hours off.

"So," Quinn said, "almost all I know about what happened to the unfortunate creature—God rest her soul, even if she was a sinful whore—is what I read in the blotter." He tapped the thick precinct diary on his desk. "And I never heard of this Alice Curry before. Which means she ain't from around here."

"Who identified her?"

"Tommy Costello. He's the patrolman who first spotted that the warehouse had got broken into by thieves. Went in there with a couple boys from the harbor patrol."

"Tom Costello—" Harp ruminated over the name for a moment. "I don't know him. New here?"

"Yeah. Got transferred to us four weeks back—from the Twenty-ninth Precinct."

The Twenty-ninth took in a good part of Satan's Circus, making it an even cushier spot than the Thirteenth Precinct, with bigger payoffs. "Sounds like a demotion to me," Harp said.

"Sounds that way to me, too. But I don't know any details about why. Costello ain't been in a mood to talk much since coming here. Anyway, it's from up there that he recognized the murdered whore. Which was a piece of luck, on account of there wasn't nothing on or around the body to identify her by. No pocketbook or nothing."

"How well did Costello know her?"

"Hardly at all, from what he says. Just her name, and that she worked in some plush parlorhouse. And *maybe* got parts sometimes in theater shows. On that Costello's not so sure."

"He know which parlorhouse? Or which theater?"

"Not from what I been told. Or what's in the blotter."

"He know *anything* else about her? Where she lived, outside of the parlor house, or who her friends or family were?"

"Nope. Just what I already told you is all, seems like."

"Costello here now?" Harp asked.

"Out on patrol duty. You can look around for him if you want. Or come back later. He's due back here for reserve duty in a few hours. Until six in the morning. Then he gets his day off, until six tomorrow night."

"Where's he stay when he's off?"

"His mother's got a couple rooms way up on the upper west side. In one of them old Dutch farmhouses what've been turned into boardinghouses. He visits with her on his days off. A good son, gotta say that for him—even if he ain't been exactly sociable since his transfer." Quinn got a ledger out of a drawer and consulted it. "Ruyter's—that's the name of the place his mother lives. A little west of Hunter's Gate, it says here."

Harp shifted the subject slightly: "Alice Curry's body in the morgue now?"

"Sure, but if you want a look at her, you'll need authorization. Which I can't give you. The captain can, if you catch him in a nice mood. Have to get it soon, though. You know how it is. If nobody claims her in a day or so, she gets quicklimed in Potter's Field."

"Who owns the warehouse where she was found?"

"Name's Monmouth Fuller," Quinn said. "Supposed to be pretty big in the import-export business, and rich as the devil. All from his dear departed dad."

Harp knew of Fuller by name and reputation. "He come through yet with a list of what was stolen?"

Quinn checked the police blotter. "Twelve cases of champagne. Fifteen cases of brandy. French booze—worth a lot of money, according to Fuller."

"Any leads to who the thieves were?"

"I think that's what Captain Redpath went over to the Tenth to talk to Brennen about. Wants to pool squealers from the other precincts, see if they can come up with a lead."

Harp said, "Thanks," stood up and slipped five dollars under the sergeant's blotter.

Quinn, pretending not to notice, turned his head away to spit another stream of tobacco juice at his cuspidor. This time he scored a bull's eye. Smiling over his marksmanship, he slid the money out from under the blotter and into his pocket as Harp walked away.

A paddy-wagon clattered to a stop in front of the stationhouse as Harp came out and down the steps. Its panting horse puffed clouds of steam into the freezing air as it stamped its shod hooves on the cobbles. Two patrolmen climbed out dragging a semiconscious prisoner in handcuffs with them. They had obviously taken Captain Redpath's advice to heart and had thumped the man into his present state of total reasonableness. There was a slanting nightstick welt decorating his face, punctuated by a smashed nose that leaked blood onto every step as he was hauled up them into the stationhouse.

The Tenth Precinct stationhouse was only eight blocks west of the Thirteenth, on Eldridge Street between Broome and Grand, in the middle of what was gradually turning into an East European ghetto. Captain Brennen was there but Captain Redpath wasn't. They had finished their conference and Redpath had strolled off ten minutes ago—to "check out the neighborhood."

Being acquainted with some of Thumper Redpath's habits, it was not difficult for Harp to think of a couple of nearby spots where he might be found.

Eight

Like the city's other first-class dance halls—some proprietors preferred to call them concert saloons—Billy McGlory's Armory Hall paid substantial weekly sums to the cops and the Tammany machine to get away with mixing sexual turpitude with its music, dancing and drinking. Unlike most of the others, which were concentrated further uptown in Satan's Circus, McGlory had established his place in the heart of the lower east side: on Hester Street, three blocks from the Tenth Precinct stationhouse.

Billy McGlory was a former bare-knuckle boxer of some repute, and he enjoyed the rough clientele of this area. Also, it was the presence of the low-life roughnecks, as well as the down-and-dirty debauchery, that drew so many affluent, eager-to-be-shocked slumming parties from uptown and out of town. They could go home and boast that they'd really "met the elephant" at Armory Hall—in perfect safety. McGlory made too much money selling rich customers cheap liquor at extravagant prices to let them get robbed or beaten in his place. He had a reputation to defend—and a number of exceptionally tough, armed bouncers to help him defend it.

Harp was let into a dim corridor by a brawny doorman with an iron club clutched in one fist and brass knuckles ready in his other. At the end of the corridor another bruiser—this one with brass knuckles on both hands, an openly displayed revolver jutting out of his waistband and a shotgun against the wall beside him—opened the door to the high-ceilinged, plainly furnished main hall of the saloon. Harp stepped into its concentration of cigar smoke and noise, and paused for a look around.

It was too early in the night for the place to be packed. But a score of men were bellied up to the bar, and half of the tables were already taken, being supplied with a steady stream of liquor by pretty waitresses in daring tights. A dozen couples frolicked to a spirited four-piece orchestra—on a dance floor that was used one night each week for a few hours of illegal bare-knuckle boxing matches; and every night after midnight for several performances of the latest import from wicked France: the illegal can-can.

And three of the boxes in the high galleries that flanked the room already had their curtains closed, to hide the goings-on inside them.

Billy McGlory strolled in Harp's direction, keeping a sharp eye on his customers, prepared to toss out any who became trouble-makers or who failed to buy enough liquor. He was a dapper fellow who hadn't lost his athletic figure, his suits always in the best of expensive taste, his mustache freshly barbered and his fingernails manicured. Still handsome despite some marks from his former profession. When he reached Harp he shook his hand and patted his shoulder before moving on: his signal to the female population of Armory Hall not to hassle Harp for drinks or sex.

All of the women in the place, including the waitresses, belonged to one class or another of what the city's clergymen called the "soiled sisterhood." No respectable female would set foot in a concert saloon; not even as part of an upper-class party of slummers.

Three of the women that Harp noted were gowned in the height of fashion and lavishly bejeweled. *Poules deluxe* accompanied by rich protectors who had no reason to hide their acquisitions: a theatrical impresario, a successful gambler and a grain merchant unencumbered by any ambition to join the social elite.

The rest were harlots slightly lower to much lower in the hierarchy. In various degrees of dishabille: from dresses that bared most of the bosom and displayed stockinged legs all the way up to the knee, to nothing but their undergarments.

McGlory didn't mind if they stripped down to nothing at all—which they often did up in the curtained gallery boxes and sometimes after midnight, on the dance floor—as long as they found male companions who kept buying drinks. In an era when it was considered daring for a woman to show an ankle, it gave the slumming tourists something incredibly spicy to tell their buddies about afterwards.

The men in Armory Hall were from every class that had cash to squander. Harp recognized some of them. Three rock-bottom hoodlums you could hire, at fixed prices, to beat, cripple or kill someone for you. The superintendent of the city's Bureau of Lamps and Gas, fondling the pretty doxy on his lap while a waitress refilled their champagne glasses. A flashy safecracker and an alcoholic poet at a table with two chorus girls from the Bowery Theater. A Court of Appeals judge and a Tammany ward heeler in a conversation too troubling for them to pay much attention to the amount of whiskey they were consuming, or to the twelve-year-old flower girl sharing their bottle. And the tipsy scion of one of society's top families, being helped up the stairs to one of the gallery boxes by a plump beauty wearing only a black satin corset, red stockings and green garters.

Thumper Redpath was easy to spot. He was the biggest man in the place, in both height and girth: and most of it was still heavy muscle. He was alone at a small table, wearing his police overcoat with every brass button fastened, up to his short, thick neck, and his helmet set square on his head. He sat erect, his huge hands flat on the table, staring with a perverse kind of sullen pleasure at a man with two women at a nearby table.

Maybe, Harp thought as he made his way toward him, Redpath liked visiting places like McGlory's because they confirmed his low opinion of mankind—and most of womankind. There was also, to be sure, the fact that it was from dives like this that he collected much of the graft he shared with Tammany.

It was no secret that Redpath was a corrupt cop. Like most conscientious churchgoers, he believed that all sin was the Devil's work and should be punished—at least financially. At the same time—like most Americans who held to the work ethic endorsed by both imported Victorianism and native Puritanism—he was convinced that earning as much as you could was what God wanted of you. It justified him collecting from what he loathed. Whorehouses, dance halls and gambling hells, he agreed with other police officers, existed so that "them as wants it knows where to find it—and human nature being weak, that's how it's got to be."

Harp had no quarrel with that opinion.

It was no secret, either, that Redpath was the most feared and fearless officer on the force. He had only to walk through a tough neighborhood for its hoodlums to turn tame. He'd beaten up so many of the hardest ones—and they'd become superstitious about trying to shoot him. He had been shot down from ambush twice. Each time his big body had absorbed the wounds and recovered from them. Each time he'd gone back out and found the shooter: beating him to a pulp before carrying him off to jail. Each time he had come up with evidence that the culprit had committed at least one murder—and had stood by to watch him hang for it.

There was yet another side to Redpath. He had twice rescued people trapped inside burning buildings that no one else had the courage to enter. One particularly frigid winter he had plunged into the ice-choked Hudson to save a child who'd fallen off a ferryboat. In the city's antidraft riots during the war he had once, alone, held off a murderous band intent on lynching a freed slave.

Harp couldn't like Captain Redpath; but he had to respect him.

When he neared Redpath he saw what fascinated him at the other table. The two women sharing drinks with the man there were good-looking young men, wearing female clothes, wigs and makeup.

Billy McGlory was one of the very few who didn't turn away transvestites or overt male homosexuals. Nobody was troubled about lesbians, since most of New York agreed that Queen Victoria was correct: they didn't exist. There *was* one place in the city where they could meet each other. A very private club run by a former ballet dancer from Germany. But Harp was probably the only man who knew about it and had been inside.

He sat down at Redpath's table and waited for the captain to acknowledge his presence.

Redpath slowly turned his head and gave him a cold stare. "What th'hell *you* want?"

"And a good evening to you, too, captain," Harp said evenly. "Are you keeping well?"

Redpath scowled at him and fingered the nightstick on the table beside his beer glass. The glass was almost full, and Harp knew it wouldn't get much emptier. Redpath had been a heavy boozer before his marriage. His wife, who had expected to become a nun, had agreed to marry him only if he swore on the Bible to stop drinking. With time, the pledge had become ingrained in Redpath. He never touched hard liquor; and he could make a glass of beer last all night and walk away leaving it three-quarters full.

"What d'you want?" Redpath demanded again. He had a surprisingly thin, reedy voice for a man of his bulk.

"I'm trying to find out about the woman who was killed in the warehouse burglary last night. Alice Curry."

"What's your interest?"

"None, personally. It's a job Howe and Hummel are paying me to do."

"What's *their* interest?"

"No idea," Harp lied. "They never tell me why they want something, just pay me to do it."

"Well, you go back and tell those two shysters I'm gonna catch her killers, and soon. All I got to do is find out which blokes burgled the warehouse. Which I got people out now checking into. I'll get 'em. And make 'em talk. And that'll solve the whore's murder, same time."

"I don't know if Howe and Hummel care that much about who killed her," Harp said. "What they want from me is information about her background."

"I couldn't help you on that, even if I had any reason to." Redpath picked up the beer glass, touched it to his lips and put it back down. An automatic movement he seemed unaware of. "I never heard of this Alice Curry before. Lucky one of my boys knew a little about her, from up in the Twenty-ninth Precinct."

"Have you checked with the Twenty-ninth about her?"

"What for? I already know she was a slut and she got killed. And I'm already hunting the gang what killed her. Can't think of anything else I got to know about her."

"I still have my job to do," Harp said. "A picture of her might help me get it done. I'd take it as a favor if you could give me a note letting a photographer I know go into the morgue and take some photographs of her."

Pictures of the dead seldom had much resemblance to what they'd looked like alive. But unless Cavalucci or somebody else turned up a picture of Alice Curry, it would have to serve.

Redpath said, "No." Flat and final.

"Why not?"

"On account of I can't think of any reason to do you a favor. Nor Howe and Hummel, neither. My opinion of them two, the way they twist the law to get off crooks and killers, they ought to be in prison themselves. And that's where I hope to see 'em one day, sooner or later."

"You better hope it doesn't happen too soon," Harp said mildly. "When these grand-jury investigations get around to you— and they will—you'll need lawyers as tricky as Howe and Hummel in your corner. Without them, the easiest you can hope for is getting kicked off the force."

"Do I look worried?"

"You should be."

"Well, I'm not. I'm ready to retire, anyway. I already got all I need, for me and the family."

Harp nodded. "Including a nice house in the city, a bigger one in the country, your own stable, horses and carriage. But the grand jury will want to know how you paid for all that, out of your salary."

Redpath curled his big hands into fists on the table and glared at Harp. "I won a Japanese lottery. Let 'em go to Japan and try to prove different."

At that moment their attention was diverted by a commotion on the dance floor. The dancers were scattering away from a waitress and a streetwalker who'd gotten into a drunken fight. A bouncer started toward them, but McGlory stuck out an arm and stopped him. The two women were wrestling on the floor now, biting, scratching, pulling hair, ripping each other's scanty costumes. It was too good a show to break up: the sort that drew the tourists. A trio of foppish slummers left their table for a fascinated closer look, joining dozens of others crowding around the battlers.

It ended as suddenly as it had started: with one of the battlers curling up on her side, clutching her stomach and gagging, and the other sitting on the floor, extracting a broken tooth from her bloodied mouth. McGlory dropped his arm, and his bouncer charged onto the dance floor, grabbed each woman by a wrist and dragged them out to be dumped into the street. Their audience drifted away, the orchestra resumed its playing and the three fops returned to their table, chattering excitedly, and ordered more of McGlory's very bad champagne.

Redpath and Harp looked at each other again, and Redpath said, "You still here? The answer's still no. And I've had all've your company I can use for one night."

Harp fashioned a grimace of reluctant acceptance. He stood up and started to turn away. Then he stopped himself and stood there frowning, as if trying to decide something. Finally he said, "You haven't been too helpful, captain. But what the hell—maybe I'll need another favor from you some day when you're in a friendlier mood."

Redpath gave him an irritated stare. "What th'Devil're you jawing about now?"

"Just before I came in I spotted two fellows pulling up in a carriage across the street. Pinkerton detectives I know, working lately as reform investigators. They're sitting out there now jotting down the names of anybody they recognize going in or out of here."

Redpath shot an involuntary look toward the Armory Hall entrance. But when he looked back to Harp, he appeared untroubled. "So what? I came in here to do my duty. Check out the place and see nothin's going on that ought'nt."

"Sure," Harp said. "But why have to explain more things to the grand jury than absolutely necessary? Those two out there came too late to see you come in here. But they'll see you come out—if you go the front way. So why do that when McGlory's got his secret way out the back?"

Having said his piece, Harp again started to turn away —but took his time about it.

"Hold it!"

Harp turned back to him.

"I can't say I think you're a regular brick," Redpath growled, "but I guess you ain't all bad." He took out a pencil and a notepad. "What's the name of your photographer?"

"Howard Ferguson."

Redpath scrawled a note on the pad, tore it off and gave it to Harp. It had Redpath's name, rank and badge number printed at the top. Under it he had written and signed an authorization for

Howard Ferguson to enter the morgue for the purpose of photographing the corpse of Alice Curry.

Harp put it into an inside pocket and said, "Thanks, captain."

Redpath said nothing at all: just picked up his club, got to his feet and marched across the saloon toward Billy McGlory.

Harp waited until the two of them disappeared into a dim rear corridor, then left the place himself by the front entrance.

The two reform investigators were not there when he came out of Armory Hall. That didn't surprise him. They hadn't been there when he went in.

Nine

Ferguson's photography studio and living quarters took up the top floor of a two-story clapboard house, above one of the Bowery's many shooting galleries. This one was closing its corrugated-iron shutters for the night when Harp reached the house.

Next door was a German beer garden that was still very much open. Blazing torches out front illuminated Prussian and Bavarian flags, and the brass band inside was alternating between polkas and military music. New York's large German population was still celebrating the devastating defeat of France in the Franco-Prussian War that had ended early that year. The band and the singing of the beer garden's well-behaved family clientele could be heard inside Ferguson's studio strongly enough to make Harp and Ferguson speak more loudly than normal.

One wall of the studio was covered with small photographs of sinister-looking men and women. Collecting pictures of criminals was a popular fad among amateur phrenologists—to be studied for proof that one's facial and skull configurations revealed one's inner character. Howard Ferguson got a kick out of mixing pictures of perfectly respectable people who looked villainous with those of genuine criminals when he sold copies to collectors.

His other major source of income was taking posed pictures of the ladies on offer in better-class brothels, for the madams to use as advertising. Alice Curry's name didn't ring a bell with Ferguson —but there was a chance he would recognize her in the morgue. Whether he did or not, Harp wanted him to have copies of her picture ready for him next morning. Ferguson pocketed Captain Redpath's authorization and promised to get to Bellevue's morgue—popularly known as the Dead House—before the night was much older.

There were flurries of snow in the air when Harp left the studio. He turned up his greatcoat collar and headed east from the Bowery, gripping his hickory walking stick a bit more securely as he neared the dark river.

Moe Saul's junkyard was two blocks from the South Street riverfront and six from the warehouse where Alice Curry had died.

Harp reasoned that the thieves would have unloaded their swag to a fence not too far from that warehouse. They would have needed a horse and wagon to transport twelve cases of champagne and fifteen of brandy. The further they traveled with it late at night, the greater the chance of their being stopped and questioned by police.

There were plenty of fences close by; but only two of them handled high-class merchandise in quantity. The other was "Mother" Mandelbaum, whose house and dry-goods shop were on the corner of Clinton and Rivington streets. Like Moses Saul, she often set up burglaries for the thieves who afterwards sold her the stolen goods. Her favorites were jewelry, silverware, works of art, antique furniture and ladies' garments of quality. But Harp had never heard of Mother Mandelbaum dealing in liquor. Moe Saul did. He had two of the best restaurants in town which were prepared to buy any imported spirits he could supply at bargain rates.

Moe's place was between a rope-and-cable factory that had closed for the night and the ruin of a brewery that had been burned by arsonists six years back for the insurance money. The rest of the block, on both sides, was filled with tenements. Some were fairly new five- and six-story affairs. The others were very old, two-story brownstones that had had a couple of extra floors piled on top of them with walls of bricks and wood planking.

The growing numbers of tenements like these, on both sides of lower Manhattan, absorbed the tide of foreign immigrants like sponges, making them the most densely populated buildings in New York. The city as a whole counted 162 inhabitants per acre; in the tenement blocks it was 732 per acre—with a death rate three times greater than that in the rest of the city.

With so many people compressed into so little space, many of these blocks had become cesspools of sordid poverty and criminal violence. But not this block.

The street was silent, deserted. The people living on this block were unskilled, low-paid workers and their families. Many further crowded their cramped flats by taking in other laborers as boarders to help pay the rent. None had reason to be out this late on a bitter winter night. Most of the men were already asleep, restoring energy for the next day's battle for survival. Those still awake—the women, children and old folks—would be bent over take-home piecework on clothing, decorative fans or artificial flowers, in a candlelit room that also served for sleeping, cooking and eating; and would keep at it until their eyes and fingers failed them.

The entrance to Moe's yard, high and wide enough for a horse and covered wagon to pass through, had an iron-barred gate. A streetlamp behind Harp shone through the bars into the yard. It was flanked by the blank walls of the factory and the fire-gutted brewery. Thousands of rags of all sizes had been hung outside for the wind and rain to clean, fluttering from high lines that crisscrossed the yard above piles of sorted junk. At the rear rose the dark shape of Moe Saul's three-floor house. The first two floors contained his shop, office and storerooms, the top, his living quarters.

The gate was padlocked and there was no sign of life inside. No light showed through chinks in the shutters of the two lower floors, nor from the grimy, unshuttered upper windows.

Harp studied the place with a stiffened, brooding expression. It was only half an hour past eleven: far too early for Moe to have closed up shop and gone to sleep. Trash scroungers and thieves did business with him until well after midnight.

Going back to the corner, Harp walked around it and into a wide alley that wandered through the inside of the block, between the backs of tenements with assorted laundry hanging from all of their fire escapes. Moe had attached a fire-escape ladder to his own back wall to obtain a lower rate for the fire insurance he might want to collect on some day. Harp's attention fixed on the window at the top of this ladder.

Its upper pane, like all of the panes in the other top-floor windows, was obscured by greasy dust from the smokestacks of nearby factories and steamships. But its lower pane was entirely clear, transparent. Which meant it was open. Moe was an old man now, prone to colds that could lead to pneumonia. He wouldn't keep a window open on a night like this.

Harp tried the handle of Moe's back door. It was locked. Tucking his walking stick under his left armpit, he dropped his right hand into his greatcoat pocket and brought it out holding a Le Mat revolver. A rare, dual-purpose weapon, the Le Mat had been designed by a Southern officer and France had manufactured a limited number for the Confederacy during the war. It had been the deadliest handgun on either side.

The revolver cylinder was chambered for nine .40 caliber shots. Under the octagonal main barrel was a shorter round one that fired a single charge of 16–gauge buckshot. The shotgun barrel wasn't long enough to be effective at a distance. But at close range its swift spread of shot was certain to inflict damage on anyone in the general target area.

Harp flicked the weapon's hammer to its shotgun position before he started up the fire escape.

He stopped when he was just below the opened window at the top. Steadying himself, he tossed the walking stick through the window, toward the left wall of the room inside. The instant it clattered on the floor there—hopefully distracting anyone inside for a vital moment—Harp jumped through the window going in the opposite direction. He dropped to the floor, rolled and sat up with his back against a corner, ready to fire a shotgun blast at any threatening sound or movement.

There was no sound. If anything moved in the darkly shadowed room, there wasn't enough light from outside for Harp to see it. He concentrated on listening. The fact that no one had attacked or shot at him when he'd come in was a good sign, but not conclusive. He stayed put for another full minute before rising to his feet, fairly sure he was alone in this room but keeping the Le Mat poised for instant use.

He knew the apartment from previous visits. The room he was in was Moe's combination living room and library. On the other side of the room would be the door to Moe's bedroom. It was possible that he would find Moe in there, peacefully asleep. If so, it wouldn't make Harp feel foolish. He never felt foolish about extreme precautions when checking out a place where he sensed something was wrong.

Hoping the furniture hadn't been shifted since his last visit, Harp moved quietly across the room. He found the big table where it had always been, and reached out his free hand to touch the armchair next to it. It wasn't there. He took a careful step and his shin came against something hard. He reached down and found it was the armchair—overturned.

His next step settled on something sticky. Harp crouched and rubbed two fingers against that part of the carpet, raised them to his nostrils then tasted them with the tip of his tongue.

Coagulated blood.

He moved on through the darkness with his free hand extended ahead of him. The bedroom door was open. He went through it quickly, side-stepping to the right with his back sliding against the bedroom wall. Then he froze and listened again. He couldn't hear anything. But that could have been because all of his senses were partially blocked by a powerful stench of death.

Sliding further along the wall, he reached out and found the oil lamp Moe always kept on his bedside table. Harp held the Le Mat covering the rest of the room, with his finger on its trigger. He got a match from his pocket and made fast work of striking it on the wall and lighting the lamp. Counting on it taking anyone else the same seconds it took him for his vision to adjust to the abrupt flare of light in the room.

There was no one else in the room except Moses Saul. A tall, skinny old man with a wizened face, a little gray beard and only a few white hairs left around the base of an otherwise bald skull. He lay neatly on his bed, fully clothed, his legs straight together, arms crossed on his chest, eyes closed, head resting on the pillow.

He was not asleep. The left side of his skull, around the temple, had been caved in. Some dried blood shone there, and on his left ear. But there was none on the pillow.

The bedroom's single window didn't face the front or the back of the house. It looked across a narrow airshaft at the blank factory wall, and it was shut and locked. The closet on the other side of the room was closed, too. Harp pointed the Le Mat in that direction, but ready for a fast switch to the open doorway, and then looked again at Moe Saul.

He was surprised by a twinge of nostalgia. He had been a little boy, and Moe had been a strong man with most of his hair when he'd first done business with him. Selling him a watch he'd lifted from a drunk outside a saloon. Moe had just clawed his way up from rag picker to pushcart junk dealer and very minor-league fence. He'd already scrimped and saved enough, though, to bring his oldest son over from the old country, to help him earn more and bring over the rest of the family. In the traditional way: the next oldest son, and then the youngest. The three sons working to help Moe make the money to bring over his eldest daughter. And, finally, his wife with their youngest daughter.

All seven of them living together in a single tenement room until there was enough saved to buy this junkyard and move in here.

For Harp, in his earliest years as an apprentice thief, they had represented a wonderland of family caring and solidarity. He'd had no father that he knew of. His mother, a consumptive Irish streetwalker whose family name neither he nor anyone else knew, had left him on a chair in a cellar saloon when he was six, and had never reappeared. As a boy, Harp had sometimes had dreams in which Moses Saul was his father and he lived here, above the junkyard, altogether with the rest of Moe's passionate, amoral family.

They were all gone now. Moe's wife and their youngest daughter had died of TB. His oldest son had joined the army early in the war, and had been killed at Shiloh. His eldest daughter was married to a schoolteacher in Brooklyn. His two remaining sons were both studying pharmacy in Philadelphia. Moe had continued to run his junk business and fence stolen goods, to pay off the mortgage on his daughter's Brooklyn home and to support his sons through college. He'd told Harp that as soon as his sons were launched with pharmacies of their own, he intended to retire and go live with his daughter and son-in-law.

Harp lifted one of Moe's hands a few inches and flexed the fingers. At a guess, Moe had been dead for many hours, perhaps a full day and night. Harp put the hand back on Moe's chest and felt through his pockets, without much expectation of finding anything informative.

A small sound reached him. He looked up in the same instant that the door of the bedroom closet slammed all the way open and a figure charged out of it swinging a fire axe at him.

Ten

The closet was far enough away. Harp wouldn't have had to react very fast to fire the Le Mat's shotgun charge before the axe got him. But the figure wielding it was a husky girl in her mid-teens. He laid his gun on the bedside table and stepped aside as the axe slashed down at him. Its blade sliced through the bedroom carpet and embedded itself in the floorboards. She was trying to pull it free when Harp seized her wrists and broke her hands loose from the axe haft.

The girl tried to yank away from him, and then tried to push close enough to knee him and bite his face. She was very strong, and determined. Harp twisted her wrists until her elbows locked, and shoved her back against the wall. When she continued to fight against his grip he twisted a little harder, making her cry out.

"Calm down," he told her quietly, "or I'll break both your arms."

Her resistance collapsed and she began to cry. He recognized her now. He'd seen her together with Moe a few weeks ago, in an oyster bar on the Bowery. They'd been holding hands. She'd been cheaply dressed then. The gray linen dress she wore now, while not quite new, was of good quality. So were her boots. Both dress and boots, Harp imagined, would be from Moe's stock.

He eased his grip on her wrists, just a little. "You wanted to kill me," he said. "Why?"

"You were going to rob him," she sobbed. "A harmless old man that's been good to me and now he's dead and maybe you killed him, too."

"First of all, I wouldn't have any reason to. Moe and I are old friends. Going back more years than you've been on this earth. Since I was a kid younger than you."

"I'll believe that when—"

"Second of all, he's been dead a long time. If I'd killed him, I could have robbed him then. Why would I wait to come back and do it now?"

The girl frowned, trying to think that out. "I don't know . . ." she said uncertainly. "*Somebody* killed him . . . and I thought . . . well, I did see you going through his pockets."

Harp sat her down in a chair before releasing her wrists and stepping back. She didn't try to spring up at him. The rage seemed to have all drained out of her, leaving only sadness.

"I was trying," Harp told her, "to see if there was anything that might tell me what happened to him. I told you, he was my friend. I'll be going after whoever murdered him. Maybe *you* can tell me something about how it happened."

She wiped her wet eyes with her sleeves, staining them. "I got no idea. All I know is I came in and found him that way in the other room. Dead and murdered."

Harp sat down on the edge of the bed, near Moe's feet. "My name's Harp. What's yours?"

"Agnes . . . Agnes Kolisch."

"All right, Agnes—how long ago was it when you found him?"

"Couple hours, I guess. I climbed in the window and found him there, on the floor in the other room. Well, I didn't want to leave him like that. So I dragged him in here and laid him out nice on the bed, like you see. Then I went and got the axe, in case whoever killed him was still around or came back. After that I just sat on the bed next to him, feeling bad and wishing he wasn't dead. Until I heard something fall on the floor in the other room and put out the lamp and hid in the closet. And when I peeked through the keyhole and saw you . . ." She let it go at that.

"How long have you and Moe been together?" Harp asked her.

"Almost a month, now. Before that, he used to visit the house where I started working. He'd come real late, about one night a week. He was too old to really do anything with a girl anymore. Said he just liked the feel of a girl warming up his old bones once in a while. He told us King Solomon used to do that. Have young girls warm him up in bed when he was real old. Mrs. Murphy— that's the madam there—she only has young girls like me. Not too young, though. Between fourteen and seventeen, mostly."

Agnes suddenly giggled and darted a look at the dead man on the bed. "Moe said I gave off more heat than any've the other girls. And he had me move in here to live with him. I guess it got too lonely here for him, all alone. My God it's been nice. All the food I could want, swell clothes, and he never hit me or talked bad, treated me like a princess."

"If you were living here with him, why'd you have to come in through the window?"

"Moe never gave me a key to the place. He said I shouldn't take it like an insult, that was just his habit, being the only one with the keys."

"He didn't mind if you went out at night without him?"

"He *sent* me out," Agnes explained. "That was last night—real late. Gave me money to stay in the Croton Hotel on the Bowery. Like he'd done some nights before that. On account of he had one of his secret meetings. Somebody coming to see him that wouldn't want anybody else being around."

"Do you know who it was, coming by last night?"

"Nope. Like I said, it was a secret."

"What about the other times?"

Agnes shook her head. "He never told me." She looked again at Moe, with a grimace of regret. "Thing is, those other times, I always came back late next morning or early afternoon. But this morning when I left the hotel I ran into an old girlfriend, and she and me and a couple fellas she knows went over to Coney Island for the day. I figured Moe wouldn't get mad at me for that. What I didn't figure was I'd get back here so late. And the place all locked up and dark. That was a surprise. And when I banged on the back door, Moe didn't come down to let me in. I got worried and went to see one of the fellas works here for Moe, lives just over on Cherry Street. He said the place was locked up when him and the other fella works here showed up in the morning, and stayed that way all day. And no sign of Moe."

"So you came back and climbed in the window."

"Yeah, because I was *real* worried by then. I thought I was gonna have to break the window to get in, but I didn't. On account of somebody'd opened it and left it like that, and Moe never did that."

Harp wanted to narrow the space of time in which Moe had been killed: "What time last night did Moe send you away?"

"Must've been around one in the morning."

So Moe had been alive at one A.M.—and almost certainly dead before seven, the hour when he normally opened the place in the morning. He'd been killed somewhere in that six-hour span.

"You're sure it was close to one when you left here?" he asked Agnes.

She nodded emphatically. "Couldn't've been much before one. I was still here when Moe got a delivery he was expecting a little after midnight. He left me out the back door right after the fellas that brung the stuff went away with their wagon and he locked up the front gate after them. Had to take 'em about half an hour to unload all them boxes and put 'em away."

Harp straightened a bit. "What kind of boxes?"

The girl shrugged. "I dunno, just boxes. Moe always sends me upstairs when he's expecting a shipment of something hot. But I heard the horse and wagon come into the yard, and went to the front room window for a look. Four fellas were unloading the wagon and carrying the stuff in. Just some kinda boxes is all I could tell."

"Do you know where Moe hid goods like that until he could unload them?"

"Sure. There's a secret part in the cellar. I even know where he keeps the key to it, in his office."

"I want a look at those boxes," Harp said as he stood up. He took the Le Mat from the bedside table, switched the hammer back to revolver-fire position and made sure it was on an empty chamber before putting it back inside his pocket. "The police are bound to get curious and bust in sooner or later," he told Agnes. "They find you still here, you're an automatic suspect. And they grill rough when it's murder."

"I ain't dumb enough to hang around for that," she said. "I'll pack my things and get out right after you go."

"I may need to talk with you again. Where'll I be able to find you?"

"Back at One-two-three on West Twentieth, I guess. The cathouse where Moe found me. I sure ain't going back to what I did before there. Sewing buttons and ironing eleven hours a day for three-fifty a week. What they call honest work, only it ain't enough to stop you being hungry all the time. Mrs. Murphy's house is paradise compared to that. And she only takes half what we make. Which everybody says is fair. She's got to pay a pretty high rent, on top of what the cops take."

The usual setup. The madams seldom owned their whore-houses. More often they rented them from reputable businessmen who distanced themselves from what the places were used for but not from what they earned. Harp knew a clergyman who collected his extortionate rents from four of them.

He took a last, steady look at old Moses Saul's dead face before he picked up the oil lamp. Using it to light their way out of the bedroom, he retrieved his hickory stick before they started down the stairs. On the way he asked Agnes if she'd ever heard of an Alice Curry. She hadn't.

In the office, she got a key out of a hidden compartment in the back of Moe's rolltop desk. The cellar below was full of old furniture, some of it antiques, the rest just used. There was a huge, dilapidated grandfather's clock flush against one wall, its face cracked and the hour hand gone. Agnes inserted the key into the clock's defunct wind-up mechanism and turned it three times, then told Harp what to do. He pulled the right side of the clock, and it swung away from the wall on oiled hinges, revealing a door-way behind it.

He stepped through and raised the lamp high. There was no surplus of merchandise in the secret chamber. Moe had usually arranged ahead of time for the disposal of the bigger and more valuable stolen goods he received; and he'd never liked keeping it on the premises more than a day or two. But he hadn't lived long enough to move his latest haul to his waiting customers.

Harp counted twelve crates of French champagne and fifteen cases of brandy.

"Did you know any of the men you saw carrying these in from their wagon?" he asked Agnes.

"Oh, yeah—one've them, anyway, for sure. With that build and the pegleg, couldn't be anybody else. You ever seen Hoggy Corcoran?"

Harp nodded. He was well-acquainted with the notorious Hoggy —and his gang.

Eleven

The Fourth Precinct consistently registered more criminal arrests than any other in the city. The next highest number belonged to an adjacent precinct, the Sixth. The hardcore of the city's crooks and cut-throats—hard even by the standards of the rest of the lower east side—had their hangouts scattered through a neighborhood that elbowed into both of those precincts. In the close-packed, decomposing blocks spreading from Mulberry Bend to the old Five Points area where Mulberry Street intersected with Park Street and Baxter.

Harp was at home in these blocks. Nevertheless, he had his walking stick in his left hand and his right on the weapon in his greatcoat pocket as he walked the ill-lit streets between the district's rotting buildings and dark, narrow alleyways.

A large proportion of this quarter's denizens slept by day and came out at night. Tonight the icy wind and increasing snow flurries were keeping many of those inside their squalid dance saloons, gambling dens and end-of-the-line brothels. Many, but not all. Segments of the most dangerous gangs—like the Whyos, the Buttenders, and Hoggy Corcoran's Boyos—would normally brave any kind of weather to carry out raids in other parts of Manhattan. Lesser nightcrawlers stuck to their neighborhood, forming small, shadowy groups in alley entrances, on the lookout for drunk sailors, lost tourists and other easy pickings.

They let Harp pass by after having assessed his size, his steady, purposeful stride, the heft of his walking stick and the way he held it, more like a cudgel than a cane. Not easy pickings. A predator, like themselves. One who knew his way around here.

The Hoggy Corcoran gang's clubhouse was a big room above a

fire-engine company. Like the members of many other gangs, Hoggy's boys were enthusiastic volunteer firemen—between burglaries, armed robberies and gang wars. But tonight Harp found the clubhouse empty, which was more than unusual. Not a single gang member. Not even somebody sleeping off a drunk or tangling with a girlfriend on one of the floor mattresses.

Harp tried another of the gang's favorite hangouts, a sagging frame house inside a muddy, garbage-strewn back alley. The ground floor was a billiard saloon, the second had two rooms devoted to gambling and the attic was an opium den. There was no shortage of hardcase hooligans on each floor; but none of them belonged to Hoggy's gang.

It was the same at the third place he checked. A dim dance hall where the women were all sick, alcoholic prostitutes, and the men came in two varieties: plug uglies and tipsy sailors who would be lucky if they wound up in a gutter, drugged, robbed and stripped instead of dead in the river. Again, neither Hoggy Corcoran nor any of his followers were in evidence.

Hoggy's gang was a fairly big one. Even if its members were involved in several simultaneous looting expeditions, there would ordinarily be some left hanging around the neighborhood. Ordinarily—but not tonight. Tonight they had all disappeared.

Harp couldn't blame them for being that scared.

Nobody really cared about a warehouse robbery any more than about rival gang members killing or crippling each other. The particularly grisly murder of Alice Curry was different. It had made all of the city's evening newspapers—and each of the stories had demanded action from the police.

Harp had read the accounts in several of the papers while he'd been in Bill Howe's office. None of them, he'd noticed, had been specific about the warehouse where Alice Curry's body was found. Nor had any named its owner. Once Harp had learned it was Monmouth Fuller, he'd understood why.

Some newspaper owners shared with Fuller the rich, roistering camaraderie of the Union Club and the Jockey Club—both of whose members took pride in their disdain for the laws and conventions of stuffier or lower forms of mankind. The rest were leery of Fuller's quickness to retaliate, in one vicious way or another, if crossed or offended. Monmouth Fuller had a reputation as an ugly customer, especially when liquored up; and he was known to have killed two men in duels well before his present age of thirty.

The pink-paged *Evening Telegram* had been the most lurid in detailing the gruesome state in which Alice Curry had been found. But the other, slightly less sensational evening papers hadn't been far behind in dwelling on the story's circulation-boosting melange of sex and blood. And none had failed to point out the lesson that this fallen woman's fate posed for virtuous maidens who might be tempted by the visions of pretty clothes and gay life that lured so many to the downward path.

Harp knew most of the newspapermen who had written these sermons into their stories; and knew most of them to be devoted to the company of "fallen women" whenever they could afford it. But they knew their readers, and pandered to them with a cheerful insincerity. The press and public shared a fascination with carnal misconduct while professing to deplore it.

All of the papers had wound up their coverage by appealing to the authorities to catch and hang whoever had committed this ghastly atrocity. And all hoped, with varying degrees of sarcasm, that a police force that had repeatedly failed to curb New York's spreading vice and corruption would not fail in its duty this time.

Under that kind of public pressure, the police would have to show *some* strong activity towards solving the crime. There would be mass roundups, intensive interrogations, merciless squeezing of informers. Payoffs to the cops, past and present, wouldn't get anybody off the hook for a while.

The prospect of getting your brains permanently scrambled by one of Captain Redpath's no-limits third degrees was enough to scare the toughest of suspects into hiding.

Even Hoggy Corcoran.

It had been a long day and a bad night for Harp, and he'd had about enough of it. His left leg, the one with the bullet-broken bone that hadn't mended properly, was beginning to ache from all the walking around. Also, he needed time to clear his emotions by putting some sleep between himself and finding Moe Saul murdered.

One more stop first. Ambrose McGowan, one of Hoggy's chief lieutenants, owned a very old brick house near Chatham Square that he had converted into a business establishment run by his father and two brothers. Back in the old days, Ambrose and Harp had been part of the same boys' gang. That didn't make them friends. But it did make for a mutually wary connection between them, which each made use of now and then.

The ground floor of the house had once been a pharmacy. Now the sign over its plate-glass front window read: MCGOWAN'S ALL-NIGHT EATERY. Harp peered through the dirt-encrusted window. The interior was hazily lit by tallow candles. Tallow gave off sooty smoke, but was cheaper than wax. There were two long tables down the length of the interior, made of planks laid on sawhorses. The customers, mostly late-night laborers and bums who'd managed to beg a few nickels, sat on backless wooden benches. All of them wore their shabby coats buttoned up, and no one took off his cap, battered derby or tattered topper. Most wore gloves of some kind. The only warmth inside came from their bodies, and from the tiny back kitchen where Ambrose's kid sister heated the meals.

There were only two meals to choose from: soup for ten cents, and stew for fifteen. The McGowans were able to keep the prices that low because the meals came from leftovers that better restaurants sold them for almost nothing rather than dump in the garbage.

Ambrose's older brother, Wade, was strolling between the long tables carrying a baling hook like a weapon, ready to throw out any diner who was eating too slowly or falling asleep. If you needed a place to sleep, you could spend the night down on the cellar floor for five cents. And for an extra penny the youngest McGowan brother, Elmus, would pour you a glass of McGowan-distilled beer that might help you sleep, if your stomach could keep it down.

As Harp had anticipated, Ambrose was not in sight inside the eatery. He didn't bother having a look in the cellar. Instead, he went around the house and rapped his stick against the back door. It was opened by Ambrose's father, a grizzled, mean-faced man that Harp had never heard called anything but Pop. He had a pistol in one hand and his other hand was automatically held out empty, palm up. When Pop McGowan saw who it was, he dropped that hand.

"I'm looking for Ambrose," Harp told him. "It's important—to him."

"Yeah?"

Behind Pop, poorly dressed men were waiting their turn on the back staircase, lit by a single candle, that led to the attic. Each had saved or stolen seventy-five cents to spend ten minutes with the woman up there.

"You know where he is?" Harp asked.

"No."

Harp didn't try to persuade him to open up. He got out a pencil and small notebook, and wrote a short message: *You're in worse trouble than you already know. Get in touch with me, while you still can. —Harp.*

A man came trudging down from the attic and went out past Pop and Harp, not looking as if he'd had a great time up there. The men waiting their turn moved up the staircase, one step each.

Harp tore off the note and gave it to Pop McGowan. "Get this to Ambrose as soon as you can."

Pop shrugged. "Sure—next time I happen to see him."

"Take your time," Harp told him, "and the next time you see him'll be at his wake."

He was a long way from Greene Street, the snow was falling harder and it was past the hour when the horsecar and omnibus lines stopped running for the night. There were no cabs in this neighborhood. But it was only a short walk to City Hall Park, where there were always hansom cabs, day or night.

Harp passed a pair of city sweepers with their nightcart, gathering up the day's horse dung accumulation. A block from the park a bill poster was dipping his long brush into his paste bucket and slapping big handbills on top of older ones wherever he couldn't find an unused portion of wall. The new ones were gaudy advertisements for Barnum's Museum on Broadway and Ann Street:

A MILLION CURIOSITIES
LIFE-LIKE MOVING WAX FIGURES
ENORMOUS GIANTS & DIMINUTIVE DWARFS
MAMMOTH FAT WOMAN & LIVING SEALS

POPULAR DIVERSION with the
TOTAL ABSENCE OF AN IMPURE SUGGESTION

The windows of the grandiose new county courthouse on one side of City Hall Park still showed lights blazing inside. Harp guessed it had to be all the members of the Tweed Ring—and the various contractors who'd gotten rich with them—holding late and worried conferences. Trying to work out how they were going to explain to the grand jury why the courthouse, originally planned back in 1858 at a projected cost of $250,000, had taken thirteen years and $12 million to complete.

There was a line of hansom cabs alongside the courthouse, each of the first three with its lamps burning. Harp slapped snow from his hat as he climbed into the first one and told the driver where to take him. He lit a slim cigar and leaned back, smoking it during the ride. The snow was spreading a pleasant blanket of white across streets and sidewalks. But the horse's hooves and the cab's iron wheels cut through it, clattering loudly across the cobbles. New Yorkers had to learn not to hear that noise, or accept never getting an unbroken night of sleep.

Harp had the driver let him off at the corner of Greene and Bleecker. He dropped the cigar in the snow and walked the final half block, automatically scanning both sides of the street as he approached his address. A second-floor window across the street from it was thrown open and a woman leaned out, signaling to him with her hand. Hilda Shaler, a street-cruiser who worked this neighborhood and kept a room up there as her business and living place. Harp entered her building and climbed the steps.

Hilda was on her way down, and met him halfway. "There's a man inside your apartment," she told him. "I saw him go into your building, and then a lamp went on in your place. I could see him behind your lace curtains moving around in there. And then he sat down, and after a while he put out the lamp. But he hasn't come back out. So he's sitting there in the dark."

"How long ago did he go in?" Harp asked her.

" 'Bout two hours ago. I ain't had anything else to do. This weather, there's hardly any business out on the streets, and anyway I got my curse right now. So I just been sitting by the window drinking tea—with a little gin in it—and watching the snow come down. Makes everything look pretty, even if it's bad for business."

"How long after he went in did he put out the lamp?"

Hilda thought it over. "Oh, 'bout half an hour later, I guess. Maybe a little more."

That told Harp pretty much everything he had to know. But just to make certain: "What does he look like?"

"Tall. Taller'n you, even. And skinny. Real good duds, though, like a swell. Walks like an old man—even had to stop and get his breath back after he climbed up your front stoop, before he went inside. But he ain't old. I saw his face when he came under the street lamp down there. No older'n you."

Harp gave her three dollars. "Thanks, Hilda."

"Thanks yourself. This way the night's not a total loss." Hilda gave him a grateful smile as she tucked the money into her bodice. "What're you gonna do, get a cop or what?"

"Don't worry about it," Harp told her, and kissed her cheek before going back down the stairs.

He crossed the street, went up the stoop into his own building and climbed the stairway to his apartment.

Twelve

Harp was quiet about unlocking his door and stepping inside. He struck a match and lit the gas jet on the wall in the small entry before looking into the front room parlor.

It was Leland Van Tromp, of course. Leland was the only other person with a key to Harp's place. Anyone who had picked the lock and come in to ambush Harp wouldn't have lit the lamp on the parlor table to advertise his presence Or have let it burn for half an hour before extinguishing it. Harp lit it again before turning off the wall jet. He hung his hat and coat on the entry coatrack and left his hickory stick there.

Leland was slumped in the parlor rocking chair, fast asleep, Harp's brandy decanter and a glass on the table beside him. It was as good a place for him to sleep as any. A bullet had collapsed one of Leland's lungs. With the damp, the cold, the insufficient food and the rudimentary medical supplies in Libby Prison, his over-worked remaining lung had deteriorated until it had little more than half of its normal capacity. That lung didn't get enough air if he tried to sleep lying down. It wasn't comfortable to sleep sitting up, but at least he could breathe that way.

He had opened his collar and unbuttoned his suitcoat and waistcoat, taking off his boots and putting his stocking feet up on an ottoman before falling asleep. His cane, necktie and hat were on the table near the opened decanter. So was an open novel—*The Moonstone*, by Wilkie Collins—that Leland had taken out of Harp's bookcase and been reading before putting out the lamp.

Talking about books they'd read in the past—along with playing chess, after Leland had taught Harp the game—had cemented their relationship inside Libby. Leland, with his education in preparatory schools and university, had been fascinated to learn that Harp's taste for reading came from tutors hired for him by a cathouse madam.

Harp noticed that Leland, as was his habit, had underlined a passage that interested him on one of the open pages of *The Moonstone:*

"Gentlefolks in general have a very awkward rock ahead in life —the rock ahead of their own idleness. Their lives being, for the most part, passed in looking about them for something to do . . . the poor souls must get through the time, you see—they must get through the time."

Harp looked at Leland's overcoat, dumped on the carpet near his boots. Leland had been taught from earliest childhood to drop his clothes on the floor, for the servants to pick up and take care of. That was the servants' job, and if you took care of it yourself, you were robbing them of part of their means of employment. Leland no longer had any servants, but he hadn't been able to entirely shake off his early training.

As Hilda Shaler had noted, Leland's clothes were of top quality, and still quite stylish. All of his clothing was from before the war: an extensive wardrobe had been made for him by fashionable tailors in London by the time his father had gone broke. It was all of choice materials that wouldn't show wear for years to come; and men's styles didn't change as quickly and radically as women's. A cut-rate tailor on the lower east side had done an expert job of altering everything to fit as though originally made for his now wasted figure.

As Hilda had also seen, Leland was Harp's age. Night and the distance had prevented her from seeing his sunken eyes and the deep lines grooved into his handsome face. Harp studied that face with a scowl. Either he'd forgotten how bad Leland had looked when he'd last seen him, three weeks ago, or else Leland had deteriorated noticeably in that short time.

Going to his bathroom, Harp got out of his boots and hung his clothing up to dry. He returned to the front room wearing a thick wool dressing gown and slippers lined with sheepskin. Leland was still asleep in the rocker. Harp picked up his coat from the floor and hung it on the entrance coatrack.

The front room was getting too cool: when Leland wasn't mov-

ing around he breathed better with warm air. Leland had made a
fire in the pot-bellied stove, but it was now down to glowing embers. Harp shook down the ashes and spread fresh coal over the
embers. When he turned around, he saw that Leland's eyes were
open and he was smiling at him. Leland could sometimes sleep
right through the most thunderous noises; but whenever he awoke
it was all the way, with no trace of sleepiness.

"Good evening, lieutenant," Leland greeted him.

Harp smiled back at him. "Good evening, captain."

Libby had been a warehouse in Richmond, the Confederate
capital, that had been converted into a prison for captured Union
officers. Harp hadn't been an officer for more than ten days before his capture. The battlefield promotion to temporary lieutenant's rank had been thrown at him haphazardly—and for much
the same reason that he'd previously been jumped to sergeant.
Too many sergeants and officers were being killed off. Company I
of the Eighty-first New York Volunteer Infantry was running short
of more qualified candidates to take their place.

Leland poured more brandy into his glass, took a sip, and
sighed appreciatively. "Good stuff. Nice of you to keep the decanter topped up just for me."

"No more than you're entitled to," Harp said. "Brandy being
the gentleman's drink, and you being a certified gentleman."

"I surely am," Leland agreed, and watched Harp get a whiskey
bottle and glass from his liquor cabinet. "You, on the other hand,
stick with that rotgut. As you should, of course, since you are not a
gentleman."

"Surely not," Harp agreed, pouring a sizable amount of whiskey
into his glass and raising it in a silent toast before taking a swallow.

Leland had another sip of brandy and said, "I also raided your
icebox and kitchen cupboard. I seem to get hungry more often
lately."

"You just have a healthy appetite," Harp said. "Like me."

"Every time I stuff myself," Leland said, "I find myself remembering Libby. You, too?"

Harp drank more of his whiskey. "Libby is something I don't
think about much, when I don't have to."

Leland, a captain from the Seventy-third New York Volunteers,
had already spent eight months inside Libby before Harp arrived

with the latest batch of Yankee officers being stuffed into that
badly overcrowded, makeshift prison. Harp had arrived in bad
shape. He was suffering blinding headaches and sporadic black-
outs from the sword blow across his forehead. He was running a
high fever from the inflammation in his torn and broken leg. A
Confederate surgeon had wanted to saw the leg off, to prevent
him from dying of gangrene. Harp had sworn that if he survived
without the leg, he would come back on crutches after the war,
find the surgeon and kill him. The overworked surgeon had
shrugged, stitched his head wound, set and splinted the broken
bone and gone to attend to less difficult wounded men, Rebel and
Yankee.

It had been night, and both the upstairs and downstairs floors
of the warehouse-prison had been covered with the stretched-out
figures of sleeping prisoners, when guards carried Harp inside.
The guards had kicked two sleepers aside to make a narrow space
for Harp, and had laid him down between Leland and a Pennsylvania captain who was hanged two days later for killing a guard in
an escape attempt.

Leland, with the help of one of the Union doctors among the
prisoners, had taken care of Harp through his worst few weeks. By
the time Harp had recovered enough to hobble around—with the
aid of a homemade crutch supplied, out of simple kindness, by a
guard who was a carpenter in civilian life—Leland's remaining
lung was in decline. It had become Harp's turn to take care of
Leland, twice fighting another prisoner to make sure Leland got
his allotted portion of food.

There was never enough food. The Confederacy couldn't be
blamed too much for that. With all of its harbors captured or
blockaded, with Sherman's army burning a wide swath across the
farmlands of Georgia, and with Grant's army eating everything in
its path during its torturous advance through Virginia toward
Richmond, the civilians and soldiers of the South didn't have
enough food for themselves and couldn't spare much of what they
did have for prisoners of war.

On top of malnutrition, there was Libby's unsanitary conditions, its plague of fleas, lice and bedbugs, being unable to get
outside for clean air and exercise, the lack of adequate medical
supplies. The location of the warehouse-prison made matters

worse. Near the gas works and only half a block from the James
River, it was subject to fumes from the one and constant damp
from the other.

A great many had died before the tenacious approach of
Grant's army persuaded the Confederacy to move the surviving
prisoners further south. Except for those considered too close to
death to be worth moving. That had included Harp and Leland.
But they'd still been there, and still alive, when their last guards
fled and federal troops marched into the Confederate capital.

"I have a short job for you," Harp told Leland. "It won't take
much effort and the money's good."

"An easy job that pays well," Leland said, "would be rather
welcome at the moment."

Harp told him what Louise Vedder had learned from Uriah
Gibbon about Daniel Drew's project for a new railroad line into
the western Catskills. "I'd like you to nose around among your
robber-baron acquaintances. Drop enough hints about the project
to whet their appetite—without giving them anything they can
operate from until we let them have the specifics. Find out which
of them would pay the most for advance information on those
specifics."

Leland considered it, nodding slowly. "I think I can do that
without too much difficulty. Do you want me to close the deal with
the highest bidder? Or would you rather handle that yourself?"

"You do it. Tycoons get to be tycoons by double-crossing people. Whoever I sold the tip to might claim it wasn't worth what
we'd agreed on when he didn't have all the facts, and pay me
whatever he felt like. None of them will do that to a Van Tromp,
not after giving you his sworn word."

"At least not the ones I'll talk to," Leland said.

"You get twenty percent of whatever you settle for," Harp told
him. "From my share."

"Naturally," Leland said dryly. "The lady in the situation must
get her full half. For a fellow who is surely not a certified gentleman, you sometimes exhibit an alarming tendency to behave
like one." Leland sipped his brandy. "I see you still have her
picture enshrined in your bedroom. Curiosity about that made me
wander in there to check."

"So?"

"You still haven't told her how you feel about her?"

"What d'you expect me to tell her?" Harp demanded. "That I fell in love with her picture and want to spend my life with her—and by the way, I killed her husband?"

"Your highly selective sense of honor has never failed to astonish me, particularly in such a basically amoral man. All you would have to do is stick to what you have already told her. Her husband sounds to you as if he was a splendid fellow, but you never met him. Why tell her anything different?"

"And then what? Wait for somebody to come along—in a year, or ten years—who knows the truth and tells it to her?"

"You'd lie your way out of it," Leland said. "For God's sake, you're the best liar I know."

Harp finished off the whiskey in his glass and stood up. "My problem, captain. Stop making it yours. You staying here tonight, or going home?"

Leland leaned back in the rocking chair and closed his eyes. "I don't feel like getting up and making the hike. And I was having such a pleasant dream. I know it was pleasant, but I can't remember what it was about. Perhaps it will come back."

By the time Harp had added more coal to the fire, Leland was asleep. Snuffing out the lamp, Harp went into his bedroom and sat on the edge of the bed, in the darkness there, looking at Louise Vedder's picture. He didn't need a light to see her face in it. He knew it much better than his own. He had looked at that picture at least once every single day that he'd been inside Libby.

One of the other prisoners of war had stopped to look at it over Harp's shoulder early during that year and had remarked, respectfully, on how lovely the woman in the picture was—and had asked if she was Harp's wife.

Harp had said yes. Perhaps he had felt, in that time when he was still drained of strength by his wounds, a need to pretend that he had someone whom he belonged to.

After that everyone in Libby, many of whom treasured similar pictures of their loved ones, accepted his lie as a fact. Leland was the only one from that period to whom, some months after the war, Harp had told the truth.

*   *   *

Halfway between Washington and Richmond, General Grant pushed his army across the Rapidan River and into the concealment of a forest known as the Wilderness. His intention was to get his forces through the Wilderness unnoticed, surprise General Lee's smaller army out in the open on the other side and force the Southern forces to fall back to defend the outskirts of the Confederate capital. But Lee read Grant's mind well ahead of time. He sent his own army to ambush Grant's inside the Wilderness. There the density of the forest would blind the Union's superior artillery, and break its greater number of troops into splinter groups unable to mount a massed charge and vulnerable to hidden sharpshooters.

Harp knew nothing of these grand plans and counterplans at the time. Combat troops seldom did: they learned about the battles they fought only afterwards, if they survived, from accounts written by reporters who stuck close to the generals.

All Harp knew was that he was alone in the middle of a thick forest, with invisible enemies all around him, the rest of his Company I scattered five minutes ago by sharpshooters firing from behind trees and fallen logs and up in the branches. There were Rebel yells nearby to his right, but he was surrounded by bullet-slashed pines and dogwoods that prevented him from seeing movement more than twenty feet away. Union cannons, firing from far back at what might or might not be Confederate positions, had set the forest on fire. The wind was blowing clouds of smoke from the burning trees and bushes in Harp's direction, further obscuring the dim light under the foliage that hid the sky. He had used up the last of his ammunition. If he ran into a Johnny Reb before he could get back to a supply wagon, he had nothing left to use against him but his rifle butt or bayonet.

And he was stuck where he was: his right foot trapped by something underneath a knee-high tangle of vines and thorn brush.

Cursing, he slashed at the tangle with his bayonet, until he'd cleared it away from his leg. And then for one long, shocked moment, he looked down in horror. His boot had crushed into the ribcage of an old skeleton. A remnant from another battle, a year earlier, when Lee had outmaneuvered another superior Union army in this same area. Harp's foot and ankle were gripped by the skeleton's broken ribs.

He wrenched himself out of his shock and hammered at the ribcage with his rifle butt. Not giving a damn if the skeleton was Reb or Yankee: it was his enemy. The bones were shattering to fragments and dust when a young Confederate officer stumbled out of the trees near him, a Colt cavalry revolver in one hand and a saber in his other. Harp yanked his leg free as the revolver was aimed, its trigger squeezed. A dry click: no bullets left. Harp charged, leading the way with his bayonet. Saw the enemy drop the revolver and swing the saber at him. Tried to duck under it but was struck a terrible blow that rocked his head and numbed his brain. Blood pouring into his eyes, blinding him, he lurched forward, driving the bayonet into flesh. Drove it in deeper, twisting it with all of his fading strength.

The rifle was snatched from his hands and he was falling to his knees, unable to see anything now but his own blood. He rubbed at his eyes and could see again. The Confederate officer was on his back, with Harp's bayonet deep in his midsection, the rifle sticking up in the air but starting to tilt as its weight dragged at the embedded blade. More blood streamed into Harp's eyes, burning them. He snatched his bandanna from his neck, wiped his eyes with it, tied it tightly around his head to staunch the flow from the wound across his throbbing forehead. He began to cough from breathing too much smoke from the nearing fires, and the coughing ended in a wave of dizziness. He fought to stay balanced on his knees, and as the dizziness subsided he heard a whispering.

It was the dying Reb. He was gesturing weakly at a pocket of his uniform coat. "Please . . ." he whispered, ". . . my wife . . . letter . . . send it . . . please . . ."

And then he was dead.

Harp found himself reaching into the pocket, though later he was never sure it was of his own volition. He was too dazed by then to think straight. Four men he knew, Company I privates, burst out of the trees in panicked retreat toward the Union rear as Harp drew an addressed envelope and a tintype out of the dead officer's pocket. When they saw Harp they stumbled to a halt, panting, and looked down at the picture in his hand at the same time he did.

"Purty gal," one of them said. "But this ain't no time for collecting souvenirs, lieutenant."

"Fire's coming this way," another blurted. "And so're the Rebs, too darn many of 'em. Gotta get outa here, fast."

Harp stuffed the letter and tintype picture into his pocket as he shoved to his feet, spreading his legs for balance, hearing the crackling of flames now, entire pine trees igniting like firecrackers, the heat of the blaze reaching through the thickening smoke. He staggered along with his four privates, but not far. They were crossing a small clearing when musket fire cracked from the underbrush off to their left.

His leg went out from under him and he fell into a bramble bush, scratching his hands and face. When he raised his head he saw one of his men crumpled near him with an ear and part of his skull shot away. The other three were racing from the clearing, vanishing into the woods. He looked at his leg. The end of a snapped bone stuck out of the bleeding bullet wound. It didn't hurt much yet, but he knew he couldn't walk any further.

He was sitting there on the ground, both hands raised high in surrender, when six Rebel soldiers came out of the trees and took him prisoner.

By then he had pushed the Confederate officer's letter out of sight under the bramble bush. In case his captors searched him, he didn't want them assuming, as his own men had, that he had been looting the Rebel dead for souvenirs.

But there was nothing on the back of the tintype to indicate where the picture had been taken or whom it belonged to. That, after looking at her face again for one hasty second, Harp kept, without analyzing why.

Thirteen

Riding a cab to Monmouth Fuller's house the next morning, Harp looked through the day's New York *Tribune*. There was nothing new in it about Alice Curry or the warehouse robbery—and nothing about the murder of Moe Saul. So he passed part of the ride reading a piece by an occasional *Tribune* reporter whose contributions were usually pertinent fun. This one concerned what New Yorkers were discovering about the extent of their city's political corruption:

A REVISED CATECHISM by Mark Twain

Q. What is the chief end of man? **A.** To get rich.

Q. In what way? **A.** Dishonestly if we can, honestly if we must.

Q. Who is God, the only one and true? **A.** Money is God.

Q. How shall a man attain the chief end of life? **A.** By furnishing imaginary carpets to the courthouse, apocryphal chairs to the armories and invisible printing to the city.

Q. What works were chiefly prized for the training of the young in former days? **A.** *Poor Richard's Almanac*, the *Pilgrim's Progress* and the Declaration of Independence.

Q. What are the best prized Sunday-school books in this more enlightened age? **A.** *St. Hall's Garbled Reports*, *St. Fisk's Ingenious Robberies*, *St. Gould on the Watering of Stock*, *St. Tweed's Handbook of Morals* and the courthouse edition of the *Holy Crusade of the Forty Thieves*.

Q. Do we progress? **A.** You bet your life.

It had stopped snowing sometime in the night. Under the morning's heavy clouds it was too cold for the fallen snow to melt, but not quite cold enough for it to freeze solid. The heavy morning traffic thundering over the cobbles of Fifth Avenue had already broken through the thin crust of ice and churned the snow into dirty slush. But after Harp's cab carried him north of Fifty-ninth Street the traffic was left behind. There were only a number of carriage tracks marking the snow to indicate that some people did live above that line.

Monmouth Fuller was one of the small number of eccentric millionaires who had built themselves new mansions "out of town": on upper Fifth Avenue, facing the east side of Central Park. It was because of the park that Fuller had done so. He belonged to a wealthy group of sporting gentlemen with a passion for racing a coach-and-four at breakneck speeds over long distances. It was no longer possible to enjoy a fast ride in the crowded city below Fifty-ninth Street, except sometimes late at night. But the miles of carriage roads in the park, especially at its northern end, afforded Fuller an opportunity for a daily practice run, making sure neither he nor his horses lost the stamina and keen edge required for the longer races to as far away as Philadelphia or Boston.

Harp took in Fuller's mansion as his cab approached. It stood alone on an otherwise empty block, like the others this far up Fifth Avenue, and had a sizable red brick stable, a corral and an exercise yard for the horses out back. The residence itself was an ungainly mixture of architectural styles: Neo-Moorish, French Renaissance, Gothic Revival. It looked big enough to house several well-off families. But Monmouth Fuller was a bachelor, sharing his mansion with only his servants and selected guests.

In his younger days he had been the target of every society couple with a marriageable daughter. He had dodged every one of their traps. By now, however, no respectable family cared to have a daughter married to a man of his reputation. His headlong career as a prankish rake, and his shocking behavior in polite society when he'd had too much to drink, had caused the important society matrons to bar him from their homes.

From what Harp had heard, Fuller didn't mind the exclusion. The long, staid society gatherings had bored him stiff; and he had too much money to fear that he would ever lack invitations from more fun-loving circles. For male company, he preferred the jolly sports at the Union and Jockey clubs. In female company his taste ran to young actresses and women from the "upper ten" of New York's temples of love. His reputation, coupled with his contempt for society's opinion, insured him against blackmail-by-scandal. Not even Howe & Hummel had ever pinned him with a breach-of-promise charge. No woman could claim to be unaware that Monmouth Fuller was a notorious womanizer with no intention of marrying anyone. And no one wanted to provoke him into an act of vengeance.

Harp told the cab driver to wait for him, went up the steps, and used the heavy, iron door knocker. It set off muffled echoes inside, as though the mansion were a giant drum. The door was opened by a butler of the kind you usually came across in Manhattan: British, with an air of being superior to the people he served but too reserved to show approval or disapproval of their doings by the slightest flicker of expression. He informed Harp that Mr. Fuller was away at the moment and yes he would return but unless Harp had an appointment . . .

At that point the butler's attention was drawn to a hansom cab drawing to a halt behind Harp's. Harp looked in that direction and saw a brawny man with a battered face and a crimson eye-patch climb out. Mike McKibbin: a professional boxer and any-thing-goes fighter who'd gotten his insides badly damaged by a stomping in his last battle, seven months ago. It didn't seem that he'd gone broke since then. His bowler hat was new, his coat was beaver fur, and the crimson patch, which covered a hole where the eye had been gouged out in an earlier anything-goes fight, looked as if it was made of satin.

His expansive smile distorted the scar tissue around his mouth as he came up the steps to Harp. "Hey, what're *you* doing here?"

Harp noted that McKibbin had an excellent new set of false teeth. "Came to see Fuller," he told him. "But it seems he's not in."

"He'll be back soon," McKibbin assured him. "We got a sparring date."

"Here?"

"Sure. He's got a big room fixed up like a gym. Punching bags,

dumbbells, ring for boxing and wrestling, the whole shootin'
match. C'mon in out've the cold.'' To the butler McKibbin said,
''S'okay, Rodgers. Harp's with me.''

The butler accepted that with a fractional, expressionless nod
and stood aside for them to enter. After closing the door he took
their hats, coats and walking sticks, their gloves and mufflers. He
was sorting them in a commodious vestibule alcove when McKibbin took Harp's elbow and steered him down a wide hallway.
''Let's wait in the library. Got a jim-dandy view've the park, and
that's where Mr. Fuller'll be right now, givin' the horses their
morning workout.''

The library entrance, its sliding doors open, was flanked by two
marble statues. One was of a jockey riding a horse in full racing
stride. It seemed as if they were trying to get at the statue on the
other side of the doorway: a nude, full-breasted nymph holding a
vase on one shoulder.

The room referred to as ''the library'' was warmed by a low
blaze in a huge fireplace. Big bay windows let in gloomy daylight.
Deep Persian carpets covered most of the marble floor. There
were mahogany and rosewood tables, leather-padded armchairs
and sofas and a large liquor cabinet. But Harp didn't see a single
book. Much of the paneled wall space had been hung with framed
pictures. Racing, boxing and yachting prints. Two large oil paintings: a luxurious harem scene, and a dancing Salome down to her
last two veils.

McKibbin gestured at the prints. ''Like you see, Mr. Fuller's a
fancier of the sporting life.''

Harp nodded at the oil paintings. ''And womanflesh.''

''He gets them paintings done special for him.'' McKibbin was
frowning at an empty space on one wall. ''The last one he put up
ain't here anymore. Shame. It'd've given you a real turn. A regular
stunner, that one. Girl with a peachy figure, not a stitch on her
and not coverin' anything with her hands, neither.'' McKibbin
headed for the liquor cabinet. ''If you want a drink, Mr. Fuller
don't mind fellas helping themselves.''

Harp shook his head and went closer to the harem painting;
then the dancing Salome. They looked as if they'd been done by
the same artist, but there was no signature on either one.

''Know who the artist is?'' he asked.

McKibbin didn't. Harp wandered over to the bay windows. Looking across Fifth Avenue into the park, he asked, "How often do you drop in to spar with Fuller?"

McKibbin came over beside him with a tumbler filled with bourbon. "Twice a week, most weeks. But sometimes he telegraphs me for an extra session, if he's been boozin' too much and needs to sweat it out've his system."

"He any good?"

"He's strong and he's quick. Can hurt you when he lands a solid punch. But he loses his temper and swings wild too much for that to happen a lot. Hot-blooded gent."

"Ever hurt him back?"

McKibbin winked his lone eye. "Just enough so's he don't catch on I'm going easy on him. Not enough to hurt his feelings. He figures he's almost a pro. Wouldn't want him hiring somebody else what's better at helping him believe it."

"Good pay?"

McKibbin nodded. "And there's the parties, too. Good liquor and lots of free and easy girls. What'cha call the good life." He pointed toward the park. "What'd I tell you, here he comes now."

Harp saw a coach-and-four careening around a tight curve in a carriage road between the bare-branched trees. The wheels skidded in the snow, and one of the lead horses slipped and almost went down, slowing the others. Fuller used his whip ruthlessly, lashing the horses to a last burst of all-out speed. Harp could see the frightened face of Fuller's coachman, who was clinging with both hands to the seat beside his employer.

"He's going to kill his horses," Harp said quietly, "if he pushes them that hard over a long run."

"He's already killed a few. Guess he figures as long as he can buy new ones without the cost bothering him any . . ." McKibbin shrugged.

Seconds later, Fuller reined the horses to a savage halt in front of his mansion, tossed the reins to his coachman and jumped to the ground. The horses were ready to drop from exhaustion: chests heaving, legs trembling, froth bubbling from their gasping mouths. There was some blood oozing from under their bits: evidence that Fuller used bit-burrs—pads punctured by sharp tacks— that made a horse hold its head up attractively, and go into a showy prance of pain when the reins were jerked. The recently formed Society for the Prevention of Cruelty to Animals had managed to have a fine imposed on anyone caught using a burr: ten dollars, which would mean nothing at all to anyone who could afford to buy prime horseflesh.

Fuller vanished from view as he stomped toward his front door, leaving his coachman to climb down shakily and lead the horses and carriage around to the stable. There was a slamming of the entrance door. A minute later Fuller came into the library, minus his hat, coat and gloves, red-eyed and still breathing hard from his race through the park.

Fourteen

Monmouth Fuller was a stocky, vigorous man with heavy shoulders but smallish hands, the fingers thick and blunt, his thumbs abnormally short. His wind-inflamed face was wide and muscular, with a prickly expression. He hardly glanced at McKibbin and Harp as he marched toward the room's largest table. Halfway there he stopped suddenly, spun around, and screamed, "Rodgers! Where the Devil's my hot rum punch!"

The butler entered a second later, carrying a steaming silver bowl. "Here you are, sir."

"Damn it, Rodgers! You know it's supposed to be ready, right here, waiting for me when I come back!"

"Yes, sir," Rodgers said impassively. "Sorry, sir."

It would be easy, Harp thought, to dismiss Monmouth Fuller simply as a thirty-year-old spoiled brat. But there was probably more to it than that. Some underworld thugs of Harp's acquaintance showed the same symptoms. Cracked in the head in a way that made them dangerously unpredictable. Like Hoggy Corcoran. The crack wasn't wide enough to get them committed to the loony bin, but it was there.

The butler had set the steaming bowl of rum punch down on the table. Fuller snarled at him, "It better be waiting right there for me next time, or you'll be looking for another job. Without any reference from me."

"Yes, sir." The butler gave one of his fractional nods and made his exit—passing a pretty, young servingmaid bringing in a silver tray with three china cups on it. She put it down next to the steaming bowl and made a little curtsy to Fuller. When she turned away, he gave her a lazy slap across her buttocks. She shot him an impudent smile and exited, hips swinging.

"She's a new one," McKibbin commented, in a deferential tone that Harp had never heard him use with anyone before.

"New," Fuller said lightly, "but already in training, one might say." He was trying to sound relaxed and amusing now, but he was wound up too tight inside for the abrasive edge to disappear entirely. He dipped a cup into the rum punch and drained half of it with one swallow.

Harp watched Fuller wince as the drink burned his tongue and throat, then force himself to empty the cup without wincing again.

His grandfather had been a hard man from Illinois who had built a fortune on transporting meat and grain to New York via the Erie Canal and the Hudson. His father, who had increased that fortune by establishing an import-export business between Europe and the Midwest, was reputed to have been equally hard. Monmouth Fuller, Harp guessed, had spent most of his thirty years trying to prove himself as hard as his father and grandfather, but still worried that some people might not entirely believe it.

"We was just saying," McKibbin told Fuller, continuing to use that deferential tone, "as how you could get yourself hurt bad one've these day, you keep racing that fast. 'Specially when it's so slippery out there. Your carriage could turn over and throw you— like what happened to that city councilman a coupla months back, that got hisself killed that way."

"Danger is healthy for a man," Fuller said, refilling his cup. "For a woman, too, come to think of it. Danger of a different sort." He smiled at the thought.

McKibbin laughed and gestured at the blank space on the wall. "Talking 'bout dangerous women, what's happened to that swell picture you put up there a coupla weeks ago?"

Fuller drank from his cup, a circumspect sip this time. "Gave it to a friend. Birthday present."

"Sure hope he appreciates it much as I did," McKibbin said. "It was a humdinger."

Fuller sipped from his cup again, looking at Harp. "So who is this?" he asked McKibbin. "A friend you've brought along as a substitute sparring partner for me? Have I been hitting you too often and too hard lately?"

"You been hitting better and harder, Mr. Fuller, that I got to admit. But Harp's just a friend I ran into outside here. We know each other from the fights. He's pals with lots of the boys in the game.''

Fuller took his time sizing Harp up. "You look tough enough, and you're certainly big enough. Care to go a few rounds with me?''

Harp shook his head. "I'm not a boxer.''

"You just like to watch?''

"Sometimes. If it's a good match.''

Fuller noted the tumbler in McKibbin's hand, and gestured for Harp to join him. "Have a few cups of this punch and perhaps you'll change your mind. There's enough rum in it to put some fight into you.''

"Too early in the day for me,'' Harp told him.

Fuller gave him a cold, bored look. "You don't fight and you don't drink this early. So what are you here for?''

"I'm hunting for information about Alice Curry.''

Fuller took a second. "Who is that?''

"The woman who was killed in your warehouse two nights ago.''

"Who told you it was my warehouse?'' Fuller demanded.

"I've got some friends with the police,'' Harp told him.

"Captain Redpath?''

"Redpath is not the one who told me. I take it you've met him.''

"Yesterday. What a disappointment. I was looking forward to knowing him. Someone with his reputation, I thought, would be a real man. But he wouldn't even let me buy him a drink. Turns out to be one of those temperance cream puffs.''

"He swore an oath to his wife that he wouldn't drink.''

"Makes it even worse,'' Fuller snorted. "A man who takes orders from a female isn't a man.'' He finished his cup and refilled it again. "What are you, a journalist?''

"No. I've been hired by a law firm that has a client who wants to know about Alice Curry's background.''

"Who is the client?'' Fuller asked negligently.

"They haven't told me that,'' Harp said. "Did Captain Redpath have you look at Alice Curry's corpse?''

"If that's the name of the whore who died in my place, yes. It's not a name that stuck in my head, though I suppose Redpath told it to me at some point when he took me to the morgue. Not an experience I enjoyed.''

"Did you recognize her?"

"How could I recognize someone I never saw before?"

"She was killed in your warehouse."

Fuller was looking quite bored with all of this. "Probably by the thieves who robbed me. And I don't know who *they* are either, naturally. Anymore than I know the dead whore."

Harp took a photograph from his pocket. It was a copy of the best one taken in the morgue last night by Ferguson, who'd told Harp he didn't know the woman he'd photographed. Harp had already given other copies to his runners, though he wasn't counting on their helping much.

He showed his copy to Monmouth Fuller. "This her?"

Alice Curry's face had been washed clean of blood and makeup before the picture had been taken; but that would have been done before Redpath took Fuller to look at her.

Fuller gave the picture a brief look. "It might be. I suppose so." He looked away with a grimace of distaste. Though cleaned, the slash across her throat was all too evident. "To tell the truth, I didn't spend much time looking at her." He grinned suddenly, baring large, strong teeth. "Dead women don't interest me. I prefer them more lively."

Mike McKibbin had come close and was looking at the photo with a self-communing frown. Harp handed it to him. "Know her?"

"Why would he?" Fuller demanded peevishly. "It's not *his* place the slut picked to die in."

McKibbin was studying the picture, frowning uncertainly. "Seems like I might've seen her somewheres. But I dunno, I could be wrong." He shook his head. "Yeah, it's maybe just the way she looks here, she could be lots've girls I've seen around."

That was the problem with pictures of the dead, especially after a day or so had passed. Unless you had known the person well, or were told who it was ahead of time, it was sometimes hard to make the connection. Even in statues, the faces had a semblance of life to them; but not pictures of a corpse more than thirty hours dead.

"Does the name Alice Curry mean anything to you?" Harp asked McKibbin.

"No." McKibbin was much surer of that than he'd been about the photograph.

Harp put the picture back in his pocket and turned to Fuller: "What time was your warehouse closed the night she was killed there?"

"I don't run the damned place myself on a day-to-day basis," Fuller said. "Naturally I pay a manager for that."

"I talked to him earlier this morning. He's the one who told me I could find you here. According to him, you were at the warehouse that night. And stayed there after he finished his day's work and left."

Fuller's frown was nothing like McKibbin's. It was full of choked-up anger. "I was checking the warehouse books for the month, and I hadn't finished when it was time for him to quit work. I saw no reason to make him stay just to keep me company."

"When did you close up and leave?"

"I wasn't clock-watching, dammit. Ten or ten-thirty, I suppose."

"Alice Curry didn't drop by while you were still there, alone? You didn't let her in?"

Fuller stared at him. "Why in the world would I?"

Harp tried a placating smile. "You do have a reputation for liking the ladies. The free-and-easy kind."

"Naturally. I'm a man. Not like the society fops that don't have anything below the waist, or that are afraid to let people know they do. That doesn't mean I'd invite a trollop I'd never seen before into my place of business in the middle of the night!"

"You *didn't* know her, then—never even heard of her before?"

Fuller switched his fury to McKibbin. "I don't like this friend you brought here. I'm good enough to answer his stupid questions —which he has no right to ask in the first place—and then he asks them again. As though he didn't believe me the first time."

"I didn't exactly bring him here, Mr. Fuller," McKibbin told him uncomfortably, not wanting to look at Harp. "He just happened to be at your door when I showed up and we kinda came in at the same time."

Harp had seen Mike McKibbin get knocked down eight times towards the end of a forty-round fight against John Morrissey, and get off the floor to knock Morrissey out cold in the final round. He had watched Bill Poole whip McKibbin to a bloody, stumbling pulp for thirty-six rounds and McKibbin had taken it without a whimper, spitting out broken teeth and accepting the defeat with a grin on his torn face and his chin tilted with invincible pride.

But he was almost cringing before Monmouth Fuller. It made Harp think of Twain's *Revised Catechism:* "Money is God."

For Mike McKibbin, Fuller was now God's dispenser or withholder. It didn't make Harp think less of McKibbin. People without money did whatever they had to do in order to get by. It was people who had more than they'd ever need, and who couldn't find reasonable ways to enjoy it, that sometimes irritated him.

Harp bade the two men farewell, shook McKibbin's hand warmly, although the anguished fighter still wouldn't look him in the face, and left. He had learned as much as he was going to here, for the time being. More than he'd expected to.

Fifteen

Outside Fuller's mansion he climbed into his waiting cab and told the driver to cross the park and take the Hunter's Gate exit to the upper west side. As he rode across the park Harp took out his two photographs.

The one of Olivia Walburton: a pretty young woman with dark hair pulled back into a severe bun and the high collar of her dress hiding most of her throat—a plump and voluptuous look to her lips but her dark eyes shy, unsure, having difficulty looking directly into the camera.

And the one of a dead Alice Curry: pale blonde hair spread out to frame a face that was composed of nicely molded features but was empty of expression, drained of any hint of what she might have been like when alive.

Harp held one picture in each hand, looking from one to the other, trying to make them tell him something. They told him nothing that he didn't already know.

There were spiritualists who claimed they could use photographs of the dead to establish contact with them. The phenomenon was called psychometry. But Harp wasn't a spiritualist, and he knew most professional spiritualists to be charlatans. He had nothing against the current craze for spiritualism, nor against the fakers taking advantage of it. It was, after all, a way of earning a living without doing too much harm. But he found even its non-charlatan practitioners—those who genuinely believed they had certain supernormal powers—too relentlessly solemn about it to spend much time with them.

Except for Tennessee Claflin, of course. Tennessee was young, picture-pretty, deliciously curvaceous, full of saucy humor and—as

others besides Harp could testify—a lot of fun in bed. Not anyone's conception of how a spiritualist was supposed to look or act.
Yet there were men and women who believed that she had healed
them of illnesses by simply touching them: the laying on of her
hands. There were others who swore that she had made contact
for them with dead loved ones. Tennessee herself, Harp knew,
believed she did have these powers.

Thinking about her made him smile. And then he stopped smiling and looked at his two pictures—while holding on to the
thought that Tennessee had triggered in him.

There was Olivia Walburton, as high in the *Social Register* before
her marriage as after it.

And there was Alice Curry, a murdered prostitute.

The gulf between them had been almost as wide when Alice
Curry was alive as it was now that she was dead.

Put aside for the moment the most easily acceptable possibility:
that someone had stolen some of Olivia Walburton's things and
given or sold them to Alice Curry. Think instead about what Olivia
Walburton had said in her last letter to her husband about seeking
a different life for herself. Suppose that Alice Curry had also been
seeking a different life for herself.

Considering events currently agitating the currents of American
society, there were two major disturbances that could have
brought these two women together across the enormous gulf between them.

One was the spiritualism craze, which attracted many more
women than men—and women from many classes.

The other was the suffragette movement: the battle by a growing number of women for the right to vote, the right to equality
with men, the right to much wider roles in life.

And these two disturbances were in many cases interlinked. Because some seekers of wider roles saw in spiritualism a power of
nature that women might possess, and men didn't.

The women's movement was still relatively small, compared with
the spiritualism craze; but it was getting much louder. Its leaders
now included some of the most distinguished names in society.
And they were being joined by increasing numbers of women
from lower classes of society.

Even by a few women whom some might put in the same category as Alice Curry.

Such as the movement's new firebrand: Tennessee's older sister, Victoria Woodhull—whom Harp knew almost as well as he did Tennessee, both socially and in the biblical sense.

Tennessee and Victoria: the two were a mutual support team, united since childhood in a life struggle to prevail against all odds. Tennessee had always been the prettier one. It was her picture their parents had used on the labels of the cure-all patent medicines they'd peddled from town to town through the Midwest when the girls were children. Victoria was just a good-looking woman with a strong figure—until she looked at you and spoke to you. Her passion, the animal and spiritual vitality in her, were magnetic; for many, irresistible.

Harp liked and respected her, but didn't see as much of her as of her sister. He didn't like being hypnotized.

But the more he thought about Victoria, the more he found in her history that could have attracted women as different as Olivia Walburton and Alice Curry.

Victoria had burst upon the New York scene in spectacular fashion: starting her own Wall Street brokerage firm, and a weekly newspaper that mixed financial news with politics, spiritualism, woman's suffrage and free-love sermons. With her sister as her chief assistant. Though Tennessee wasn't really interested in finance, journalism or politics, she always went good-naturedly along with anything Victoria wanted.

The notion of female stockbrokers, and of a woman-run newspaper that included highly unladylike opinions, was scandalous enough to start reporters digging for other scandals in the sisters' past and present.

The first to surface: it was rich old Commodore Vanderbilt who had backed the sisters' entrance into the worlds of finance and the press—in gratitude for their rescuing him from his deathbed by getting into that bed with him and administering nightly applications of their own version of hands-on healing.

Other scandals began turning up from other parts of the country. Victoria, and later Tennessee, were said to have engaged in child prostitution at times, when their parents failed to sell enough of their patent medicines to support the family.

The same reason had compelled Victoria, when she was fifteen, to wed middle-aged, alcoholic Dr. Woodhull. She had since divorced him—another scandal—and married a second husband: a much-wounded war veteran, Colonel Blood. Much more outrageous: she not only kept the family name of her first husband, but she was presently living in the same house with both her former husband and her present one. Victoria's explanation that Dr. Woodhull had become too feeble to be cast out on his own did not diminish the professed shock of this disclosure for the delighted press.

Well before their arrival in New York, the sisters had joined the spiritualism craze. Setting themselves up as young mystics, giving seances as clairvoyants and go-betweens with the other world. Until forced to flee, with their family, from charges of prostitution and bilking sick people who came to them for cures.

By then Tennessee had become a convinced spiritualist. Harp could never be sure if Victoria was also a true believer or not. She did swear that it was a ghost that had finally directed her to New York City—and to the richest man in that city, the aging and ailing Commodore Vanderbilt.

They had cured him too effectively for their own good. He finally felt so chipper that he'd gotten married again. To a lady who denied the sisters access to the Vanderbilt home—and purse. Without that, the brokerage firm had collapsed and Victoria's weekly was in trouble.

But by then she was already moving on from those careers and plunging into the women's movement with all of her passionate energy and eloquence. The press was quick to point out the incongruity of it: a fallen woman presuming to speak in the name of a sober group of respectable—if misguided—suffragettes. And at first the upper-class ladies who led the movement had been horrified to find such a notorious woman in their midst. But most had finally welcomed her after she went to Washington, seduced Congressman Butler into helping her and became the first woman ever allowed to argue the case for female voters before a congressional committee. At the next meeting of the women's movement she had been seated on the podium with its other leaders.

The press professed to regard that as shocking: "Her career as a trance-physician, her brazen immodesty as a stock speculator and the open, shameless effrontery with which she has paraded her name at the head of her newspaper—all this has proclaimed her as a vain, immodest, unsexed woman with whom respectable people should have as little to do as possible.''

In spite of which, early that summer, Victoria had made herself the very center of the battle over votes for women, with a rousing oration before the Woman's Suffrage Association that headlines called the "Great Secession Speech":

"If the very next Congress refuses women all the legitimate results of citizenship, we shall call another convention expressly to frame a new constitution and to erect a new government. We mean treason! We mean secession—and on a thousand times grander scale than was that of the South. We are plotting revolution! We will overthrow this bogus republic and plant a government of righteousness in its stead!''

One reporter was so impressed that he acknowledged it in print: "Mrs. Woodhull reminds one of the forces in nature behind the storm, or of a small splinter of the indestructible."

Others, however, retaliated by calling her the "Queen of the Prostitutes."

To which one of the most distinguished ladies in the movement's leadership, Mrs. Elizabeth Cady Stanton, responded with a defense of Victoria that stunned many of the city's elite: "Admit for the sake of argument what all men say of her is true—that she has been or is a courtesan in sentiment and practice. When a woman of this class shall suddenly devote herself to the grave problems of life, brought there by profound thought or sad experience, and with new faith and hope struggles to redeem the errors of the past, shall we not welcome her to the better place she desires to hold?''

With that going on, yes—it was a possibility that a whore named Alice Curry might have been drawn to the women's movement. And if Olivia Walburton had also been drawn to it, by . . .

Harp arrested the speculation with an angry grimace. He was indulging in guesswork, and without a single solid fact to base it on.

Nevertheless, he *would* get around to checking with both Tennessee and Victoria. Call it guesswork or call it cognizant speculation, either of them might have something he needed.

He looked again at the pictures he was holding. The basic problem was that he knew almost nothing about either woman. If he could dig more out of Vance Walburton than Howe and Hummel had managed to, it would help. So would finding a picture taken of Alice Curry when she was alive. Until then . . .

Harp put the pictures away as his cab crossed the as-yet unpaved upper stretch of Eighth Avenue—eventually to be renamed Central Park West—leaving the park behind and entering the wastelands of the upper west side.

Urban maps showed block after block of paved cross-streets cutting through the upper west side from the park to the Hudson River. Everyone knew that the anticipated building boom could not occur without those connecting streets. But few of them had actually been started, let alone finished. Antediluvian glaciers had torn the region into a broken jigsaw puzzle of hills, cliffs and high outcrops, all of hard rock. Between them were ravines, hollows and tight little valleys with innumerable ponds and meandering creeks. So far the city hadn't gotten down to the preliminary work of blasting, filling, leveling and draining necessary before the cross-streets could be put through. A great many speculators who had invested in land here hadn't taken a realistic look at the difficulties and expense of trying to extend the city north into such rugged terrain.

Harp's cab maneuvered around the terrain's obstacles via twisting paths. On and around those the fallen snow had been trampled to brown mush by the thousands of squatters whose shanties, pigpens, goat enclosures and chicken coops spread over areas that had once been woods or Dutch farms. These squatters were no richer than the tenement dwellers in the lower parts of Manhattan, but they did live somewhat better lives. They had their animals and eggs and summer vegetable gardens for food, cleaner air to breathe—and no rent to pay.

There were, it was true, certain drawbacks. One was the sporadic outbreaks of malaria, yellow fever and cholera from the marshes created by the ponds and creeks overflowing every spring and summer. But such outbreaks were even more common in the slum areas of lower Manhattan, where sewers leaked noxious gases into tenements, and garbage dumped into the streets and alleys was usually left to rot.

The other drawback was the fact that the squatters could be evicted without notice the instant the expected building boom did get under way. But the squatters had less belief than the urbanists and speculators in the boom arriving in the near future. That accounted for so many of them being new arrivals: those who'd been forced out of their former squatter haven on Dutch Hill, in the east forties, by recent construction. Harp had watched some of them making the move. They had simply taken their shacks apart, carted the planks, tar paper and sheets of tin northwest through Central Park, along with their animals, and put them back together up here.

His cab didn't pass a single tree left from what had been the wooded areas. The squatters had chopped the last of them down for firewood. There were some of the old Dutch farmhouses left; but they'd been converted into taverns or boarding houses. Harp had the cab halt at one of them to get further directions to Ruyter's boardinghouse. But the cab finally reached a dead end: blocked by a steep, rocky hill slope with a wide pond on one side and massive boulders on the other.

Harp decided he would have done better to take the long way around. Back down to Fifty-ninth Street, then up again, further west, along the continuation of Broadway named the Grand Boulevard—which was used by the only omnibus that went all the way north to Washington Heights.

His driver had turned the cab around, and was looking for a way to bypass the pond, when Harp spotted two children coming through the boulders in his direction. A boy and girl of about ten, dragging along three snarling dogs leashed to a two-wheeled cart carrying coals the kids had picked up along some stretch of railroad tracks or had stolen from a coal wagon south of Fifty-ninth. Harp had the cab stop, and climbed out to question them.

Ruyter's place, they informed him, was only a little way beyond the top of the hill slope. Harp instructed his driver to stay put, and climbed the slope on foot.

Perched at the top was a clapboard beer saloon that he had seen from the bottom. It was roofed with rusty tin and tar paper. Smoke rose from a chimney that looked like it had once been a drain-

pipe. A hundred yards beyond it was Ruyter's: a large, two-story
house with a verandah around three sides. Beyond and below that
was a view all the way to the river and the New Jersey bluffs on the
other side. Between the river and this broad hilltop, Harp could
see the Grand Boulevard, with an easy pathway winding up from it
in this direction.

He nodded to himself as he walked on toward the boardinghouse. The long way around, though more time consuming,
would have been simpler.

Inside the saloon, two men sat at a three-legged, burn-scarred
table by the soot-smeared window. The one whose left ear had
been partly chewed off was a squat man, appearing at first glance
to be as big around as he was in height. The other was much taller,
and almost as thick in body and arms as the squat man. Nobody
would have had trouble guessing their occupation. They were professional thugs and street brawlers—usually called ruffians or
"roughs." Heavy muscle, brutal expressions, primitive brains.

"That's him," the squat man said as they watched Harp go past.

"You sure?" demanded the bigger one.

"Dead sure. That's Harp, no question."

The bigger one tilted his head to watch Harp going up the steps
to the boardinghouse verandah. "We'll get him when he comes
back down," he said. "Meantime let's make sure his driver's in no
shape to butt in."

They waited until Harp disappeared inside the boardinghouse
before leaving the saloon and going down the slope to the waiting
cab.

Sixteen

"Nope, I don't think I know her," Tom Costello said. "Am I supposed to?"

"You knew her when you saw her a couple nights ago, dead in a warehouse office."

"Alice Curry?" Costello took a more careful look at the morgue photo that Harp was holding with his thumb hiding the slashed throat. "Well, sure, now you tell me I can see it's her. That's her face. But . . ."

"But you wouldn't make the connection if I didn't pin her name on her first."

Costello shrugged. "Maybe I'm just not sharp this morning—but I don't think anybody would. I got a darn good memory for faces and the coroner said she wasn't dead more'n an hour when I found her. See what I'm saying? She still looked like her, even with all that blood smearing her warpaint. But in this picture . . ." He shrugged again.

They had settled into rockers on an enclosed part of the boardinghouse verandah. They had it to themselves. Its big windows, facing west, kept out some of the winter cold; and a certain amount of heat was given off by the back of the parlor fireplace. But Costello's mother and the other boarders were inside the house where it was much warmer.

Harp put the picture away. Knowing he might as well tear it up. Getting it taken had been a waste of his money and Ferguson's time. It wasn't unexpected; but you always had to give it a try.

He studied the young patrolman again. Costello was about twenty-four. He had the usual size and sturdy build of a New York cop, but hadn't yet developed the usual gut. Blue eyes with quick intelligence in them dominated a freckled, very Irish face that still retained traces of choirboy.

"I've seen you somewhere before," Harp said, "but I don't remember where. I got the impression when I introduced myself that you remember me. And know how I make my living. You weren't surprised when I said I had some things I wanted to ask you about. Not worried I might be a reporter or some grand jury investigator."

"Oh, I know what you are." Costello grinned. "Like I said, I got a good memory for faces. Live ones, anyway. I saw you one time at my old stationhouse. Going out with Jenkins, back when he was still captain of the precinct there. He acted like you was a friend, and I got a curious streak. One of the other fellows told me the sort of stuff you do. And later Captain Jenkins told me you and him used to be part of a gang when you was kids. Said you and him—and somebody pretty big in Tammany—are the only three out've that gang that didn't wind up out-and-out jailbirds."

"Sounds like Jenkins had a lot of trust in you."

"Trusted me enough to make me his bagman, collecting for him from the cheaper joints around the precinct. You know how it works. I take my little share out've what I collect, and pass the rest to the sergeant. Who takes his share out and gives the rest to the captain."

"Who takes his share," Harp said, "before turning the big slice that's left over to Tammany Hall."

"Right. It knocked the bejeezus out've me when Jenkins suddenly up and retired. He knew I was always on the up and up. But the new captain, he claimed my tally on what I collected wasn't on the level. Said I was taking more than my fair share before turning it over. Which is pure baloney. He just wanted me out so he could give the job to one of his pals."

Costello stared angrily through the verandah windows. Harp was sure he was contemplating the injustice done him rather than the view below.

It was an extensive view that included the Bloomingdale Insane Asylum, with its spacious landscaped grounds that the militia used to practice its drills. And further south the public dump at the edge of the Hudson. Harp could see tiny figures moving slowly through the dump. Scavengers who lived in the dump and spent their days searching through the garbage for anything remotely usable or salable, before the barges hauled the rest off to the outer bay. And squatter kids collecting swill to feed their pigs.

"So they kicked you down to the Thirteenth Precinct," Harp said, to nudge Costello out of his hurt silence. "The pickings there aren't bad either. Not as good as up around Satan's Circus, but not bad."

"Yeah, but I ain't one of Captain Redpath's close boys, so I don't get much of it."

"You may be better off that way, for the time being. Until all the grand jury investigations run their course."

"That may be so, but the thing is, this place ain't cheap. And I pay 'em extra so they'll take special care of my mom. Sometimes she's okay, but sometimes she forgets to eat, or even who she is."

Harp took out a five-dollar gold piece, held it in his open hand. "I'm after anything you can tell me about Alice Curry."

"Glad to help you out," Costello said, eyeing the gleaming coin and holding down his eagerness for it. "You bein' friends with Captain Jenkins and all. But I got to be honest with you. I ain't sure I know enough to be worth that much."

"You can give me two dollars change if we decide it's not."

"Fair enough." Costello took the gold coin and stuck it into his breast pocket. "Main thing I know about her is she used to work in a fancy parlorhouse run by Emma Wells. It's on Twenty-eighth, between Fifth and Sixth. Nearer to Sixth, but I don't remember the exact address."

"I know the place," Harp told him. He figured that Costello had already earned his five dollars.

"Then you know it's a real tony joint. Nothing but posh gents for clients. Gotta be wearing evening clothes and sober enough to mind their manners. Emma don't let 'em in unless they're regulars she knows, or they got an introduction from somebody she does know. She never has more'n seven girls working at her place. Strictly the best, naturally. Have to be, the prices she charges.

"Anyway, I sometimes saw this Alice Curry going into the place or coming out've it. Tell you the truth, I paid special attention whenever I did see her. She was always turned out elegant, day or night. Pretty enough to make you weep, and a grand figure."

Costello surprised Harp by suddenly blushing and looking away.

"Once I even told the priest in confession about having these sinful thoughts about a professional harlot. Wishing I had the money and clothes for an hour with her in Emma Wells's house."

Through the verandah windows, Harp saw an omnibus come north along the Grand Boulevard and make a stop at the bottom of the path that led up to this hilltop. A small figure got out and began trotting up the path.

Costello had gone silent again. Harp said, "Ever get up the nerve to speak to her?"

"Yeah, finally. It was one day I was off duty and went into an ice cream parlor on Fifth and Thirtieth. She was in there, having tea and cookies. Well, like you said, I screwed up my nerve. Went and introduced myself. Bein' sure to do it real respectful, like. She said she'd seen me around, like I'd seen her. Which was flattering, her noticing and remembering me. And she told me her name, Alice Curry. Because I'd told her mine, and it was the polite thing to do. Polite, that was her. Not exactly friendly, but not unfriendly, either. Formal, but in a nice way, you understand? So I asked if I could join her, and she was too good-mannered to say no."

The figure trotting up the path was close enough now for Harp to see who it was. Billy Doyle. The street kid who worked for Howe & Hummel—and currently for Harp. His tattered army jacket was buttonless, flapping in the wind behind Billy's short, scrawny figure. Harp remembered when he could still run uphill all the way without stopping to catch his breath.

"I can tell you one thing sure about Alice Curry," Costello said. "The refined way she acted and talked, that wasn't something you could just put on. She didn't come up from the gutter, like some. She'd come down, from class."

"What did she say about that?" Harp asked him.

"Not a thing. And I couldn't ask her. She was being so nice and polite, it woulda been like slapping her in the face, if I'd gone and asked how did she fall and become a whore."

"What did she talk about?"

"The weather. How bad traffic was in the streets." Costello made one of his shrugs. "Mostly she asked about me. About my work as a policeman, and about my mom, after I told her about that. The only thing she told me about herself was that she wouldn't be working for Emma Wells anymore. Said she'd gotten herself a job as an actress.''

''Where?''

''She didn't say. And I didn't push to find out. You know how the harlots are, high or low. So many of them pretending they're really actresses. So I don't know if it was the truth or not, in her case.''

Billy was outside the verandah now, panting just a little. He'd spotted Harp through the windows, and seen he was with somebody. Harp hadn't signaled him to come in, so he just stood out there and waited.

''When she was ready to leave,'' Costello said, ''I asked if I could pay for her tea, and she let me. We said goodbye outside the ice cream parlor and that's the last I ever saw of her—alive.''

''How long ago was this?''

Costello thought back over his days off. ''A little more'n three months, I guess.''

Harp watched Costello's expression: ''Do you know Moe Saul?''

Costello looked a bit puzzled by the abrupt switch of subject. ''Just by reputation. Never met him. I know he's a fence, is all. Why?''

Harp switched back: ''Is there anything else you know about Alice Curry? Friends, relatives, anything at all?''

''Not a thing. What I told you's all of it. I told you it wasn't worth five bucks.'' Costello tapped the pocket into which he'd put the gold piece. ''Want two back?''

''Keep it.'' Harp got out of the rocker. ''I may want to do business with you again.''

Costello grinned as he stood up and shook hands. ''Any time. You bein' a friend of Captain Jenkins.''

He went back inside the house as Harp went down the verandah steps to Billy Doyle.

He had assigned Billy to hang out around the Suze la Rousse today. A lot of Harp's contacts knew he used the restaurant below his apartment as a message center. He'd told Billy he would be at Ruyter's sometime during this morning, and had given him a couple of places where he might be later in the afternoon, in case a message did come in.

Billy had two for him. One was in an envelope, from Carson, the old ex-pimp who'd been combing Satan's Circus for some trace of Alice Curry. He'd written: *The Curry woman used to work in a parlorhouse, 62 West 28th Street. I asked about her there but the madam, Emma Wells, claims she never heard of her, wouldn't open up.*

So now Harp owed Carson five dollars. He'd already paid Costello that for the same information, but fair was fair.

The other message was on a folded scrap of paper. Harp unfolded it and read: *Millie's pier after dark.*

It wasn't signed but it had to be from Hoggy Corcoran's lieutenant, Ambrose McGowan. Millie had been Mildred Hertz, a teenage prostitute who had sold her favors to Harp, Ambrose and the other boys in their old gang for a special rate of ten cents for five minutes. When not working the sailor's joints along the waterfront, Millie had lived and plied her trade in a wrecked tugboat permanently moored to a pier on the lower west side. The abandoned tug had been towed away, and Millie had drowned herself in the Hudson years ago, but the pier was still there. And "after dark" meant that Harp had the rest of the day to pursue other leads before meeting Ambrose.

Harp gave Billy two dollars for bringing the messages. Then another dollar: "This is for delivering one for me. We'll go back to town together and I'll write it on the way."

Billy said, "Thanks," but didn't crack any smile of appreciation. He wasn't a smiler. He belonged, like Harp had, to one of the roughest parts of the slums, where a scowl was the smartest permanent expression and a smile was considered a show of weakness.

He stuffed the three dollars in his pants and hurried along after Harp, past the shanty saloon and down the slope to the waiting hansom cab.

Seventeen

The cab driver wasn't waiting up on his box, or anywhere else in sight. Harp had no reason to expect trouble up here. He figured his driver was probably catching himself a snooze inside the cab. He was striding toward it, with the short-legged Billy lagging a little behind, when the two roughs stepped out from the boulders. One in front of him and the other behind.

Harp recognized the squat one in front of him. A bone-breaker for hire named Jake Roach. He wore brass knuckles on his left fist. His right gripped a slungshot—the longer and heavier street-brawler's version of a blackjack—that he lashed at Harp's head.

Though Harp wasn't expecting it, you didn't survive a child-hood in the alleys around the old Five Points without developing instant reflexes, and nothing in his life since then had inclined him to let those reflexes go slack. The slungshot flew out of Roach's hand when his wrist broke under the impact of Harp's hickory stick.

Billy yelled a warning in the same instant. Harp dodged side-ways, keeping watch on Roach while turning just enough to see the hulking bruiser swat Billy out of his way. The kid sprawled in the brown slush, stunned or unconscious. The bruiser came on at Harp, brandishing a crowbar.

Harp surprised him by charging to meet him. Surprised him again by doing a dodging turn around him. Putting himself in position to deal with the bruiser and at the same time see Roach, who was going after his fallen slungshot, broken arm pressed against his chest. The bruiser spun to face Harp, swinging the crowbar two-handed, like a baseball bat.

Harp dropped to one knee. The crowbar slapped his hat off his head. He clubbed the thicker end of his stick across the bruiser's left kneecap, shattering it. The bruiser fell on top of him, losing his crowbar and snarling with pain but not ready to quit. His fingers groped for Harp's eyes.

Squat Jake Roach snatched up his slungshot with the hand that still functioned, the one with the brass knuckles, and was lumbering back toward them as fast as he could. Harp was too entangled with the bigger man to use his stick. He dropped it, seized two of the bruiser's groping fingers and broke them, punched him in the throat. The bruiser gagged and rolled off him. Harp lunged to his feet and kicked him in the head with the heel of his hobnailed boot. The head bounced and then lay as inert as the big body it was attached to.

Roach was almost on them by then. Harp bent down and then jerked upright. Roach stopped abruptly, panting and looking across his partner's unconscious form at Harp, who stood waiting with his stick in one hand and the crowbar in the other.

Jake Roach was not a coward, but experience had taught him that sometimes in a brawl there came a moment when you knew you were going to lose if it went on. He'd heard things about Harp that had just been confirmed. And with his partner out of it he was all alone. Roach turned and ran.

Harp kicked the unconscious man's head again to make sure he stayed out of it, tossed the crowbar away and went after Roach. Roach wasn't built for speed. Harp caught up and tripped him with his stick. Roach fell to his knees, swiveled on them and tried to strike at Harp's legs with the slungshot in his left hand. Harp deflected it with his stick and kicked Roach's broken arm.

Roach howled. The slungshot spilled from his left hand as he reached with it for his agonized right wrist. Harp kneed him in the jaw, knocked him flat on his back. Planting his right foot on the ground, he dropped down on Roach's midsection with his left knee, all of his weight behind it. Roach's face contorted and the air gushed out of his sprung-open mouth. But seasoned roughs didn't fold up just because they were hurting. Roach had enough primitive stubbornness left in him to let go of his broken wrist and drive his brass-knuckled fist at Harp's face.

Harp caught the wrist behind that fist in his free hand and gripped it, forcing it back. Roach was brute-strong, but Harp was much stronger. Roach couldn't break his grip; and when he tried to heave Harp off, the hickory stick slid across his throat and pressed down, pinning him to the ground. Harp continued to force Roach's good arm back and down, until its elbow was locked across his raised knee.

"One more push," he told Roach, "and your elbow's busted. You'll be walking around with both arms useless, easy pickings for fellows who don't like you. For a couple months, maybe longer."

He emphasized his point with a bit more pressure on the trapped elbow.

"Don't be a rat." Roach had to force the words through the constriction of the stick against his throat. "You're not the one got hurt, so why get nasty? We wasn't goin' to do the big job on you, for crissakes."

"What were you going to do?" Harp demanded, maintaining the pressure on Roach's elbow.

"Just bust up your face a little. And break a leg is all."

"How much did you get paid to do it?"

"Thirty bucks. Take it easy on my arm, will ya?"

That added up right. The current rate among thugs like Roach was ten dollars to break somebody's nose and jaw, twenty for each arm or leg. The big job, killing someone, cost a hundred or more. How much more depended on the difficulty of carrying out a particular job, and how much trouble the victim's death was likely to cause. But if Roach and his partner had been hired for that, they would have come at him with guns or daggers.

"Who hired you?" Harp asked. He didn't apply more pressure on the elbow. It was already near the breaking point.

"A buckaroo named Smuts Coon." Buckaroos being hoodlums who specialized in acting and dressing like sailors so they could lure real sailors to a place where they could be drugged or knocked out and robbed.

"I never heard of him," Harp said.

"Well he's heard of you," Roach said. "And he knew I know you by sight. Me and Andy, that big lunk sleepin' it off over there, was in Little Becky's when Smuts came in and made us the proposition."

"When was this?"

"This morning, 'round four, I guess. Will you for crissakes let go've my arm now?"

"When you've told me all of it, and if I think it's the truth. How'd you know I'd be up here this morning?"

"Smuts Coon's the one knew that. He wasn't sure exactly when you'd be here, but he thought you'd pay a visit to that boarding-house sometime today. Told us to get up here early and hang around till you showed up."

"He say anything about why he wanted me busted up?"

"Naw, they don't usually bother. Just told us what he wanted and paid us for it."

"Where's this Smuts Coon hang out?"

"Lotsa places near the South Street docks," Roach said. "But he's gonna check into Little Becky's place now and then to see did we get the job done like he wanted."

Harp looked away, past the big bruiser's inert figure. Billy was up on his knees, slowly shaking his head. Harp saw him put both hands against a boulder to help himself get to his feet.

"What'd you do with my cabbie?" he asked Roach.

"In his cab. Ain't hurt much. Just knocked him out a little so we could tie and gag him. C'mon, quit leanin' on my damn arm."

Harp let go of it and stood up. Roach sat up and flexed it, wincing, and then drew his broken wrist protectively against his chest again, cradling it. Harp rapped him behind the ear with his stick. Not as hard as what he'd done to the big one; but hard enough to put him out until the cab was gone.

Billy Doyle had a swollen jaw and was still dazed. But his head would clear; and for any street kid it was part of normal life to get banged around now and then. Roach had told the truth about the cab driver. Once the gag was out and his hands and feet were untied, there was nothing wrong with him but the lump on his forehead and a bad headache. But he was too shaken by the experience to drive his cab back downtown. It was Harp who drove it to the livery stable the driver worked out of. There he paid him a small bonus, and wrote out a message for Billy to deliver.

It was to Cavalucci, the former tenor. Most of the theatrical agents were concentrated around Union Square, along with the actors' hangouts. If Cavalucci hadn't found someone among them who knew Alice Curry by now, he wasn't going to. The note told Cavalucci to switch to checking with artists and try to find the one who did those erotic paintings for Monmouth Fuller.

Billy took a horsecar going south to search for Cavalucci. Harp went into a businessmen's saloon on Broadway and sat at a quiet table for a time, sipping whiskey and smoking a cigar while he thought it out:

Someone had killed Alice Curry in Fuller's warehouse. And someone had killed Moe Saul the same night. The stolen liquor moving from the warehouse to Moe's place that night made it more than possible the same someone had done both murders.

And someone had directed this Smuts Coon to hire a couple of hoodlums to attack him. Someone who'd made an educated guess that he was likely to visit Costello up there. Costello didn't know enough about Alice Curry to worry that someone much. Whoever it was just wanted to make sure Harp wouldn't be in any condition to dig further, for some time to come.

The same someone who'd killed Moe and Alice Curry?

Harp flicked his cigar into a cuspidor, finished off his drink and found a cab to take him down to the lower east side.

Little Becky's was a small cellar saloon half a block from the Croton Temperance Lunchroom on the corner of Division Street and the Bowery. With no window to let in daylight, the kerosene lamp hanging from the splintery plank ceiling and the other on the bar were always burning. With the doorway at the top of the rotting wooden steps the only way for air to get in or out, the kerosene smell was permanent, mixing with the odors of cheap cigar smoke and the nickel beer that was Little Becky's standby. The bar was two kitchen tables pushed together. Wooden stools crowded most of the floor space, but there were no other tables. Little Becky didn't want her customers using them to fall asleep on.

It was a few minutes before noon when Harp came down the cellar steps. There were only three customers, on stools against the back wall so they had something to lean on while they nursed their beers. The early-morning alcoholics were gone, and the afternoon crowd of loungers hadn't begun to arrive. Little Becky was using the interval to rest her swollen legs, sitting in the padded armchair behind her bar, with her sledgehammer and sawed-off shotgun close to hand. Customers learned not to make trouble in her place.

She was a massive black woman who dyed her hair and eyebrows red. When Harp sat down on a stool across the bar from her she filled a shot glass with whiskey and passed it to him. It wasn't something she served her customers. She kept a bottle of good whiskey for herself and special acquaintances.

Little Becky had a cold hatred for most men. Harp was one of the exceptions. That dated back a couple of years. Her niece, a very pretty, light-skinned girl of seventeen, had gotten involved with the son of a well-off tobacco merchant. The father had learned of it and had been appalled. He had warned his son that a liaison with a colored girl, if continued, was certain to blight the boy's future. But the boy was too smitten to give her up. The father had finally done what he felt any devoted parent would do under the circumstances. He'd sent his son off on a European vacation and paid a thug to throw acid in the girl's face. She was left permanently scarred and blind. An understanding judge had let the father off with a two-hundred-dollar fine.

Little Becky had told Harp about it. By then the thug who had thrown the acid had been found dead in a gutter with most of the bones in his body pulverized. Little Becky had difficulty holding in check a burning desire to do the same to the merchant who'd hired the thug. But what was left of her niece's life had to be taken into consideration first, she'd explained to Harp. He'd paid the merchant a visit. The merchant had agreed, in writing, to pay the girl a monthly sum: sufficient for her to live decently, in a Hoboken apartment, and hire a woman to live in it with her, take care of her and be her guide outside. The agreement, witnessed by the merchant's lawyer and banker, stipulated that these payments would continue to be made by his estate after his death.

Little Becky never asked Harp how he had gotten the man to agree to this.

And he never asked her any questions when, a couple of months later, the merchant, working alone late one night, apparently tripped or slipped on his establishment's second-floor landing and broke his neck tumbling down the flight of steps.

"Has Smuts Coon been in yet today?" Harp asked after taking a sip from the whiskey glass Little Becky handed him.

"I serve just about anybody what comes in here," she told him. "But never no ghosts."

He took another sip and waited, sure of what was coming.

"You got good timing," she said. "I just heard about it myself, less'n an hour ago. They fished Smuts out from under the Christopher Street ferry pier 'bout an hour before that. Drowned. You gotta wonder about a feller crazy enough to go for a swim in the river this time of year."

Harp drank the rest of his whiskey.

Somebody was wiping out tracks before anyone could follow them too far.

From Little Becky's he went directly to his Greene Street apartment. He wanted to get what he needed while it was still broad daylight—and before whoever had paid to have him busted up learned that the ambush had failed. With Smuts Coon dead it was unlikely that would happen for at least a few more hours. But he didn't intend to walk into another, better-prepared ambush without being ready to deal with it.

He left the apartment with the Le Mat revolver in his greatcoat pocket, and circled two blocks on foot, until certain he was not followed.

Then he went to see Emma Wells.

Eighteen

There are very few first-class houses of ill-fame in the city, and they are located in the best neighborhoods. The inmates are chosen for their beauty and charm, and are frequently persons of education and refinement . . . competent to grace the best circles of social life. The visitors to these places are men of means. No others can afford to patronize them. Governors, congressmen, lawyers, judges, physicians, and alas that it should be said, even ministers of the Gospel are to be seen there.

—JAMES D. McCABE, 1868

Having penned these accurate comments about Manhattan's first-class or "parlor" houses in one of his several behind-the-scenes books, McCabe may have worried that guardians of the city's morals would charge him with making the life of a high-class harlot sound altogether too attractive to girls and women who had not yet fallen into sin. Whatever his reason, McCabe devoted the next few pages to warning tempted females that they could not expect to last long in a first-class brothel. As soon as their freshness began to fade they would start the inevitable descent, through second- and third-class brothels to a death within five years of misery and disease in some filthy waterfront dive.

Which was quite true for the majority of prostitutes. But McCabe and other commentators on the subject often detoured around a couple of related factors.

One was that for a young woman born in abject poverty, or one who fell into it after a father's or husband's business failure, the wages of virtue could also be a short and brutish life ending in a sick and miserable death. McCabe's warning meant little to an underpaid seamstress who saved her pennies by walking fifteen or

twenty blocks to her place of employment through a winter rain-
storm and then worked her twelve hours in drenched clothing
inside an unheated loft. She might consider her existence as de-
moralizing and debilitating as the ultimate fate of a whore—and
that a few years of warmth and comfort, of eating well among gay
company and taking a streetcar or even a cab when it rained was
more than she could hope for from a life of honest toil.

The other factor usually avoided was that, as in all professions in
which one started low and most never clawed themselves higher, a
minority of prostitutes—those with a sharp mind, stubborn ambition and luck—wound up doing rather well for themselves. Some
saved enough to move to another part of the country, open a shop
there and marry respectably. A very few did much better than
that: like Victoria Woodhull, destined to settle down to a third
marriage with a wealthy banker; and her sister, Tennessee, who
would end her life as the wife of a British lord. Others stuck to the
trade they'd learned and invested their savings in a brothel of
their own—much like an ironworker who succeeded in opening
his own foundry.

Emma Wells was one of this last group. She owned the house on
Twenty-eighth Street. It was set back from the street, surrounded
by a garden with many evergreen trees, and appeared, from the
outside, no different from the home of any prosperous middle-
class New York family. Inside, it was rather more luxurious.

The large dining room where Harp had joined Emma Wells for
a meal of roast duckling, boiled potatoes and champagne—lunch
for him, breakfast for her—had a magnificent chandelier imported from Venice. The long rosewood table was from England,
the flowered carpet from Persia, the tapestries and drapes from
France. It was here that one night each month the madam had
her dinner party for a select group of gentlemen and her ladies,
all in formal evening attire.

But at this time of day Harp and Emma Wells had the big room
to themselves. She never received paying guests until evening. Her
butler and her cook were in other parts of the house, where she
could summon them by bellpull when she wished. Her ladies, having been occupied with their visitors into the wee hours of the
morning, were still asleep. Emma, who never went to bed until the
last visitor left, no longer needed much sleep. Though she'd awak-

ened only shortly before Harp's arrival, there wasn't a trace of residual drowsiness in her eyes, voice or appetite.

"Was Alice Curry her real name?" Harp asked, after finishing off a juicy bite of duckling with a sip of champagne.

Emma thought about it while cutting two more slices from the carcass of the duckling, forking one slice to Harp, depositing the other in her own dish. "I had a feeling it wasn't," she said, "but I don't really know. So many girls make up new names for themselves when they enter this business. But if Alice did that, she never told me and I never asked. The past of my ladies is their business, unless they care to talk to me about it. Some do, others don't. The only things it's my business to know about them is that they're well-bred, healthy and attractive to gentlemen callers."

Emma chewed another forkful of gravy-soaked potatoes with undisguised relish. She was dressed like any proper dowager, in a black muslin dress with its sleeves buttoned just above her knuckles and its high whalebone collar tight enough to create a roll of fat between it and her double chin. If she was wearing a corset, it had been let out to make room for her expanding midsection. Harp remembered when, in a tight corset, she'd had a waist that looked as if it could be completely encircled by a man's hands.

"She never told you anything at all about her past?" he asked.

"Little bits and pieces. Once she mentioned she was from Concord, up in New Hampshire. Which may have been true. She did have a special sort of New England accent, rather charming. Another time she told me her father owned a cotton mill, but went broke when the cotton supply dried up during the war. Alice—or whatever her name really was—woke up one morning, she said, and she and her mother saw he'd hanged himself from a tree in front of their house. Seems he'd gambled on the stock market with money he didn't have. All he left were debts that couldn't be paid off, even with what they got for selling the house and everything in it. Her fiancée was dreadfully sorry, but he couldn't sully his own family name by marrying a girl whose father died in such scandalous circumstances—and without even leaving his daughter a dowry."

"A pretty common story," Harp said.

"Oh, yes. I hear variations on it all the time in my business."

Emma shrugged. "Sometimes it's probably even close to the truth."

"Think it was the truth in her case?"

"Who knows, lovey? I stopped giving a whoop if the stories these girls tell are history or fairy tales long ago." Emma's laugh was soft and melodic. "Sometimes I even forget which of the tales I spin about myself are partly true." She drank the last of the champagne in her glass and got on with her eating.

She had recognized Alice Curry immediately from the morgue photograph of her. But that was because of the slashed throat—and because she had been thinking about her ever since reading in the papers about her murder. Preparing herself to lie to the police or anyone like Carson who came by with questions.

Harp didn't ask why Emma hadn't gone to the police with whatever she knew after reading about Alice Curry's murder. No one who was part of the city's underworld would do so. It would draw unwanted attention to their activities. Emma's house sold privacy as well as pleasant feminine companionship. Newspaper notoriety would drive away the prominent gentlemen who were her clientele—none of whom had so far cared to tell police and reporters that Alice Curry was a name known to them from their visits to a parlorhouse.

Harp refilled Emma's champagne glass. "I need a picture of what she looked like when she was alive. One from that album you show to new clients would be perfect."

"I don't have one of her anymore," Emma told him. "When one of my ladies leaves here I give her the photographs, to keep or destroy. That's one of the rules I made for myself. I don't keep anything that could embarrass her later, she never has to worry about that, not with me. I figure her past is her own private business—so is her future."

It was a disappointment; but experience had taught Harp to take those in stride. "Do you think this was the first house she worked in?"

"That I'm sure of. From the way I had to explain everything to her. She wasn't a virgin, but she wasn't far from it. My guess is she sold that little treasure for her fare to New York and enough to live on for a short period while she looked for work that paid reasonably. When she couldn't find any, and struck up a chance acquaintance with one of my ladies, she came to me."

"Was it hard for her to adjust to what was expected of her here?"

"Not at all," Emma told him. "She was ripe for it. Even eager. You got the feeling she was getting even—with society, or fate—for what they'd done to her. I see that in other new girls, at this level."

"When was it she came to you?"

"Be a year ago, soon. A few weeks before Christmas."

"When did she leave you?".

"A few months ago," she told Harp, as Costello had.

"Somebody who knew her casually," he said, "told me she quit here for a job in the theater."

"I suppose that's possible," Emma said. "But if so, she didn't say anything about it to me when she left. What she did tell me was that her dead father spoke to her during a seance. Asked her forgiveness and begged her to get out of the business."

Harp went silent for a long moment. Then he said, "She was involved in spiritualism?"

"Apparently. Though that was the first I knew of it. It was obvious she really believed she'd been in contact with her father."

"Do you know where she went for these contacts with the spirit world?" Harp asked. "Or the name of the medium?"

Emma shook her head. "I've no idea at all."

It was interesting how often he heard those exact words, or variations on them, in his work. He asked Emma to describe Alice Curry for him, as closely as she could.

"Natural blonde hair, big blue eyes, nice neat features. Marvelous figure—tiny waist, nice and full in the bust and hips. Nothing unusual that would distinguish her from other pretty girls, if that's what you're looking for."

"It would have helped," Harp said. He took out his picture of Olivia Walburton and showed it to Emma. "Ever seen this one?"

Emma studied the picture. "No. Is she in the business?"

"I don't know." He put the picture back in his pocket. "It's one possibility."

They had finished their meals by then. Emma used the bellpull to summon her cook, who cleared away the dishes and went off to get them coffee. Emma opened a box of her best cigars for Harp, and he selected one. She struck a match and lit it for him, with an expertise and coquetry learned long ago.

Over their coffees she suddenly said, "I wonder if old Kouwenhoven is still alive."

Polly Kouwenhoven was the brothel madam who'd unofficially adopted him when he was thirteen—because she'd thought he looked like her son who had died at that age. Emma Wells had come to work for her when Harp was fourteen, a year before he'd gone out on his own again.

"She was the last time I visited her," Harp said. "A month ago. She's got a little house in Paterson, New Jersey. And a woman there who takes care of her."

Emma was staring at him in surprise. "You go all the way over there to see her?"

"Now and then."

"Will wonders never cease! You've got a sentimental streak."

"I owe her."

"Sentimental," Emma repeated. "Most men are, of course. Irresponsible but sentimental. But I wouldn't have suspected it in you. Well—how *is* the old harpy?"

"Getting older. Like you're getting fatter."

Emma laughed again. She patted her ample stomach and said, "You'll never know how wonderful it is, not having to lace up tight enough to bust anymore." She eyed Harp. "I sometimes used to wonder if she ever took you to bed with her—the way some of us did."

"That wasn't part of what she felt about me," Harp said, and switched the conversation back to Emma's memories of Alice Curry.

There was nothing further in them of use to him. But Emma had already given him two trails to follow into the murdered woman's recent past. That neither might get him any closer to Olivia Walburton didn't trouble him. Finding Vance Walburton's wife was no longer a priority. He was sure the murders of Alice Curry and Moses Saul were connected. It was getting Moe's killer that had become Harp's priority.

That it was Walburton's money he was using, for a hunt that Walburton didn't know about, didn't bother Harp either.

* * *

His follow-up on the first lead Emma Wells had given him was taken care of with a brief visit to one of the city's leading evening papers: the New York *Telegram,* at the corner of Broadway and Ann Street. A veteran reporter there, Jack Goodhue, still owed Harp fifty-six dollars from a poker session a few weeks ago. In exchange for cutting the debt down to thirty-five dollars, Goodhue agreed to telegraph a colleague in Concord, New Hampshire, asking him to check in his own newspaper files for a cotton-mill owner who had gone broke and hanged himself from a tree outside his house, sometime more than a year ago.

If it had actually happened, Harp wanted to know the name of the mill owner's daughter; and whether her mother or any other relative could be contacted. He offered a twenty-dollar bonus if the Concord journalist could also find a picture of the daughter. Goodhue promised to send Harp word by messenger as soon as he got a response from Concord, negative or positive.

To initiate his probe into Emma's other lead, concerning Alice Curry's visits to a spiritualist medium, Harp took a cab to Fifteen East Thirty-eighth Street—the home that Tennessee Claflin shared with her sister Victoria and the various relatives who had been living off the two of them since they were kids.

Nineteen

**H**ow to account for the astonishing spread of spiritualism in the United States during the second half of the nineteenth century, growing in numbers and organization until it posed a challenge to both established religions and accepted scientific dogma?

Many attributed it to a reaction against an increasingly materialistic society in which wealth and position became the only values that mattered. The two decades following the Civil War were called the Flash Age. Flash as in show-off and conspicuous consumption. Men trampled their fellow beings underfoot to achieve business and political success, and flaunted a contempt for anything that did not contribute to it. The Old Guard professed a disdain for these parvenu vulgarians but based their own pride on the material accomplishments of their ancestors.

Whether that explained the phenomenon or not, the fact remained: there were millions of followers of spiritualism—or "spiritism" as some preferred to call it—and their numbers were growing and organizing at an impressive rate, with well-attended regular meetings in every city of any size.

The spiritualism movement shared with orthodox religions a faith in life after bodily death; and in certain supernormal manifestations that the orthodox called miracles. But it differed drastically from them concerning the nature of and reasons for those manifestations. Its followers included adherents to many beliefs, not all of them compatible: clairvoyance and telepathy; animal magnetism and faith healing; mesmerism and hypnotism; telekinesis and psychometry; automatic writing and reincarnation. But almost all predicated their beliefs on an assurance that a gifted medium—also called a "sensitive"—could establish communication with the dead. And almost all believed that it was women who possessed these supernormal powers.

Prominent intellectuals were among the movement's leaders: doctors, sci-

entists, teachers, philosophers, social reformers. They held to the ancient definition of spiritualism as "idealism": a certainty that the ultimate reality of the universe had to be something beyond tangible matter like flesh and gold. They were basically antiestablishment. Their aim was to dismantle entrenched society's stagnant ideas and break through to a better way of life.

That goal brought them into close alliance with another growing movement attempting to do the same: the woman's rights movement. In some cases leaders of one movement also became leaders in the other. By 1871 the outstanding example was Victoria Woodhull, who was attracting more newspaper coverage than any other person in either movement.

"The sublime mission of spiritualism," she told the audiences that came to see and hear her during her lecture tours, "is the sexual emancipation of woman, and her return to self-ownership."

As a child she had, like her younger sister, Tennessee, been used by their charlatan parents to conduct seances and perform miracle cures. Even back then, Tennessee had been more gifted at it. Since Victoria had pushed her way into the spheres of finance, journalism and politics, she had left seances and cures behind her. There was, however, one claim to supernormal powers that she never dropped: "I owe all I am to the education and constant guidance of spirit influence."

The spirit who gave her this guidance, across the more than two thousand years that separated her from him, was the Greek orator, Demosthenes. When he wished to instruct her, she said, she would find herself falling into a trance, from which she would emerge saturated with his wisdom.

Harp, who had seen her slip in and out of these trances, considered it a form of self-hypnosis that she could induce whenever she wanted, and that lasted for whatever period served her purpose. He guessed that in that state Victoria, who had virtually no education but was a very fast learner, was better able to absorb and render into her own terms what she learned from the small group of erudite gentlemen who had attached themselves to her vibrant public personality. Whether the ghost of Demosthenes was one of those advisers was not a question Harp spent time pondering.

At the moment it was Tennessee he wanted most to speak with. Unlike her older sister, she had never dropped mediumship and spiritual healing.

"I *am* a clairvoyant," she'd told Harp—and though she'd been sitting on his lap at the time, with her soft, uncorseted curves pressed against him and a merry smile on her lips—there'd been no doubt that she'd meant it. "I have humbugged people, I know. But if I did it, it was to make money for my parents and the rest of the fools in our family. I believe in spiritualism. I have power, and I know my power."

There was no one at the Thirty-eighth Street house when Harp got there that afternoon except Dr. Woodhull, Victoria's first husband, and their two children. Drink had made Woodhull a sick man, aged beyond his years. But he was a dignified alcoholic, and never out of control when he was minding the kids.

"Vicky's gone to Steinway Hall," he told Harp. "She's giving a talk there in about half an hour from now. The rest of the family is off doing God knows what—if He cares."

The acid he put into the word *family* made it clear it included neither Tennessee, of whom he was very fond, nor Victoria's present husband, Colonel Blood, whom Woodhull had come to regard as his closest male friend.

"Is Tennie with Vicky?" Harp asked him. She usually was there lending moral support when her older sister gave a speech, even when she didn't know or care much about the subject, because Victoria was her favorite person in all the world.

"No. Vicky plans to speak in Albany and then Hartford and Boston next week. Tennie went up to make advance arrangements for the places and advertising."

The uninhibited Tennessee was often handed that chore, because she was good at wheedling reduced rates out of the managers of local halls and journals. "What is a middle-aged man of normal impulses to do," an Ohio newspaper owner had explained to Harp during a visit to Manhattan, "when a girl so fresh, so plump and entertaining lights up his lonely office for him? By the time she's left, you find you've given her what she wants for a ruinous price."

"When'll she be back?" Harp asked Woodhull.

"I don't really know. The colonel could probably tell you. He's at Steinway Hall with Vicky. Mrs. Vedder took them there in her landau."

Harp was the one who had introduced Victoria and Louise Vedder. He'd figured they would like each other, and they did. Louise was not active in the woman's rights movement. She was not a joiner. But she admired Victoria's unabashed dedication and passionate spirit. And Victoria, who burned under the continuing scorn of many well-bred women, liked being with a cultured woman who respected her and to whom she could speak without holding anything back.

Harp thanked Woodhull, shook his hand and headed for Steinway Hall.

Latecomers were still climbing the stairs above the Steinway piano salesrooms on East Fourteenth Street when he arrived. Harp stuffed his gloves into his greatcoat pockets and draped the coat over his arm as he reached the top of the steps. With his hickory stick and hat in his left hand, he went to Col. James Blood, who stood by the auditorium entrance making sure there were no further last-minute arrivals of importance.

Blood was a tall, good-looking man with a short beard and an athletic figure. A Union war hero, he had been wounded five times while leading the Sixth Missouri Regiment into battle. After the war, and before he'd met and married Victoria, he'd been both the St. Louis city auditor and president of that city's Society of Spiritualists.

And he'd been living in New York long enough since then, so that he probably knew more of this city's mediums than even Tennessee did.

Harp shook Blood's outstretched hand and said, "I have to talk to you."

"Not right now," Blood said. "Vicky will begin at any moment."

"Afterwards, then."

"Fine, but I won't be able to spare you more than half an hour, at the most. I have to pack and catch a train to join Tennie in Boston. We just received a telegram. The governor of Massachusetts is threatening to ban Vicky's appearance there."

Harp nodded and followed Blood into the auditorium where Charles Dickens had drawn a full house seventeen times in a row during his American lecture tour three winters ago.

It was more than three-quarters full for Victoria. Women made up the bulk of the audience, but there was also a sprinkling of men. Among them Harp recognized four reporters. You could count on some being present whenever Victoria spoke in public. Almost everything she said, or could be provoked into saying, made juicy newspaper copy.

Colonel Blood seated himself in the front row, next to Stephen Pearl Andrews, an elderly man with a long black and white beard. Author of a highly regarded book, *The Science of Society,* Andrews was a radical philosopher whose friendship was valued by such celebrities as Henry James and Horace Greeley. He and Blood wrote most of Victoria's speeches and newspaper articles.

That didn't make her their mouthpiece, as some charged. She would listen to what they had to say, tell them what she wanted to say and often push them to rewrite the result until it felt right to her. And neither man could control the times when she seemed to catch fire, dropped a prepared speech and launched into something that was unadulterated Victoria Woodhull—and more eloquent than anything Blood or Andrews could come up with.

Harp wandered along the central aisle until he located Louise Vedder in the third row from the front. Most of the women in the hall were dressed in Quaker gray, pale lavender or brown, their hair drawn back in buns under no-nonsense hats with loose veils. Among them, Louise looked like a touch of spring. Her thick auburn hair was up in a coronet of seed pearls and lilies-of-the-valley. She wore a torso-hugging, rose-red jersey over a satin dress of fresh green trimmed with lace, a jade brooch fastening its high collar, an embossed silver chatelaine attached to its girdle.

A young woman seated next to her was looking around uneasily, as if suddenly discovering she was too conspicuous so far forward. Harp asked if she would mind letting him sit next to his sister. She agreed eagerly, relieved at having an excuse to make the move, and hurried toward the rear of the hall. Harp took the seat she'd vacated.

Louise smiled at him. "So now you are my brother."

"Everyone should have a black sheep somewhere in the family."

"I thought you never attended these meetings."

"I'm here on business," Harp told her.

"You seem to be on business most of the time." Louise paused and then asked him, "Will you be, tomorrow evening? Because tonight is when I bid Uriah farewell. After that, I would be pleased to have you come by for that dinner we spoke about in the park."

He shook his head. "I've got too much ground to cover over the next two or three days. Too many things to be done at the same time. Too many people to be found and asked the same questions."

She regarded him for a moment. "Could I possibly do any of it for you?"

He started to say no but stopped himself and thought about it. There was nothing dangerous in talking to dozens of mediums, trying to find the one Alice Curry had consulted. And Louise wouldn't need to keep finding cabs—and paying for each. She had a choice of her own two carriages for getting around town quickly from one medium to the next. It would free him to follow other leads.

He returned her gaze with a slight smile. "Working for me doesn't pay what you would consider real money. And it would be time consuming."

"After tonight I'll have more time than I'll know what to do with—for a while. And I don't expect to be paid. After all, we are already in business together."

Harp gave it more thought, nodded and broke the electrifying contact between her remarkable eyes and his own. "I'll tell you about it, together with Vicky and the colonel, after she's finished here."

People in the audience had begun to applaud. Victoria had appeared and was walking to the podium.

Twenty

She took her place on the podium, a good-looking woman in her thirties with a bold figure and an erect stance, whom many regarded as an incarnation of an ancient earth-mother goddess. There was a smile on her pale face as she waited for the applause to die down. It was a smile that had warmth and controled energy in it; but also, as always, a suggestion of restrained sadness—as though she knew things others didn't, which made it impossible to regard life as something gay.

She wore a promenade dress of stiff black silk without the traditional stylish flounces, its bodice molded to her strong curves but her trailing skirt voluminous. Her trademark white rose was pinned over the generous swell of her left breast. Her hair was cut to short curls, in defiance of the fashion that a woman's hair was her crowning glory, to be grown very long and gathered up into a chignon or a Grecian coil, and to be let down only in private, before no one but her husband or personal maid.

She began to speak as she usually did before an audience, in a voice that was low and slow, somewhat hesitant. But it gathered volume and sureness as her speech progressed. It was an attack on what Victoria saw as destructive elements in the most sacrosanct institution of all: the wife's role as an extension of her husband.

Harp didn't give it much of his attention. He had heard most of it from Victoria in the past. And his awareness of Louise so close beside him was too intense. The intoxicating scent of her delicate perfume. The whisper of silk under her skirt whenever she stirred a bit in her chair. The gentle rise and fall of her bosom. The warmth of her body seemed to penetrate his flesh, prodding a physical response too strong to be ignored. His hand itched to cross the scant inches between them, and to touch her. He had to will the hand to remain still, gripping his hat and walking stick.

Victoria was more than halfway through her speech when his attention was snapped back to what was being said in the hall. A reporter had risen to his feet, pencil and notepad poised as he interrupted her: "Mrs. Woodhull, are you saying that it is *all right* for a woman to desert her husband?"

Victoria paused, and then answered firmly: "If her will takes her away from a man, she surely ought to go. I hold that any man or woman, whether married or unmarried, who consorts for any reason but love is a prostitute."

Another reporter shot to his feet, scenting blood. "Since you yourself have brought up the subject of prostitution, Madame, some people had charged that *you* have on occasion prostituted yourself to improve your position in the world. Is that charge true or false?"

There was a hush in the audience. Harp watched something he had seen before. Victoria's face went utterly blank, as though her mind had left her body and gone off to some other place. It lasted no more than seven or eight seconds. When her eyes focused again on her questioner there was a ruddy glow in her cheeks, and her voice took on an increased strength:

"The spirits have entrusted me with a mission, and I have done and shall do everything and anything that is necessary to accomplish it. I used whatever influence I had to get the money for my work, and that's *my* business and none of yours. And if I devoted my body to my work and my soul to God, *that* is my business and none of yours."

The reporter looked buffeted but remained standing. "That phrase you just used, Madame—*devoting your body*—are we to take that as meaning . . . sexual intercourse?"

"*Sexual intercourse,*" Victoria repeated slowly, looking at the reporter as if he were a block of stone she was going to have to work hard at sculpting. "*That* phrase seems to discomfit you. This sexual intercourse business may as well be discussed now—and discussed until you are so familiar with your sexual organs that a reference to them will no longer make a blush mount to your face anymore than a reference to any other part of your body."

The reporter tried to interrupt, but there was no stopping Victoria: "Nothing," she told him, "is as destructive as intercourse carried on habitually without regard to reciprocal consummation. I need not explain to any woman the effects of unconsummated intercourse. But most men need to have it thundered in their ears. A woman demands a return for all that a man receives. She demands that he shall not be enriched at her expense. Demands that he shall not, either from ignorance or selfish desire, carry her impulse forward only to cast it backward with its mission unfulfilled, to breed nervous debility or irritability and sexual demoralization. And that, dear sir, involves a whole science and a fine art, now criminally repressed."

The reporter was sitting by then, looking a bit stunned as he scribbled furiously in his notebook—but a third one had popped up with his own question: "Madame, regarding your assault on marriage today, do you really believe that the practice of free love is preferable for society?"

She nodded. "I do advocate free love. In the highest and purest sense. As the only cure for the immorality which corrupts sexual relations today—when men preach against free love openly and practice it secretly."

"On the subject of immorality, Madame, you advocate free love —but do you *practice* it?"

"I do not like your lewd tone, sir," Victoria told him with a sharp anger. "So many of you reporters make that grievous blunder when they encounter free-love women. I have had to repeatedly free myself of their lascivious allusions and gross conduct. And they, repulsed, then write pious articles against free love."

"That is not an answer to my question, Mrs. Woodhull."

"Oh, I'll answer it, no fear." Victoria took a breath, and then let him have what he was after: "Yes! I am a free lover! I have an inalienable, constitutional and natural right to love whom I may, to love as long or as short a period as I can, to change the love story every day if I please—and neither you nor any law that you can frame has the right to interfere."

By the time Victoria concluded the meeting a number of women in the audience, and a few of the men, had fled from the hall. As soon as it was finished most of the others hurried out, some with their heads down, praying no one would notice them. But when Harp and Louise went backstage they found a group of women clustered worshipfully around Victoria outside her dressing room door.

She broke free of them to kiss Louise on the cheek, then put her arms around Harp's neck, rising on her toes to kiss him on the lips. Turning back to the group of women, she thanked them heartily for their kind words and good wishes, bade them farewell and ushered Louise and Harp into the little dressing room.

"Well," she asked after closing the door, "how do you think I did out there?"

"No one can say you didn't speak your mind," Louise said with held-down humor. "Perhaps not wisely, but very well."

"There's not a paper in the country with the nerve to quote you verbatim," Harp told Victoria with a dry smile. "But they'll hint at enough of it to scare away some of your supporters. May pull in some others, though."

"Anyone frightened off by plain speaking," Victoria said, "doesn't belong in my movement anyway."

Harp didn't comment on her reference to the women's movement as hers. He'd already warned her, recently, that if she really tried to take its leadership away from the ladies who presently headed it, she would lose.

Colonel Blood entered the room saying, "Vicky, if we don't go soon, I'll have to board that train with an empty satchel."

"Give me two minutes first," Harp told him, and brought out his picture of Olivia Walburton. "Do any of you know this woman?"

Blood looked and shook his head. Louise did the same. Victoria took a longer look at the photograph before saying, "No. Who is she?"

"Doesn't matter." Harp put that picture away and showed them the one of Alice Curry. None of them recognized her. All three knew her name when he gave it—but only from the newspaper stories about her murder.

Victoria gave him a knowing look. "You're trying to catch the monster who killed her."

"Among other things."

Colonel Blood took a silver watch from his waistcoat pocket and snapped open its cover to check the time. "Harp, if there is more you want to talk about, why don't you come along in Louise's carriage, and we can discuss it on the way to the house."

"I'm pressed for time myself," Harp said. "For one thing I have to find a medium whose name I don't know, that Alice Curry consulted before she was murdered." He gave Louise an inquiring look. When she nodded he told Blood, "Louise has offered to help me with that. I'd appreciate it if you and Vicky would give her the name and address of every medium you know of in New York."

"You're going to be a busy woman," Victoria told Louise. "There are so many of them—if you include the fakes. When we get home I'll tell you about the ones I know."

"No need," Blood said. "I have a fairly complete list of them in my desk." He looked at Harp. "Louise can start copying from it after I've gone to the train station. Will that do?"

"It'll do fine."

"Consider it done, then."

Blood helped Louise into her ankle-length, caped overcoat. Harp did the same for Victoria. The two women covered their heads with scarves and knotted them under their chins while Harp and Blood put on their own coats and hats.

Harp gave Louise a copy of the Alice Curry photograph before accompanying the three of them outside to her carriage. As he handed Louise up into it he told her, "If you do locate the medium she went to, don't ask any further questions yourself. Just contact me the usual way."

Then he realized he was still holding on to her hand. He let it go, slowly. As her carriage pulled away he gazed after it, cursing himself and the nasty game that a vicious fate was playing with his life.

He turned abruptly, walked one block west on Fourteenth Street and went into the saloon section of a plush restaurant facing the southeast end of Union Square. He needed a drink.

More than one would be better.

Twenty-One

He ordered his first whiskey as soon as he'd taken his seat at a window table. A double. He downed half of it with one swallow, and had to force himself to go slower with the rest. A waiter brought him a menu. Harp looked at it. It would be wise to have an early supper before going to meet Ambrose McGowan at Millie's pier. No telling what the rendezvous would lead to, and whether it would allow him any time for a meal later.

But he had no appetite. His hunger for Louise was too strong. And the knotty problem of what to do about her was too disturbing.

He put the menu aside and ordered another double whiskey instead.

Leland was right: his reluctance to simply lie to Louise was ridiculous. He wouldn't even have to tell her a lie. Just avoid the truth. And enjoy whatever time he would have with her—before someone who knew the truth told it to her. That, he knew, was not likely to ever happen. The men who'd seen him take her picture from her dying husband were New Yorkers, but they might not have survived the war. The same was true for any others in the Eighty-first New York Volunteer Infantry that they'd told the story to. If any were still around, Harp hadn't run into them. The chance of Louise becoming acquainted with one of them was infinitesimal. Though not impossible.

But the uncharacteristic hesitation that tormented Harp went deeper than that. He'd invested too much of himself in Louise, back when he'd had no expectation of ever meeting her. Her tintype had become an icon for him. But she wasn't an icon. She had materialized as a flesh-and-blood woman, and he was in love with her; yet unable to take what he wanted.

He had too much imagination. That was the trouble. He could see the look of horror that would come over her if she did learn about his killing her young husband. A horror that there'd be no getting past. The image burned in him.

His second double arrived. He took small sips and looked out of the window. Trying to push the problem aside by observing the activity out there.

There was plenty to observe. The Ladies Mile started here. Union Square, surrounded by theaters and first-class hotels and expensive restaurants, by theatrical costumers, piano showrooms and some of the city's best shops, was one of the two hearts of fashionable Manhattan. The other was uptown around Madison Square, where Broadway's Ladies Mile reached Twenty-third Street.

The streets around Union Square were crowded with carriages, cabs and horse cars. This was one of the few places in New York City where a policeman with a rattan signal baton was stationed to bestow some order on the heavy flow of traffic. And where the streets had been swept clear of snow and mud, and there were frequent daytime pickups of horse manure.

Scores of women shuttled between fashionable stores, stylishly bundled up against the cold. Strollers were coming out of the fenced park in the center of the square. Along with mothers and nursemaids ushering children and pushing baby carriages—hurrying home as the thin light of winter day faded towards evening. Street vendors and musicians at the many street corners around the square did their best to entice nickels and dimes from prosperous passersby. Sellers of colored balloons and heated doughnuts, matches and toothpicks, artificial flowers and puppies. An Italian organ grinder with a monkey on his shoulder. A Scotsman in kilts playing a bagpipe, his knees bright pink from the cold. A ragged little girl with a violin. A three-man German brass band.

Among the women shoppers Harp spotted one he knew. Georgiana Judson, a middle-aged, well-dressed lady with a sprightly step, indistinguishable to the unknowing eye from the others. She was coming from the Tiffany building, closely following a younger woman dangling a beaded purse from one gloved hand. Georgiana's hands were not gloved.

She was one of the most accomplished pickpockets Harp knew.

She concentrated on the rich women shoppers who usually carried substantial sums of cash on them. No male pickpocket could get close enough to a respectable woman before she reacted to a man she didn't know having the bad manners to move in on her. That left female victims to female pickpockets like Georgiana. Though she was after cash, she often wound up with jewelry and expensive ladies' watches. When she had enough of those she would take a train to Philadelphia, where she had a fence who paid her reasonable prices because she was a steady source.

She had a nice house in Trenton, New Jersey, where she lived a blameless life with the husband and children her skill supported. She came into New York only once every couple of weeks, or when needful. If her first day's prowl of the Ladies Mile didn't net enough, she would stay overnight at the St. Bernard Hotel at the corner of Prince and Wooster, and sally forth again the next day. The St. Bernard was a favorite resort for well-to-do pickpockets. The police knew about it, of course. So the hotel had to charge its clients enough to pay off the authorities and be ignored. An arrangement that Harp guessed was due for a temporary interruption, now that the Tammany political machine was collapsing.

Harp watched Georgiana and her quarry turn out of sight around a corner. He took another sip of whiskey, beginning to feel its warmth relaxing him, and turned from the window. The restaurant tables were beginning to fill up. The women were all stylish, most of them in their twenties or early thirties. The men with them—no respectable restaurant would serve a woman without an escort—didn't appear to be their husbands, judging by the attitude of guarded complicity. Some of the men looked prosperous, the others presentable. Harp knew a few of them to be actors who appreciated having a lady treat them to an expensive meal when they were between jobs.

Harp also knew two of the women: members of the *demimonde* who lived in nearby boardinghouses and regularly attended nearby churches. The rest looked to be upper-crust or middle-crust wives—bored with having nothing to do at home but supervise servants who didn't need supervision, and nothing purposeful outside their homes that it was considered proper for them to occupy themselves with.

An observer of the city's sins had not long ago published a

rebuke to women like these who frequented the high-priced restaurants around Union Square with men other than their husbands: "Suppers and rich wines, and low voices and delicious flattery are dangerous, dear Madame, even if you think it not."

Harp hadn't noticed business dropping off at any of these places since that had been published.

There was a rack of newspapers and magazines near him. He pulled out a copy of *Leslie's Weekly* and leafed through it in search of something to grab his interest. The only one he found was an item by the reporter of scientific and medical discoveries:

> SLEEPING TOGETHER.—More quarrels arise between husbands and wives owing to electrical changes through which their nervous systems go, by lodging together night after night under the same bedclothes, than by any other disturbing cause. There is nothing that will derange the nervous system of a person who is eliminate in nervous force like lying all night in bed with another person who is almost absorbent in nervous force. The absorber will go to sleep and rest, while the eliminator will be tossing and tumbling, restless and nervous, and wake up in the morning fretful, peevish and discouraged. No two persons, no matter who they are, should habitually sleep together.

Harp laughed softly and tossed the magazine aside. *That* was what he needed, to get the Louise Vedder problem out of his head: a night of having his nervous system deranged by some other woman. He looked again at the women in the restaurant. Some were pretty, and a few were beautiful. He knew women just as desirable he could spend tonight with if he contacted them. It usually worked. At least for the one night . . .

He drank the rest of the whiskey in his glass and felt its soothing glow spread through him. That was another way: and one without complications. Simply get drunk. And come out of it a couple of days later with nothing on his mind but a violent headache, a parched mouth and throat and a sick stomach.

And to hell with meeting Ambrose.

Harp signaled his waiter to bring him a third double whiskey.

But by the time it arrived he was remembering the way he'd last seen Moe Saul. Laid out so neatly on his bed, with the side of his skull bashed in.

He paid and tipped the waiter, put on his hat, coat and gloves and left the drink untouched. Outside he took a deep breath and headed towards Millie's pier on foot. That was yet another way to clear his head of a cleft-stick predicament he couldn't solve.

A long, brisk hike through the evening's freezing city air.

Twenty-Two

There was now a large tenement house on the site of the freight company stables where Harp had often slept in the haylofts—huddled together with other kids for shared body warmth—during the bitter winter in which he'd reached the age of ten. The slaughterhouse building on the other side of the street had been converted into another tenement—after complaints about the stench wafted to more affluent blocks finally forced the removal of Manhattan's west side abattoirs across the river to Communipaw, New Jersey.

Walking past there now, Harp experienced a sudden, sharp memory: the taste of the soup the gang used to make out of animal entrails they stole from the place in the slaughterhouse where the fat was left to be rendered into lard. He remembered, too, the time he'd watched from hiding when two of the scuddlers who scraped bristles from slaughtered hogs got into a fight and fell into the big scalding-tub. They were screaming incoherently when they'd scrambled out; and they'd gone on screaming until they'd died.

Harp walked on past a row of storage sheds in the direction of the North River: the official name of the stretch of the Hudson that flowed past New York City. It wasn't quite sunset yet, but thick cloud cover let none of the sun's warmth reach the city below. Piles of garbage thrown into the streets and left to rot didn't stink the way they did in the summers. They were frozen with snow and ice, forming hard, uneven hills. Freight wagons lurched and bounced over them, passing Harp on their way from the docks.

A bunch of little boys and girls in rags, bare feet showing through cracks in their shoes, were roasting chunks of meat and toasting a bread loaf over a fire in the mouth of a wagon alley between the sheds. The bread, if stale, might have been begged from a bakery. The wood for the fire would have been snatched in a grab-and-run raid across a lumber dock. The meat was probably stolen from the back of a delivery wagon while its driver's attention was focused on cursing a kid who had fallen down in front of his horse's hooves. Harp knew. He had been one of those kids once. Part of him still felt one of them.

There were screams of raucous laughter as they took turns leaping across their fire, its flames singeing their torn skirts and trousers. Street kids weren't much for smiling, but they laughed a lot. Laughing proved that nothing could get you down.

Continuing west, Harp crossed the part of Tenth Avenue locals called Misery Row. Gutter-poor Irish families crowded every room of its old, two-floor-and-attic houses. Houses without gas or water that tilted crazily because they'd been built over a filled-in patch of swamp where the ground was still in the process of settling.

Next came Eleventh Avenue—and that was called Death Avenue because of drunks killed on its railroad tracks at night by shuttling locomotives.

This was the neighborhood Harp had fled to after escaping from the orphanage on Randall's Island in the East River. His previous neighborhood had been on the lower east side, and he'd reasoned that if the authorities came hunting for him they would look over there, not all the way across Manhattan on the west side. He'd been only nine at the time. But his reasoning powers—like those of the other street kids that one observer likened to a swarm of cockroaches—were razor-sharp when it came to such basics as survival and freedom from authority.

It hadn't been difficult to win acceptance into this neighborhood's band of juvenile vagabonds—after the obligatory fistfights and a display of his skill at picking pockets. Every gang could use a tough newcomer with special expertise. And Harp wasn't the only kid from outside the area. Though most were from around Misery Row, others came from as far away as the Midwest, working their way on the canal boats that still carried more merchandise between the Great Lakes and New York than the railroads. Wherever they came from, the kids had much in common. They were orphans, or unwanted castoffs, or runaways from situations they hated. Roving the streets and alleys with others like them was an improvement.

By the time Harp had felt it safe to rejoin his old gang on the east side of town he'd gotten an idea. It was for an informal linkage of the west side gang he'd joined and his home gang on the east side. They were too far apart for any territorial disputes between them. And each could serve as a haven for the other. Any time a member of one gang had police too hot on his heels he could move across town and become an accepted part of the other gang, as Harp had done, for as long as it took for the heat back home to dissipate.

Both gangs had liked the idea, and it had been activated often enough to become standard practice. That was how Ambrose Mc-Gowan and other boys from the east side had gotten to know Millie. She'd been one of the street girls, not too bright, who'd roamed the west side with the boys. Until she'd gotten old enough to earn more than most of the boys could make or steal, by selling her body. She'd been very proud of that, for a time. Harp had estimated her age as a little short of seventeen when she'd drowned herself . . .

The noise ahead, getting louder as he approached, became an uproar that hurt the eardrums when he reached the West Street docks. The clash and screech of iron wheels and iron-shod hooves on cobblestones from the multitude of freight wagons milling about. Steam whistles, bells and hooters. Teamsters and stevedores shouting to be heard through the din. Night was closing in but the loading and unloading of docked vessels went on full blast under the yellow glare of quayside gas lamps.

Millie's pier was like most of the others stretching north and south of it like wide-spaced teeth in an endless comb. It was made of timber that was showing the wear and tear of some decades of hard use. Officials talked about modernizing the docks but never got around to it. Improvements cost money that would have to be taken out of profits that belonged in the pockets of merchants and politicians. Harp guessed nothing would be done until the piers collapsed; and maybe that would be the end of New York's career as one of the world's great commercial harbors.

There was an oyster-and-coffee booth, covered by a tin awning, near the quayside end of Millie's pier. Harp took an early supper

—oysters spread thickly inside a long half-loaf of crusty bread—there, standing where Ambrose or whoever he sent would see him. He ate his sandwich and watched the activity around Millie's pier.

Moored against one side of it was a Dutch sail-and-steam freighter, with three masts and two smokestacks, taking on a cargo of buffalo hides and beaver skins. Further out along that side of the pier large blocks of ice were being carried to waiting wagons from two barges that had just arrived from the ice factories up the Hudson at Barrytown. Far out along the other side a floating grain elevator was drawing grain out of a canal boat and spouting it into a three-mast bark from Spain. Closer to the quay on that side dockworkers were unloading hogsheads of sugar and big sacks of coffee beans from an iron-hulled square-rigger back from the Caribbean.

Harp spotted four boys in their early teens lurking in the deepening night shadows between two transit sheds nearby. He didn't need to see their eyes to know they were watching each stevedore pass them carrying a load from the square-rigger to wagons on the quay. Waiting with tensed excitement, tin cans ready in their hands, for a hogshead or sack to fall and break open. So they could dash out and scoop up as much as they could before darting away from a dock guard's club or a teamster's whip.

Harp didn't want them to mistake him for a suspicious guard and get put off their game. He looked away: out to the sail and steam vessels still plying the darkening river. Tugboats and lighters, sloops and schooners, barges and canal boats. A Europa-class clipper ship with a mermaid figurehead glided along the middle of the river on its way out to the sea. A Hudson River night liner steamed past it in the opposite direction, its paddlewheels churning the water, its long saloon and three tiers of staterooms ablaze with lights, looking like a multilayered, candlelit wedding cake. Off to the right and left ferryboats were crossing the river between New Jersey and Manhattan, escorted by flocks of seagulls.

This had been one of the grand pleasures of a street kid. Wandering along the docks as long as you liked. Sharing in the drama of its hustle and bustle while keeping an eye out for something you could steal. Sitting on the end of a pier watching the river traffic go by and daydreaming of distant, exotic lands. Swimming around the piers in the summers.

Life on the streets did have its compensations for a kid. Being able to rove through the city at will; with nobody you had to account to and no fixed hours when you were expected somewhere. Hanging onto the back of a wagon for a long-distance ride. Dropping off to explore prosperous neighborhoods and ogle their stylish ladies and gorgeously dressed tarts. Cadging pennies from shoppers. Hanging around outside the better hotels and theaters at night, on the lookout for well-filled pockets to pick and rich drunks to roll.

Picking up short-term jobs could be fun too: because you didn't have to if you didn't want to. Sweeping out stables, shining boots and polishing carriages; running errands, delivering messages, helping to clean out breweries. And swiftly spending the money you got, from working or stealing, for other pleasures. Gambling and going to bawdy shows at the Bowery theaters. Splurging on a winter night's comfort in a halfway decent hotel's warm room and soft bed. Treating your chummies to a good meal in a cheap restaurant where you could swap noisy jokes and smoke cigars . . .

Harp finished his oyster sandwich and ordered a cup of coffee. He had taken off his gloves and stuffed them in a back pocket, so they wouldn't slow him if he had to put a weapon to use in a hurry. He held the steaming cup with both hands, keeping his fingers warmed and supple while he drank. He drained the cup and was about to order a refill when a head popped up above the edge of Millie's pier. The face under the bowler hat was Ambrose McGowan's. As soon as Ambrose saw that Harp had spotted him, his head ducked back down out of sight.

Harp put down the empty cup, strolled over to the spot where the head had been and looked down. Ambrose wasn't there, but a pier ladder was. Harp climbed down and peered between the tarred piles that held up the pier. Ambrose was in deep shadow under the pier, seated at the oars of a small rowboat, holding the boat in place by gripping a pile with one hand. Harp swung himself into the boat and sat down facing him.

Ambrose had small, neatly chiseled features and dark blue eyes framed by long black lashes. His face would have been almost girlishly pretty if it hadn't been deeply pitted with smallpox scars. He was short and thin, lacking the brute strength of most gang members. But he had developed a skill to compensate for that. He was a knife thrower of uncanny accuracy. A rare accomplishment that had won him instant acceptance as one of Hoggy Corcoran's key men.

Harp remembered Ambrose practicing it as an undersized young boy, hour after hour, until he'd perfected the skill.

"Sure nobody followed you here?" he asked Harp.

"When was the last time you heard about somebody shadowing me and I didn't know about it?"

"Okay," Ambrose said, and before Harp could begin trying to pry what he wanted out of him he went on: "Hoggy wants to see you. So you can tell him what that note you left for me means. About us being in more trouble than we know about."

This wasn't what Harp wanted or had planned. "I don't give a damn about the trouble Hoggy and the rest of them are in," he said. "You're the only one I've got any reason at all to help. And I can't do that unless you level with me about the night your gang swiped the liquor from the warehouse."

Ambrose blinked. "What makes you figure we're the ones copped the liquor?"

"I know you did. So do the police by now. We've got to talk before they find you."

Ambrose shook his head. "I can't. Hoggy said not to talk to you about *anything*. Just bring you. He's the one you got to talk to."

Harp didn't like it. The prospect of a confrontation with Hoggy Corcoran made his nerves creep. Hoggy was more intelligent than most hoodlums, and he could sometimes be reasonable. But he was also a massive bundle of volatile ferocity—prone to rages during which he might kill or maim over a fancied slight, or just in a spasm of bad temper.

"I've got other things to do," Harp said. "You and me trade information, here and now. You can tell Hoggy about it after."

"I can't," Ambrose repeated. "He said bring you and that's what I got to do."

It wasn't a stubbornness that could be budged. Ambrose, like every other member of the gang, was simply too scared of Hoggy Corcoran to disobey his orders. Harp had to go along with it or walk away from it without the information he wanted. His nerves settled down as soon as he accepted that. He felt a concentrated cooling of blood and brain that came each time he set himself to walk the razor's edge.

"Okay," he said, "let's go."

Twenty-Three

Ambrose rowed them south, going under piers where he could and maneuvering between docked vessels from one pier to the next. He had to swing further out into the dark river when they got to the floating wholesale oyster market. There the barges, equipped with saltwater wells for the oysters brought by sloops from Long Island, were permanently moored with no space between them. But as soon as that was behind them Ambrose swung back to the protective cover of the piers and moored vessels. The Canal Street depot for ferryboats to and from Hoboken was a short distance ahead when he angled sharp left underneath one of the piers.

It resounded with the bellowing of frightened cattle and the thunder of their hooves as they were driven up a wide gangplank onto an ocean steamer from Liverpool. Fat bars of shadow cast by the piles on either side crosshatched the meager gaslight filtering down from the docks above. Harp had to squint to make out exactly what Ambrose was doing: fastening his bowline to a rusted ringbolt in the brick embankment under the quay. Next to it equally rusty iron bars formed an interlaced barrier across a water drainage outlet about six feet in diameter.

Back in the previous century lower Manhattan had been full of open streams, ponds and swamps. As the city had expanded north from the Battery these had been filled in and canals had been dug to drain them into the East River and the Hudson. By early in the nineteenth century the canals had disappeared from view under new-built streets. The earliest was Broad Street, down in the financial district; the longest and best known was Canal Street, reaching from river to river. But there were dozens of others, intercon-

nected by innumerable drainage sewers leading from cellar cesspools to the covered canals, built by neighborhood companies and
even by individual house owners.

After the city had finally built an organized system of water
supply and drainage, most of the earlier covered canals and sewer
tunnels had become relatively dry, except during heavy, pro-
longed rains. By 1871 the existence of many had been forgotten
by city officials. But not by the poorer denizens of lower Manhattan. Many used the underground networks to walk from one place
to another during rains and snowstorms. And for local criminals
they provided places to hide loot and a means of escape when
police came calling. Some established gangs had dug their own
underground passages connecting one abandoned drainage system to another.

Nobody knew all of the ways in and out of these many intercon-
nected networks. Harp knew a lot of them. But he didn't know this
one.

Ambrose reached a hand through the bars and twisted something inside. Then he gripped the bars with both hands and swung
them open—on what were probably fairly new and well-oiled
hinges. If they squeaked at all, Harp couldn't hear it through the
noise of the cattle crossing the pier overhead. Ambrose motioned
to Harp and climbed into the opening. As soon as Harp was inside
with him, he pulled the barrier shut.

In the total darkness the flare of a match was bright enough to
make Harp's eyes narrow defensively. Ambrose was lighting a lantern, one of a pair that hung from nails on one wall of the drainage tunnel. He worked a lever in the opposite wall, locking the
bars in place across the opening before taking down the lit lantern
and leading the way through the tunnel. Ambrose was short
enough to walk upright, but Harp had to lower his head and bend
forward as he followed.

Not much water had drained through this tunnel recently. It
was thickly carpeted with partially solidified sludge that was only a
little spongy under their boots, absorbing the sound of their foot-
steps. They passed sewer pipes opening into the main drain from
left and right. Some of crumbling bricks, others of cast iron or
hard-fired clay. A few very old ones were constructed of hollowed-

out tree trunks. Nothing came out of them at the moment but
sewer stink and the scratching and squeaking of rats.

The drain tunnel meandered, following the course of a creek
that no longer existed. Twice they came to places where the tunnel forked. Ambrose took the one to the right the first time, the
one to the left the next. It was hard to calculate distances pre-
cisely. Harp guessed they'd passed beneath three or four city
blocks when Ambrose stopped by a mound of broken bricks.

The bricks had been dislodged from the tunnel roof overhead.
Through the gap, the lantern showed a stout new trapdoor set
into much older floorboards. Ambrose stepped up onto the
mound, reached above his head with his free hand and rapped his
knuckles against the underside of the trapdoor. Two raps, pause,
one rap, pause, two raps.

The trapdoor was opened, showing nothing but darkness above
it. Ambrose raised the lantern to show his face to whoever was up
there. A ladder was lowered. Harp followed Ambrose up, into a
small cellar room that might have originally been intended as a
storage place or a coal bin. Ambrose's lantern showed two hefty
thugs putting revolvers back in their coat pockets. Harp knew both
slightly. Dutch Duffy and Sheeny Max Cohen, veterans of Hoggy
Corcoran's gang.

Duffy took a curved cover off a large tin pan in the middle of
the plank floor. The pan contained burning coals that gave the
room some heat and a little light. Other than that, the room had
only two very old easy chairs, one facing the trapdoor and the
other near a narrow, glassless window through which Harp could
see only black night outside.

Cohen was pulling the ladder back up when Ambrose asked,
"Hoggy upstairs?"

Cohen closed the trapdoor and spat tobacco juice on the floor
before answering: "Just went across to the other house."

Ambrose and Harp went up a short flight of stone steps, raised
the slanted cellar door at the top and climbed out into an enclosed courtyard. There was no light there except from Ambrose's
lantern; and most of that was absorbed by the night. Vague shapes
loomed over them from every direction. The backs of half-seen
buildings, looking like moldering ruins in the darkness. Bulging
walls, crooked roofs, lopsided gables, collapsing turrets, askew

chimneys. Harp didn't spot any way in or out of the court except through these buildings.

He stuck with Ambrose and his lantern as they crossed the courtyard, their boots breaking through thin crusts of ice into a sucking mire of mud, refuse and half-frozen snow. They climbed four sagging wooden steps to the back door of a tightly shuttered three-story house. Ambrose knocked: the same signal sequence as at the trapdoor. There was the sound of lock bolts being drawn inside.

The one who opened the door was new to Harp. Young, beefy, hard-faced. Standard street brawler. His right fist held one of the multipurpose handguns turned out by craftsmen during the war: a six-shot knuckle-duster revolver with brass knuckles for a grip and a wavy-blade dagger sprouting from the left side of its iron frame. He jerked his left thumb over his shoulder and relocked the door. Harp saw it was sheathed inside with iron, and that the lock bolts were long and thick. Ambrose extinguished the lantern, left it on the floor and led him toward the front of the house. They went through a cold, bare corridor that exuded a musty odor of rot and mold. A single candle in a wall bracket lit their way. Splintering floorboards bent under their weight.

They entered a front room where the smell was of soft coal burning in a pot-bellied stove and cigar butts pickling in three cuspidors full of chewing-tobacco juice. Wavering light from an oil lamp, its wick turned low, made room shadows move like ghosts stirring in their sleep, and didn't penetrate into dark corners. Heavy velvet drapes covered two windows facing the street, so no chink of the feeble light would show through the outside shutters.

Flowered wallpaper, with huge roses predominating, hung in shreds from the walls and ceilings, exposing large patches of crumbling plaster and laths. Most of the splintery flooring here was covered by rugs. A few were threadbare but most looked like money: loot from various robberies. The furniture came in the same variety: junk and booty. The oil lamp rested, with a nearly empty pitcher of beer and some glasses, on a delicate writing table that might have been Louis XIV. There were more glasses and an empty whiskey bottle on another table improvised from a large beer keg. One of the three much-used cuspidors was an enameled bowl with gilt trimming, the others were rusty tin cans.

A tall, cadaverous character named August "Smoky" Poole sat on a new leather sofa, dressed like an undertaker. He had a half-filled beer pitcher and a glass on the floor by his left leg, and he held a pistol on his right thigh, shifting it slightly to point at Harp.

Harp sidestepped and put his back against a wall.

"Don't move around," Smoky advised him, in a lugubrious voice that went with his clothes and physical appearance. "You don't want to make me nervous."

He didn't have to be more emphatic about it. Smoky had a reputation as a dead shot with a handgun. There were rival gang members who could have testified that he'd earned the reputation, if they were still alive. He'd gotten the nickname from having "smoked" quite a number of them.

"Where's Hoggy?" Ambrose asked him.

"Upstairs. Waking up some of the boys to take their turn keeping watch outside in the street."

"Wait here," Ambrose told Harp, and left the room.

Harp remained standing with the wall at his back, not quite leaning on the walking stick in his left hand, his right inside his coat pocket with the Le Mat revolver. Smoky leaned back in the sofa, eyes and pistol fixed on Harp.

The pistol had a short barrel, not more than two and a half inches. Its stock and forearm were of checkered and polished hardwood, the butt curved like a bird's head. It looked to Harp like the kind of pocket pistol made by Deringer of Philadelphia.

"That one of the Lincoln Murder models?" he asked Smoky.

"One of 'em, hell," Smoky said. "This is *it*. The one what did the deed."

Harp doubted that Smoky believed that. The pistol John Wilkes Booth had used to kill President Lincoln was supposed to be under government lock and key. Con men sold exact copies to wealthy collectors for extravagant prices, claiming each was Booth's weapon. But Smoky wouldn't fall for that scam. He'd been a part-time con man himself, though never very successful at it, before discovering his talent as a gunman.

Smoky had been much lower down the criminal scale when Harp had first known of him. He'd been called Augy back then, and he'd been a hair thief. An abundance of hair was a woman's crowning glory, and many women didn't have enough to fashion themselves a fat chignon. Those who could afford it bought false hair to rectify nature's failure. Those who could afford better than that paid more for real hair that matched or blended with their own.

Smoky—Augy back then—would hang around Castle Garden watching the latest shiploads of poor immigrants entering the city. When he spotted among them a woman with a generous amount of hair, he would follow and try to get to her before she discovered for herself that she had a marketable commodity. Using the promise of a job, he would lure her to some place where he could drug or slug her unconscious. When she'd come to, she would find most of her hair shorn.

Stealing hair was still a moderately lucrative minor-league activity. But being a killer with a handgun paid better; and it earned you a lot more underworld respect.

Harp stopped thinking about Smoky's background when he heard a *thump-thump-thump* coming down a stairway and approaching along the corridor.

Hoggy Corcoran—announcing his approach with every alternate step. He'd had his pegleg shod with a sharpened angle-iron. So that when he stomped a fallen man he could drive it into the man's guts all the way to the backbone.

Harp flexed his shoulders a little to ease the tension. He managed to look relaxed, almost sleepy, when Hoggy stomped into the room.

Twenty-Four

Hoggy was massive. A solid block from shoulders to hips. The floorboards shuddered and spurted dust each time his shod pegleg thudded down on them with all that weight on top of it. Harp knew the stump of that leg hurt all the time where it was strapped at the knee to the pegleg; and that accounted for some of Hoggy's explosions of rage. It was almost nine years since a rival for the affections of a Water Street whore had shattered the rest of the leg with a shotgun. Hoggy had disappeared from the city for over a year after that. The first anyone had known that he was back was when the rival was found in an alley with his arms tied behind him with baling wire, dead from loss of blood. Both of his legs had been hacked off with an axe.

Ambrose came in after Hoggy and sat down on the edge of a flaking kitchen chair. Smoky's eyes and pistol stayed on Harp.

Hoggy slapped the empty bottle and glasses off the beer keg and settled his broad buttocks on it, facing Harp. His flat, snub-nosed face was cobwebbed with pain wrinkles. His head was shaved to show off the scars on it. Souvenirs from his days of winning head-butting contests. He'd given that up after losing part of his leg. You needed more than an abnormally thick skull to butt heads. You needed two sound legs under you to ram your head against the other man's with enough impact to knock your opponent unconscious.

"Why'nt you take a seat," Hoggy suggested. His voice was as heavy as the rest of him, even when he whispered.

"I've been sitting too much today," Harp said. "I'm fine this way."

"Suit yourself," Hoggy said. And then: "It too cold in here for you?"

"No."

"So why've you got your hand in your pocket?"

Harp just smiled at him. Hoggy smiled back. Harp didn't look away to see if that exchange altered Smoky's expression.

"Ambrose says you figure us for the ones took the liquor out've the warehouse," Hoggy said. "Why d'you figure that?"

"It's not a secret," Harp told him. "I don't know how it got out but the word's around. I heard it—and so have the police."

Hoggy reached down behind the beer keg and brought up a brown paper bag. He took out a walnut and cracked it apart between thumb and finger. He dropped the pieces of shell on the floor and munched the meat while offering the bag to Harp.

Harp shook his head, and relaxed a notch. Hoggy wanted something from him; something more than information. His patient manner said so. And that meant that Hoggy would keep his violence banked. If he could.

Hoggy cracked and ate another walnut. "So far this ain't news. So what's the worse trouble your message to Ambrose said we don't know about?"

"The first one," Harp told him, "is that Moe Saul was murdered in his place the same night as Alice Curry, and the police will have found his body by now. And think you did it, like they think you did Alice Curry."

"Moe?" Hoggy's surprise wasn't faked. Harp knew him well enough to be sure of that. "Why would we kill Moe, for crissakes? And that whore they found in the warehouse, we didn't know anything about that until we read it in the papers next day."

"I had a talk with Thumper Redpath," Harp said. "For him it's crystal-clear you must've killed her while you were robbing the warehouse. And what you stole is still in Moe's place. So now the Thumper will be figuring you boys for both killings."

Hoggy made a dismissive gesture. "Redpath's east side. And we're holed up here, a long way from his precinct. His reach don't spread this far."

"Wrong," Harp said. "My second chunk of bad news is that he's been seeing the other precinct captains. Getting them to cooperate with him and pool squealers. There's people in this neighborhood who must know you're here. With all the pressure on this one somebody's bound to squeal. No question. Just a matter of time before Redpath gets his hands on you. Only one way out of it."

Hoggy's laugh had a chill undertone that warned Harp he'd better not relax too much around him. "You mean get out've town and never come back."

"Or take the pressure off you. Help me get the ones who did kill Moe and Alice Curry. Tell me about the night you looted the warehouse, nothing held back."

Hoggy chewed another walnut while regarding Harp, then asked the same question Redpath had: "What's your interest?"

"I knew Moe since I was a kid. I want whoever killed him."

"Sure it wasn't us?"

"Pretty sure," Harp answered. "Like you said, why would you kill him? You always need a fence you can trust. And Moe always played straight with people like you. He had too much good sense not to."

"And the whore in the warehouse?"

"If you'd killed her, you wouldn't have left her there. You know there's always a chance of somebody seeing you go in or out of a place you're looting. You would have taken her body away and dumped it someplace else."

"Damn right I would've."

"So tell me your side of it."

Hoggy started to take another walnut out of the bag. Changed his mind and tossed the bag aside. "I hear you're thick with Bill Howe and Abe Hummel."

"I do jobs for them now and then."

"What I want," Hoggy said, "is for you to talk to them about this mess me and my boys are in. All we did was cop the liquor. Nothing else. Okay, that's easy for 'em to square. Some cash to the right judge and we're out've it. Tell 'em I'll pay whatever they say if they can get the rest of it off our backs."

"They can't do a thing without knowing your version of what happened that night—in detail. I can't tell them that until you tell it to me."

Hoggy nodded and scowled, and seemed about to say something. Whatever it was, Harp never got to hear it.

There were splintering crashes as the shutters facing the street were ripped open. Followed instantly by the windows being smashed in. Hoggy's sentries out there must have been silenced beforehand. Broken glass scattered across the floor as the drapes were ripped away by long steel hooks.

Ambrose was the first on his feet, yanking a pistol from his pocket and firing blindly at the dark street outside. He was answered by a fusillade of rifle and pistol shots. Harp threw himself flat on the floor. Ambrose staggered and his bowler hat flew across the room. He crumpled to the floor near Harp. There was a groove across the top of his head where a bullet had gouged away hair and scalp, creasing his skull hard enough to knock him out. Harp couldn't tell if it had done worse than that. Blood welled from the groove; but much more was soaking through his left coat sleeve where another bullet had torn into his upper arm just below the shoulder.

Hoggy had jerked his bulk off the beer keg and was turning to extinguish the oil lamp when a bullet thudded into the side of his skull. He spun around on the pegleg and toppled to the floor, landing ponderously on his back. His head rolled limply and came to rest facing Harp. There was a hole in his face where his right eye had been, with a trickle of blood leaking out.

It seemed incredible, and somehow unnatural, that so much animal ferocity could be snuffed out that abruptly.

Smoky Poole had moved in a low crouch to the wall by one window and was peeking out. He had transferred the short-barreled pistol to his left hand, and now had a revolver with a long barrel in his right. It looked like a Colt five-shot Officer's Model. He had both weapons ready, but was holding back, waiting until he could see a target to aim at in the dark street.

The fusillade from out there intensified, bullets thunking into walls and ceiling, breaking exposed laths and chopping down chunks of plaster.

"Police!" a reedy voice outside screamed through the noise. "Come out with your hands up and empty!"

It sounded very much like Thumper Redpath.

Harp snaked across the floor to the kitchen chair Ambrose had used. He gripped one of its legs and threw it at the lamp, knocking it off the antique table. It crashed to the floor and flickered out, plunging the room into darkness.

Smoky began triggering spaced shots through the window.

Other gang members were now shooting from another downstairs room and from upstairs windows. The gunfire from the street slackened. Harp picked up his hickory stick, crawled to Ambrose, seized one of his wrists and dragged him out of the room into the corridor.

Close to him, a heavy axe began slamming into the outside of the front door, chopping through the wood. But the inside of that door, like the one in back, was sheathed with iron that couldn't be broken through quickly. The attackers wouldn't be in a hurry to climb through windows defended by the gang's guns. Finding a way to get to the rear of the house, by going through or over other buildings, would take time, too. The lack of any gunfire back there meant the attackers hadn't done so yet.

Harp got his feet under him, lifted the unconscious Ambrose off the floor and slung him across his shoulders. He was light, an easy carry. Harp went toward the back of the house, hunching forward so he didn't need his hands to keep Ambrose's slight figure securely balanced.

The back door was wide open and the young thug who'd been guarding it had fled. Sensible fellow. Harp snatched up the lantern Ambrose had left there, but didn't light it. He made his way across the dark courtyard, testing the ground with each step to avoid holes and entangling debris, holding down the need to hurry. Getting away from here quickly was vital; but he wouldn't go far or fast with a sprained or broken ankle.

The slanting cellar door of the other house was open. The coals burning in the tin pan below showed him the way down the stone steps. Nobody was left in the cellar room. The trapdoor in the floor was open. The door guard from the other house was gone, and so were Dutch Duffy and Sheeny Max Cohen and any others of the gang who'd been upstairs in this house.

The ladder into the drain tunnel under the cellar was in place. Harp went down with his unconscious burden. When he reached the bottom he struck a match and lit the lantern he was carrying. There was no point in heading back in the direction from which Ambrose had brought him here. The other escapees would have gone that way. The boat under the pier would be gone by the time he got there. At this time of year a swim in the river, pulling Ambrose along with him, was not an appealing notion.

Harp started off in the opposite direction, lighting the way through the tunnel ahead with the lantern and moving fast. These under-city networks always had a number of ways in and out of them. All he had to do was to find one before the police found this tunnel, swarmed through it and caught up with him.

Twenty-Five

The underside of this trapdoor had a bright red TWO DOLLARS sign painted on it.

There was what looked like a knothole in the trapdoor, and hanging down beside it was a short, thin chain. First Harp tested, pressing the tip of his stick up against the trapdoor. It didn't give. He pulled the chain. There was a tinkling sound somewhere above, faint and far away. He got two silver dollars from his pocket while he waited.

About thirty seconds later a light showed through the knothole. It disappeared a second later: hidden, Harp guessed, by the head of somebody bending to look at him through the hole. He showed the two dollars in the light of his lantern. Light showed through the peephole again, and something scraped across the top of the trapdoor. It was pulled open and a ladder was lowered. Harp carried the unconscious Ambrose up the ladder, into a windowless room not much bigger than a closet.

A brawny, gray-haired woman in an old calico dress stood waiting with her hand out. Behind her and a step to one side was a skinny woman with wispy white hair and a similar dress. She held a lantern in one hand, and a six-barreled Sprague & Marston pepperbox aimed at him with the other.

The only furniture in the little room was an army cot with a thin, patched blanket on it. Through an open door Harp saw wooden steps leading up inside the house. He dropped the two silver coins in the brawny woman's waiting palm, then extinguished his lantern and lowered it and Ambrose to the floor.

Ambrose's bullet-ripped coat sleeve was entirely soaked with his blood, some of which had leaked onto Harp's coat. He was still breathing. Harp hoped he was going to continue to do so—at least until he could tell what Hoggy hadn't gotten around to.

The brawny woman regarded Ambrose thoughtfully as she put the coins away in a skirt pocket. "If he's gonna die, he ain't doing it here. I got enough sick people renting beds in my house without another one dying on me."

"We're just passing through," Harp told her as he began to strip the coat off Ambrose. "There a cab rank near here?"

"The Christopher Street ferry depot's only two blocks away. Always lots there."

Harp gestured at the lantern he'd put down. "You can have that and an extra dollar if you get me a cab. Tell the driver I've got a friend who got drunk and passed out, and I'll pay him a one-dollar bonus on top of the fare to take us uptown."

"Drunk, is he?" Her laugh was harsh and short. *"Bleedin'* drunk is what I'd say. The cabby ain't gonna like that."

"He won't see the blood in the night." Harp wasn't entirely sure of that. If the driver did notice it, the bonus would have to go higher than a dollar.

The brawny woman shrugged and held out her hand again. Harp gave her another dollar. She put it away with the first two, then pulled up the ladder, shut the trapdoor and pushed an iron drawbar in place to lock it. Picking up the lantern he'd offered her, she trudged out and up the steps. The white-haired woman, who hadn't uttered a word, stayed behind with her own lantern and her pepperbox.

Harp finished getting the coat off Ambrose. All of the left shirt-sleeve was bloody, and so was the rest of the shirt on that side. Harp ripped the sleeve away at the shoulder and peeled it off Ambrose's wiry arm. The bullet had torn the biceps apart and the wound was still bleeding. Harp used the bloody sleeve as a tourniquet, tying it tightly just below the shoulder. He ripped off the other sleeve and wadded it against the wound, using his own neckerchief to bind the wadding in place.

Ambrose's head wound had stopped bleeding, but his breathing was becoming disturbingly shallow. Nothing to be done about that here. Harp had him back into his coat and was buttoning it when the brawny woman reappeared and nodded at him.

He settled Ambrose over his shoulders again and followed her

up the steps, with the white-haired woman following them. He had
to bend low to get himself and Ambrose through the small door at
the top. It opened into a recess under another stairway. They
maneuvered between boxes and baskets stored there, and went
through a hallway carpeted by dust and mold. The house smelled
like a tomb for the barely living, untouched by fresh air. They
passed what had been a dining room and a drawing room. Both
dim rooms were packed with narrow bunks, on which shadowed
figures stirred and snored and moaned.

There were dozens of lodging houses like this in parts of lower
Manhattan. The brawny woman might earn an occasional two dollars from some fugitive who needed to use her escape hatch to or
from the drain tunnel. But her basic income was from people who
had no other place to sleep, who didn't want to go into a police
shelter for the homeless, and who could come up with the fifteen
or twenty cents to bed down here for the night.

The hansom cab was waiting at the curbside out front. There
was no street lamp nearby, and the cabby stayed up on his box as
Harp carried Ambrose down from the porch. He didn't notice the
blood; and he displayed no interest in Ambrose's unconscious
state. This wouldn't be the first time he'd ever had a passed-out
drunk as a passenger. For a cab driver an unconscious drunk was
preferable to a conscious one. With a drunk who was still awake
there was more of a chance of his throwing up during the ride.

Harp eased Ambrose inside the cab and gave the driver an address before climbing in after him. The cabby twitched the reins
and got his horse moving, heading uptown toward Satan's Circus.

The city area known to police and sporty ladies and gents as Satan's Circus spread roughly one block east and west from Sixth
Avenue, from Twenty-fourth Street up to Thirty-sixth. It was an
area with many pleasant, gardened family brownstones, tree-lined
streets, normal shops, restaurants and business offices. But at
night the shops and offices closed, and respectable women vanished from the area's streets.

That was when the other element took over. The more expensive brothels and houses of assignation. The fancier dance saloons
and fashionable gambling hells. Flocks of the more elegant street-

walkers. Sixth Avenue was the Main Street of Satan's Circus, and it was coming to garish, noisy life as the hansom cab carried Harp and Ambrose up it through the still-early night. Big gaslit globes and signs radiated red, gold and blue glitter across sidewalks in front of prosperous establishments. Horses drew cabs, carriages and one-man gigs up and down the avenue to their nightlife destinations. Gorgeously dressed women, and men with silk top hats and gold-headed canes, strolled past each other along the pavements; the women sometimes slowing so the men could circle back for a closer look and a bit of flirty conversation.

Harp had his cab turn west on Thirtieth Street and stop at an alley entrance. A ten-piece German band was playing on the corner at the far end of the block. Much nearer, two beauties casually let their furs slide open to display bare shoulders and bejeweled upper bosoms while they engaged in confident negotiations with a pair of nervous young rakes wearing velvet-trimmed opera capes. Their conversation fumbled to a momentary halt as they watched Harp carry Ambrose out of the cab and past them into the alley.

The back door of Quincy Coyne's gambling house was never locked during business hours. The kitchen help needed to use it frequently to take garbage and empty bottles out to the big dump-boxes that were emptied each dawn by a private garbage collection firm. Harp opened the door and carried Ambrose inside.

Most of the kitchen staff paused in their work to gape at him and his limp, bloody burden. But the head chef knew Harp. He came over with an uncertain smile and watched Harp stretch Ambrose out on the floor against one wall.

"You've got the wrong place, Harp. The Dead House is over in Bellevue, and I haven't gotten around to making cannibal steaks yet."

"He's not dead." Harp checked whether that was still true. Ambrose's arm didn't seem to be losing any more blood. But his breathing was even more ragged now. The scalp on either side of the furrow across the top of his head was acquiring an ugly color. And his face was ashen.

"Mrs. Honeyman up front now?" he asked the chef as he straightened up.

The chef nodded. "Last I looked, she was just coming in with some Texas cattlemen."

Mary Honeyman often spent part of a late evening—with a paid escort—dining or nursing a sherry cobbler at one or another of New York's best hotels. It was seldom that she didn't manage to lure adventurous out-of-town businessmen to this house of chance.

Harp took off his bloodstained coat and left it beside Ambrose with his hat and stick. The chef clapped his hands and ordered his staff back to their tasks as Harp crossed the kitchen and pushed through swinging doors into the establishment's dining room. A bouncer with a build that strained the seams of his formal evening attire was on duty there. He nodded recognition as Harp stopped to look around.

The dining room was lit by a huge gas chandelier with ground-glass shades, and warmed by logs burning in a big marble fire-place. The wall to wall carpet had an intricate pattern of entwined vines and flowers. Mirrors and oil paintings hung in ornate gilt frames on mahogany-paneled walls. Three black waiters in white dinner jackets were at work behind a long buffet table. It was covered with crystal bowls of iced lobster, crab and shrimp, steam-ing silver tureens of meat stews, heated platters of steak and eggs.

Men taking a break from the gambling rooms were at the bar renewing energy and faith with champagne and brandy, hot tod-dies and whiskey punch. Pretty women in low-cut evening gowns glittered with jewels at small tables with embroidered linen table-cloths and the finest silver and chinaware. Some were with the men who'd brought them. Others sat alone, dawdling over their food and drinks while they waited for their escorts to return flushed with victory or numbed by loss.

The woman Harp needed wasn't in sight. He walked on through the first floor gambling rooms. Like the dining room, they had magnificent chandeliers, rich carpeting, marble fire-places, frescoed ceilings. The paneled walls were hung with more gilt-framed paintings. But no mirrors.

Quincy Coyne, who'd been a Mississippi riverboat gambler be-fore the war, was in the main room keeping a sharp eye on the gamblers, the dealers and the flow of chips across the roulette, brag and euchre tables. He was a tall, lean man in his mid-sixties, with an aristocratic face, white hair and a gray goatee.

Though the casino bore his name, Quincy Coyne was actually only its most important employee: a reliable assistant manager.

Some of the casino's regulars knew it was Mary Honeyman who owned the place. Very few knew she was the one who ran it, on a day-to-day basis, and who made every important decision. It wasn't odd for a woman to own a business. After all, many widows inherited complicated, thriving enterprises from deceased husbands. Nothing wrong with that—as long as the woman put a man in charge of operating it and didn't intrude herself into the serious matter of its direction.

Mary Honeyman had been the mistress of one of the most successful bank robbers in America. He'd married her shortly before police shot him dead coming out of his last bank. She had given a third of the fortune he'd stashed away to various Tammany politicians, and had used the rest to open her gambling house—hiring Quincy as her front man. In the beginning she had deferred to his experience and taken most of his advice. But by now she knew as much about gambling as he did. And she'd turned out to have a better head for business.

Harp shook hands with Quincy and asked, "Where's Mary?"

"Upstairs making sure a bunch of Texans she snagged are well oiled."

Harp followed a waiter who was carrying a tray loaded with bourbon bottles and glasses up a black marble staircase. On the second floor they passed the room devoted to *vingt-et-un,* a card game for wealthy gentlemen that would become much more popular when renamed blackjack. The waiter entered the next room: occupied by players of bluff—which most players now called poker —a favorite of rich visitors from the West and South. Harp stopped in the doorway.

Each of the three large tables had a house dealer, with a box beside him into which the players donated one dollar each before every new deal. Mary Honeyman stood by the table around which her Texas cattlemen had settled, chatting flirtatiously with them while the waiter distributed their bottles and glasses and the dealer broke open a fresh deck of cards. She had the cattlemen's full attention. And not only theirs. Gamblers at the other two tables had paused in their betting to gaze at her.

Mary Honeyman was something to gaze at. She was what the

sporting set called "a fine figure of young womanhood." Tall and regal, in a dark red gown with sequins that glistened like tiny rubies, and that displayed her splendid arms and shoulders and a daring amount of deep cleavage.

Ten years ago she had just begun a career as a sixteen-year-old streetwalker. But then the war had begun, and she had volunteered her services to the federal army as a nurse. As she'd explained to Harp later, she had regarded that vocation with awe ever since her brother, whom she'd thought dead from drowning in the Hudson, had been brought back to life by a professional nurse. That nurse had, like ninety-nine percent of them, been a man. Female nurses were a rarity—and at first the military had balked at accepting any. Even those who had training, let alone those like Mary Honeyman, who had none.

But as the war had ground on and on, with casualties mounting to staggering numbers, the medical corps of both armies had become grateful for any help they could get. Even from inexperienced women. By the war's end Mary had acquired a great deal of practical medical experience—and a dream. She wanted to become a doctor. But female doctors were much more rare than female nurses. The two she'd managed to locate had told stories of disrespect, and of being prevented from fully performing the function for which they'd trained, which were too discouraging.

She had instead become Jack Honeyman's mistress—then wife and widow. But she hadn't given up entirely on her dream. There were people who couldn't pay a real doctor; and others who could pay but didn't want the police notified. And nowadays Mary could afford to buy all the medical equipment and supplies she needed in order to practice what she'd learned in the war—and to bribe authorities to look the other way as long as she did so discreetly.

When she noticed Harp waiting in the doorway she raised an inquiring eyebrow. He nodded, and stepped back out of sight into the hallway.

He heard her voice inside: "Please excuse me for a while, gents. I'm sorry, but it seems the boss wants me."

When she came out Harp told her quietly: "I've got a friend on your kitchen floor. He's been shot in the head and arm."

"How bad?"

"His skull's creased and I don't know if it's fractured. The bullet's not still in his arm, but it's torn it up pretty badly. He's unconscious and he's lost a lot of blood."

"Take him across the alley and wait in the garden behind my house," Mary told him. "I'll join you as soon as I alert Quincy, throw on a coat and tell the kitchen staff they never saw you or your friend."

Twenty-Six

Harp boiled a fresh kettle of water on the stove that warmed the room while Mary Honeyman bandaged Ambrose McGowan's head. The room, in the basement of her row house across from the rear of her gambling casino, was fitted out as a combination surgery, recovery room and pharmacy. It had a padded operating table with a square metal table beside it, several hospital chairs, a pair of covered, white enamel disposal bins. There was a sink and a bunk with clean sheets and blankets against one wall. Extending along the opposite wall were glass-doored cabinets with shelves crowded by a diversity of doctors' instruments, medications, surgical dressings and other clinical supplies.

The shutters and curtains of the single high window were closed. Wall gas-jets and a tall oil lamp on the square table supplied all the light needed. Harp had stripped Ambrose above the waist, removed his boots and stretched him on the operating table while Mary had gotten out of her red gown and put on a long white smock much like a monk's cassock without a hood. There were now damp blood spots on its sleeves.

She had cleaned and examined Ambrose and decided his skull wasn't cracked. But he'd obviously suffered a bad concussion, or he would have regained consciousness by now. Pain had almost shocked him awake when Mary had cauterized and stitched his severely torn arm. Harp had kept him under with a chloroform-saturated wad of cotton.

Now he poured half the boiling water into a basin by the stove and prepared a poultice: adding linseed oil to the water, stirring it with a wooden spatula, and lowering in a thick pad of muslin to soak up the mixture. He poured the rest of the water from the kettle into a pan on the square table. Mary had finished dressing Ambrose's head wound. She dipped cotton into the hot water and wiped his arm where some blood had leaked from the cauterized wound while she was sewing it up.

"He was lucky," she said, "that the bullet didn't break bone when it went through his arm. But unlucky, the way it ripped the muscles apart. I doubt if he'll ever get back the full use of this arm."

"He won't mind that too much," Harp told her. "It's his left arm. He throws knives with his right."

Mary dipped another cotton wad into the hot water and used it to wipe blood from her hands. "Okay, that poultice should be ready now."

Harp got the big muslin pad out of the mixture of hot water and linseed oil with the spatula, wrung excess moisture from it and gave it to Mary. She covered the stitched wound in Ambrose's upper arm with it and began wrapping wide strips of gauze around the arm over the poultice. When the bandaging was thick enough to satisfy her, she knotted it securely and stepped back a little to admire her workmanship.

"Nice job," Harp said. "Thanks."

She blushed with pride, ducking her head like a praised little girl. Then, once more the doctor, she pressed two fingers against Ambrose's throat and placed her other hand flat on his naked chest. After a minute she straightened and nodded. "His pulse is steady and he's breathing a little better. He should be all right if he takes it easy for the next few days."

"What do I owe you?" Harp asked her.

"Between old lovers? It's on the house, naturally."

"Thanks again."

"Sure." She gathered up the used cotton wads and dumped them in one of the disposal bins. "I've got to get back to work now. Until we close up. That's between three and four in the morning, depending. I guess you'll stay here with your friend?"

"Until a little before dawn. I want to take him away when the first morning ferries start operating. Will it be okay to move him by then?"

"Probably. Long as you don't shake him up too much. If you want, I can have Quincy hitch up my carriage and help you."

"I'd appreciate that."

"I'll tell Quincy."

She took off her bloodstained smock and dropped it into the other bin. That left her in her chemise and drawers, both diaphanous pink, with a black satin-and-silk waist cincher, red-gartered black stockings and her red-tasseled pearl-gray boots. An erotic vision that caused Harp to experience a strong surge of pure lust as he watched her stroll to the sink to use soap and water on her hands.

When she turned around, toweling her hands dry, she saw the way he was looking at her. She cocked her head slightly to one side and looked back at him with a small smile. "If you want to stay for something more exciting than watching over your sick friend, Quincy could take him wherever you want. And I *could* arrange to come back before three."

Harp considered it. He and Mary Honeyman had enjoyed a number of mutually pleasurable nights together. But that was back when he'd only been bewitched by a tintype photograph. Even when that tintype had come to life it hadn't been quite real. Louise had been another man's mistress, and Harp could tell himself she was still unobtainable. Now it was different. Now it had become possible. If he could only decide between living a lie with her, or risk having the truth destroy that possibility, finally and forever.

And that didn't leave enough of him—right now, anyway—for the kind of passion and affections a woman like Mary deserved. Telling himself he was a fool didn't change that.

"I'll have to stay with Ambrose," he told Mary, regretfully, "so I can question him whenever he comes to."

Mary's smile became knowing, unoffended. She'd seen other men trapped in the illusion of only one woman, and she recognized the symptoms. There were men who felt that way about her —but never the right ones.

"He'll be hurting when he comes to," she said, striding over to one of her cabinets. She took out a bottle of laudanum—tincture of opium—and gave it to Harp. "Put fifteen drops in a full glass of water, stir it well and have him drink it. If that doesn't do it, repeat the dose. But not too often."

Harp put the laudanum on the table, took her bare shoulders in his hands, drew her close and kissed her. It lacked the fire she was accustomed to from him, but she knew he meant well. She kissed him back, patted his cheek and said, "Got to go. You know where the liquor is."

And with that she left the room to get back into her petticoats and gown and return to her business establishment across the alley.

Harp woke up slumped in a chair beside Ambrose and the operating table, his boots off, his legs up on another chair. He stood and flexed his shoulders to ease a cramp in his upper back while he studied Ambrose. He was still out, but his breathing was much improved: the deep, regular breathing of real sleep. No blood had seeped through the bandages around his head or arm. Harp took his watch from his waistcoat pocket. He'd slept for more than an hour.

He padded up the stairs in his stocking feet, went into the first-floor pantry and poured himself half a tumbler of whiskey. He took a healthy swallow and carried the glass down to the basement room. Ambrose's condition hadn't changed. Harp sat down, took another drink of his whiskey, put the glass on the square table beside the laudanum, put his legs back up on the other chair and let himself drift back to sleep. He knew the slightest sound from Ambrose would wake him.

When he opened his eyes it was a little after three A.M. and Mary was entering the room in her red sequined gown. Ambrose was still comatose. She took his pulse, listened to his breathing, felt his forehead. Harp got out of the chair and stretched and watched.

"He's running a temperature," she said, "but not enough to start worrying about. Outside of that he seems okay, no worse than you'd expect. Has he come to at all?"

"Not yet."

"He should, before too much longer. Unless he's got some bad brain damage." A worry groove deepened briefly between her eyebrows. Then she turned to Harp. "Quincy is upstairs, going to sleep in my spare bedroom. He says to wake him whenever you want and he'll get my horse and carriage from the stable."

They kissed goodnight—just affectionate friends for the time being—and she went upstairs to bed. Harp had a sip of whiskey, lowered himself into the chair and slept again.

A whimper brought him to his feet. The sound was coming from Ambrose. He wasn't conscious yet, but his senses were groping, getting close enough to the surface to react to the pain in his arm and head. His legs stirred aimlessly. His hands quivered. The whimpers were subterranean protests.

Harp got a glass of water from the sink, stirred in fifteen drops of laudanum and set it on the square table ready for use. Ambrose was breathing through his open mouth now, dragging spasmodic gulps of air into his lungs. His whimpering ceased, but pain-sweat beaded his pockmarked face and bare, heaving chest. Harp went back to the sink, soaked a towel in cold water and used it to wipe Ambrose's face, neck and chest.

Ambrose rolled his head to one side, then to the other. His right hand rose off the operating table and reached toward his left arm. Harp caught the hand and pulled it away from the bandages, forced it down. Ambrose's eyes snapped wide open, glazed, staring up at Harp.

"Take it easy, Ambrose," Harp said, enunciating each word distinctly. "You've been shot, but I've had that taken care of and you're going to be okay. Understand what I'm saying?"

Ambrose's stare began to focus. "Harp . . . ? Wha' happened?"

"The police hit your hideout. Remember that?"

"Yeah, but . . . Hoggy . . . ?"

"Hoggy's dead."

"That's . . . how'd you get me . . ." The rest of what Ambrose was trying to say was ripped apart by a wild groan as a spasm of agony shook him. His hands squeezed into tight fists and the muscles of his face and neck clenched, his eyes narrowing to slits. He drew a shuddering breath and gasped, *"Christ!"*

Harp raised his head and put the water glass with the laudanum mixture to his lips. "Drink this. All of it. It'll stop the hurt."

Some of the drink spilled from the corners of Ambrose's mouth, but Harp managed to make him swallow most of it. He put down the empty glass and waited, watching as Ambrose gradually relaxed—his gasps becoming slow, steady breathing, his eyes drooping as his face smoothed out.

Harp continued to wait, but knew he couldn't afford to wait too long. Tincture of opium usually acted in three progressive stages. First it blotted out pain and anxiety. Then, if the drinker was prodded, it could act as a mental stimulant. And finally it carried the drinker off into a trancelike slumber. Harp needed some answers before that final stage took hold.

After a few more minutes, he pinched Ambrose's nostrils shut, cutting off his air. Ambrose made a strangled noise and his eyes snapped wide open again. Harp let go of him and let him take a couple of deep breaths before speaking.

"Hoggy was going to tell me all about the night your gang stole the liquor from that warehouse," he said. "Do you remember that?"

It took a couple of moments of concentration. Then Ambrose said, "Yeah . . ."

"But he got killed before he could. And the rest of your gang is either in jail now or on the run. That leaves you—and you owe me. I saved you from the police and I've probably saved your life. The cops will be hunting for you and the others who got away. I can get you out of town to a place where they won't find you. *If* you tell me everything I want to know about that night."

It took time, and prodding from Harp, but Ambrose did tell it— as much of it as he knew about.

Twenty-Seven

"It was Moe Saul gave us the job've swiping that liquor," Ambrose said. "He told Hoggy he'd got an order from some swell hotel for imported brandy and champagne. And Moe knew this warehouse'd just got in a big shipment of the stuff from France."

"How'd Moe find that out?"

"Search me. He was always gettin' tipoffs on things like that. That's part've what made him a great fence. He even told Hoggy when the warehouse would shut that night. And when the precinct patrolman would be making his next round and checking the doors around there. The time between was tight—just enough to take out the stuff and get away before the patrolman came by."

"Moe didn't give Hoggy any idea where he got this information?"

"If he did," Ambrose said, "Hoggy didn't tell the rest of us. Anyhow, that wasn't any've our business. All we cared about was the stuff was in there, it was an easy job if we worked it fast at the right time—and Moe was giving us a fair share. Thirty percent of what the hotel was gonna pay when he delivered the stuff."

"So you went there with a wagon," Harp said, "and got in and out in the time limit Moe gave you."

"Yeah. With fifteen cases of the brandy and twelve cases of champagne. That's what Moe had a deal for with the hotel."

"Was the dead woman already there?"

"If she was, we didn't see her. In the papers next day it said they found her in the warehouse office. Moe told Hoggy there wouldn't be anything in the office or its safe worth lifting. So with our having to get in and out fast we shouldn't waste any of the time checking in there. So we didn't."

Harp took a moment to digest this tantalizing disclosure. "Moe knew an awful lot," he said slowly.

"He usually did. I don't know who he got his tips from, but they were always good."

"So you took the liquor to Moe's place, and he paid you for it and he was okay when you left him."

"He didn't pay us," Ambrose said. "The deal was he was gonna pay us after the hotel paid him."

"What hotel?"

"Don't know . . ." Ambrose's voice was getting draggy now.

"He had an appointment with somebody at his place shortly after you left," Harp said. "Any idea who?"

"No." Ambrose's eyelids were drooping again. "Maybe somebody from the hotel?"

"Maybe." But Harp doubted it. He went over in his mind what Ambrose had told him about that fatal night. What he hadn't been able to tell was more intriguing. Who had tipped off Moses Saul that that many cases of French brandy and champagne would be inside the warehouse that night? Who had been able to tell him when the warehouse would close, and how long they would have after that before the beat patrolman—Tommy Costello—would come by? The same person who had seen to it that the gang didn't bother with the office—which almost certainly meant that Alice Curry was already dead in there.

If Hoggy Corcoran had known the answers to any of those questions, he'd taken them to the grave with him. Like Moses Saul had.

Harp was satisfied that Ambrose didn't have any of those answers, and had divulged all he did know. Which was good, because Ambrose was now sinking back into sleep with a peaceful smile on his face. And it was difficult to get coherent answers out of somebody you yanked out of an opium dream.

Harp went to the sink and sloshed cold water on his hands, face and the back of his neck. He pulled on his boots and stood by the operating table with his hands in his pockets, gazing at the medical cabinets and mulling over what he'd gotten from Ambrose. Thinking about what each part of it meant.

At five-thirty in the morning, while it was still pitch-dark outside, he went upstairs and woke Quincy Coyne.

* * *

Quincy drove the carriage. It was a covered landau, big enough inside for four passengers, six in a squeeze. Ambrose lay on the rear seat with his booted feet on the floor. Harp sat on the facing seat watching over him and making sure he wasn't thrown around too much whenever the carriage hit a hole in the dark streets. There was hardly any other traffic. Carts delivering coal and milk. Some empty covered wagons heading for the docks. An occasional horsecar taking workers to pre-dawn jobs.

The carriage pulled up at the address Harp had given Quincy: Three Hudson Street. It was part of a block of three-floor row houses, most of them now taken over by small tradesmen. Signs crossed the front of each house at all three floors, advertising the firms inside. The ground floor of the house flanking one side of Number Three was a drug broker's store and the two upper floors were occupied by a card-and-job printing plant. The house on the other side contained the shops of a saddle and harness maker, a sign painter and a repairer of whalebone corsets.

Number Three's two lower floors belonged to a carpentry shop. The top floor had a big sign rising from the roof's edge above its two front windows:

OLD CLOTHING
Shirts, Drawers, Over-Alls
Cart & Wagon Covers

But that firm had moved out five months ago: three weeks before Harp took over its floor as his current emergency retreat.

Now that Quincy knew the address Harp would have to shift to somewhere else. A minor inconvenience: he changed the location of his secret refuge regularly, anyway. A hideout stopped being secure if you stuck to the same one too long.

He climbed to the top floor and did a fast job of changing into fresh clothes. His bloodstained coat, folded inside out, went into a camouflaged cache above the rafters. He put on a different one and went back down the stairs carrying an extra coat and shirt, and a floppy slouch hat. When he was back inside the carriage,

Quincy snapped the reins and headed for the ferry depot at the west end of Christopher Street.

Harp got Ambrose out of the ripped and bloodied coat, being careful with his injured arm, and put his own spare shirt and coat on him. Ambrose made some complaining sounds and movements, without emerging from his sleep. His being too small for Harp's clothes made it easier. His head was smaller, too; so the slouch hat fitted low enough to hide the bandages there.

A cold dawn light was leaking through fissures in the sooty clouds hanging low and heavy over the city when they reached the depot. Street traffic was already building up near it; but almost all of it going away from the depot. This early in the morning ferries began filling up for the trip to Manhattan, and went away virtually empty. Aboard the sidewheel steamer re-crossing the North River to New Jersey, Mary Honeyman's carriage had the central horse-and-vehicle section to itself.

Fred Sigfried's drugstore was in Hoboken. Fred lived in the two floors above the store, together with his wife and his widowed brother, Paul, a retired animal doctor. Four years ago Paul Sigfried's eighteen-year-old daughter had vanished while shopping in Manhattan. The police hadn't been able to find her, but Harp had. She'd made the romantic blunder of accepting an invitation to a tearoom from a handsome stranger. He'd fed her knock-out drops and sold her to a Water Street whorehouse notorious for starving its captives into submission.

Harp had pried her out of there, returned her to her family and made sure no one else learned what had happened to her. She was now safely married to an oilcloth manufacturer in Jersey City; and the gratitude of the Sigfrieds remained something Harp could count on.

They settled Ambrose in a small spare room behind the drugstore. Paul Sigfried examined him and pronounced him no worse for the trip. Harp told them to get rid of him as soon as he recovered enough to travel—and to advise him to head for some other part of the country and not come back.

If Ambrose didn't have the good sense to follow that advice, Harp was not going to give a damn what happened to him.

He rode up on the driver's seat with Quincy Coyne on the return trip. Outside the Hoboken depot they had to get at the end of a long line of horse-drawn vehicles waiting their chance to board one of the ferryboats. The line moved forward each time a ferry pulled away.

A newsboy came out of the depot hawking a special edition of the New York *Morning Sun,* the newspaper with the biggest circulation in the country. Shivering with cold in his tattered jacket and pants, he moved along the line shouting: "Awful gun battle between police and gangsters! Dozens shot! Read all about it!"

Harp bought a copy from him, paying double for it. He read the story while they waited.

It was written by a reporter who'd accompanied the police attack against the gang suspected of robbing the warehouse where Alice Curry had died—and of her murder. According to the story the raid had been led by Captain John Redpath, commander of the Thirteenth Police Precinct, supported by his own men and others from the west side precinct where the gang had been hiding out. The gang had refused to surrender to the law at first, and a gun battle had erupted. The gang's leader, Horace "Hoggy" Corcoran, and two of his men had been killed—and three others wounded—before the others finally gave themselves up. Four policemen had been wounded, one seriously. The captured gang members were being questioned by Captain Redpath concerning the Alice Curry murder.

The story contained unstinting praise for the determination of Redpath, who'd shown unusual initiative in enlisting the cooperation of other precinct commanders throughout the city in hunting and capturing the gang. If those other commanders would only follow his example in the future, the reporter wrote, the New York police might finally become a force to be proud of.

Harp looked through the rest of the paper and found no mention of Moses Saul. He gave it to Quincy to read, and took over the reins while they waited for ferry space. During morning and evening rush hours, departures were every ten minutes. After twenty minutes of waiting and moving forward, they reached a steamer that could take their carriage. While it churned its way across the river they watched the church steeples ahead, the tallest structures in New York, flash reflections of morning sunlight above the hazy gloom of the city.

Hunger, intensified by his having gotten little sleep last night, was gnawing at Harp by the time they got off the ferryboat. More hunger than could be satisfied by the typical French breakfast of pastry and coffee served at the Suze la Rousse. He had Quincy drop him off at Fourteenth Street and Fifth Avenue, and went into Delmonico's for a full-scale American breakfast.

Oatmeal and fried eggs with biscuits. Followed by steak and bacon, with corn on the cob. Finishing up with buckwheat cakes and honey. All of it washed down with several cups of coffee.

Harp emerged from Delmonico's replenished and revived, and in need of a walk. Fat snowflakes were adrift in the windless air; but they were too feathery and occasional to herald the coming of a real snowfall. He walked downtown to check for messages at the Suze la Rousse.

He didn't see any of his watchers when he entered his block on Greene Street. The kids weren't out playing. If Hilda Shaler was in her room, she didn't open her window to signal an all-clear or a warning. When he neared his building he saw why. A uniformed policeman came up off the steps to the basement there. Another stepped out of a doorway on the other side of the street.

Harp knew both of them. Tommy Costello and Dick Crowley. They converged on him, looking embarrassed but ready to carry out their assigned duty. Harp came to a halt and waited for them.

"Captain Redpath wants to talk to you," Crowley said awkwardly.

Harp nodded, his expression bland. "I always look forward to conversations with the Thumper."

Costello brought out a pair of handcuffs. "I'm real sorry about this—but the captain said to bring you in with these. Behind your back."

Harp had stopped fighting cops a long time ago. He said, "Okay," gave his walking stick and Le Mat revolver to Crowley and put his hands behind him.

Costello locked the cuffs on his wrists, but took care not to make them too tight. They escorted him around the block to a narrow, empty lot, and apologized again when they carried out Redpath's orders and locked him inside the paddy wagon waiting for him there.

Twenty-Eight

They took Harp to the back of the Thirteenth Precinct stationhouse. A horse-ambulance from the hospital ward of the Tombs was waiting there. The station's rear door opened as Costello and Crowley unlocked the paddy wagon and helped Harp climb out. A pair of Tombs guards came out of the opened door carrying an unconscious man on a stretcher. The man was coatless and most of his shirt and wool undershirt had been ripped away, revealing livid club-bruises on his torso and shoulders. His face was too smashed to be recognizable. But one bared arm hung from the stretcher, and there was a tattoo on it. A red rose inside a black heart. Harp had seen it before, on one of Hoggy's boys whose name he didn't know. The dangling hand was badly swollen, and the thumb looked as if it had been broken.

Captain Redpath's interrogation methods usually got results, but they were not pretty.

The guards lifted the stretcher into the ambulance. Harp was taken into the back of the stationhouse. There was a bare hallway leading ahead to the rest of the station, and a narrow stairway to the left that led underneath it. Harp was taken down the steps and into a windowless cellar room lit by a large hanging kerosene lamp.

The walls and floor were dirty stone. A scarred table held a nightstick, a water pitcher and an empty glass, and a small pile of thick white towels. There was a chair behind the table. In the center of the room, facing the table, was a much heavier chair with manacles chained to all four legs. On the floor by this chair lay three bloodied towels that looked as if they'd once been part of the pile on the table.

Redpath was at a sideboard with a tin basin and another pitcher on it, his uniform coat off and his shirt sleeves rolled up to his elbows, rinsing his face and hands. He took a damp towel from a wall hook, used it and hung it back on its hook. Then he slowly turned around and gave Harp a long, expressionless stare.

His rinse had missed part of his forehead. A small spot of dried blood glistened between his left eyebrow and his hairline. There were dark pouches under his eyes and his cheeks were grooved by fatigue. If he'd been grilling the captured gang members ever since the raid, he hadn't gotten any sleep at all last night. He was getting a little too old for that kind of dedication, even if he still had the physical strength of an ox.

Crowley put Harp's stick and gun on the table beside the white towels. "His weapons, captain."

Redpath pointed a thick finger at the chair with the manacles. "Take the cuffs off," he told his patrolmen, "and attach him." His voice had a weary rasp.

"You're making a big mistake," Harp told him, and was relieved to hear his voice come through with a controlled calm. "It'll just get you in trouble you won't be able to get out of."

"I don't think so," Redpath said, and growled at his two patrolmen, "Are you deaf? I told you to do something."

They didn't like it, but they obeyed his order. Harp's cuffs were removed; then his hat and coat. They sat him down in the grilling chair. Crowley knelt, pulled off Harp's boots, and fastened his ankles to the chair's front legs. Costello manacled Harp's wrists to the chair's back legs.

"Get out," Redpath told them. "Tell the sergeant I don't want no interruptions. Nobody comes down here before I give the word."

They left without looking in Harp's direction, and shut the door behind them.

Redpath sank into the chair behind the table, filled the glass with water from the pitcher, and drank all of it. He wiped his mouth with the back of a hand, picked up the Le Mat revolver and sniffed it.

"I haven't fired that in almost a year," Harp said. "And I clean it regularly. Last time less than two weeks ago."

"Maybe you cleaned it more recently," Redpath said. "Like right after you used it against us when we hit Hoggy's hideout."

"I wasn't anywhere near there at the time."

"So how d'you know where and when it was?"

"It's in a scoop edition of this morning's *Sun.*"

Redpath put the revolver down and folded his big hands on it. "Smoky Poole told me you were there."

Something cold and hard formed inside Harp's chest. "It's not true," he said evenly. "Smoky wouldn't even tell you his mother's name unless you were hurting him so bad he was ready to say anything at all to make you stop it. He'll retract it when he's feeling better."

"I doubt it," Redpath said. "You could call it part of his death-bed confession. He had a coupla bullets in him when we got him. He conked out on me—from his wounds, I guess—while he was answering my questions."

"That doesn't make what he said true. It won't hold up against my word."

Redpath ignored that. "Another thing Smoky said was you told Hoggy somebody killed Moe Saul. He told me that's the first they knew about it. And he said you knew the liquor from the ware-house was still in Moe's place. So how would you know that? 'Cause I ain't given out anything about that or Moe's killing to the papers yet."

"But you're not the only cop who knows about it," Harp told him. "And some of them are friends of mine. Including a couple higher up than you. Something you'd better think about before you start on me."

That didn't seem to touch Redpath either. "You knew how to get to Hoggy's hideout before I did. You knew about Moe Saul and the liquor bein' at his place. You know things about the murder of that whore that you don't want to tell me. But you will."

He wrapped a clean white towel around his nightstick, stood up and came around the table with it.

Harp held down panic. "I'm not one of Hoggy's gang that you can beat up without it coming back to hurt you. I'm just doing the same as you. Trying to find out who killed Alice Curry, and why."

"But you know things about it you're keeping from me, and I got to know what they are." Redpath's tone was quietly reasonable. He seemed to be almost entreating Harp to open up. "Y'see, I *got* to know. It's not my fault some whore got herself killed inside my precinct instead of somebody else's. But all the pressure's on *me* to catch her killer."

"The last time I talked to you," Harp said, "you were sure that when you found the gang that looted the warehouse it would solve her murder at the same time. Well, you've already got the robbers."

"Yeah, and every one of 'em I got admits they did the robbery. Trouble is, they keep on swearing they didn't kill that whore. Say they never saw her, dead or alive. Never heard of her before they read about her in the papers. And," Redpath added reluctantly, "I'm starting to believe them."

"My guess," Harp said, "is that it's probably true."

"So where's that leave me?" Redpath demanded with an aggrieved scowl. "Covered with horse manure, that's where. I got to try and solve the whore's murder, dammit! It'd make a lot of other stuff easier for me. Let me retire with my record clean. And anything you know about her might help me do it."

"Be glad to help any way I can, captain. Let me out of this chair and we can discuss it like two civilized men. But I doubt if I know anything vital that you don't."

"Yeah, you do." The padded nightstick in Redpath's fist flicked a few inches up, a few inches down. As if it were a living thing with a volition of its own. "One thing, for starters. Last time I saw you, you wouldn't say who's paying for you to dig up information about the dead whore. And whoever that is has got to have some kinda connection with her. And maybe with her getting killed. You can see that, can't you? So tell me who it is. Okay?"

"Ask Howe or Hummell," Harp said. "Maybe you can get them to tell you who their client is, but they still haven't told it to me."

Redpath's expression didn't alter. He drew back the towel-wrapped club, took a step forward and swung it at Harp's head.

Harp threw himself to one side with all his strength. He fell to the stone floor, taking the heavy chair with him. It hurt his arm and shoulder. More than his skull hurt from the glancing impact of the club as he'd toppled over. But his ear went numb and his head did a dizzy spin.

He got a dazed impression of Redpath walking around behind

him and heard him say, "It's okay by me if you wanta hurt yourself worse falling over every time I thump you. Suit yourself."

With a slight grunt of effort, Redpath raised the chair, with Harp in it, and set it upright again. "The important thing is, you're gonna stop telling me lies. After a while."

He was positioning his padded nightstick for another clubbing blow at Harp's head when the door behind him opened and Sgt. Pat Quinn stepped into the cellar room. "I'm sorry, captain, but there's—"

Redpath turned on him. "My orders were not to bust in on me, sergeant!"

"I know, captain, but this is something you got to know about right away."

Quinn stepped aside so the man behind him could enter the room. Big Bill Howe—his customary dark-blue yachting cap at a rakish angle, diamonds flashing on the lapels of his fur coat, his fingers, and the gold handle of his walking stick, and a polite pink smile in place under his flamboyant white mustache.

"How d'you do, captain," Howe said pleasantly, and drew a folded paper from his coat pocket. "I have here a court order, from Judge Barnard, for you to release my client into my custody—immediately."

He unfolded the paper and placed it on the table. Then he took out an envelope. "And this, captain, is a personal letter for you, from Richard Connolly. I have not read it, naturally, but I have reason to believe it is of some urgency."

Redpath stood like a statue for several moments, his face brick-red from the effort it took to choke down his rage. Then he moved slowly to the table, as though he were pushing himself through some invisible barrier, and put down his nightstick. He ignored the order from Judge Barnard, who was on the verge of being indicted for accepting bribes to render judgments favorable to the Tammany political machine, and opened the envelope from Richard Connolly.

Connolly, known fondly to insiders as "Slippery Dicky," was the comptroller of the city's Department of Finance. He was in as much danger as other Tammany bigshots of being toppled by the current grand jury investigations. But unless and until that happened, he remained too powerful a politician to be ignored.

Redpath had his emotions under control when he finished reading Connolly's note and stuck it in his back pocket.

Behind him Bill Howe said gravely, "I hope none of *that* is from my client there?"

Redpath turned and saw that Howe was looking at the bloodied towels on the floor around Harp. "Naw," he said, "all I was doing was showing Harp how we handle the worst kinda criminals—the kind you can't make behave theirselves any other way."

Harp said nothing to that. His head was clearing, the rate of his heartbeat was almost back to normal and there was nothing to be gained from making accusations that couldn't be proved.

"I hope," Howe said, "that the demonstration is over. Because Harp and I have an appointment we'll soon be late for."

"Sure." Redpath tossed the key to the manacles to Sergeant Quinn.

When Harp's wrists and ankles were freed he pulled his boots on, then stood up and put on his coat and hat. He still felt a little shaky when he walked to the table and picked up his hickory stick.

Redpath made no objection when Harp put the Le Mat revolver back in his coat pocket. "No hard feelings? I was just trying to do my duty."

"As you saw it," Harp said dryly. "According to the *Sun,* your methods are much to be admired."

Redpath's laugh was a short bark. "Okay. But if you do come across something that might help with the investigation, I'd still like to hear about it."

"You can count on it," Harp told him.

Outside, the snowflakes had stopped fluttering down, as Harp had expected. But the air was bitter cold, and the city's cloud cover wasn't breaking up. Bill Howe's carriage was a two-passenger brougham. As its driver got the horse trotting in the direction of the Howe & Hummel law offices Howe told Harp, "You were lucky. Billy Doyle was waiting with some messages for you at that French restaurant in your building when the police arrested you. He came running to us with the news."

"If he hadn't," Harp said, "somebody else around there would have."

"You take it all rather calmly."

"Now I do. A little while ago calm was not what I was feeling."

Howe patted Harp's knee with a fat, diamond-beringed hand. "Vance Walburton dropped by to see me early this morning. He's anxious about whether you're making progress in locating his wife. Anything I can let him know?"

"I'll be talking to him myself," Harp said. "Right after I find out what Billy Doyle's got for me."

His private priorities hadn't changed. It was Moe Saul's killer he was after—not Walburton's wife. But to get what he was after he needed to find out why Alice Curry had been murdered. Because he was certain now that Moe had been killed so he couldn't tell anyone who had tipped him off about Monmouth Fuller's warehouse—and had seen to it the robbers didn't bother with the office where she had died.

So far he had turned up that much. And some background on Alice Curry. But it was not enough.

Unless one of the messages Billy had waiting for him at the Howe & Hummel offices gave him a strong new lead, he was going to have to try a different tack for a while.

Maybe—just maybe—Walburton's runaway wife knew something that would explain Alice Curry's death. And Moe's.

But to find that out, he had to find Olivia Walburton.

Twenty-Nine

Billy Doyle had three messages for Harp.

One was a short note in Leland Van Tromp's lazy scrawl: *I have received an offer for your lady's information about the railroad project. I would like to be sure you approve before closing the deal. The weather being rather unpleasant, you will find me at home reading, resting and playing invalid.*

It reminded Harp that he should make time, before too long, to check on whether Willem Jacobs had finished substituting fake rubies for the real ones in Louise's choker.

The second message was from Ralph Cavalucci, whom Harp had switched to looking for Monmouth Fuller's painter of erotic pictures. Cavalucci's handwriting was small and neat, with an occasional flourish at the end of some words:

> I believe the artist you are interested in may be a Belgian named Philippe Preud'homme. He has been in this country less than two years, does not seem to have made a very good living with his painting so far, and if he has made any close friends, I haven't found them as yet. He sometimes goes to Neal's, a bohemian hangout at the corner of Grove and Bedford, to drink. According to people there he is a heavy drinker, as well as a passionate but unlucky gambler.
>
> While getting drunk in Neal's one night he was complaining that he needed money so badly that he was reduced to painting lewd canvases for "a stupid, self-indulgent young millionaire businessman." Does this sound like your Mr. Fuller? Preud'homme told some of the

Neal's regulars that the latest painting commissioned by
this millionaire was a nude, and the model was a young
lady supplied by the millionaire.

Philippe Preud'homme lives and has his studio in a
house at 55 West 16th Street. But he is not there now. He
left yesterday afternoon with a single suitcase, telling his
landlord that he had come into an inheritance and was
going to take a long vacation. The landlord was impressed. He told me that Preud'homme was usually behind in his rent payments. But before leaving yesterday
he not only paid his back rent, but also enough in advance to keep his rooms waiting for him for the next
three months.

The landlord doesn't know where Preud'homme went.
Nor does anyone else I have talked with so far.

Harp didn't have to strain his imagination to come up with a
source for the artist's sudden financial windfall—and an explanation for his abrupt exit from the city, and perhaps from the country, yesterday afternoon. Yesterday afternoon was only hours after
Harp had upset Monmouth Fuller with questions about Alice
Curry. And after Mike McKibbin had asked Fuller, in front of
Harp, about the nude painting missing from Fuller's wall.

It added to what Harp had already concluded about Fuller. But
not something that Fuller couldn't deny. It still wasn't enough to
break him down with.

Harp would need something stronger for that.

The third message was from Jack Goodhue, the *Telegram* reporter who'd wired a colleague in New Hampshire for Harp:

Your story about a Concord cotton mill owner hanging
himself from a tree outside his house did happen. Almost
two years ago. His name was Elisha Willard Olcott. He
had only one daughter. Her name: Alice Olcott. Unmarried when she left Concord—some say to attempt to
recoup her fortunes in Boston or New York. Her mother
left Concord about the same time. Maybe to go live with
some distant relative in Kansas or some other depressing
place in the West.

There doesn't seem to be anybody around Concord who has heard from Alice Olcott or her mother since then, and my Concord contact can't find any picture of Alice Olcott.

Okay, that does it. Brings what I owe you down to $35. Which I'll win back the next time you sit down to a game with me. Cheers . . .

Harp wrote a note to Louise: "Alice Curry's real name was Alice Olcott. Try that name first on the mediums you talk to. If it doesn't mean anything to them, then try the Alice Curry name. And thank you, again, for helping me with this."

He reread the note and saw how stiffly formal it was. But he didn't change it. He put it in an envelope, wrote her name and address on it and gave it to Billy to take uptown to her home.

Then he went to Washington Square, got Leland out of the two back rooms that had once been part of the servants' quarters in his home and took him to Huber's Eating House two blocks away for lunch.

They ordered lavishly, and nursed beers while they waited for their food. Harp studied Leland's gaunt face and said, "You look worse every time I see you."

"Compliments are always welcome."

"You should see a doctor."

"What for?" Leland said carelessly. "They always tell me the same thing. I should stop drinking and stop smoking. Since I seldom feel lusty enough to indulge in fleshier pleasures lately, what would that leave me? Don't worry so much about me, lieutenant. Everyone is going to die, of something or other, sooner or later."

"I'd prefer later to sooner. For both of us."

"But we don't often get to choose that, do we?" Leland eyed Harp's bruised and swollen ear. "Speaking of looking worse than when last we met, *that* is not a pretty sight."

"I had a slight collision with the law," Harp told him.

"That sort of thing seems to happen to you from time to time."

"Yes," Harp agreed. "It does."

Their meals arrived at that point. Leland didn't get down to business until they'd finished eating.

"The offer," he told Harp over their coffees, "is from Collis Huntington. He'll pay us thirty thousand dollars—if my business tip is as interesting as I've assured him it is. Since Mrs. Vedder's information about Drew's projected railway line is surely worth that much to him, I'm certain he will pay up. And I don't believe I can better Huntington's offer elsewhere."

"There's Gould and Fisk," Harp suggested "That partnership keeps grabbing at everything in reach."

Leland nodded. "True. But Jay Gould is a sour scoundrel. And Jim Fisk, though I know you are on friendly terms with him, is a cheerful one. They might agree to more, then not pay in full once they have all the information. Neither of that pair of scoundrels has the romantic respect for my fading family name that Huntington clings to."

Harp considered that aspect. It didn't take him long to come to a decision. "You're right, go with Huntington. Put his payment in your bank account and divide half of it between us the way I said. Make out a check to Louise Vedder for the other half."

Leland drank the last of his coffee and asked, casually, "Have you decided yet what you are going to do about you and her?"

"No."

"Louise Vedder is not a woman who will lack for eager suitors, lieutenant. Procrastinate too long and you won't have any decision to make. The lady will no longer be available."

It was not a new thought for Harp.

"Leland," he said heavily, "please mind your own business."

There was nothing new or fancy in Vance Walburton's dark-paneled inner office. Its furniture was considerably older than Walburton himself. The gold lettering on the brown leather volumes of law and finance in his bookcases had lost its shine long ago. The carpets, though of excellent quality, were worn. The general impression, in the gloomy daylight coming through the windows that looked across Wall Street to the Stock Exchange, was of aged-in-discretion sobriety. A reminder that this was a venerable law firm with an established tradition of prudent service to the city's best families.

"I have had to employ a few private detectives in the past," Walburton said. "For certain of my clients, of course. Families suspicious of a suitor's background. Business firms worried about embezzlement. Nowadays there seem to be dozens of these detective agencies in New York. Most of them utterly fraudulent, I'm aware of that. So I have been careful to deal only with those who have a good previous record as members of the police. Even so, my opinion of them has not been entirely favorable. The very nature of the profession is of doubtful propriety, since a detective must use unscrupulous methods to—"

"I'm not a detective, Mr. Walburton," Harp interrupted. "Not private or otherwise."

Walburton frowned, and the leather-padded swivel chair squeaked under him as he leaned forward a bit. "Then what *are* you? Forgive me, but Mr. Howe was vague about that."

"I'm just somebody who is trying to find your wife for you."

"By your own admission, you haven't made much progress at it." Walburton said it as politely as he could. Good upbringing. One was not supposed to be rude to one's inferiors. "And I must point out that I am paying a good deal more for your efforts than I would have to pay any detective I have dealt with in the past. The best of them charge only ten dollars a day plus expenses."

"I have made some progress," Harp lied. "But as I explained, I've reached a point where I can't go further without knowing something more about your wife."

"There is nothing of an unusual nature to tell. Olivia is a normal, well-bred young lady from a good, respectable family. Intelligent, a fine wife—"

"But she ran away from you. Why?"

"As I explained to Mr. Howe and Mr. Hummel, we began to have some very personal and private problems between us—which I do not wish to discuss."

Harp got to his feet. "Then you can hire one of the private detectives you know to hunt for your wife. And I can stop working on it. Because what I said is true. Without knowing more about your wife, and her problems, I don't have a chance of finding her."

"Wait! Please, sit down . . ." Walburton watched anxiously until Harp settled back into his chair. Then he turned in his swivel chair and stared out the window. After a long silence, still looking through the window, he said, "I don't want you to stop. I simply . . ." He went silent again. Finally: "Losing our child, only one month before it was born, was a physical and mental shock for Olivia. She didn't want to . . . to risk trying again, and possibly losing another. Mr. Harp, this is extremely difficult and embarrassing."

"I know," Harp said gently. "I appreciate your trying in spite of that. Take your time."

Walburton did take time before speaking again. "I *think* that was the whole root of the difficulty between us. If we had children, she could employ all of her energies in caring for them. Olivia has a great deal of energy, you see. It makes her nervous—restless. She began to feel she needed to find some means of using it. Outside of our home, I mean. Running the house and supervising the domestics didn't seem to be enough for her."

"Doesn't your butler take care of that?"

Walburton turned his head with a slight smile. "We don't have a butler, Mr. Harp. We are not *that* grand. We have a housekeeper."

"She's in charge of your house and the other servants?"

"Yes."

"Your wife didn't feel telling the housekeeper how to do her job was a full use of her energies?"

"No."

"What did she want to do?"

"God knows!"

"But you don't."

"Not a clue."

Outside the window a small hawk landed on one of the telegraph wires. It bent its neat head, studying an alley below. You didn't see many of those in the city now. When Harp had been a kid there'd been more. For a bird of prey New York City was as good as the countryside for hunting mice and rats. But possibly they weren't as tasty here, nowadays.

"You told Howe and Hummel," Harp said, "that your wife reads books you don't approve of. You blamed that for part of her . . . restlessness."

"Novels," Walburton said with undisguised distaste, "that involve impulsive, headstrong females who act in ways utterly contrary to a Christian woman's natural reserve and modesty. Who abandon the restraints of convention and do things no refined person would—or should—wish to read about."

"What sort of things?"

"I don't have time to read fiction. And certainly not those sort of novels. What I read *about* them is quite enough to persuade me that they cater to tastes of a lower order than mine. So of course it embarrassed me that my own wife, a young woman of breeding, doted on them so."

"She didn't try to get you interested in any of the ones she liked?"

"Never," Walburton said. "She knew my opinion—even if she stubbornly refused to yield to it."

"You didn't get curious and have a look through her books after she left you? On the chance something in them might explain what was on her mind?"

"Olivia didn't leave her books scattered about the house where one might pick them up on impulse. They are in her private rooms. She knows I respect her privacy and would never intrude there uninvited. Certainly not in her absence."

"But I would," Harp told him. "Give me a note to your housekeeper. Tell her to let me in and then leave me alone in your wife's rooms."

Walburton spun his chair around to face Harp fully. "Certainly not!"

"There may be something in there, besides her books, that could tell me where she is."

"Mr. Harp, I adhere to certain rules of behavior. What you propose is entirely out of—"

"If you want to get your wife back," Harp cut in flatly, "you'll have to relax those rules. Either that or I quit looking for her. Your choice."

In the end, Walburton grudgingly gave in. "But how the devil can I explain it to our housekeeper?"

"Tell her I'm a home decorator. You want to prepare a surprise for your wife, when she returns from her trip, by having her quarters spruced up. And I need time in there, alone, to plan the redecoration.''

Walburton continued to look squeamish about it. But he did write the note.

Thirty

There had been a brief shower while Harp was in Walburton's office. It had stopped minutes before he'd left, but the rain that had fallen had frozen. In Waverly Place—one of the established residential purlieus of sedate society—the slim, leafless branches of the trees lining both sides of the street were sheathed in thin, translucent ice.

The Walburton home was red brick with brownstone trimming, a French mansard roof and a spacious front porch. It was smaller than Monmouth Fuller's mansion, but roomy enough to house comfortably a large family with its servants. The housekeeper was a broad-bodied woman with a ruddy face and a Bavarian accent. She read Walburton's note and looked curiously at Harp. Perhaps he didn't fit her notion of an home decorator. As she showed him where to leave his hat, coat and stick in the vestibule, she asked if he knew when Mrs. Walburton was expected to return.

He said he didn't, and followed her rustling skirt and petticoats deeper inside the house. There was a wide, dim hallway with dark wallpaper and heavily framed paintings of pastoral scenes and, presumably, family ancestors. They passed between a double drawing room and a morning room full of large rubber plants and ferns. Turning into a narrower hall, they climbed a gracefully curving, carpeted stairway with a black oak banister to the second floor.

The housekeeper stopped at a closed door and said, "This is Mrs. Walburton's apartment." She gave Harp an uncertain smile as she took a bunch of keys from her belt. "Mr. Walburton's instructions say you'll want to be left to yourself in there. But if you want me to show where things are . . ."

"Thank you, no," Harp told her.

"Well then—" She unlocked the door and opened it for him. He thanked her again, stepped inside and shut the door.

He was inside a smallish antechamber with hazy daylight coming through a round, overhead window in its slanted ceiling. There was a thick Smyrna rug, and a wall-table of inlaid marble on which were a pair of sculptured silver candelabra, an ebony comb and an ivory-backed brush. On the opposite wall a mirror in an embossed bronze frame rose from the floor to the height of Harp's head. This would be the place for the mistress of the house to do a last-minute primp of hair and dress before issuing forth. Harp turned away from his reflection in the tall looking glass and walked out of the antechamber. He didn't like what mirrors showed him. His figure seemed to him too large and clumsy-looking. His face was too hard, and its expression too guarded. And that damned scar across his forehead made it worse. From the moment he'd first met Louise Vedder, and realized she was the woman in the tintype he'd stolen from a dead man, it had felt like a brand left on him by her husband, to warn her that Harp was his killer.

The next room was Olivia Walburton's boudoir. It was a good-sized room, with a pair of windows overlooking a rear garden. Harp wandered around it very slowly, touching things, trying to absorb a feeling of Olivia Walburton.

But there was nothing that spoke to him of an individual person, different in any way from other gentlewomen of Victorian New York. It was a cozy nest for a pampered and sheltered status symbol. A young woman whose main function was to show people that her husband could afford a wife who need exert herself in no other direction.

The ceiling was painted with modest cupids and sun-shot clouds. The wallpaper had the customary profusion of blossoms and vines. There was a luxurious bed with silk cushions and over-hanging folds of a pale-blue canopy. There were antique tables and upholstered chairs covered with embroidered chintz. There were wardrobes and chests of drawers full of the great variety of expensive clothing one would expect. There was a small fireplace with a marble-and-ormolu mantelpiece, and a tall pier-glass in a burnished gold frame. There were Venetian watercolors and Japanese prints, collections of French ceramics, tropical seashells and Florentine cameos.

But no books.

Harp left the boudoir, and entered Olivia Walburton's dressing room.

Her books were in there.

Along with the usual things one found in the dressing rooms of most well-to-do women. A dressing table with its toiletries and spindly gilt legs. A looking-glass over it flanked by gas jets in brass wall-brackets shaped like lilies. A satin brocade sofa and a fringed, horsehair armchair. A lace-curtained window framed by pink-and-gold draperies. A big steamer trunk and a corner washstand with a flowered skirt.

What was not usual was the plain oak writing table with an ink-stand, pens and pencils on its leather-cornered blotter, and a straight-backed chair in front of it. And all those books. Two walls with floor-to-ceiling shelves crammed with them.

That many told Harp one thing that gave Olivia Walburton a distinct identity. She did not entirely live in what most people considered the real world. Part of her life was inside these books.

Or had been, before she had left home and husband. Was she out there somewhere now, trying to live in reality something from these books?

Harp tried to read their titles. But the north light seeping through the window's lace curtain was too dim. He struck a match, lit one of the gas jets, turned it up high and tried again.

Her reading tastes seemed to be all-embracing. History and literature, science and travel, novels and poetry. Plutarch, Shakespeare and Moliere. Macaulay's essays and Andersen's fairytales. *Mawe's Gardener. Cities and Cemeteries of Etruria. Exploring Mexico. Treatise on Mechanics. Origin of Civilization.* Many novels by Balzac, Dickens and George Sand. Two of the Wilkie Collins mysteries digging into the underpinnings of Victorian society.

She had made no attempt to arrange books according to categories; nor to separate fiction from non-fiction. But it was easy for Harp to spot, amid this undisciplined hodgepodge, some of the books he knew, and could imagine her husband regarding with disapproval.

Lady Audley's Secret—its central character a lovely, gracious, titled woman who was a secret bigamist attempting to murder her first husband. Dickens's *Great Expectations,* with its young hero whose benefactor was a thuggish escaped convict; and with the two patrician women in his life vengeful sadists intent on humiliating men. Swinburne's *Poems and Ballads*—with its heavy accent on masochism. *East Lynne,* which postulated that an adulterous wife might eventually be forgiven. *The Woman in White,* with its assertive, "masculine" secondary heroine and its hints of perversion.

The translations of French novels were stronger meat. Balzac's *The Girl with the Golden Eyes,* with its lesbian relationship, and his *Splendour and Misery of Courtesans.* The younger Dumas' *The Lady of the Camellias,* also about a courtesan. Gautier's *Mademoiselle de Maupin,* about a bisexual actress. Prevost's *Manon Lescaut,* another professional harlot.

And from the Italian: *Orlando Furioso,* with its invincible female knights in armor defeating all male challengers in tournaments and single combat.

Whores and murderesses, lesbians and women warriors, adultery and sexual ambiguity. Did it add up to what was on Olivia Walburton's mind? Or was it simply another indication of the wide range of her literary curiosity?

There was a book on one shelf that seemed to Harp to have no connection with her tastes in literature. *Home Topics*—part of a simplistic popular series of "common sense" volumes of advice for right-minded females. He took it down and opened it. On its first page, in a large bold hand, was written: *My Dearest Livvy—To prove to you that I am not alone in my opinions, please read the chapter beginning on page 32. Then, one hopes, you will understand that I have nothing but your best interests in my heart.—Your Loving Husband, Vance.*

The chapter that began on page thirty-two was titled, "Our Girl and Doubtful Books." A number of passages in it were heavily underlined:

> In the doubtful class of literature that now floods the market, one often, however unwillingly, stumbles upon some book that would bring a blush to the cheek. You may despise the morals of a bad book, but once read it

and Memory cannot be cleansed—a sin against the purity of your mind. My dear Girl! you cannot afford to run the risk of reading *any* book that makes even a feeble attempt to undermine your faith in purity and Christianity . . .

And what is to be gained by the perusal of immoral literature? Knowledge of the world, perhaps. The same kind of knowledge in which dwellers in the slums and *habitués* of rum-holes delight. If you are a *woman,* in the noblest, truest sense of the word, your own instinct will enable you to travel through life to your final resting place, unsullied and unspotted from the world. Close your eyes resolutely against such vile literature . . .

Innocence and purity are so sweet! so unusual, in this world of ours! Sooner have your face scarred than sully the whiteness of your soul.

At the end of this chapter a comment had been written in a neat, stylish script: *This author would tell a blind man he was lucky, because he didn't have to see what was going on around him.—O.B.*

O.B.? Then Harp remembered: her maiden name was Bixby. A secret declaration of independence? Telling herself that she had an identity outside the circumscribed role society assigned her?

Harp took other books from the shelves at random, skimming through them in search of other notations by her. But there were none: no passages underlined, no jotted comments. He gave it up, and opened the drawer of her writing table.

The first thing he saw in it was her diary.

Why had she left it behind, so easily accessible?

Had she hoped that her husband might "intrude into her privacy"—and learn something about her?

Harp sat down and opened the diary. It was a disappointment, at first. It wasn't a diary about her life, but a literary journal. Quotations from some of the books she'd read; and her observations about them.

On an early page she had written:

So many of our so-called literary critics seem to me to
be prejudiced fools. In the latest Harper's Monthly there
is a review of George Sand's *Monsieur Sylvestre*. The critic
says her moral is summed up in its final sentence: "Be an
unbeliever rather than selfish. God does not love cowards." To which this critic responds that such advice
"might, perhaps, serve a useful purpose in France. It is
not needed in America."

What can one say in the face of such smug stupidity?

Some of Olivia Bixby Walburton's comments became more personal as Harp read further in her diary:

Our eminent American historian, Mr. Francis Park-
man, writes, "It is among women who have no part in the
occupations and duties of the rest of their sex that one is
most apt to find that morbid introversion, those restless
cravings, that vague but torturing sense of destinies unfulfilled." Yes, very true. But *what* in God's name is a
woman to do with herself whose husband doesn't need
her help in earning their living, who has no children,
who has servants capable of taking care of the house
without her, and who has become bored beyond toler-
ance of repeating the same empty social rounds, over
and over again, within polite society?

Some pages later:

A review in the Spectator attacks the novel *Armadale*
for "overstepping the limits of decency, and revolting
every human sentiment." Well, I myself find many of the
sentiments expressed in this book my own. Such as this
one: "In the miserable monotony . . . anything is welcome to women which offers them any sort of refuge
from the established tyranny of the principle that all human happiness begins and ends at home." True! True!
True!

And further on:

In her book, *Cassandra,* Florence Nightingale writes about the illnesses that wives of successful men are prone to. One sentence, in particular, strikes deep into my soul: "The accumulation of nervous energy which has had nothing to do during the day, makes them feel every night, when they go to bed, as if they were going mad; and they are obliged to lie long in bed in the morning to let it evaporate and keep down."

It is as though Miss Nightingale knows me—much too well.

Reaching one of the last diary pages, Harp came across something, at the end of the final paragraph, that gave him pause:

Self-Culture and Perfection of Character, a recently reissued book by O. S. Fowler, seems to me a mish-mash of ridiculous phrenology and rigid Puritanism. But in his section on self-esteem, though I seem to lack the head bump denoting "small self-esteem" that he describes, I cannot deny the symptoms: "Lacks self-reliance and independence; underrates own capabilities and worth, and is therefore liable to be underrated by others."

But when we come to his section on Love, we find this insufferable sentiment: "How omnipotent the power wielded by a husband over a wife who loves him." Mr. Fowler considers this like a parent's power over a child, and approves of it highly.

As Vicky says, too many supposedly cultured men feel that once a woman is "honorably bedded" she should act like a helpless, insipid little girl until Nature transforms her into a dull old lady.

Vicky . . .

Harp looked through the other things in the drawer. Finding nothing else of interest, he tried the steamer trunk. Unlike the drawer, it was locked. He took two hairpins from the dressing table and used them to open the lock. They did the job as efficiently as his thief's picklock would have, if he hadn't left it in his coat downstairs.

The trunk contained an assortment of neatly folded summer dresses. But she wouldn't have locked the trunk for those. He delved deeper. At the bottom he discovered something other than dresses. Back issues of *Woodhull & Claflin's Weekly*. With its front-page motto: "Progress! Free Thought! Untrammeled Lives!—Breaking the Way for Future Generations!"

That explained why the trunk was locked. Husbands concerned for the innocence of their wives forbade them to attend Victoria Woodhull's lectures or to read her newspaper. Only last month Governor Hawley of Connecticut had published a warning about "this disreputable weekly journal which is edited by a woman. The journal is taken and read by woman spiritists and woman suffragists, who may shut their eyes to its immorality, and who introduce it into respectable households where there are virtuous girls."

Harp leafed through the issues. In the second one, Olivia Walburton had underlined in red Victoria's published answer to a judge who had accused her of being "a strong-minded woman." Victoria's underlined answer: "I consider that a compliment, not an insult. I *hope* I am a strong-minded woman—rather than one of the shrinking violets that men try to make of us. This judge's tone of ridicule does not intimidate me. Women who defy the present rules of society, by pushing themselves into activities that men pretend to consider unladylike, must expect derision and animosity—and not be put off by it."

There was more red underlining inside another issue, under a statement by the distinguished suffragette Elizabeth Cady Stanton: "Victoria Woodhull has done a work for woman that none of us could have done. She has faced and dared men to call her the names that make women shudder, while she chucked principle, like medicine, down their throats."

And then, in the seventh issue Harp looked through, he came across one of Victoria's editorials that Walburton's wife had underlined: "At present the profession of prostitute is illegal. To prevent arrest she gives the patrolman $3 to $10 a week and the privilege of visiting her gratis. Police captains and sergeants get $20 to $30. The amount of degradation and bodily injury to which you must daily submit to meet these combined charges may be imagined

. . . Prostitution exists. As it cannot be extinguished, its evils should be palliated by legalizing it.''

Next to this, Olivia Walburton had written, *Get more information about this from Vicky.*

Victoria had lied to him.

Thirty-One

He didn't find her at her home on Thirty-eighth Street. Dr. Woodhull said she had left for Boston, to join Tennessee and Colonel Blood in their efforts to prevent the authorities from banning her scheduled lecture. The three of them, Woodhull told Harp, were sharing a pair of connecting rooms at the Tremont House there.

Harp took a hansom cab down Broadway and had it stop and wait for him outside a stationer's shop on the Ladies Mile. He came out with an envelope and three sheets of letter paper, and the cab carried him the rest of the way downtown to Howe & Hummel. There he found Ralph Cavalucci hanging around the waiting room with nothing to do. Cavalucci told Harp he hadn't been able to turn up a single thing about Monmouth Fuller's artist, Philippe Preud'homme, beyond what he'd put into his earlier message.

Evening was approaching through the gloom of the day when Harp and Cavalucci walked to Pontin's, a restaurant on Franklin Street favored by lawyers and judges from the nearby Tombs criminal courts. They took a small table near the bar. Cavalucci ordered a glass of red wine, and Harp a cup of black coffee. While they drank, Harp asked, "Did you get a chance to look around Preud'homme's place?"

"No," Cavalucci said, "the landlord wouldn't let me in without Preud'homme's permission."

"Does the landlord live in the same house?"

Cavalucci shook his head. "In the house next door."

"What floor's Preud'homme on?"

"The ground floor."

"Anyone else live on that floor?"

"No, he has the whole floor to himself. Why?"

"I just like details," Harp said.

Especially details that would help him do what he intended to do, when it got later and darker.

"Have you got anything you have to do tonight and tomorrow?" he asked Cavalucci.

"Not if you have something remunerative for me."

"I want you to take the next train you can get to Boston and deliver a letter for me," Harp said. "And bring me back the reply if there is one. I'll pay you twenty dollars, plus the expenses for your train fare there and back, your meals, and an overnight stay at a *cheap* Boston hotel."

"I like visiting Boston," Cavalucci said. "But could you make it twenty-five dollars?"

"No."

Cavalucci sighed. "Could I have another glass of wine?"

Harp said he could, and wrote Victoria Woodhull's name and the name of her Boston hotel on the envelope he'd purchased. Then, while Cavalucci nursed his second glass of red wine, Harp composed his letter to Victoria.

> I understand why you claimed not to know Olivia Bixby Walburton. I imagine she must have sworn you to secrecy. But I *have* to talk with her. And soon. As you know, I am trying to find out who murdered Alice Curry. That, I think, is something a woman of Olivia Walburton's character would want to help me accomplish. And she may be able to. I have reason to believe she may have known the murdered woman, though perhaps under a different name: Alice Olcott. If not, she may at least know something about her that helps me.
>
> If you know where Olivia Walburton is, please telegraph her asking her to contact me as quickly as possible. When I showed you her picture, you naturally figured her husband must have hired me to drag her back to him. I give you my word that I have no intention of doing so. And that I won't tell her husband where she is, if she doesn't want me to.

You know I sometimes lie to people—but you also
know that if I give *you* my word, I will never go back on it.

He sealed the letter inside the envelope, gave it to Cavalucci and
hoped for the best.

He ran into Hilda Shaler when he entered his block on Greene
Street. She looked as if she was returning to her room from a not-
too-successful day of streetwalking. With a guilty grimace, she told
Harp she'd spotted the two cops lurking in wait that morning, and
she apologized for not having yelled a warning before they'd
grabbed him. But she didn't need trouble from police she didn't
know, she said; she had enough with the ones she had to pay to
stay in business. As soon as they had taken Harp away, Hilda told
him, she'd rushed down intending to go to Howe & Hummel. But
Billy Doyle had appeared out of nowhere and told her he'd take
care of it.

Harp thanked her for her good intentions and went into the
Suze la Rousse. There was no message waiting for him there from
Louise Vedder, or from anyone else. He went up to his apartment,
took a leisurely bath, and put on a change of clothing. From a
drawer in the front room he took out a bull's-eye lantern. It was a
compact version, made especially for him by a metal worker with a
shop on Hudson Street. It fitted easily into Harp's coat pocket,
and made a nice balance for the Le Mat handgun in the other
pocket.

The night was dark enough for what he had in mind when he
came down from his apartment. But not yet late enough. The
owner of a newspaper-and-cigar store a block away was preparing
to close when Harp got there. Harp bought a copy of the *Evening
Telegram,* and returned to the Suze la Rousse for a leisurely supper.
While he ate, he read the paper.

It had a story about a conference Captain Redpath had given
the press that afternoon concerning the aftermath of his raid
against the Hoggy Corcoran gang.

After intense questioning, Redpath told reporters, the captured
gang members had all confessed to stealing the liquor from the
warehouse where the prostitute, Alice Curry, had been found

dead. And they had told him where they'd taken their plunder: to a notorious dealer in stolen goods named Moses Saul. Redpath had obtained a court order, and he and his men had broken into Moses Saul's place of business and found the stolen liquor there. They had also discovered Moses Saul, murdered by some unknown hand.

Unless evidence to the contrary turned up, Redpath told the reporters, this did not necessarily establish a connection between his death and the death of the prostitute. Men like Moses Saul, who worked hand-in-glove with violent criminals, had to expect violence to visit *them* one day.

Redpath said that none of the captured robbers had confessed to knowing anything at all about the death of Alice Curry—or of Moses Saul. Redpath admitted to reporters, with evident regret, that he was now beginning to doubt that they were the killers. But he wanted to assure everyone that he would press ahead with other lines of investigation, with all of his energy and resources. He would never give up on finding the killers.

Since the paper couldn't come up with anything new about Alice Curry's murder, it tried to keep her story going by using her fate as its reason to publish a debate between a doctor from the Metropolitan Board of Health and a minister of the Gospel. The question debated was one most officials shied away from. Whether prostitution should be made legal—and thus legally controllable —in the United States as it was in some European countries.

The doctor went into detailed facts and figures about the spread of syphilis in New York. Then:

> It will continue to spread at its present alarming rate so long as our lawmakers refuse to acknowledge the consequences of prostitution remaining illegal. There is little sense in attempting to ignore a thing that every one knows to exist. To acknowledge a vice is not to applaud it.
>
> In order to preserve society from the ravages of syphilis, every prostitute and every house of prostitution must be subjected to regular medical inspections. This cannot be done until prostitution is licensed by law, and thus brought under the law's control.

The minister, whom Harp knew to be sincerely concerned about society's unfortunates, acknowledged that every point made by the doctor was true:

> We admit that the present condition of the whole matter in New York is terrible. Fearful diseases have spread through not only the prostitutes, but have communicated to the virtuous and innocent, and are undermining the health of society. Medical men almost exclusively advocate licenses to prostitutes. They consider exclusively the frightful effects on society, and see that legislation would at once check the ravages of these terrible maladies.
>
> On the other hand, those of us who deal with the *moral* aspects of the case have a profound dread of anything which, to the young, should appear to approve or even to recognize prostitution. A wise legislator cannot consider physical well-being alone. A license system for prostitution is plainly toward recognizing this offense as legal or permissible. It removes one of the safeguards of virtue.

Harp put the paper aside and ordered a strong black post-supper coffee.

One of the French chess-players, the exiled aristocrat, came in and looked around for his usual opponent, the anarchist. Not seeing him, he looked questioningly at Harp. Harp took out his watch, looked at the time, and nodded. The Frenchman ordered a glass of wine and brought the restaurant's chessboard and pieces to Harp's table.

Harp lost the first game in a little more than an hour. He gave the second game more concentration, and it lasted almost two hours. In the end he won it by sacrificing his queen and his remaining rook in order to checkmate the opposing king with two pawns and a knight.

The Frenchman wanted another game to try for best out of three, but Harp checked his watch again and said, "Sorry, but I can't. I have an appointment."

"At this hour? It is quite late."

"Yes," Harp said. "It is."

* * *

It had turned into a heavy, wet night, with sullen mists crawling toward each other from the East and North rivers. Nobody was out on this stretch of West Sixteenth Street. The only sounds were the crackling of the ice coating tree branches stirred by brief gusts of wind. No light showed in the windows of Number Fifty-five, where Philippe Preud'homme had his apartment, nor in the house next door, where his landlord lived.

There was a narrow alley between Number Fifty-five and a Presbyterian church. That made it easier. Harp left the pavement and went through the alley. Behind the house was a little garden with a split-rail fence, a bedraggled hedge and an old chestnut tree that looked as if it had died in the previous century. Harp used his picklock on the back door and had it opened in less than twenty seconds. It had not been made to withstand a skilled invader. Inside, he shut the door and lit his bull's-eye lantern, holding it low and aiming it at the floor.

He was in an old-fashioned dining kitchen, its floor of cracked tiles that hadn't been scrubbed in a long time. There was a pile of dirty dishes, cutlery and glasses in a wooden hipbath in one corner. A small tin pail on the table was half full of beer gone stale. Harp closed the window curtains and moved on.

The next room was a bedroom without windows. After that came a windowless washroom with another hipbath, this one of tin. The rest of Preud'homme's apartment was a big, untidy artist's studio with two windows facing Sixteenth Street, both with their curtains closed.

There were gobs of dried oil paint of different colors on the bare timber floor. The room smelled of fruit going bad, from an arrangement of overripe apples, bananas and pears on a table between a copper vase and a blue-and-white ceramic bowl. There was a partly finished oil painting on an easel near it. A still-life of the arrangement on the table.

Harp prowled the room, searching. There were no erotic paintings. But there were three stretched canvasses with oils of the city's prettiest squares—Washington, Union and Madison—in which the technique was very much like that of the artist who'd done the paintings on Monmouth Fuller's library walls. There were many watercolors, and charcoal and pencil drawings, that seemed to be studies for planned oil paintings. In one sketchbook Harp came across six pages of studies of a nude woman striking different poses. But her face was barely sketched in: of no use to Harp.

He didn't find anything else in the studio, nor in any of the other rooms, that was of any help at all. Nothing about where the artist had gone. Nothing connecting him with Fuller. Nothing about Alice Curry—or Alice Olcott.

He sat on a stone bench in the icy darkness of Louise Vedder's rear garden looking at the only window in her house that still had lamplight inside it.

That window belonged to her combination music and reading room. Harp knew that from the two times he had been inside her home. Both times as one of a group invited for supper when Uriah Gibbon had been out of town on business.

Her dead husband's picture was on the piano in that room. A handsome young fellow with a likable smile. Harp couldn't recall actually seeing his face when he'd killed him.

The light he was watching diminished and then was gone. Louise had carried the lamp out of the room. After a time the lamplight reappeared, inside an upper window. Probably her bedroom. Harp hadn't gotten above the first floor during either visit.

It began to snow. A gentle but steady snowfall that felt like it intended to continue through the rest of the night. But Harp didn't leave the garden until the lamp up there was extinguished.

He had a strong desire to get drunk. Instead, he walked all the way back to Greene Street. Thirty-two blocks through the falling snow.

Thirty-Two

The night's snowfall had spread blankets of white over New York's streets and roofs before ending shortly after dawn. The cloud cover had broken apart. Only a few scattered clouds were left, drifting across an otherwise clear sky that brightened the city below without warming it enough to melt any of the fallen snow. Jingling harness bells sounded below as Harp prepared to leave his apartment that morning. He glanced down through a front room window. A businessman with a fur lap robe and with earmuffs showing below his top hat was driving past in a one-horse sleigh, instead of his carriage, to make sure he didn't bog down in the snow on the way to his office.

Madame Letessier had a telegram waiting for Harp when he entered the Suze la Rousse for breakfast. It had been delivered last night after he had left the restaurant, and the Letessiers had closed up before he'd returned to his apartment.

The telegram was from Louise Vedder: THE MEDIUM SHE CONSULTED UNDER OLCOTT NAME IS MARIE DEVOL AT 20 WEST 46 WHOM COLONEL BLOOD LISTS AS A CHARLATAN.

Harp made fast work of his breakfast and went out looking for a hansom cab to take him uptown. But between the snow and the morning rush hour, which was not quite over yet, there were no cabs immediately available. Too impatient to wait, he paid a nickel and a penny to board a Sixth Avenue horsecar. None of the eight hundred six-cent streetcars operating along the city's sixteen "horse railway" lines offered comfort. You got packed-in standing room, more often than a seat on the hard wooden benches, on a floor covered with straw that was soaking wet in rainy or snowy weather.

If you insisted on comfort, and could afford it, there were the less-frequent "Palace" and "Drawing Room" horse cars. Aboard those a twenty-cent fare bought you upholstered seats, curtained windows, a carpet and an absence of smelly rabble. But there were none of those on the Sixth Avenue line.

The tracks had been cleared much earlier that morning by one of the city's huge wooden snowplows pulled by a team of ten horses. It had left the snow piled high on either side. Work crews were now shoveling those onto wagons that would dump their loads into the city's rivers. It was hard, slow, underpaid work; but with so many immigrants, New York didn't have to shell out much to get all of the unskilled labor it wanted.

Except for stops to squeeze more passengers aboard, Harp's horsecar made its way uptown at the customary five miles per hour until it reached Union Square. There, in bumping across the intersecting Fourteenth Street line, it jumped its tracks.

This was so frequent an occurrence that no one had to be told what to do about it. All of the passengers got out. Then, while the driver held his team under control, Harp and the other able-bodied men among the passengers joined together and lifted the streetcar back onto its tracks. After which everybody piled back into the car and it resumed its northward journey.

Harp got off at Forty-sixth Street, and walked a half block east to Marie Devol's place.

She had basement rooms in a boardinghouse a few doors from Fifth Avenue, across from the Bull's Head Hotel and Hamilton's draft-horse market. Six stone steps led down to a door under the boardinghouse's front stoop. Tacked to the door was a cardboard sign:

MARIE DEVOL OF PARIS
Spiritist & Magnetic Healer
$1 per visit

She was a tall, handsome quadroon wearing a shapeless black Mother Hubbard and a black headscarf with silvery stars sewed to it. Her fingernails were painted blood-red, and there was heavy kohl darkening her eyelids. She took Harp's silver dollar and led him into a small, windowless room with astrological signs in bright crayon colors on its walls. An oval table was covered by a sky-blue cloth, and there was a crystal ball on it. Marie Devol sat down and gestured graciously for Harp to take the chair across from her.

"And now," she said softly, "tell me what it is that you are seeking."

Her accent sounded more like Boston than France, and was surprisingly cultivated.

Harp placed a five-dollar gold piece on the table and gave her a second to look at it before pinning it down with the tip of his forefinger. "Colonel James Blood recommended that I consult you about a young woman named Alice Olcott."

Marie Devol's smile was loaded with humor. "It would seem that the good colonel has changed his mind about me. I assume you are associated with the elegant lady who came here last night asking about the same young woman."

Harp nodded. He raised his fingertip an inch and tapped the gold coin with it. "I'll double this if you tell me everything you know about Alice Olcott."

Marie Devol looked at his finger and the coin, then raised her dark-rimmed eyes to his. "Your name is Harp."

"You've seen me somewhere before," Harp said.

"I could say I read your mind, with spirit help. But yes, last summer in Madison Square. I was with a friend who knew you and she told me your name. And your profession."

Harp tapped the gold coin again. "That doesn't change my offer."

She studied his face, thinking about it. Then she took out the silver dollar he'd given her and flicked it across the table. It spun and came to rest touching the gold coin under his fingertip. "My friend also told me you can be depended on to always return a favor," she said. "There may come a time when I will need a favor. If I don't take your money, you will owe me one."

Harp picked up both coins, put them back in his pocket, and waited.

"Why this interest in Miss Olcott?" Marie Devol asked. "The elegant lady yesterday didn't explain that, and you haven't either."

Harp passed a copy of the morgue photograph across the table to her. "Recognize her in this?"

She studied the picture with a sharp intake of breath. It was a few moments before she could speak. "Since you've told me it's her, yes. Poor soul . . . Who did this to her?"

"I don't know," Harp said. "Not who or why. Anything you know that helps me find out adds to the favor I owe you."

Marie Devol looked at the picture a moment longer, then shuddered and passed it back to Harp. "But I don't know anything about that."

"Tell me what you do know about her."

"She came to me several months ago. I don't remember the exact date, but I do remember her. She was so pretty. And cultured, almost like your lady who visited me yesterday. But I could sense that she was deeply troubled. Trying to come to a decision about some important change in her life."

"You sensed it," Harp said, "or she told you?"

"I could sense it. I *am* unusually sensitive to other people. Although unfortunately not in the way some mediums are. The very few lucky enough to have been born with the genuine gift in them. But I do have an understanding of people, and I do try to help those who come to me. What she did tell me was that she was worried about what her dead father felt about her and her way of life."

"She believed the dead can observe the living and communicate with them?"

"Of course." Marie Devol looked at him as if he'd said something foolish. "Don't you?"

Harp thought about Louise Vedder's dead husband, and said, "I hope not."

"The spirits are all around us, always," she told him, with obvious faith in what she was saying. "Sometimes I sense their presence. Sometimes I can almost establish contact. Almost—" She shook her head, looked down at her hands, clenched on the table. She opened them with a sigh.

Harp leaned back in his chair and waited again.

"I told her that the one dollar she'd paid me was just for a preliminary consultation. I explained that acting as a conduit for the shade of a departed one required an enormous struggle inside a medium, and drained one, for a time, of one's life force.''

"For which you'd have to be paid more than the one dollar,'' Harp said, careful to put no special intonation into the way he said it.

"Yes,'' she said, without embarrassment. "Ten dollars more is my usual fee. She paid it, and I asked for her name and the name of her father, to help me in establishing contact between them. She said she was Alice Olcott, and her father was Elisha Willard Olcott.''

"You have an unusually good memory.''

"I do. It is a help in my work. Anyway, once I had the names, I closed my eyes and went into a trance state.''

"Or pretended to.''

"It is not exactly a pretense. I do leave my normal state, and sink into some other part of my mind. I don't know what that part is, but it is there. In a woman, at least.''

"But you remain aware of what you're doing.''

"Partly. And I do use what I call my spirit voice. Very different from my normal one. It is never like the voice of the departed person, naturally. But that isn't expected by most questioners, since it has to reach me across an infinity of ether, which distorts it.''

"In this case the voice of Alice Olcott's dead father.''

"Yes.''

"What did you have him say to her?''

"Well,'' Marie Devol said, "I already understood from her that she thought her father would be upset about her present way of life. That had to mean that *she* was troubled by some aspect of it. So I told her—that is, her father did, through me—that the time had come for her to stop doing what troubled her. I kept it that vague at that point. A medium has to feel her way by slow stages, giving the questioner time to furnish more information of her own accord, often without realizing it.''

"And she did?''

"Yes, in an angry way at first. Anger at her father. She told him that a man who committed the sin of suicide and left his wife and child to fend for themselves had no right to tell *her* to stop sinning. That she didn't do it out of choice, but from necessity. I hadn't, as her father, spoken of sin. But she did in responding to him. So then I understood why she was troubled, of course."

"That she was a whore," Harp said.

"That she was a sinner of some sort, in her own eyes. And that she had reached a stage where it troubled her. So I told her what I thought was best for her. Or her father did, through me. Begging her to forgive him for what he had done, and not to use it as an excuse for continuing to do what she was doing. Oh God, I hope nothing I said to her led to her death . . ."

"I doubt it," Harp said, though he was not sure if her anxiety about that was justified or not. "Tell me about the rest of the seance."

"There is nothing more to tell," Marie Devol said. "She broke down and wept at that point—and I came out of my trance state."

"Acting as if you didn't know what had happened during it."

"Yes. The usual thing. It's what they expect of a medium"

"She did quit what she was doing after your seance," Harp told her. "Or at least she quit the place where she was doing it. She may have gotten a job in the theater. Would you know about that?"

"Not a thing. Everything I know about this poor Alice Olcott is what I have already told you. I urged her, before she left here, to return for further contacts with her father. But she never did come back."

Harp tried, but couldn't pry a single thing more out of her memory.

"From the look on your face," Marie Devol said, "I haven't earned much of a return favor, have I?"

He tore a page from his notebook and penciled the address of the Suze la Rousse on it. "This is where you leave a message for me, when you need that favor." He showed her his picture of Olivia Walburton, on the very slim chance. But the face and name meant nothing to Marie Devol.

He left without having gotten what he'd hoped for. But then, you seldom did.

Thirty-Three

When Harp came up the steps from Marie Devol's place he saw Louise Vedder's landau waiting at the curb several doors further west, her footman standing by its closed door. Louise leaned out of its opened window when she saw Harp, and waved to him with a fur-gloved hand.

This late in the morning the snow covering the sidewalk had been compressed to a starchy solidity by pedestrians tramping across it. It crunched under Harp's boots without giving way as he walked to the carriage. The footman opened the door for him, closed it after Harp was seated inside with Louise, and climbed up beside her coachman.

"I went to the Suze la Rousse to make sure you had gotten my telegram," Louise told Harp. "They said you had, so I came here. Curiosity. Did you learn anything from Marie Devol?"

"Not much," Harp said. "Not enough."

"I would like to hear about it," she said. "But I've an appointment at the Fifth Avenue Hotel. Do you have the time to accompany me there?"

Harp nodded, and Louise rapped the carriage roof with the handle of her small winter parasol. While the carriage made its way over the packed-down snow towards Madison Square, Harp told her what little Marie Devol had told him. He also found himself confiding in her the rest of what he knew about Alice Curry-Olcott. This uncharacteristic relaxation of his habitual taciturnity surprised him as much as it did Louise. He brought it to an abrupt halt.

"The poor girl," Louise said, unconsciously echoing Marie Devol. "That could have been me—if Uriah hadn't taken a fancy to me."

"If he hadn't," Harp said, "some other rich protector would have showed up."

"That is far from certain. I think the difference between her destiny and mine is nothing but a matter of luck. Good luck or bad."

"That plays a part in everyone's destiny," Harp said. "It starts with whether you're born rich, poor or in between."

"Yes. By the way, I did finally bite the bullet and tell Uriah it is finished between us. He is not happy about it, but he does realize I won't change my decision." She went on without pausing for a comment from Harp: "And I am already preparing my future without him. That is the reason for my appointment at the hotel. I am meeting with Adam Kershaw—my banker. He has been checking into locations along the Ladies Mile that might be suitable for my boutique. Places available, their rents, the costs of refurbishing them the way I would want."

"Does he know about you and Uriah Gibbon?"

"Oh yes. As I once told you, it is simply too much effort to be secretive and watch what one says every moment. I don't think it shocked Adam *too* much. He is fairly openminded, for a banker."

Harp registered her use of the banker's first name, but showed no reaction to it.

"He is going to tell me what he has found out so far," Louise said. "Over an early lunch at the hotel, together with his sister."

"His sister?"

"Adam thinks she may want to invest some of her own money in a partnership with me. She is a widow now, and Adam feels she is beginning to find time hanging heavy."

"Does *she* know about you and Gibbon?"

Louise gave Harp a small, slightly conspiratorial smile. "I doubt if Adam has had the nerve to tell her. I gather she is a rather conventional sort. That is part of the reason for this luncheon. I want a chance to sound her out, and see if I can relax with her. An extra investor would be useful, but I *can* manage to open the boutique on my own."

Harp told her then about the offer Leland had gotten from Collis Huntington.

Louise nodded approval. "With an additional fifteen thousand dollars in my bank I can really afford to be choosy about taking on a partner. Thank Leland for me."

She had gotten to know Leland when Harp had brought him along to her second supper gathering. The two of them had spent much of the evening in conversation; so at ease with each other that Harp had experienced a pang of jealousy.

"It's possible we could have gotten a better offer elsewhere," he told Louise. "But Leland felt safer with Huntington, and I agreed."

"I trust Leland's judgment," Louise said. "How is his health lately?"

"Not good," Harp said, and looked out the carriage window.

They were approaching Madison Square—which was gradually taking New York's carriage trade away from Union Square seven blocks south. Another example of the city's inexorable march northward.

Only some fifty years earlier it had been a Potter's Field, a desolate hinterland where New York deposited the corpses of people who had nobody who cared or could afford to give them a decent burial. Now it was a pretty park, where stylish people strolled and where expensively dressed children played under the watchful eyes of nursemaids, building snowmen and pelting Admiral Farragut's statue with snowballs.

Around the square the homes of the wealthy were being taken over by luxury businesses as the wealthy moved their families further north. Even the Delmonico brothers were talking about shifting their famous restaurant uptown from Union Square to Madison Square. A number of other top restaurants were already there. Along with fashionable shops, theaters and gentlemen's clubs.

And the hotels—of which the six-floor Fifth Avenue Hotel, with its white marble facade and opulent interiors, was considered the city's very best.

Harp escorted Louise into it—out of gentlemanly courtesy, not unmixed with curiosity. They crossed the imposing lobby and rose above it, in one of the new water-powered elevators, to a lavishly decorated hallway. Passing a vast dining room that the hotel boasted could seat three hundred at the same time, they reached the wide, crimson-curtained entrance to the ladies drawing room.

Adam Kershaw was waiting for Louise there, seated with his sister on a sofa of plush and gilt.

Kershaw looked young for a banker: not more than forty, though he tried to add a bit to that age with a respectable set of Galway whiskers. His sister was much as Louise had anticipated: straitlaced and tight-lipped.

Kershaw introduced Louise to his sister; and Louise introduced Harp to both of them. The way the sister's eyes crawled over Louise told Harp a number of things. That Kershaw was either a bachelor or a widower. That she considered her brother to be both extremely eligible and dangerously vulnerable. And that she intended to protect him by taking the measure of any woman she suspected him of being interested in.

Louise's banker gave Harp a polite smile and a firm handshake. But when he asked, as good manners dictated, if Harp cared to join them for lunch, there was restraint in the invitation. His smile became warmer when Harp declined.

Leaving the hotel, it occurred to Harp that Louise had not, during their carriage ride, mentioned again the possibility of his coming to her home for a supper for two. In a way it was a relief. But it was also worrying.

That afternoon, after eating at Gallat's Oyster & Lunch Room on Union Square, and resisting a recurring impulse to drink too much, he returned to the Suze la Rousse to check again for messages.

There was an envelope for him that had been delivered by messenger. Inside was a short note, in handwriting he recognized from Olivia Walburton's literary diary:

Vicky has sent me a telegram asking me to see you. She has given me certain assurances, and she is one person in whom I know that I can place my entire trust. I am at Number 26 Monroe Place, in Brooklyn City.

It was signed *Olivia Bixby Walburton.*

Thirty-Four

This was the year they had begun to construct a bridge across the East River between New York City and Brooklyn City. There was talk of someday connecting the two cities via a tunnel underneath the river; but most New Yorkers treated that notion as a joke, saying it might serve a purpose for people who had to go to Brooklyn but wouldn't want to be seen doing so. The only way across was still the ferryboat. Harp boarded one at the foot of Wall Street. It took longer than normal to reach its Montague Street terminal in Brooklyn, because it had to keep dodging big blocks of ice swept along on the river's powerful winter currents.

Brooklyn's thriving commerce and industries echoed New York's. Its waterfront had as dense a concentration of ships, docks and warehouses. Its population was nearing three hundred thousand people. Some of them had been drawn there by the claim that the air was better for one's health in Brooklyn than in New York. But most had come for the practical reason that Brooklyn was not yet as overcrowded as lower Manhattan; decent houses and rooms cost less. The neighborhood Harp entered as he walked away from the ferry terminal was basically middle-class residential.

Monroe Place was a long, pretty block lined on both sides with three-floor row houses, most of them dating back to the 1830s. The Church of the Restoration rose at one end of the block, and the Church of the Savior at the other end. The address she'd given him was halfway between the two churches. The house had a somewhat neglected appearance. Its entrance door and the wood framing its first-floor bay window needed paint. The iron fence around a small stone yard outside its basement floor and the ornamental wrought-iron railings mounting its front stoop were rusty. One of the twin ironwork basket urns topping the stone pedestals at the foot of the stoop had been bent askew.

There was a husky man in his fifties shoveling snow from the front steps. He had steel-rimmed pince-nez eyeglasses clamped to the bridge of his hawklike nose, and wore a fur hat and gloves with an aging plaid overcoat. Watching him carry a shovel full of snow from the bottom step across the pavement to the street, Harp realized he knew him.

The Reverend Stephen Clay. The last time Harp had seen him, Reverend Clay had just been booted out of his job of running the Christian Ladies' Moral Reform Mission to the Poor, in the old Five Points district. The charitable ladies who funded the mission had fired him after discovering that he was spending more of his time teaching semi-skilled trades to the poor than in saving their souls by preaching the Gospel and warning them of hellfire. In addition, the ladies had been horrified to learn that he'd been providing refuge for homeless and penniless women known to have been streetwalkers.

Reverend Clay was coming back to the stoop for more snow when he saw Harp. He stopped and smiled, took off a glove and held out his hand. "What on earth are *you* doing here?"

"I was about to ask you the same question," Harp countered as they shook hands.

"Me? I've been hired to help Miss Bixby manage the place." Reverend Clay gestured at the house. "And its inmates. Not many of those as yet. We're just getting started. Still in the process of fixing it up."

"Fixing *what* up?"

"Well, don't shout it in the street. And we're not going to put up a sign outside. Don't want to alarm the neighbors before they catch on and start complaining. But what we have here will be a refuge and training school for young women who have fallen from the virtuous path. In other words, whores—those who want to get themselves out of that profession."

"You've finally found yourself another mission," Harp said.

The reverend laughed. "Yes, another. But with a difference. Oh, I may preach at them a bit. Can't help doing that. My nature and training. But more important, we'll give them a place to rest and think things out in peace, without the pressure of need. We'll give them a bed and meals—and when and if they are ready for it, Miss Bixby will teach them to operate the latest types of sewing machines."

"She's a sewing-machine expert?"

"Oh yes, she took instruction on the different makes while in England. The point is, most of these unfortunate women have already tried needlework, and found they couldn't get by on the little more than three dollars a week that pays. But with the ready-made clothing business growing so fast, a woman who can operate sewing machines with the latest improvements earns two dollars a day. That adds up to twelve dollars a week—and a frugal person can live decently on that. Also—"

Reverend Clay interrupted himself and gave Harp an uneasy look. "I have a feeling I've been preaching at you."

Harp smiled at him. "Just a little. How did you and Miss Bixby get together on this idea?"

"It's her idea. She spoke about it to Victoria Woodhull, who then introduced us to each other. We found that we were made for each other, in a manner of speaking. And now, what *are* you doing here?"

"Came to see Miss Bixby on a private matter," Harp said. "Is she around?"

"Inside the house," Reverend Clay said, and he opened the front door for Harp, "sprucing things up. There's so much still to be done. But she is a dedicated worker."

"Mind if I tell her you're a friend of mine, in case I need it to help break the ice?"

"Go ahead. Just so long as you don't claim I think you are a saint."

"What *do* you think I am, Reverend?"

"A genie who toys too often with the powers of darkness."

He didn't have to go far inside the house to find her. The vestibule opened into a large front room with an uncarpeted, freshly sanded floor. It was unfurnished except for five brand-new sewing machines of different makes, their manufacturers' names brightly displayed: Isaac Singer, Wheeler & Wilson, Bartlett & Demorest,

Weed, Grover & Baker. The machines had been pushed together
in the middle of the room, and three young women were at work
putting up wallpaper full of flowers in cheerful orange, green and
yellow colors.

One of them, with a nicely rounded figure under a dark gray
housedress stained by paint and wallpaper paste, stood on a ladder
doing an amateurish but adequate job of adding a strip to a place
that had been missed just below the ceiling. Her hair was tucked
up out of sight under a head scarf; but her eyebrows were dark
and her face was the one in the picture Walburton had given to
Howe & Hummel.

Harp knew one of the other two: Celia Jane Touhy, a Water
Street cruiser of about twenty, with old age starting to wrinkle a
still pretty face. The other was a thin girl of about sixteen with a
pale face scarred by smallpox.

They looked in Harp's direction when he shut the vestibule
door and stepped into the front room. Celia Jane let out a whoop
of laughter. "Hey, if it ain't old Harp! What'cha doing, come to
see what the lost sisterhood looks like working our hands to the
bone, 'stead of our fannies?"

"Come to see the boss," he told her, and watched Olivia Bixby
Walburton come down off the ladder and turn to study him.
There was a smear of dried plaster on her plump right cheek, and
paint stains on her hands. One thumb was bandaged. Her lips had
the voluptuous look he'd seen in her photograph, and her dark
eyes were still shy—but no longer unsure. They met his gaze with a
determined steadiness.

"You are the one Vicky wired me about?"

"I'm the one," Harp said. "Is there some place we could talk in
private for a while?"

"Of course." She looked to the other two and said, "Please
keep at it, as best you can. I'll be back to help soon." Then she led
Harp through a bare hallway and into a large dining kitchen.

There was a big pot of coffee keeping hot on the stove. She
gestured at it after inviting him to take a chair at a long table
covered with green oilcloth. "May I serve you a cup?"

"Yes, thank you."

She filled two cups, brought them to the table and sat in a chair
facing him. She took a small sip, made a face and put her cup back

down. "Too hot. Better wait a bit and allow it to cool." And then: "What is it you wish to speak to me about, Mr. Harp?"

"Vicky didn't let you know?"

"Her telegram asked me to contact you immediately. She said it was important that I talk with you. She also said that you are in contact with my husband. But that I could place the same confidence in you that I have in her. That is all." Her eyes continued to meet his, but he could see it was something that still required an effort of will on her part. "Was it my husband who asked you to speak to me?"

"He wants me to find you."

Her chin came up a bit and her plump lips tightened. "And you have found me."

"That's something he's not going to know unless you want him to," Harp told her. "And it's not what I'm here for."

He put the photograph of Alice Curry-Olcott on the oilcloth in front of her. "Do you know her?"

She looked at the picture, then flinched and looked away. The gaping wound in the dead woman's throat was all too evident.

"I'm sorry," Olivia Walburton said. "I'm afraid I am still much too squeamish."

"You'll have to get over that if you're going to run a mission for prostitutes."

"I know . . ." She made herself look at the picture again, forced herself to study it closely. "No. I don't know her."

"Her name was Alice Curry," Harp said.

She thought about that, then shook her head. "You say the name as though you expect it to mean something to me. But it doesn't."

"It's a name that's been prominently featured in all the newspapers this week."

"I have not had time to read newspapers lately. I'm much too busy trying to launch this mission. From the moment I wake up to the moment I fall into bed exhausted each night."

Harp tapped the photograph. "You may have known her under the name of Olcott. Alice Olcott."

She looked quickly at the photograph. Started to flinch again but stopped herself. She was still looking at it when she spoke again. "She had such hopes . . ." Her voice held a deep sadness.

"I can't blame myself for not recognizing her. I only met her twice and she was nothing like this . . . How in God's name could such a horrible thing happen to her?"

"I'm trying to find out. *That's* why I'm here."

"I don't see how I could help you with that."

"You knew her," Harp said. "I haven't found many people who did. Or who'll admit they did."

"How did you find out I knew her?" Olivia Walburton asked.

"She was wearing a gown and petticoats with your name sewed in them when she died. Your husband was asked to identify her corpse but he told the police he didn't know her."

"Of course he didn't. Poor Vance."

"You're quite sure he didn't know her."

She looked at him with a puzzled frown. "I've no reason to believe he did. Why do you ask that?"

"A stray thought . . . You're not surprised that she had some of your clothes."

"No. I gave them to her."

Which meant there'd been some sort of real relationship between the two women. Harp put that on hold for the moment. "She died in a warehouse owned by Monmouth Fuller," he said. "Do you know him?"

"By reputation. I've never met him and wouldn't care to. A thoroughly unpleasant person, from all I have heard about him. Are you telling me that Alice had a . . . a relationship with him?"

"I think so. She never mentioned him to you?"

"No." She gave it some thought. "I'm certain she didn't. I would remember if she had. I would have warned her against having anything to do with a man like that."

"Tell me whatever you know about her. In any way it comes to you."

She tried another sip from her cup, and nodded at his. "It is cool enough now."

Harp drank some of his coffee and waited for her to speak again.

"I actually know so very little about her," Olivia Walburton told him. "Both times we met were by chance, and the first was so

brief. It was at the theater. One of Joseph Jefferson's performances in *Rip Van Winkle*. Mr. Jefferson has played that role so
often, and I know people who have seen the play twice or even
three times. But I never had. My husband is not fond of stage plays
but I had heard so much about Mr. Jefferson's performance that I
finally insisted. Rather angrily in the end, I'm afraid. And Vance at
last agreed to buy the tickets and take me."

"When was this?" Harp asked her.

"Less than three months ago. Not long before I went to England."

That placed it at about a couple of weeks after Alice Olcott had
quit the parlorhouse of Emma Wells.

"I was in the theater's ladies room during intermission when
Alice came in," Olivia Walburton said. "She sat down next to me
and began to touch up her makeup. The makeup caused me to
suspect she might be some kind of courtesan. But she smiled at
me in the looking-glass, and it was such a nice smile that I smiled
back and we spoke to each other. And once we did, I realized she
was a person of good education and background. Which made me
wonder if my guess about the sort of woman she was had been
correct."

"What did you speak about?"

"Mr. Jefferson's acting in the role of Rip Van Winkle. We agreed
he was marvelous and deserved his reputation as one of our best
actors. Perhaps the very best."

"Nothing else?"

"That was all we had time for. An attendant was going along the
corridor outside ringing the bell for the next act. We wished each
other well and parted to return to our seats."

"Did you see her in the audience or when the play ended? See
who she was with?"

"No. But I met her again less than a week later, and again by
chance. I was buying a scarf at the Lord & Taylor drygoods shop
on Broadway and Twentieth, and I saw her there as I was paying
for my purchase. We recognized each other—and somehow it was
as though we were old friends. She told me she wasn't actually
there to buy anything. Just looking and longing, as she put it.
Because she was temporarily low on funds—a situation she anticipated improving in the near future."

"How?" Harp asked.

"She didn't say—not while we were in the store. We talked again about Mr. Jefferson's performance as we went out together, and I found her to be such pleasant, intelligent company that I asked if I could treat her in Bond's ice cream parlor on the same block. Alice said she would be delighted. That Bond's was one of her favorites but she'd had to be too frugal lately, with the little money she had left, to patronize it. And she said she would be pleased to invite me, in turn, when her finances did improve.

"But then she hesitated. I remember how seriously she looked at me for a moment. Before looking away and saying it might not be good for my reputation to be seen with her. I asked what on earth she meant. Though of course I understood, then, that my first suspicion about her had been correct. She still couldn't look at me when she told me—that she had only recently broken away from an impure means of earning her living."

Olivia Walburton looked again at the photograph that showed, so brutally, how the woman she was talking about had ended her life. "I felt so sorry for her. She was so horribly embarrassed. At the same time I felt tremendously flattered that she had confided in me about what was obviously very painful for her. Perhaps that was a contributing factor to my organizing this place. Though I think the idea had been developing in me for a long time . . ."

She covered the photograph with her hand. As if that were the only way she could stop herself from looking at it. "Well. I insisted, and she did join me in the ice cream parlor. After we exchanged names she told me how much she had admired the gown I'd worn to the theater. A green velvet gown that I had never worn before. She said she had an offer to go on the stage and that if she was lucky and proved to have talent she would one day be able to afford to buy clothes that fine."

"Did she mention the name of the theater?" Harp asked. "Or its owner?"

"No, she didn't. And I didn't think of asking."

Harp held the disappointment in check and said, "Go on."

"It was a pleasant day out, and Alice said she lived only a few blocks away, so after we left Bond's I walked her there. It was a roominghouse of the better sort. We parted there and I took a cab home."

She was about to say more but Harp interrupted: "I'd like the address of her roominghouse."

"It is on the north side of West Twentieth Street. I don't recall the number, but is only one door from the house on the northeast corner of Seventh Avenue. I went back there the next afternoon. With the gown she'd admired, and some of my best petticoats, ones I hadn't worn yet. I was already making plans to go away and I didn't intend to take many things with me. It felt good to give some to a woman who could appreciate but couldn't afford them."

"You said you only met her twice," Harp mentioned. "That makes a third time."

"Alice wasn't there that afternoon. I left the gown and petticoats with the landlady, to give to Alice when she returned. The next day I received a grateful note from her saying she looked forward to one day being able to do as much for me. I boarded a steamer for England not long after that."

"And you never saw Alice Olcott, or heard from her, again."

"Never." Olivia Walburton looked down at her hand, still covering the photograph. Without uncovering it, she pushed it back across the oilcloth to Harp. "Please take this away with you. I don't wish to look at it again."

Thirty-Five

He was getting up to leave when Olivia Walburton suddenly asked, "How is my husband?"

"Worried about you," Harp told her. "Afraid you're in trouble."

"Please tell him that I am not. That I am involved in doing something useful and needful, and that I feel good for doing it. Tell him there is no reason for him to worry about me."

"He'll want to know how I know that," Harp pointed out. "And that'll lead to his insisting that I tell him where you are."

"I don't want him to know. I am not ready to see him again, not yet. Not until what we have started here is fully established and I am more sure of myself and what I am doing. Please do not tell him anything except that I am perfectly all right."

He could imagine Vance Walburton's reaction to that. A violent protest to Howe & Hummel; accompanied by a threat to sue the firm for Harp's refusal to disclose what he'd paid good money to find out.

Olivia Walburton was studying him with some anxiety. "You did promise you wouldn't tell Vance where I am," she reminded him. "Vicky assured me you would keep that promise."

"Don't worry," Harp told her, "I will keep it."

But that didn't rule out, Harp decided, giving Walburton her literary diary to read. The man was entitled to a chance to adjust his thinking, if he could, to the fact that he was not married to a Victorian doll.

"Thank you," Olivia Walburton said. "It's not that I no longer care for my husband. I do. But I don't know if I can ever live with him again. In a way, that will depend on Vance. When the time comes for me to invite him to come see me. On how he reacts to what I am doing here."

"Running a house for whores."

She blinked, and her face started to flush. But she controlled it and after several seconds said, "That is one way to describe it. I am afraid that will be all that Vance will see in it. But it is far from describing all we hope to accomplish here. Or I would not have invested so much of my money into obtaining this house."

"You're not renting it, then."

"No. Reverend Clay—he's my partner in this project—advised that I had better buy the house outright. He said if we rented, the owners would take us to court and get us evicted, once what we are using the house for became known."

"He gave you good advice," Harp told her. "I know Reverend Clay. And the problems he's had with other projects he's tried to start in the past."

"I know about those, too," Olivia Walburton said. "He was very frank about them."

"I ran into him outside," Harp said. "He told me this one was entirely your idea."

"That's so, though I depend very much on his greater experience. I got the basic idea after attending a lecture by Charles Brace at the Children's Aid Society. About a lodging house he opened for homeless street girls. Do you know of it?"

Harp nodded.

"Did you know that he finally came to a decision not to accept any of what he called 'polluted souls' into his shelter?"

"He's a good man who's done good work," Harp said. "But he's not like our Reverend Clay. For Brace, religious and moral instruction come first. And he got scared. Afraid if he let in fallen women, they might corrupt the morals of the other girls. The ones who were, as he put it, still trembling on the line between purity and vice."

"Exactly. And that's why I decided to open a place like this. Just for the sort of girls and women he rejected. This way, there are no other kind here for them to corrupt."

"Except for you," Harp said.

Olivia Bixby Walburton smiled for the first time, shaking her head. "I don't believe my moral fiber is vulnerable to that sort of discomposure." And added, "Sometimes I almost wish it were . . ."

The sun was setting when Harp returned to Manhattan and reached West Sixteenth Street. The attached houses forming the north side of the street between Sixth and Seventh avenues looked like vertical slices of French Gothic flamboyance. Mullioned stained-glass windows on the ground floor. Small second-floor balconies with decorative balustrades of stone tracery. Pointed-arch third-floor windows. Thin turrets rising on either side of steep-sloped attic roofs. The ornamented facades had become dingy from New York's coal-smoke pollution, but otherwise all of the houses remained in fairly good condition. Including the rooming house Alice Curry-Olcott had moved into after quitting Emma Wells.

The landlady there told Harp that Alice Olcott had been a tenant for over two and a half months—but that she hadn't seen her in almost a week and was beginning to worry because her weekly rent was due the next day.

Other than that, the landlady proved to be another disappointment. Alice Olcott had told the landlady that she was employed by a theater; but had never said which theater, nor in what capacity. No, she had never had any visitors. Except for a very nice lady who'd come by, shortly after Miss Olcott had moved in, to leave a ballgown and petticoats for her. Miss Olcott had certainly never had any gentlemen callers: the landlady didn't permit that. And no, she'd never seen any man waiting outside to escort Miss Olcott to the theater or wherever. Miss Olcott had sometimes received telegrams or letters brought by messenger—but the landlady had of course never read any of them and so had no idea who or where they'd come from, except that they'd all been sent from inside New York.

For three dollars extra—on top of the two Harp had given her to answer his questions—the landlady allowed him inside Alice Olcott's room; though she stayed in the open doorway watching while he looked around. Clothing, toiletries and other articles belonging to the room's tenant were still there; which told him she hadn't made a stealthy move to someplace else before her death.

But there was nothing in the room that added anything to what Harp already knew.

It was dark out when he left, but Willem Jacobs often worked late at night, especially when he had illicit jobs to complete. Harp took a Sixth Avenue horsecar downtown and went to the cubbyhole workshop in Nassau Street.

Jacobs was there. He hadn't finished cutting and polishing all the copies of the rubies in Louise's choker, but he had estimated the value of the real stones.

"You should be able to sell them to a gem buyer for at least eight thousand dollars," he told Harp. "Maybe even nine thousand if you drive a hard bargain."

"Fine," Harp said. "When'll they be ready?"

"Gem cutting is not like carving a chicken. It is a fine art, and a gem cutter who hurries the job does it badly. You want the copies to be exactly the same as the genuine rubies, so why do you sound so impatient this time?"

"No reason," Harp admitted. "I'm just feeling irritable, about something else."

"So don't rush me. Come back in three or four days. I should have the last ones copied by then."

Harp left him to his work and went back uptown to the back of the Van Tromp house on Washington Square. Leland had good news for him. Collis Huntington had agreed that Louise's railroad tip was worth the full amount he'd promised. He had given Leland his check, and Leland had already deposited it in the bank. They could divide up the money as soon as the check cleared. Which it surely would in the next few days.

They celebrated by going to a late, leisurely and ridiculously expensive supper at Delmonico's. Harp kept his drinking under restraint. Leland did not. It was after one A.M. when Harp helped him into a cab, accompanied him to the mews behind his house and took him inside his rooms there. By the time he got Leland out of his coat, hat and boots and deposited him in the big easy chair he used instead of a bed, Leland was already falling asleep.

Harp spread fresh coals on the fire in the heating stove and doused the lamp before letting himself out and locking the door from outside with a key Leland had given him some time ago.

* * *

It was raining when he walked across Washington Square in the direction of his Greene Street apartment. The raindrops were tiny, but the ones striking his face felt like bits of ice. Winter had definitely settled in to stay awhile.

The Suze la Rousse had closed for the night, so he would have to wait until next morning to find out if there'd been any more messages for him. He used the back way into his apartment. His hat and coat dripped rainwater on the carpet as he lit the lamp on the front-room table. He took them off and hung them to dry inside the entry.

He was walking back, past the front-room lamp, when the lower pane of his front window shattered and something burned the back of his neck before thudding into the wall.

There were two more gunshots as Harp dropped to the floor.

Staying flat down, he felt the back of his neck and brought his hand away with a single small drop of blood on it. The bullet had scraped away some skin, no worse than that. Shards of glass and shreds of lace curtain lay scattered across the floor. Harp regarded the height of the three bullet holes in the opposite wall. They had been fired from approximately the same level, across the street, as his broken window.

Possibly from the roof there, but Harp doubted that. Not with the cold and rain outside. The shooter must have waited a long time for him to come home. Much more likely was the third-floor room facing his apartment. That had been empty and for rent the last couple of weeks.

Harp did not raise his head to see if the window of that room was open. Nor did he reach up to extinguish the lamp on his table. The shooter was probably still waiting: watching for any sign of life from Harp. Harp figured as long as he kept down well below the level of his windowsill he couldn't be seen from over there. After a time the shooter could persuade himself that the first shots might have done the job. But he wouldn't stay put over there for too long.

Harp crawled to the entry and got the Le Mat revolver from his coat. Crawled back across the front room and did not stand until he reached the rear of his apartment. Moving faster now, he went through the two closets, into the next building and ran down the back stairs to the alley. The cold rain had not let up. He circled around his block and the one across the street to reach the alley behind the houses over there without being seen by the shooter.

An iron fire-escape ladder led up the rear wall of the house the shots had come from. The window at the top was wide open. That could mean the shooter was already gone. But Harp kept his gun ready and his attention sharp when he climbed inside and felt his way along a short dark corridor. The door he wanted was ajar. Light from a Greene Street gas lamp came through the partly opened front window into the room behind that door.

There was nothing in the room but the lingering fumes of burnt gunpowder.

Harp wiped rain from his face and hair, went out the way he had come in and hurried back to his apartment. People living nearby would have been awakened by the shots. Hilda Shaler, with her room on the floor just below the one the shots were fired from, certainly would have. Hilda wouldn't go running to the police. But others would. Harp's last interview with the police was enough to last him for some time to come.

Rain was coming into his front room through the broken pane. He tacked a blanket across the inside of the window to stop that and to prevent the breakage from being noticed from below or across the street. He put on his hat and coat, put out his lamp, used his rear exit from the apartment and walked back through the rain to Washington Square.

Leland was still sound asleep in his easy chair. He did have a bed—for the rare overnight guest. Harp climbed into it after hanging up his wet clothes and toweling himself dry. It took time and effort, but he finally got his brain turned off and sank into sleep.

Thirty-Six

Harp woke next morning to the smell of perking coffee. He got dressed and found Leland seated at the kitchen table, hunched over a coffee cup cradled between his trembling hands. He tried to nod at Harp, but the nod made him wince with pain and he gave up on it. There was no point in trying to talk with Leland when he had that bad a hangover. Harp poured himself a cup of coffee and drank it in silence. Then he touched Leland's shoulder in farewell and went out into the cold.

It was no longer raining, but icicles hung from porch roofs and some tree branches in Washington Square were bowed almost to the ground by the weight of additional ice that had formed on them during the night. Harp bought two morning papers from a newsstand on the south side of the square and carried them with him to the Suze la Rousse.

Billy Doyle was huddled in the doorway next to the restaurant, his nose, cheeks and ears an angry red from the frosty air. Harp asked if he had a message for him. Billy said he didn't, he was just hanging around to make sure he didn't miss the chance to earn a little if any did come.

Harp took him into the restaurant and asked Madame Letessier if her husband could possibly come up with bacon and eggs this early in the day. For Harp, she said, they would stretch the rules a bit. But he was not to tell people about this. She didn't want others to start demanding anything other than the habitual coffee and pastry for breakfast.

Harp shared eight eggs and a heaping plate of crisp bacon with Billy. Plus coffee and a stack of rolls with butter and jam. When they'd finished, Harp gave the boy four dollars and a key to his apartment and told him to take the glazier from down the street upstairs to replace his broken windowpane. He said Billy could keep whatever was left from the four dollars, after the glazier's charges, in exchange for cleaning up the mess the broken window had left on his front-room floor. After Billy left, Harp ordered another cup of coffee and looked through his morning papers.

There was nothing new on the investigations into the murders of Alice Curry and Moses Saul. But there was something else in one of them, the *Herald*, that instantly grabbed his full attention.

A *Herald* reporter returning to New York from Boston had gotten lucky and recognized Tennessee Claflin—the notorious sister of the notorious Victoria Woodhull—among the passengers on the same train late the previous afternoon. In the article the reporter wrote that in spite of her reputation he had to confess to finding her not only extremely pretty but also sweet and unassuming and, unlike her elder sister, entirely feminine, with no masculine leanings at all.

He'd asked if he might interview her and she had replied, most graciously, "Sure, why not?"

What had she been doing in ultra-conservative Boston?

"I was helping my sister make arrangements for a lecture she's due to give there," Tennessee had told him. "I would do anything for Vicky. She's a wonderful sister and the best thing in my life and I just adore her. Though I can't say I adore most of those phony intellectuals that hang around her all the time. And they don't think much of me, either. When I decided to come home to get away from them, they were just as glad to see the back of me."

Why did she think they didn't like her?

Tennessee: "They think I'm a dummy. I'm nearly twenty-six years old and yet they treat me as if I were a child of five who doesn't understand serious matters. But I do. After all, I did help Vicky run a financial brokerage. So I can't be such a dummy."

Did she feel, then, that she held financial opinions that practical men of business should take seriously?

She had laughed, the reporter recorded, and had answered: "I have at least one financial opinion, and that is that gold is cash, and that to have plenty of it is to be pretty nearly independent of everything and everybody. Even that most terrible personage, public opinion."

How did she feel about much of society's public opinion of her?

"Were I to notice what is said by what they call society," Tennessee had answered, "I would be afraid to ever leave my house. But I despise what squeamy, crying girls and powdered dandies say of me."

There was more of the same in the article. All of her replies very much in character for the Tennie Claflin that Harp knew so well. She got a kick out of saying things calculated to upset or confuse people who had preconceived ideas about her.

The important thing was that she was back in town.

The odds were against her knowing anything that could help him. But at this point he was running out of other people who could or would.

There was a big advertising handbill, dating back to when Tennessee Claflin had been about ten years old, and now brown-spotted with age, framed in gilt in the roomy antechamber to her part of the house:

MISS TENNESSEE
THE WONDERFUL CHILD
has established a
MAGNETIC INFIRMARY
at No. 265 Wabash Avenue
Chicago, Ill.

Tennessee turned from closing the door she'd opened to let Harp in, and saw him looking at it.

"For a kid," she said with a nostalgic smile, "that was a darned exciting time. And not just the cure business. I told such wonderful things as a child, my father could make fifty to a hundred dollars a day simply by letting folks see and listen to his strange, clairvoyant daughter."

Though it was almost noon she was indulging in a lazy period after her trip with no intention of going out soon. Her hair hung in careless ringlets, and she didn't appear to be wearing much underneath her thin Mother Hubbard. A visual impression confirmed by the press of her body against Harp's when she hugged and kissed him. Tennessee didn't like the restriction of corsets; and she didn't need the bosom-and-behind bolsters many women used.

When he gave her buttocks a friendly pat, she drew back a step and looked up at him with a mocking glint in her gray-blue eyes. "If it's love you've come for, I'm sorry to say you've picked the wrong time. I've got my curse."

"I'm here about a professional problem," Harp told her. "Hoping you can help me with it."

"Sure. You tell me your problem and I'll try my best. But let's have a drink first. I was just going to get myself a nip of gin when you knocked."

"It's a little early in the day for me."

"Oh, come on, Harp. You don't want to let a girl drink all by her lonesome."

"Okay," he said, "but just a short one. I've been trying to taper off."

"Good boy. Make yourself comfortable while I dig the bottle out've where I hid it."

"You hide your liquor these days?"

"On account of Vicky," Tennessee told him. "You know she never drinks the hard stuff. And she's begun to act upset every time she sees me reach for a drink."

"You can't blame her," Harp said. "She's got some scary examples right here at home."

"Yeah, our besotted mother and poor Dr. Woodhull. I don't blame Vicky and I don't want to worry her. But taking a drink now and again won't make me like them."

Harp watched her saunter off into her other rooms, her fulsome curves moving pleasantly. When she was gone from sight he sat down in one of the overstuffed armchairs around a table covered by a Turkish rug. Tennessee's antechamber was a nest of satin, silk and brocade, the predominant colors dark red and deep purple. It often reminded Harp of rooms in a better-class brothel. Tennessee had never gotten any lessons in moderation. Or wanted them.

She returned carrying two small glasses of gin. After putting them on the table she went to lock the door to her quarters. "Mother sometimes busts in without knocking," she explained. "I don't want her catching me drinking and threatening to tell Vicky unless I give her and Pop more money. We already give them more than enough but they always want more. I can't stand it sometimes, the way they don't want to do anything but be dead weights on us."

"Your father wasn't such a dead weight when he managed to put you and Vicky together with Commodore Vanderbilt," Harp reminded her. "Without that you two wouldn't have done so well in New York."

"Yeah, I know. I don't forget we owe him for that." Her frown ended with a sudden giggle. "Vanderbilt—now there's one funny fellow. Thought he was gonna die soon because he kept falling asleep in the daytime." Tennessee giggled again. "I used to slap him on the back and yell, 'Wake up, old boy!' in his ear. He liked that. Had enough people treating him like he was God Almighty."

She settled into an armchair facing Harp across the table and raised her glass. "Well, here's looking at you."

"And you." Harp touched his glass to hers and they drank. He took only a sip. He'd never cared that much for gin.

Tennessee put her glass down half-empty and said, "Now, what's your problem?"

"Do you know anything about a woman named Alice Curry?"

"Sure, she's been in all the papers, even up in Boston. And Vicky told me you're hunting for her murderer."

"That's all you know? What was in the papers and what Vicky told you?"

"Never heard of her before that."

"What about Alice Olcott?" Harp asked. "Ever heard of her?"

"Nope . . . You're interested in *two* women, both named Alice?"

"They're the same woman."

"One's her maiden name, the other her married one?"

"She was never married as far as I know," Harp said. "Olcott was her real name. Curry was an alias she used when she became a prostitute. But you're sure you didn't know her under either name."

He watched Tennessee's expression for any hint of holding something back but saw nothing to suggest it.

"I hate to disappoint you," she said. "But I can't tell you what I don't know."

Harp put the morgue picture of Alice Curry-Olcott down in front of Tennessee.

She looked at it and grimaced. "That's her, eh? Your two Alices."

"That's her. Ever seen her before? Under any name, or no name."

"No." But she went on looking at the picture. For so long that Harp finally asked her, "What is it?"

"I don't know," Tennessee whispered, frowning.

She covered the picture with her hand. Much as Olivia Walburton had. But not for the same reason. Not to hide it from her sight. Tennessee was trying to absorb something from it.

Harp watched her eyes close as she rested her palm on the photograph. He didn't believe or disbelieve in what spiritualists called psychometry: the ability to find out things about the dead by touching their picture or something that had belonged to them. It didn't matter whether he believed or not. The important thing was what it stirred out of Tennessee, wherever she got it from.

Tears began to leak from her closed eyelids and run down her cheeks.

"What's the matter?" Harp asked her.

"I don't know," she said again in that same hushed voice.

She opened her eyes and stood up. "Wait a minute," she said, and went off into another room.

When she came back she was carrying a short candle in a plain pewter holder, a small bowl with a lump of something inside it and an embossed silver matchbox. After putting them on the table she closed the window curtains, plunging the room into shadow, before sitting down. She hadn't wiped the tears from her cheeks. Harp watched her rearrange the candle and bowl: behind the picture of the dead Alice Curry-Olcott. She struck a match and lit the candle, then set fire to the lump inside the bowl.

Smoke rose from the bowl, and its sharp odor told Harp the lump was incense. Tennessee looked again at the morgue photograph; then again placed her hand on it and leaned back in her armchair, gazing at the candle flame through the incense smoke.

Her eyes didn't close again. They remained open, fixed on the smoke and the flame.

Tennessee never went in for the long rigmarole and elaborate hocus-pocus of some other mediums whose seances Harp had witnessed. Her approach was as direct and uncomplicated as picking up a pencil. Sometimes she came through with what a questioner wanted, and sometimes she couldn't. Whether it was deception, self-deception or supernatural probing, when it worked her results could be startling.

Harp watched her and waited. She appeared to be waiting, too. He saw a deep groove form in her normally smooth forehead and was careful not to break the silence.

Tennessee spoke again, her voice muted: "I think it's her I see . . . but I can't seem to establish communication . . ."

Harp kept his own voice low: "Is there a man with her, or near her?"

"No . . . only her."

"Who killed her?"

Another silence from Tennessee, her eyes fixed on the wavering flame of the candle seen through the smoke. Then: "I can't . . . she . . . I can't hear her . . . or it may be that she doesn't know the answer . . ."

That was possible. The murdered woman had been knocked out from behind. A blow across the back of her head before her throat was cut.

"How did she get into the warehouse?" Harp asked.

After some moments Tennessee said, "A key . . . I see a key turning . . ."

"Is she the one using it or someone else?"

"I don't know . . . I only see the key."

"Is she alone? Is someone waiting inside for her?"

"I can't see anyone else. Only her . . . and a door opening . . . she's inside now . . ."

"Where? What does the inside look like?"

"Only mist . . . she seems to be moving through a fog . . . there is a sound now . . . something behind her . . . oh, damn it! She's gone. I've lost her . . . no, *wait* . . ."

Tennessee's hand spasmed, closing around the photograph, crushing it inside her fist.

"There's a stage . . . a big stage, in a theater . . . girls in tights . . . singing and dancing . . ."

"Is she one of them?"

"No. She's not there . . ."

Perspiration was streaming down Tennessee's face now, mingling with fresh tears.

"I think I'm seeing what she sees . . . the girls on the stage . . . and I hear music . . . an orchestra playing . . ."

"Do you recognize the tune?"

"Some kind of marching music, I think . . . but the girls are dancing to it . . . singing to it . . ."

"Can you hear the words?"

"No, I can't . . . I *see* them singing but . . . wait—that's very strange . . . there's a *train* . . . crossing the stage on railroad tracks! A real one . . . big, with smoke pouring from its locomotive . . . but no one pays attention to it . . . the girls are still dancing and singing . . . with that train chugging past them off the stage . . . but I think another is coming, following it . . . no . . . nothing . . . nothing."

Tennessee's eyes closed. She shook her head vigorously back and forth, making her ringlets dance around her face, then used both hands to wipe the tears and sweat from her eyes and opened them.

She looked at Harp with a disparaging smile. "That's just plain silly," she said in her normal voice. "That train went right *through* those girls on the stage and they never even noticed it. Makes no sense at all."

"It does to me," Harp told her.

He didn't know where she'd gotten it from. Out of previous knowledge she'd kept from him—or from some region he had never explored.

But he did know the theater she had described.

Thirty-Seven

This was the first time Harp had been inside the place since the extravagant party Jim Fisk had thrown here when he and his business partner, Jay Gould, had bought it.

The Grand Opera House—a massive structure of cast iron and white marble shouldering around both sides of the northwest corner at Twenty-third Street and Eighth Avenue.

Its previous owner had gone broke trying to pull upper-crust audiences away from the Academy of Music with grand opera and symphony concerts. Jim Fisk had turned it into a success by serving the bourgeois public what it—and he—liked: light operas with lots of lightly clad girls.

That was one aspect of the Grand Opera House. The other was that its upper floors were the headquarters of Fisk and Gould's Erie Railroad. And its basement contained the steam-powered printing press on which they turned out the watered shares that had bilked so many suckers who'd invested in their railroad.

Entering the building through its theater lobby, Harp remembered exactly where he'd first seen Louise Vedder during Fisk's party.

Remembered, too, the numbing shock of realizing who she was.

There was a staircase leading up from the lobby to the theater's thirty-three private boxes. A journalist had dubbed it the most magnificent stairway in New York. Harp had been climbing those stairs, and Louise had been coming down escorted by John Gilbert, a stage star Harp knew. When Harp had come to a frozen halt, staring at her, Gilbert had been obliged to introduce them to each other.

This time Harp crossed the lobby without looking at the staircase and opened a door to the back of the theater's auditorium. Its sixteen hundred seats were empty, but some of the gas-fueled footlights illuminated the stage. A chorus line was rehearsing steps to the tune of a piano and violin while a choreographer shouted exasperated instructions and reprimands. It wasn't a martial number; but there was seldom a night at the Grand Opera House without one, with the chorus girls wearing elaborate military hats to top off their displays of leg and *décolletage*.

Jim Fisk loved martial music almost as much as he loved pretty girls.

He also like to watch rehearsals. Harp looked around but didn't see him there now. Walking halfway around the auditorium to a side door, he climbed a stairwell leading to the directors' section of the Erie Company headquarters.

The big, sumptuous vestibule at the top was flanked on one side by Jay Gould's business apartment, on the other side by Jim Fisk's. But it was Fisk's full-length portrait, alone, which hung facing the vestibule's main entrance. Gould was too shy to display himself in that way.

The portrait was an oil painting, with Fisk's florid moon face beaming and his superb mustache waxed to sharp points. He was dressed in a resplendent uniform he had designed for one of the two military titles he had assumed for himself. One was as admiral of a fleet belonging to the Narragansett Steamship Company—a subsidiary of the Erie Railroad. But in the painting he wore his army uniform: as colonel of a Union regiment he had equipped and uniformed at his own expense during the Civil War.

He had never actually gone to the war with his regiment, however, having too healthy a respect for his own life to endanger it unnecessarily.

Harp never blamed him for that decision. If you had the choice, that was the sensible one. And if you had the money, you did have a choice. In the North, you could escape the draft by either paying the government three hundred dollars or by hiring a needy man to go in your place. In the South, you were not required to serve if you owned thirty or more slaves.

There had been a song popular with combat troops on both sides: "It's a Rich Man's War, and a Poor Man's Battle."

There were rich men who, unlike Fisk, had fought and died in that war's battles. But in combat, as in peace, the rich were a tiny minority. Even General Lee had never been a wealthy man. And General Grant had been almost a pauper at the war's start.

Grant, it was true, had a peculiar personal problem about money. Hard-headed in war, he was a pushover when it came to other practical matters. Even now that he was president, none of the cash that Washington lobbyists distributed stuck to him. Money flowed over and under and around him; and wound up in the pockets of the sharpers he trusted.

Men like Jay Gould and Jim Fisk.

They made an effective working team. Gould, scrawny and cold-eyed, secretive and puritanical about sex, was a brilliant financial manipulator. Fisk was a cheerful fat man who enjoyed having fun and liked having others join in the fun: the jolly salesman and convivial con man.

Harp's business this day was not with Gould. Jay Gould had many interests beside the Erie Railroad: stock manipulations, cornering the gold market, gaining virtual control of America's telegraph system; speculating in real estate, coal mines, harbor leases; undercutting rival tycoons and snatching pieces of other railroad lines. Some of these ventures were shared with his partner. But he was not interested in the theatrical side of the Grand Opera House. That was Jim Fisk's expensive toy.

The pair of uniformed guards stationed at the entrance to Fisk's business apartment knew Harp and let him pass between them into a carpeted corridor. He went by a room where three book-keepers toiled over thick ledgers and pushed open the ground-glass door to the office of Fisk's private secretary, Jacob Applegate. Applegate, an elderly man with a dreamy expression, presided behind a low iron railing at a desk flanked by speaking tubes painted in different colors. Applegate and Harp had met during the war when the man had been a supply sergeant. It was Harp who had recommended him to Fisk.

"Is Jim inside?" Harp asked him.

"Naw, he's off to Washington for a couple days. Having a quiet pow-wow with Grant's treasury secretary."

There was a whistling noise from a green-painted speaking tube. Applegate blew into the tube and put it to his ear so that all that Harp could hear was faint whispering. Applegate transferred the tube from ear to mouth and spoke into it: "Tell him Mr. Fisk don't see nobody without an appointment. Tell him he's got to write a letter first so Mr. Fisk can fit him into his schedule."

Applegate hung up the tube, spat tobacco juice into an ornate bronze cuspidor and grinned at Harp. "Fisk ain't never gonna fit that one in. Feller wants to know what's happening with the money he gave Fisk to invest in a Pennsylvania coal mine. Feller with no more sense'n that deserves to go bust."

There was a peal of feminine laughter from the other side of the carved-oak door to Fisk's private office. Harp cocked an eyebrow at Applegate.

"Josie's in there," Applegate told him. And after the barest of pauses: "With Mr. Stokes."

Josie Mansfield, Harp decided, might be of as much use to him as the absent Fisk. She did a lot of the recruiting of girls for his shows—as well as for the special parties he arranged for businessmen whose gratitude would be useful to him.

Harp opened Fisk's door and stepped into his office.

Josephine Mansfield was lounging back in Fisk's upholstered swivel chair, her feet up on his desk. It wasn't, Harp thought, exactly a graceful pose for a woman. But grace was not what Josie sold. A plump and pretty strumpet from San Francisco's Barbary Coast, she oozed uninhibited sensuality—in any pose—and Fisk was crazy about her. For the last two years she had been living in a house he had bought for her just one block away from his Grand Opera House.

Her skirt and silk petticoats were rucked up above her chubby knees, showing off black-and-yellow-striped stockings. Her red tasseled boots rested on either side of a caricature statuette of Fisk. It showed him striding along in military uniform, his rotund body disproportionately small, his head very big and his imperial mustache enormous. Fisk kept it in a place of honor on his desk, having a good sense of humor about himself.

Harp wondered if he would take it with the same good humor when he discovered what some others already knew: that his mistress had recently become the mistress of Edwin Stokes, as well.

Stokes was at the moment rinsing his hands in a gold-rimmed

blue basin at the marble washstand in one corner of Fisk's office.
He was a handsome, athletic gentleman from Philadelphia's Main
Line who was involved with Fisk in a number of Wall Street deals.
Josie had been gazing fondly at Stokes's wide shoulders and lean
hips when Harp came in. Swinging her gaze from Stokes to Harp,
she said, without rancor, "Ain't nobody ever taught you to knock
first, Harp? You coulda walked in on an embarrassing situation."

Stokes dried his hands with a flowered towel as he turned to eye
Harp. "Fortunately, there is nothing embarrassing going on
here."

"Not this second, anyway," Josie added, grinning at both of
them.

Stokes hung up the towel and shook Harp's hand. "If you're
looking for Jim . . ."

"No," Harp told him. "It's Josie I want to talk with."

"Go right ahead," Stokes said, settling into a padded leather
visitor's chair and gesturing for Harp to take one of the others.

Harp could think of no reason to exclude Stokes from this conversation. He sat down and asked Josie, "Do you know of a young
woman named Alice Olcott? Jim may have given her a job on the
stage sometime in the past few months."

Josie dropped her legs off the desk and took a cigarette from a
gold-and-silver box while she frowned over the name. Stokes came
smoothly to his feet, plucking a match from a porcelain holder on
the desk, striking it against the holder's ribbed side and leaning
across the desk to light Josie's cigarette.

She took a drag and let the smoke trickle from her lips.
"Thanks, Eddie." She looked to Harp as Stokes sat down. "Eddie's always such a perfect gentleman," she said with a touch of
mockery but more of fondness.

"Alice Olcott," Harp repeated.

"Yeah, sure I remember her," Josie said. "Pretty girl with nice
blonde hair and a juicy figure. And a funny New England accent."
She turned to Stokes. "Remember, Eddie? We were there when
Jim gave her a stage audition and we talked about that accent."

Stokes nodded. "Actually, her accent was an excellent one. I was
fairly sure she must have gone to one of the better private schools
for girls in Boston. And I remember she had a nice singing voice."

"Yeah, but she couldn't dance worth a damn. Not chorus-girl

dancing. But they can teach a girl how to do that right, if she's ready to really work at it."

"Did Jim hire her?" Harp asked.

"Sort of." Josie gave him a smile. "This Alice Olcott with the funny accent is a little over the hill for just starting out in a chorus line and having to be taught how. But you know Jim. He can always find a use for somebody like her. Even in her late twenties. You'd be surprised how many tough businessmen, smart in other ways, feel beholden to somebody who can keep introducing them to different pretty women. Or no—I guess it's not much of a surprise to *you.*"

"What would surprise me," Harp said, "would be if she went along with the idea of becoming one of his party girls."

Especially when she was trying to climb out of what she considered a life of sin at Emma Wells's parlorhouse.

"Oh, Jim is never dumb enough to lay it out in the open like that with a girl, not first thing. He told her he'd like to give her a job on the stage, only his chorus line was full up right then. But he'd say he wanted her to be available when an opening did come up. And to make sure of that, and prove he was serious about it, he'd pay her in the meantime what he paid any starting chorus girl. Fifteen dollars each week."

That was the normal salary. Not much but enough to live on, frugally. Most regularly employed actors earned forty to fifty dollars per week, and a woman ambitious for a stage career could dream of rising higher than that if she proved to have talent. The stars earned a hundred to two hundred a week. The big audience-pullers like Edwin Booth, Lily Langtry and Joseph Jefferson got five hundred for each performance.

But being a party girl wasn't a single step up that ladder.

"Did Alice Olcott fall for it?"

"Sure, for a while. Jim's good at stringing them along."

"Making sure they're so hungry for that chance on the stage that they're afraid to say no when he asks them to be entertaining at parties for his business friends."

"That's the general idea," Josie agreed.

Stokes, looking a little troubled, said, "It must have been hard for someone like her to accept. She's a girl of good background. That was obvious to me."

Both Stokes and Josie, Harp had registered, spoke of Alice Olcott in the present tense. He didn't think it came out of an attempt to mislead. It was always possible that he was reading them wrong; but he doubted that either knew Alice Olcott was dead.

Josie had turned an irritated look on Stokes. "What's good background got to do with anything? All that does is make a girl too starchy to be any use to a real man."

"Was Alice Olcott too starchy?" Harp asked her.

"Well, she didn't like it. And I guess she caught on pretty soon that Jim only wanted her as a shill. Wasn't ever gonna put her on the stage. Because she quit on him. Stopped dropping by here to check with him. Told him not to bother ever contacting her again."

"When was this?"

"Oh, 'bout three, four weeks ago, I guess. Jim told her if that was her attitude, he'd stop paying her wages. She said he could keep his measly fifteen dollars, she didn't need it anymore." Josie winked at Harp. "Want my guess? I bet one of the big spenders she met at Jim's parties took a real fancy to her. Became her sugar daddy."

"From what I've heard," Harp said, "Jim is friendly with Monmouth Fuller." He hadn't heard it; but it sounded possible and was worth a try.

Josie laughed. "Naturally. Jim's friendly with anybody's got a lot of money. And Fuller, he's friendly with anybody's got a lot of fresh girls."

"Any chance Fuller met Alice Olcott at one of Jim's get-togethers?"

Josie shrugged a plump shoulder. "I don't know, but could be."

Stokes spoke up again: "Why are you so curious about this Miss Olcott?"

"Somebody's paying me to find her," Harp told him. Apparently they really didn't know she was dead.

"Why?"

"That he didn't tell me."

"If that's all you're after," Josie said, "I can tell you where she lives. In a roominghouse on West Twentieth. I'm not sure of the number but I could look it up for you."

"I know the number," Harp told her. "She's not there anymore."

"Then I don't know where you can find her."

Harp turned to Stokes. "Do you?"

"Me? No—why would I know that?"

"If you ask enough silly questions," Harp said, "sometimes one of them turns out lucky."

"Not this time," Stokes said. "Sorry."

"I can tell you who *might* know," Josie told Harp. "Kate Flint. She used to be Jim's main girlfriend, before I came along. And she's the one brought Alice Olcott to Jim's audition. So they must be pals. Trouble is, I don't know where Kate is these days, either."

Harp didn't know where Kate Flint might be at that very moment, but he was pretty sure where she would be by five o'clock that evening.

"Jim used to get pictures taken of his party girls," he said. "To show to interested pals."

"Still does," Josie said. "Keeps them at my house."

"I'm hoping there's one of Alice Olcott."

"Could be. 'Less Jim threw it away after she quit. Me and Eddie were just gonna go over there, anyway. Want to come along and help look for it?"

Harp took a look at his watch. There was plenty of time left before five o'clock. He tucked the watch back in his vest pocket and said, "Let's go."

Thirty-Eight

Pier 28 jutted into the North River at the west end of Murray Street. The steamer depot there was of whitewashed brick. Rising from its roof, front and sides, were huge painted signs:

OLD COLONY ST'M'BT CO.

FALL RIVER LINE

BOSTON VIA NEWPORT AND FALL RIVER

The twin smokestacks rising above the signs, on the river side of the depot, belonged to the vessel that departed on that overnight run each evening, except Sundays, at 5 P.M. It was one of the wood-hulled, paddlewheel coastal steamboats that they called floating palaces. Kate Flint had called it home for the past five weeks. She seldom went ashore for more than an hour, except on Sundays when she visited with friends in the city.

Harp reached the depot at 4 P.M. Passengers, visitors and freight wagons were still arriving. He joined well-dressed latecomers pressing through the passenger entrance with the porters carrying their luggage and made his way with them across the pier and up the ship's gangplank.

A floating palace could be utterly bewildering for anyone unfamiliar with its labyrinthine interior. This one—half-ship and half-hotel—had three passenger decks with 260 staterooms, plus its public rooms, cabins for passengers' servants and a complexity of corridors and stairways. But this was not Harp's first visit. He climbed a narrow internal stairway to a corridor in which passengers, the people seeing them off and porters clustered at the opened doorways to each stateroom. He eased past them and climbed another stairway.

That brought him to a long, oak-railed gallery above one side of the ship's white-and-gold two-story main saloon. The door to the stateroom Kate Flint rented by the week was ajar, like most of the others this close to departure. The interior had a thick carpet, tapestried walls with full-length mirrors, lamps in frosted pink globes and a sculptured rosewood ceiling. And the bed: wide and soft with a velvet-padded headboard, crimson brocade spread and a profusion of silk pillows.

A private detective named Pete Bliven came along the gallery and shook hands with Harp. Every hotel, department store and floating palace employed at least a half-dozen detectives like him to keep a sharp lookout for thieves. They were all former policemen, and Harp knew most of them.

"If you're looking for Kate," Bliven said, "she's on her stroll right now, making sure the gents know she's on board."

Harp stepped to the oak railing and scanned the vast, richly decorated saloon under the crystal chandeliers below. Black waiters in blue-and-gold uniforms moved back and forth across it, serving tea and snacks to small gatherings of passengers and visitors. Several round tables were already occupied by top-hatted card players smoking fat cigars and making frequent use of the gilded cuspidors arranged at convenient intervals on the saloon's wall-to-wall carpet. But Kate Flint wasn't down there.

Leaving Bliven, Harp prowled the ship in search of her and found her, finally, strolling very slowly across the vestibule outside the open entrance to the gentlemen's bar. In the moment that he spotted her, Kate came to a halt, took a small hand mirror from her purse and pretended to become engrossed in a critical examination of her bold makeup.

She was a tall woman in her mid-twenties with a shapely figure and a winsome face topped by a jaunty alpine hat with a perky red feather. Her lace shawl was draped with seeming carelessness to display her smooth white shoulders. Her black velvet gown had a bodice that was a bit daring but not quite scandalous, revealing the upper rounds of her bosom. As Harp stopped to watch her go through her act, she drew a lace handkerchief from her cleavage and used it to correct an invisible flaw in the makeup at one corner of her lips.

What Kate was doing was letting potential clients in the gentlemen's bar get a good look at her. Never returning their glances. She wouldn't do that until after the ship set out on its voyage. You never knew if some of the other men were gossipy relatives or friends seeing your target off.

Kate didn't want anyone to be embarrassed. Continuing to be a permanent passenger required a certain amount of discretion in the conduct of her trade. She couldn't afford to be barred from future voyages. It would wreck her retirement plan.

Reserving that stateroom for herself cost a great deal. But a goodly number of prosperous businessmen often made the trip between New York and Boston, preferring the comforts of a sea voyage to the sooty and spine-jarring train ride. Some had already become regular clients, and her charms snared new ones. Her savings were mounting. Even after what she had to pay out for her shipboard rent and meals—and the generous tips to Bliven and the purser to make sure they didn't let any red-blooded gentleman suffer through a lonely overnight voyage.

Kate finished her little advertising chore and tucked the lace handkerchief back into her cleavage to provide a modicum of modest concealment. When she resumed her slow stroll, Harp moved to meet her.

She halted in surprise. "Hello, Harp—you off to Boston on business?"

"No, I'm here to see you. Can I buy you a drink?"

"Just a small sherry. I don't want to get tipsy before we've even left the dock."

Harp escorted her to the main saloon, which was as good a place as any for her to catch the interest of lonesome gentlemen. They settled into overstuffed armchairs at a coffee table with legs sculptured in the shapes of entwined leaves. An efficient waiter reached them immediately. Harp ordered a small sherry for Kate, black coffee for himself.

"You off the booze?" Kate asked as the waiter left.

"Just cutting down."

"Glad to hear it," she said with motherly concern. "Last time I saw you, you were coming off a three-day drunk and you looked just awful. You're getting too old for that, Harp. Got to think about your future."

"I am thinking about it."

"Me, too. I mean, thinking about my own future. That's why I stick to business now. No more getting lazy and just having fun. I've only got a couple more years at this level. If I don't sock away enough now, I'll be too old for it, and you know what that'll mean. It'll be scummy bars or the river for me. Not a swell choice."

Harp saw the waiter on his way back with their orders. "You've got more than couple good years left," he told Kate. "I hear you're doing well for yourself here."

"Not bad," Kate admitted. "This boat is perfect for it. Fellows with the money, on their own with just enough time to enjoy themselves between two cities where they got to stick to business."

She paused while the waiter set down their orders and Harp paid and tipped him. As the waiter walked off she resumed: "But I'm thinking ahead to summer. When the resort season's going full-blast in Newport. I could get off the boat when it makes its stop there and look for business at Newport's better hotels. That's if I don't have a live one on board who wants my company all the way to Boston. Or coming back from Boston to New York. What do you think?"

"It's worth a try."

"That's what I think too. If it doesn't pan out, I go back to staying on board for the whole round trip."

From the ship's nearby banquet hall came the sounds of a symphonic orchestra tuning up for the supper concert it would begin when the voyage began.

"When was the last time you saw Alice Olcott?" Harp asked abruptly.

It startled her for a moment but then, without hesitation, she told him, "Three Sundays ago. Sunday's when I get off the boat and take in the town, and that's when I saw her. Why?"

"I have a client who wants to find her."

"Oh." Kate didn't ask who the client was or why he wanted Alice Olcott. She knew Harp wasn't open about his doings. You either trusted him or you didn't. "I can tell you where she's living. On Twentieth Street, in a rooming—"

"I've been there," Harp cut in. "She hasn't showed up at that roominghouse in almost a week."

Kate Flint frowned over that, then smiled. "Maybe she's gotten lucky. Maybe Monmouth Fuller's had her move into his place for a while."

Harp had just been about to bring up that name. He was silent for about five seconds, experiencing a tightening at the small of his back, then said, "She's one of Fuller's girlfriends?"

"She was when I saw them together that Sunday."

In Harp's experience this was how it usually happened. You kept pulling at loose threads and most of them turned out to be connected to nothing. But if you were stubborn enough to stick with it, eventually one of the threads began to unravel the entire fabric.

He said, "And you think Fuller's a lucky connection for her."

"It's a lot better'n what Jim Fisk was doing to her. I mean, Jim's got his good points, but he's such a bastard. The way he uses girls for business purposes and pays them almost nothing for it. Fuller can get rough when he's drunk, but at least he's generous with a girl."

"It sounds like you know Fuller pretty well," Harp said.

"Well enough." Kate had a sip of her sherry. "Met him at a party, long ago, and I ended up spending three nights in his place with him. Just three nights, but he gave me a bracelet I was able to hock for almost three hundred dollars, and that ain't bad."

"Not bad at all," Harp agreed. "Where did you see the two of them together?"

Kate took another sip of sherry. "I was taking a Sunday stroll with a friend along Broadway, by Madison Square. Fuller drove past us with his gig and pulled up in front of the Hoffman House. He had Alice with him. A gig's a tight squeeze for more'n one person, but they didn't act like they minded the squeeze."

"Did you speak to them?"

"Just Alice. Fuller had hurried into the Hoffman House before we got to it. I told my friend I'd meet him at Lauch's ice-cream saloon and he went on ahead alone while I said hello to Alice." Kate paused, giving Harp a worried look. "She in some kind of trouble?"

"No," he told her. After all, the dead were free of troubles, as far as he knew. "What did the two of you talk about?"

"Fuller, naturally. Alice said she'd met him at one of Jim's parties and Fuller liked her a lot. She'd caught on by then that Jim was just conning her with his promise of giving her a chance on the stage. So she was gonna break with him, and she'd spent most of the last week with Fuller. I warned her not to get serious about him, on account of Fuller was never serious with any girl for long. But that wasn't news to her."

"Meaning she already knew about that?"

"She said she did. But meantime Fuller was being nice to her. Except sometimes when he drank too much and called her names and slapped her around some. But Alice said he was always sorry afterwards and tried to make up for it. Gave her jewelry, told her he was crazy about her looks and figure. And he was paying her rent and giving her money to buy good clothes. Alice said it gave her time to think about what she was going to do with the rest of her life. Jim playing her for a sucker soured her hopes for a stage career. She thought maybe she'd leave New York and try for a fresh start out West, where her mother is."

"Where in the West?"

"Somewhere in Iowa," Kate told him. "I don't know where exactly. But Alice didn't want to go without any money. She said she was going to wait, anyway, until Fuller paid what he'd promised her to pose for a painting by some artist he knew."

"What kind of painting?"

"Alice didn't say, just a painting. Alice told me Fuller was going to pay her more for posing than he was giving the artist." Kate drank the last of her sherry and shook her head when Harp asked if she'd like another glass. "Maybe she's still with Fuller. Why don't you ask him?"

"That's an idea," Harp said dryly. The carpeted floor shuddered under him as the ship's engine started warming up for the voyage. "What else did the two of you talk about?"

"Nothing else. Fuller came out of the Hoffman House then with Captain Redpath."

Harp repeated the name quietly: "Redpath . . ." It didn't come as a complete surprise at this point. But there was still a jolt in knowing for sure what he'd only suspected before.

"You must know him," Kate said. "The one they call the Thumper?"

"I know him." Harp's mouth was dry. He drank some of his coffee, which had gotten lukewarm. "And this was three weeks ago?"

"A little less. Three Sundays ago. Fuller barely nodded to me. I think the bum didn't even remember he ever met me."

"Did he and Redpath act like friends?"

Kate shrugged. "Friendly enough. They shook hands before Fuller got back in the gig with Alice."

"Did he introduce Redpath to her?"

"No, but they said hello like they already knew each other. Then Fuller drove off with her, and Redpath walked away across the square. And I went to join my friend."

Harp thanked Kate Flint, kissed her goodbye and left as the gong began sounding the ship's departure warning.

Thirty-Nine

What Harp needed now was a conference with Junius Slowly. The fame the Pinkerton Detective Agency had gained in running military intelligence for the Union's General McClellan during the war was more a tribute to its founder's flair for self-advertisement than a result of accomplishments. The Confederacy had delighted in feeding misinformation to the agency, which caused it to grossly overestimate the strength of Southern forces. The small number of Confederate spies it caught were caught after they'd already accomplished their missions. And the Lincoln assassination plots that Pinkerton agents investigated had led none of them to the one that actually resulted in the president's death.

But once the war was behind it, the agency had begun to acquire a number of highly qualified agents. The best of these had since been hired for the grand jury investigations into corruption in New York City's politics, business and law enforcement.

One of the very best was Junius Slowly.

Slowly was not Harp's kind of hunter. He was an accountant with a genius for plucking hidden lives out of accumulations of complicated bookkeeping.

He also had a hidden life of his own, known only to two persons: himself and Harp. When Slowly's fellow investigators told Harp that Slowly was up in Albany looking for something in the state government's records—and Slowly's wife told him the same—Harp knew what it meant.

Slowly was a bigamist. There were his wife and two kids in New York City. There was also a wife, with another of his children, in Albany—and he was employing his usual excuse to visit with them.

He was due to return the following morning. Harp decided to

wait. He didn't want to do anything more until he had milked Junius Slowly.

When the hansom cab entered Bleecker Street in the early night, Harp had it let him out half a block before Greene Street. He became increasingly wary as he walked through the back alley of the block on the other side of Greene Street from his own. The Le Mat revolver was ready in his hand when he climbed the fire-escape ladder and went through the short corridor to the room the shooter had used the other night to fire three rifle bullets into his apartment.

No one was in the room now. Harp looked through its single window toward his apartment across the street. He couldn't see inside it because he'd taken the precaution of closing the heavy inner curtains of both front-room windows after the broken one had been replaced. The curtains were still closed. But a thread of lamplight inside showed through a thin gap in one curtain.

He held himself still for a moment, contemplating that thread of light. It was probably Leland Van Tromp over there, come to pay him a visit.

Harp went down the inner staircase to the floor below and knocked at the door to Hilda Shaler's place. No response. Hilda was already out, starting her nightly rounds. He descended the rest of the stairway and stopped when he stepped out into Greene Street and looked up at his apartment windows, hesitating over whether to go in the front or the back way.

A ten-year-old girl named Francine Bourignard, who shouldn't have been outside this late, came running over to him.

"There's a *lady* up inside your place!" she told him excitedly.

"*Inside?*"

Francine nodded vigorously. "Went in there a couple hours ago. Ain't come out."

Harp experienced a jolt of premonition and with it a sinking feeling. He hadn't given a key to his place to any woman.

"A lady, you said?"

"A real swell," Francine assured him. "All wrapped up in a beautiful fur cloak. *She's* beautiful, too."

Harp gave Francine a nickel and went up the stoop into his

house. He took off his gloves and stuffed them in his coat pocket
as he climbed the inside stairs to the third floor. His door was not
locked. He opened it and stepped inside. The entry gas-jet was
burning. A hooded fur cloak he recognized was on his coat rack.
He took a deep breath and hung his coat and hat next to it.

Louise Vedder's winter parasol and headscarf lay near the glowing lamp on his front room table. She sat in the rocker beside it,
her head leaning back as if she were asleep. But when he moved
around the table he saw those remarkable eyes open, giving him a
steady look.

"Leland gave you the key," he said. His throat felt constricted.

"Yes," she told him, her voice quietly controlled. "He said he
thought I should come here and have a look around. Leland said
you would probably be very angry with him, but he felt it had
become necessary."

Harp glanced toward his bedroom and was not surprised to see
that the lamp in there was lit, too. "I'm not angry," Harp said.
And that was true. What he felt was strong enough, but it wasn't
anger.

"I found something," Louise said in that same restrained tone.
She moved the scarf on the table. Under it was her dead husband's tintype of her, face up. "I think it is time you told me about
this, don't you?"

Harp sat down heavily and looked at her across the table and
the tintype.

"Yes," he said finally. "I guess it is."

He stood in the middle of the room, staring at the door that had
shut behind her when she'd left.

She had listened to him without once interrupting while he had
told her the truth. The look of horror he had imagined so often
had not appeared in her face. She simply looked dazed, disori-
ented. Though she surely must have guessed at enough of it when
she had discovered her husband's picture of her in Harp's bedroom.

He had told her all of it. The whole thing. Her husband's death
at his hands. Why he'd kept the picture. What having it had meant
to him, before he'd ever met her—and since then.

When he had finished she had continued to sit there without a word. Staring at him. And at her husband's picture of her. She shook her head several times, slowly. As if she were trying to clear her mind and not succeeding.

At last she had gotten up and left. Still without speaking to him.

But she had picked up the tintype he had gotten from her dead husband, and had taken it away with her.

Harp turned and went to his liquor cabinet. Filled a big glass with whiskey and gulped down half of it without taking it from his lips. Not stopping until his burning throat choked up on him. Gasping, he lowered the glass and looked at the liquor remaining in it.

Then he hurled it and watched it smash against the wall.

Forty

The next morning was a nasty one, with cold rain pouring out of a gloomy sky and striking the hard-packed snow on the ground with the impact of buckshot. The weather did not help to lift the savage mood that had continued to ride Harp since the previous night. He sloshed his way from a horsecar stop to Junius Slowly's street with his coat collar turned up and his hat brim turned down, head bowed in a vain attempt to keep his face reasonably dry. He stationed himself in a covered doorway across from Slowly's house, wiped his face and waited with water dripping from his hat, grateful that at least his heavy boots let no water in.

When Slowly climbed out of an omnibus at the near corner Harp intercepted him before he could reach his house. He took him into the nearest barroom and sat him down, ordered coffee laced with whiskey for both of them and began milking the grand jury's ace accountant-investigator.

It took Harp almost an hour to get everything Junius Slowly knew out of him. But it proved to be worth that hour, as well as the overnight wait.

The sign above the front entrance of the warehouse dated back to another generation:

FULLER & SON
Dealers in Imported Wines & Liquors
Fine Foreign Groceries
& Havana Segars

A black two-passenger brougham with the initials *M.F.* embla-
zoned in gold on it was at the curb outside. Neither Fuller's horse
nor his coachman looked happy as they stood there waiting in the
steady rain.

Harp went inside, took off his hat and swung it, spattering water
across the small waiting room. He told the receptionist he had an
appointment with Fuller and pushed through the swinging gate in
the wooden railing fencing off the waiting area. Ignoring the receptionist's protest, he marched through a short rear corridor.

The warehouse manager was coming out of the office where
Alice Curry-Olcott had died, carrying a sheaf of business forms
and a black bookkeeping ledger. He stopped and looked at Harp
uncertainly. Harp smiled, gave him a reassuring nod and stepped
past him into the office. He shut and locked the door, hung his
hat on the hatrack next to it, leaned his hickory stick against the
wall.

Monmouth Fuller was crouched at his office safe, locking it.
The coal stove near the safe was red hot, and after the cold outside
the office felt overwarm. Harp unbuttoned his dripping coat as
Fuller stood up and turned to stare at him. Anger hardened
Fuller's jaw when he saw who it was.

"What the devil d'you think you're doing in here?" he demanded.

"We need to talk," Harp told him.

"You came to my home uninvited and now you're here uninvited. We've nothing to talk about. If you are not gone in exactly
one minute, I'm sending for the police."

"We need to talk." Harp took off his coat and hung it from the
rack.

Fuller's reputation for explosions of rage was not exaggerated.
He came at Harp as though launched by a spring, feinting a left at
his chest and driving his right fist at his face. But Mike McKibbin
was right. When Fuller got mad, skill went out the window. Harp
slapped the right fist aside, seized hold of Fuller's left arm and
threw him away. Fuller slammed against the wall, got his ankles
tangled when he bounced off it, fell against the desk and went
down on his knees. A drop of blood oozed from his earlobe where
he'd scraped it on the edge of the desk. But he already had one

foot braced on the floor, preparing to come up and renew his attack.

"Don't be stupid," Harp said. "I'm here to help you, not hurt you. And right now you do need my help."

Fuller hesitated, balanced on one foot and one knee, scowling up at Harp. "What do you mean?"

Somebody was trying to open the door, and finding it locked.

Harp took the photograph Josie Mansfield had given him from an inner pocket of his jacket and held it so Fuller could get a good look at the pretty blonde woman smiling from it. He said, "Alice *Olcott.*"

Fuller stared at the picture, his mouth opened as if he had sudden difficulty in breathing through his nose.

There was a knock at the door. "Mr. Fuller? Everything okay in there?"

"Go away!" Fuller shouted at the door. "I don't want to be disturbed!" He stood up and reached for the photograph.

Harp drew it back out of Fuller's reach and returned it to his pocket. He sat down in a visitor's chair and gestured for Fuller to take the swivel chair behind the desk. "As I said, we need to talk."

Fuller backed around his desk and sat down. The drop of blood fell from his earlobe to his shirt collar. He made an attempt to control his fear. "Talk about what, exactly? I still don't understand what it is you are—"

"Let's not waste time, Mr. Fuller. You claimed you never saw Alice Olcott before. Like you claimed you never met Redpath before he showed her to you in the morgue. But now I've got a good picture of her—of what she looked like alive. That plus her real name changes everything for you. And you know it does. The name Alice Olcott is known to a number of people. People who will recognize her from this photograph. And they'll remember seeing you and her together. Put that with her being killed right here in your office, and you're nailed into a corner you can't lie or buy your way out of. Even Redpath won't be able to save you. Not when it's murder."

There was a long moment before Fuller could find his voice. "I didn't kill her!"

Harp looked at him. "I've already talked to one person who

knows you and Alice Olcott were lovers. I haven't told that person she was the woman who was murdered here—not yet."

"I *didn't* kill Alice, why would I, for God's sake? I had no reason to—" He shut himself up, his eyes narrowing on Harp. Gradually, his look of panic gave way to one of hard, accustomed authority. "All right. Enough of this. How much do you want?"

"To do what?"

"You *know* what. You've already hinted strongly enough. Telling me you've kept what you know from somebody who knows about Alice and me. So don't play games with me. Redpath told me what you are."

"You went running to him after I came to your house asking questions that scared you."

"You take money for finding things out—or for concealing them. Fine, that's something I can understand. How much money do you think you're entitled to for burning that picture—and seeing to it that no one finds out she's the whore that died here?"

"A lot," Harp told him.

"Name a figure. Then we'll discuss it in a businesslike manner and come to a reasonable agreement that satisfies both of us."

Fuller *was* spoiled, Harp decided. He'd been born into wealth and all of his life it had bought him anything he'd wanted—and kept away things he didn't want. It made him easy to dupe. Like anyone surrounded by yes-men who kept reality at a distance.

"I haven't figured out how much yet," Harp said. "How much have you paid Redpath for what *he's* done for you?"

"Not one red cent."

"He's depending on you to show your gratitude later?"

"He knows he can count on that," Fuller said, with a certain amount of pride. "So can you. You have my word on that."

"What's Redpath done so far, exactly, to earn your gratitude? I'd like to compare it with the value of what I'll be doing for you."

Fuller hesitated, studying Harp.

"Let's start with what I already know," Harp said. "First, Redpath pretended he didn't know who she was when he came here with his patrolmen to look at her body. But he did know her, and he knew she was one of your girls. I guess he got to you fairly soon after that, to warn you that you had a serious problem."

Fuller opened a desk drawer. Harp tensed, but what Fuller

brought out was a silver liquor flask. "Let's have a drink. A few drinks always helps to make a business discussion go more smoothly."

He sounded confident now. Fully in charge here. Dealing with greedy inferiors was something he was accustomed to and could handle.

"I don't need a drink," Harp told him. "I need to know what you and Redpath worked out between you."

Fuller uncapped his flask and drank from it—two long swallows.

"Come on, Fuller," Harp said impatiently, "if you want me to cover it up for you, I've got to know how much Redpath's already covered—and how well. If he hasn't done it right, I'm not going to expose *myself* to a charge of concealing knowledge about a murder. Tell me what I need to know, or I spill what I do know. To the authorities and to the press. That way, at least I cover myself with glory for solving the crime. Good advertising for me."

Some anxiety crept back into Fuller's expression. "I told you I didn't kill Alice. That's the absolute truth, I swear it."

"I'm not concerned about that," Harp told him. "I have to know how much Redpath's been able to cover up so far. And what he hasn't."

Fuller took another swallow from his flask. He lowered it to his desk blotter and held on to it, looking at it rather than Harp when he spoke again.

"Redpath came to my house late the night they found Alice's body here. The next morning, actually, but it was still dark. He told me about her murder. I told him I didn't do it. But he pointed out that unless he could prove she was killed by the thieves that broke into my warehouse, it was going to look very bad for me if her real identity and my relationship with her became known."

"He was right," Harp said. "It does."

"What made it worse," Fuller said, "was something Redpath found here, after the first patrolmen overlooked it. Alice's purse, behind my safe. It had her identification in it—and a letter she'd addressed to me."

"What kind of letter?"

"Crazy—it made no sense at all. It said I had promised to make sure she was well taken care of for life, in return for her—as she put it—having surrendered her virtue to me. And that I wasn't keeping my promise. It said that unless I did, she was going to get a lawyer and expose me in court and sue me for all the money she was entitled to."

"You read this letter?"

"Of course. Redpath brought her purse when he came to my house that night. To make sure I realized how much trouble I was in."

"And to make sure you understood the risk he was taking to protect you."

Fuller shrugged that off. "Anyone who does me a favor," he said pointedly, looking at Harp now, "can be certain I will prove my appreciation. Generously."

He took another drink. "I told you her letter made no sense, and it didn't. Alice *knew* I am not vulnerable to that sort of blackmail. It's been tried before, by some of the sharpest shysters in town. They couldn't get a penny out of me with stories like the one in her letter."

"Do you think she wrote it?"

"It did look like Alice's handwriting, but I'd been quite generous with her. And I didn't think she was the sort to try something like that. I can only assume that she was forced to write it by the gang that killed her. So *they* could blackmail me later."

"Redpath," Harp said, "is beginning to have doubts about them being her killers."

"No, no—he just hasn't been able to get a confession out of any of them yet. But he will, in time. I'm certain of that."

"Where's her letter?"

"Destroyed," Fuller said. "Redpath took her purse with the letter and Alice's identification in it away with him and burned them for me."

"An artist named Philippe Preud'homme painted a nude of Alice Olcott for you," Harp said. "After I came to your house the other day you paid him to go away."

"So you did find out about him. I was afraid you might. Or someone else might."

"And that could lead to uncovering the fact that the woman killed here had been your mistress."

"Yes."

"What happens when he comes back?"

"If Redpath has gotten a confession to the murder by then," Fuller pointed out, "I won't have anything further to worry about. If he hasn't, I'll simply send Preud'homme away again—for a longer period."

"What's happened to the painting of her?"

"Redpath took it away for me and burned it together with Alice's purse." Fuller had another bracing drink, put the flask aside on his desk. "All right, now you know what Redpath has done to help me—and to earn my gratitude. Now we come to the question of what *your* help is worth to me. I asked you before, name a figure."

Harp got out of his chair. "I'll think it over."

Fuller experienced a spasm of panic. "No, wait! We have to settle this *now.*"

"I can't do that," Harp told him. "I need a few more days to decide." He got his hat off the rack and put it on.

"*I'll* name a figure," Fuller rushed on. "Five thousand dollars. I'd be willing to bet that's a good deal more than you'd dreamed of getting out of me."

"Not nearly enough," Harp told him as he put on his coat and buttoned it up.

"*Ten* thousand! That is absolutely my final offer. I won't go higher than that, I warn you."

Harp picked up his stick. "The thing is," he said as he unlocked the door, "I'm starting to wonder if *any* offer you make is worth the risk I run if I don't spill what I know." And on that note he opened the door and left.

The thought of Monmouth Fuller suffering nerve-wracking anxiety for the next few days did not perturb his conscience.

Forty-One

Sleet was mixing with the rain when he reached the Thirteenth Precinct police station, and the temperature was dropping steadily. Inside the station house Harp found Sergeant Quinn upstairs in the dormitory, relaxing during his stint on reserve duty. Captain Redpath wasn't in the station at the moment, which was a relief. But he was expected to return before long. So Harp made short work of his conversation with Quinn. Less than five minutes —and Harp was outside again, striding away.

Gusts of wind were now whipping the rain and sleet. Overhead, the multitude of telegraph wires strung between the high poles were beginning to sag under the weight of ice. There was talk of moving the telegraph system underground because of interrupted service every time the wires broke during storms. So far it was still just talk.

In this weather all the hansom cabs were taken. Harp took a crammed omnibus, and then an equally packed horsecar to its terminus in the Battery at the southern tip of Manhattan.

Redpath's townhouse was uptown on East Thirty-seventh Street. But it was unlikely that what Harp wanted would be hidden there. According to Junius Slowly, too many people in addition to Redpath lived in that house. His wife, his widowed sister, an unmarried daughter, a married son with his wife and three children and four servants. Redpath couldn't construct a secure place of concealment without some of the others noticing and getting curious. And any one of them might happen on a less secure hiding place by chance.

Harp boarded the *Middletown*, one of the ferryboats to Staten Island, at Pier 1 at the foot of Whitehall. The gusts had settled into a hard, steady wind from the south, blowing the falling rain and sleet at an almost horizontal slant. It was going to be a choppy crossing, but he couldn't wait for less stormy weather. Fuller would, Harp figured, get to Redpath as fast as he could and tell him about his visit to the warehouse. Might even be doing so at this very moment.

Ferry service between Manhattan and Staten Island went once each hour. By crossing the bay now, even if Redpath moved very quickly, Harp would be at least an hour ahead of him.

Within minutes after the *Middletown* pulled away from its slip, the rain and sleet turned into a heavy snowfall. Harp, standing in the forward cabin with his feet braced apart against the roll and bounce of the deck, looked toward Governor's Island, close by off to his left. He saw it—and then it was gone, vanishing behind a slanting wall of white.

By the time the ferry was halfway across the bay there was hardly any visibility at all in any direction. It surged ahead through the choppy water, steered by compass, its foghorn blasting without letup, its pounding engine and churning paddlewheel battling against both a rising wind and an incoming tide.

Other vessels materialized out of the heavy snowfall and were swiftly swallowed up by it again. A schooner heeling over dangerously, close to capsizing as it disappeared. A stubby tugboat bounding up and down in waves that broke across its deck. A ferryboat returning from Staten Island, the moan of its foghorn joining that of the *Middletown* as they passed each other.

The wind was nearing gale force and the snow had become a blizzard when Harp's ferryboat managed to nose into its slip at Staten Island's Old Quarantine landing. A snowdrift had piled up against the south wall of the shabby depot, almost to its gabled roof; but the wind had blown its north side clear of the falling snow. A sign was being hung up inside the depot as Harp walked through it, announcing that there would be no more ferries between Staten Island and Manhattan until further notice.

That was good news. It gave Harp that much more time for an undisturbed search. Until ferry service resumed—which wouldn't happen until the storm dwindled.

* * *

The road outside the depot was covered with powdery snow too deep for hansom cabs or any other wheeled vehicles to get through. But there were seven horse-drawn sleighs waiting there, driven by bundled-up farmers. Snowstorms presented them with a golden opportunity to charge extortionate prices to transport disembarking passengers to their destinations.

Harp got in line and waited until one of the sleighs returned and it was his turn. He told the farmer where he wanted to go, explaining its location the way Junius Slowly had.

"That'll be an awful hard trip," the farmer told him. "But I'll give her a try for thirty-five dollars."

That was an enormous amount to pay for a sleigh ride. But it was too far to walk all the way in this storm; and the farmer was already looking around for other customers when Harp dug the money out. The farmer pocketed it with a grunt of satisfaction, gave Harp a blanket when he climbed onto the sleigh, snapped the reins and started off. Harp wrapped the blanket around himself against the biting cold, tugged his hat brim down in front and wrapped his scarf around his lower face to protect it from the wind-whipped snow.

They went south along the coast road that skirted the east shore of the Narrows. Nothing could be seen of the opposite shore, usually clearly visible from this part of Staten Island. There was nothing out there but the dark, turbulent water and the moving curtain of white. The farmer turned right after they were past the stretch of handsome villas between Fort Tompkins and the village of Stapleton, heading inland via a series of narrow country roads.

The wind was capricious. It broomed some roads almost clear as fast as the snow fell on them. Along other roads it dumped high drifts across their route. Their horse floundered on through the drifts, while the sleigh it was pulling glided over them with ease. They passed dimly glimpsed woods, farms, hills and marshes. The only sounds were the howl of the storm, the snorting of the horse, the hiss of the sleigh's runners on the snow.

Tilted gravestones, some mantled in snow, others swept bare, appeared behind a split-rail fence to their left. The old Dutch

cemetery Junius Slowly had told Harp about. Immediately beyond
it was the access lane that led to Redpath's country house.

Harp couldn't see the house through the flying snow but he
could see that the lane was now impassable. It cut between rugged
banks of rock, and the wind had swept snow into the lane, filling it
almost to the tops of both banks.

The farmer did try: using his whip to make the horse enter the
lane. But the snow was too soft and deep. The horse sank into it to
its belly and gave up after its first plunging steps. Harp agreed with
the farmer: there was no point in continuing the attempt. He
helped extricate the horse from the blocked lane, and watched
the sleigh head back toward the coast. Climbing the lane's left
bank, Harp trudged across Redpath's property through snow that
came up almost to the tops of his boots, detouring around higher
drifts.

According to Slowly, the house was only a short distance from
the road. For Harp, buffeted by the wind, clutched by the intense
cold and half-blinded by the swirling snow, it was not a short hike.
By the time he could see the house ahead of him, he was gasping
for breath through his open mouth, sucking in snowflakes along
with air to melt inside his heaving lungs. Ice weighted his hat brim
and eyelashes. More was encrusted around his nostrils and lips
and clinging to his coat and gloves.

Redpath's new country house, with nothing around it but empty
fields and the old cemetery, was as Junius Slowly had described it.
A sprawling two-story-and-attic structure in mid-Victorian style of
stone and timber, with gingerbread decorations around its shuttered windows and tall chimneys. And it was not quite finished.
Pillars stood waiting to support a ground-floor porch and second-
floor balcony, but they had not been roofed as yet.

The house faced south, and snow was banked against it there,
partly blocking the front door and the ground floor windows to
either side of it. Above that, icicles as thick and long as cow legs
hung from a rain gutter under the eaves.

Harp, shivering and sweating inside his ice-sheathed coat, did
not pause for a long study of the exterior. Its sheltering interior
was what he wanted, urgently. He circled around the building,
ploughing through the snow to the area behind it. The back of the
house, facing north, was in the lee of the storm, and the bulk of

the house acted as a windbreak, protecting it from most of the blown snow.

He did not waste time on trying to open the back door with his picklock. Inside his frozen gloves his fingers were too numbed to make quick use of it. He rammed his boot heel against the door just above the latch, breaking the lock, trudged inside and shoved the door shut behind him.

Forty-Two

With all of the shutters closed, the interior was dark. Harp felt his way along the wall until he touched a window. Unlocking and opening it, he reached through and unlocked and opened the shutters. The gloomy daylight coming through showed he was inside a large uncarpeted room with no furniture except a large dining table, a pair of rustic chairs and a carpenter's table with its tools. A wide break in the room's east wall, constructed to accommodate sliding doors that were still absent, opened into an unfinished drawing room. In the opposite wall a smaller doorless opening led to a kitchen and pantry awaiting completion.

Redpath had told Harp, in Billy McGlory's dance saloon, that if he was forced to leave the police department now, it wouldn't trouble him because he already had all the money he needed to support himself, his family and his town and country houses. That, according to Junius Slowly's detailed audit of bookkeeping records, was not true.

Slowly said that Redpath had underestimated the cost of building this country house on the property he'd bought, and had badly overextended himself in trying to complete it. His savings were used up, he had borrowed heavily from two banks and was behind in paying back those debts and he'd had to mortgage his family's townhouse.

Redpath hadn't plunged into debt blindly. Until the grand jury investigations had gotten well underway, he'd had every reason to believe it was safe for him to borrow to the hilt—that he would always be able to pay everything back out of his large, continuing slice of the city's graft. But Slowly's methodical investigation—plus statements recently forced out of people who had made payoffs to

Redpath—were accumulating enough evidence to send Redpath to jail or get him kicked off the police force. Or both.

Once Redpath was no longer a police captain, his share of the graft would come to an abrupt end. He would not be able to pay off his debts. He would lose his country house, and perhaps the townhouse as well. Everything he'd created for himself and his family would be lost.

That was why he had done what he had done.

What was of more immediate interest to Harp, in his half-frozen state, was a large stone fireplace that took up much of one dining room wall. With a stack of sawed and split logs on one side of it, and a bin of kindling wood on the other. Fastening the shutters open for the light, he shut the window and dropped his hat, gloves and stick on the dining table. He unbuttoned his coat with stiff, fumbling fingers and draped it over one of the chairs to dry. Snow was melting off his thick boots onto the floorboards; but inside them his feet, though cold, remained dry.

He was turning toward the fireplace when habitual wariness made him turn back, take the Le Mat revolver from his coat and stick it into his jacket pocket. Then he devoted himself to thawing out. The kindling was old and dry. Harp arranged enough of it in the fireplace and had it blazing in minutes. He added the smallest of the split logs, and when those were burning steadily enough he piled bigger splits on top. Then he stood up and basked in the blessed heat reaching out of the fire to engulf him.

He lit one of his slim cigars while he thawed. But the cigar smoke, combined with the water from melted snow in his lungs, started him coughing. After a few puffs he gave it up and tossed the cigar into the fire. He turned slowly now and then to let his sides and back absorb the heat, and while turning he noticed a hot-air grate in the floor. There would be a cellar furnace to supply the hot air to the different rooms. Unless Redpath had run out of money before installing one. But there was no way from the dining room for Harp to go down and find out.

When he was sufficiently thawed out, he began a preliminary prowl of the rest of the ground floor. To get acquainted with the basic layout, and to spot potential hiding places. He opened each window he came to; then closed them after fastening the shutters open to let in light. Except for those at the front of the house.

Those faced south, and he couldn't push the shutters open against the heavy weight of snow piled against them.

Little warmth from the dining-room fireplace reached into the other rooms. It was like walking through a series of large iceboxes, and the cold began to grip him again as he explored. None of the rooms had their doors installed. Every room had a floor grate.

Harp found one thing he was looking for when he reached the entry hall. A wide staircase, minus a banister, rose from there to the second floor. Behind it a passage led to a washroom and two narrow flights of steps: one leading up, the other down. A paraffin lantern hung from a brass hook just inside the down stairway. Harp lit it and descended.

The cellar wasn't large. Most of the space was taken by a cast-iron soft coal furnace, by fat charcoal-tin hot air pipes radiating upward from it in different directions, and by a well-filled wooden coal bin. Stamped on the furnace's coal door was: PALACE QUEEN FURNACE—WHEELER & CO., UTICA, N.Y. Harp looked into the water pan and found there was enough in it. Checked the draft regulator, and opened the coal door, shoveled a good amount of coal into it and got the fire going.

Within minutes the cellar was almost too hot. Harp unbuttoned his jacket and searched the underground room. He couldn't find any part of it that offered a place to conceal things . . . unless what he was after was under the soft coal in the bin—and that search he would leave to the very last, if everything else failed.

Harp climbed to the ground floor and returned to the dining room. He left it carrying one of the chairs—for something to stand on when examining ceilings and upper walls—and with a chisel and two different-sized screwdrivers from the carpenter's table stuck in his back pocket. He climbed the passage steps to the second floor. More steps led from the landing there to the attic. But he left the chair on the landing and went through the second floor first, opening windows and reclosing them after opening the outside shutters. Up here even the shutters facing south could be opened. None of the snowdrifts banked against that side of the house had as yet reached that high.

There was no letup in the force of the freezing wind or the density of the falling snow outside. But the interior of the house was already becoming warmer with the air from the furnace fire rising through the floor grates.

When all of the shutters were opened, letting in daylight, Harp strolled back through the unfurnished second floor, doing a preliminary scan. Well-off families were fond of incorporating hiding places in their new dwellings. After a while you got to know the most likely places and the giveaway indications. Spotting nothing obvious, he retrieved the chair and climbed to the attic.

There were only two windows up there, one at either end. Neither was shuttered. The attic was subdivided into small rooms. Apparently it was intended to be the living quarters for the "domestics": New Yorkers who could afford them considered it vulgar and undemocratic to refer to domestic help as servants. Only people who had to work as domestics called themselves servants.

Harp began his detailed search with the attic. It took time before he was convinced nothing was hidden there. He carried the chair down to the second floor. But he didn't start his search there until he'd first looked through a window to make sure the blizzard was still raging too fiercely for the ferries to be operating.

It was.

If the house had been furnished, it would have presented him with a more formidable task: requiring a detailed examination of every sizable piece. As it was, there were only the walls, floors and ceilings. Harp tested those as he went from room to room.

It also helped that the house was still uninhabited and, according to Slowly, no workmen had been employed here since autumn. Nobody but Redpath would have had any reason to come here over the past week. And Redpath could expect that no one else would visit the house for at least the rest of winter. He wouldn't have felt a need to get overcomplicated in choosing a way to cache things out of sight.

Except for a bathroom, two dressing rooms and two corridors, the second floor was occupied by "chambers." To call them bedrooms was considered too suggestive. Domestics had bedrooms. Proper people had chambers.

The largest chamber faced south. It had French doors that were supposed to give access to the still nonexistent second-floor balcony. Nothing had been erected out there as yet, other than the tall pillars, half sunk in the snowdrifts below, that were intended one day to support both the balcony and the ground-floor porch. With the shutters outside opened, the French doors, their glass panes glazed with frost, trembled from the force of the wind.

There was something else in the room that none of the other chambers had. A bookcase, its shelves empty, built against one wall. Harp could detect nothing odd about it. But one of the favorite hiding places, he knew, was behind bookcases that looked immovable.

Harp examined every inch of it. Rapping the back of each empty shelf. Using the chisel in an attempt to detach it from the wall. Lying down on the floor to check underneath it for a hidden catch. Getting up on the chair to investigate its top and the ceiling above it with a screwdriver. He found nothing.

He left the bookcase and began to study the room's floorboards. Walking over them slowly, sounding each board in turn with his bootheels. Trying to pry some of them loose with the chisel. None of the boards looked, sounded or felt different from the others.

He was passing the floor's hot-air grate when he noticed the first deviation from the norm that he had come across in his search. There were tiny, shiny scratches in the slotted heads of the screws fastening the grate to the floor.

Harp sat down on the floor beside the grate. He spread out the three carpenter's tools and tried first with the smaller screwdriver. It fitted perfectly into the screwhead slots. Each screw could be turned counterclockwise with unnatural ease.

When they were all out he pried out the grate, put it and the screws down with the tools, then tried to pull up the floorboard ends it had been screwed into. The second one he tried came loose. Under it was an open space between interior beams. Inside the space was a tight roll of stiff artist's canvas.

He pulled it out and unrolled it, face up, on the floor in front of him as he rose to his knees. There were nailholes around the edges of the canvas where it had been detached from its frame.

It was a full-length oil painting of a pretty blonde woman posed nude in front of an oriental carpet hung behind her. She had a young, full figure; highlighted by the artist's touches of golden-pink on some of her curves, making them glow as though touched by warm sunlight.

Harp didn't know the figure. But the face was the same as the one in the photograph Josie Mansfield had given him.

Alice Olcott. Who had for a short period of her young life used the name of Alice Curry. And who was now dead and disintegrating under the dirt in Potter's Field.

Behind Harp, a reedy voice he knew said wearily, "Stand up. Real slow. And keep your hands away from your pockets."

Harp turned his head first.

Captain Redpath, covered with snow and ice that half-masked his face, stood in the room's doorway, his hat and gloves off, holding a police revolver aimed directly at Harp.

Forty-Three

Harp stood up—slowly, as ordered. Increasingly conscious of the gun's weight in his jacket pocket. But not foolhardy enough to try for it as he turned to face Redpath.

"Don't tell me the ferries are running again."

"No," Redpath said. "I got a tugboat to bring me across."

He didn't look or sound triumphant about it. He seemed drained, almost sick as he stood there with the melting snow and ice streaming off him and forming growing puddles around his boots. A powerful man who had reached an age at which his struggle to get here through the blizzard had brought him near the end of his strength. But the gun aimed at Harp's chest didn't waver.

"I should have thought you might do that," Harp said. "Dumb of me."

"We all make mistakes," Redpath said. "I must've made some or you wouldn't be here."

"You made some," Harp agreed.

"Like I shouldn't've left that picture here." Without shifting his attention from Harp, Redpath tilted his head toward the painting on the floor. "How'd you figure I'd still have it?"

"Obvious," Harp told him. "You're not stupid enough to depend on Fuller's future generosity. You murdered three people to get Fuller under your thumb. You wouldn't destroy something that makes it look like *he* killed the woman. You'll need it to scare him into paying off your debts. And to go on blackmailing him into taking good care of you and your family. I didn't find her letter, though."

"It's there," Redpath said slowly. "You just didn't look deep enough."

He seemed to be trying to work something out in his mind. But it didn't diminish the attention he kept fixed on Harp.

"So you forced her to write that letter before you killed her," Harp said. "And then you killed Moe Saul so he couldn't say you were the one who told him about the liquor in Fuller's warehouse, and when it would be safe to rob the place. Like you killed Smuts Coon so he couldn't say it was you that got him to pay some roughs to bust me up."

"How do you figure I'm the one killed Alice and Moe?"

Harp forced a tight smile. "You want me to tell you where you made mistakes. So you can cover them over. Why should I, if you're going to kill me, too?"

"Maybe I don't got to kill you." Redpath took a deep breath. He used his free hand to wipe water from his face, without once covering the eyes that watched Harp. "I'll offer you a fair trade. You tell me the stuff I want to know—and I don't kill you. Not if you give me your sworn word to keep your mouth shut."

"You've *got* my word on that," Harp said. Knowing Redpath wouldn't believe it. Any more than *he* believed in Redpath's fair trade.

"You swear it, before God?"

"Sure. Why not? Alice Olcott didn't mean anything to me. Neither did Moe Saul or Smuts Coon."

"They didn't mean anything to *anybody*," Redpath said. "A whore, a fence and a hoodlum. Scum, all three of 'em. So why should anybody decent care? They're better off dead and the world's better off without them, see what I mean?"

"I see what you mean," Harp said.

"So tell me how you figure *I* killed 'em."

"First of all, there's Moe Saul. I doubt if Fuller would know somebody like him. And if he did know him, why would he have him set up a robbery of his own warehouse? And if he did have some reason to, he wouldn't kill Alice Curry there, and leave her there knowing thieves were about to break in. But *you* did know Moe Saul. You got some of your payoffs from fences like him, for letting them stay in business. According to one of your own men you got extra for tipping them off about big hauls. Plus, *you* did have a reason to want the warehouse broken into. So Costello would spot it, go in to check the place out and find Alice Olcott's body. Setting things up so you can blackmail Fuller into getting you out of financial ruin and keeping you out of it.

"Everything else," Harp told Redpath, "you could have done to cover for Fuller so you could blackmail him. But setting up the warehouse robbery and its timing pins Alice Olcott's murder on *you*. Plus a couple other bad mistakes you made."

A powerful blast of wind rattled the French doors, threatening to blow them open. Harp half-turned to look at them.

"Hold still!" Redpath ordered. And then: "What other bad mistakes?"

"Lower that gun so I can think straight," Harp told him. "Looking into it's making me nervous."

"Not till I'm sure you're being square with me," Redpath said. "And speaking of nervous, let's get rid of *your* gun. The one bulging your pocket there. That way we can both stop thinking about it. No, don't take it out. Just take off the jacket and toss it over here."

"Okay," Harp said easily, took off his jacket—and threw it at Redpath.

Redpath fired in the split-second before the jacket hit him in the face. But it was already blocking his view and Harp was already on the move: jumping aside and hurling himself against the French doors with all his strength and weight, smashing them open. Redpath fired again as he clawed the jacket from his face, but the bullet found nothing but air. Harp had dived through the opening and dropped out of sight.

He landed on one of the high snowdrifts the wind had piled against the front of the house and sank partway into its powdery softness. He was still sinking when he began rolling himself, fast as he could, down the far side of the drift. There was another shot, from above, as Harp reached the bottom. It missed because by then he was plastered with snow from head to foot, blending with the whiteness of the drifts around him, an extremely difficult moving target at that distance.

Redpath must have realized that because there were no more shots as Harp plunged through other drifts, away from the house. Redpath would be making fast work of getting out of the house to catch up with him for a sure shot. And Harp suddenly registered a discomfiting change in the storm. Very little fresh snow was falling now. Though the air was filled with white powder the fierce wind blew off the snow already fallen, it wasn't covering his tracks fast enough to keep Redpath from following his every step.

Under normal conditions that wouldn't have been a problem. Harp was younger than Redpath and would have had no difficulty in keeping and increasing the distance between them. But these weren't normal conditions. The cold was more intense than when it had been snowing, and the wind was like moving ice. Redpath had the protection of his overcoat. Harp was down to boots, pants and shirt.

For the first hundred yards or so the fear driving Harp away from the house seemed to supply enough inner heat. But then the cold began to fasten its grip on him, penetrating his body and reaching for the organs that kept him going.

He ploughed ahead through the snow, detouring around higher drifts, pushing himself to move faster. The faster he moved, the more body heat he would generate to counter the cold. But with no coat to hold that heat in it was lost to the shrieking wind as it reached his skin. And he knew the loss would soon add exhaustion to the ravages of exposure.

The snow plastered to him since his jump from the house had soaked through his shirt, trousers and underwear, and was now freezing them to his body. Icicles were forming in his hair and eyebrows. The cut of the wind brought tears that threatened to freeze his eyelids shut. He had to keep wiping them clear in order to see. His bare wet hands were turning red, burning with frost. If he couldn't soon lose Redpath, or find a way to counter the advantage of his revolver, he was a dead man. Killed by the cold or by Redpath, it didn't matter which. Dead was dead, either way.

He was pushing through snow that came up to his knees, around a drift that rose higher than his head, when his boots slid on iced rock underneath. Before he could catch his balance the wind had bowled him over and he fell against the base of the drift. Snow avalanched down its side on top of him. He slapped some of it off him as he shoved himself up on unsteady legs, and panting and shivering violently, he looked back in the direction he'd come from.

The house had disappeared behind wind-driven veils of powdery snow, but through the veils he glimpsed a dark figure moving between himself and the vanished house. It was indistinct but it had to be Redpath, moving faster than Harp could: because he was using the passage it had cost Harp time and effort to trample through the snow.

Which, Harp realized, shrank his options. Even if he could somehow manage to ambush and disarm Redpath, he knew he couldn't survive against him in a hand-to-hand struggle. Redpath's age hadn't diminished his enormous strength. Not enough. He wouldn't need a weapon once they came to grips.

There was only one way Harp could think of to come out of this alive. What he couldn't predict was whether he could last long enough to accomplish it. At a guess it had taken him at least a half-hour to get this far through the snow, and it had drained him.

He turned away from the oncoming figure and drove himself toward his goal. Every step began to require a separate act of his will to live. Snow had gotten down inside his boots. His feet and ankles were going numb. And his heart was losing its battle against wind and cold, no longer pumping enough blood to his extremities. Nor to his brain. He was fighting a wave of dizziness when he almost walked into the split-rail fence of the old cemetery.

Harp tried to grasp and remove the top rail but couldn't force his hands to close around it. His fingers had gone from red to a dead-white and felt brittle enough to break off. He hooked his forearms under the rail, lifted it and let it drop inside the graveyard. Then, awkwardly, he climbed over the middle rail—and fell to his knees in front of an old granite tombstone.

The propelling force of the wind had broomed the tombstone's face. The weathering of more than a century had not yet quite obliterated its inscription:

HERE LIES YE BODY OF

RACHEL BART

AGED 6

RETURNED TO GOD JUNE YE 3, 1769

Drawing on reserves he was not sure he had, Harp made it back up on his feet. Swayed by the wind, he again looked back the way he had come. It seemed a very long time since he had last done that. Redpath was out of sight behind one of the high drifts between them. But he wouldn't have had to see him enter the graveyard in order to follow him in there. The trail he had ploughed through the snow was deep and clear.

Harp was near the front of the cemetery. He began making his way toward the rear, angling toward one of the higher tombstones. Reaching it, he turned behind it and headed for the next high one. They were arranged in close haphazard order, not in straight lines. That would help. Redpath wouldn't be able to see where his tracks went on until he passed each tombstone in turn. He'd be wary of ambush, and would swing wide each time to a point of view where he couldn't be jumped before using his gun. That was at least going to slow him down . . .

Harp reached the back fence, climbed through the rails and fell down again. This time he felt an almost irresistible urge to stay down. The snow under him seemed to be exerting an intent of its own, pulling at him, coaxing him to lie down in its softness and close his eyes. He remembered the peaceful look on the face of Moe Saul, lying dead on his bed. That peace could be his if he obeyed the magnetic summons of the snow and stretched out in it to freeze to death. There was no pain in dying like that, once you stopped fighting against it. You went to sleep, that was all. Usually with a smile, because you no longer felt cold or hurt.

His numbed legs and arms didn't want to push him up again. Most of his body seemed to have joined in a revolt against doing so. Part of his mind had, too: whispering to him about the bliss of surrendering to the strengthening grip of the glacial cold. He pitted the part of his mind he still controlled, and all of a furious drive to survive, against that insidious, lethal pull.

Somehow he found himself standing again without knowing how he'd done it. Little muscles just under his skin jerked uncontrollably and his nerves seemed to be shrieking in protest. But he was up. He spread his feet apart to keep his balance and looked back over his shoulder. He couldn't see Redpath anywhere behind him, and could only hope that Redpath still couldn't see him, either. Stumbling away on his unsteady, trembling legs, Harp went around the end of a long row of bushes against which the snow had piled up like a high white wall.

When he had that wall between him and the cemetery, he staggered off in the direction of the house.

With his vision becoming blurred, he failed to see a drift directly in front of him and blundered into it, not realizing it until the snow cascaded down around him and buried him to his waist. Cursing, fighting down hysterical spasms of laughter, he battled his way out of it and went on: knees bending under his weight with each step; lungs heaving painfully, gasping frozen air through his open mouth.

He could no longer feel his feet at all. They seemed to have become chunks of lead dragged along at the ends of his shaking legs. His ankles tangled with each other and tripped him. He went down on his side, rolled himself over onto his hands and knees without allowing sleep the seconds it needed to engulf him. Lurching upright, he floundered ahead again, his heart thudding with an ominous slowness.

He fell again. And this time could not force himself all the way up. But the protected back of the house was in sight now, very close.

Harp forced himself to crawl the rest of the way.

Forty-Four

Redpath had left the back door slightly open when he'd rushed out after Harp. Pushing it now with his head, Harp crawled into the dining room, then shoved the door shut with his shoulder. Wishing he could lock it but unable to because he'd broken that lock.

The warmth from the room's fireplace and hot-air grate wrapped itself around him and was sucked in by his panting lungs. He got his boots loose by dragging their heels against the floor, then kicked them off so the heat could reach his feet. It would have helped to rip off his soaked stockings, too, but his frozen fingers wouldn't respond to his will.

Most of the split logs he'd put into the fireplace had burned away by now. But small flames were still eating at a last one, and there was a bed of glowing embers under it. Harp felt an almost irresistible impulse to crawl over there, push his feet close to the embers and hold his hands over the last burning log. But he knew that if he did that, in their condition his fingers and toes would burst and he would lose them forever. Instead, he began frictioning his hands and stockinged feet against the floor, having to use sight rather than feeling to do it right. It was a much less dangerous method for stimulating circulation in them. But it was also very, very slow.

He still couldn't feel either feet or hands but he was too acutely conscious of time running out to wait any longer. He crawled to one of the rustic chairs, shouldered it across the floor until it was against the closed door. It wouldn't keep Redpath out, Harp knew, but at least he would hear it topple over if the door was shoved open while he was away from the dining room.

Harp braced his forearms on the chair's seat and levered himself up to a standing position. Sliding first one numbed foot across
the floorboards and then the other, he made it out of the dining
room and reached the main stairway to the second floor. But his
ankle turned under him on the first step and he fell heavily
against the higher ones. Pains shot up his leg, announcing that he
had probably sprained the ankle. Harp actually welcomed the
hurt. It meant the heat inside the house was starting to awaken
cold-paralyzed nerves.

He dragged himself up the stairway on his knees, and by the
time he was on the second-floor landing welcome needles of pain
were stabbing through his hands and feet, too.

There was no warmth in the master bedroom. Wind and flying
snow dust blew in through the French doors he had smashed
open. His jacket lay crumpled on the floor, one sleeve across the
nude painting of Alice Olcott. He crawled to it, praying that
Redpath hadn't taken time to remove the Le Mat revolver before
rushing out.

He hadn't.

But it was a hard job to get the gun out of the pocket. His hands
felt on fire, his fingers were twitching as the agony of thawing
spread into them. But he still couldn't make them close sufficiently to grasp the weapon. Finally he used the heels of both
hands to pry it out and held it pressed between his palms. He
crawled to the bookcase, braced his elbows on its shelves and
pushed himself upright. His feet hurt badly now, and his swelling
ankle hurt worse. Moving carefully, Harp limped to the stairway
and worked his way down to the ground floor.

The chair still held the dining room door shut. And Redpath
couldn't have broken in anywhere else without him hearing it. He
hadn't expected it to take this long for Redpath to follow his trail
back to the house. He was grateful for what the time allowed him;
but he wondered about it.

Using his knees, he pushed the other chair into the position he
wanted beside the dining table and let himself drop into it. From
there he had a view through the back window of the area behind
the house that Redpath would have to cross to reach the door.
Resting his forearms on the table, Harp separated his quivering
hands and let his gun settle on the table top between them. He

began rubbing his hands back and forth on the table and scraping his feet against the floorboards, which increased their agony as more blood forced its way into them, but he didn't stop. He felt very weak. The warmth of the house had almost dried his clothes; but it had also brought a drowsiness he had to keep fighting against. The torment in his hands and feet helped some with that.

When Redpath finally came into sight outside, Harp understood why it had taken him so long. He was reeling from side to side, unable to walk a straight line. His overcoat had given him a certain amount of protection against wind and cold: but not enough for someone his age. Exposure and exhaustion had sapped his great strength. His arms swung loosely as he tottered closer. But the revolver was still clutched in his massive right fist.

Harp watched him stumble and sink to his knees. He stayed that way for what seemed a very long time, his head sagging and his broad shoulders hunched. But at last he pushed his left hand against the ground, got his feet under him and came on in a wavering crouch.

Harp picked up his own gun with both of his shaky hands. He pressed hands and gun against the table top to still the shaking but still couldn't make his finger curl around the trigger. Holding the gun so that his left hand would hide that inability from Redpath, he pointed it at the inside of the door.

Redpath moved out of Harp's line of sight. A moment later he pushed against the door, then crashed against it. The door slammed wide open, overturning the chair and sending it skittering across the room. Redpath fell inside, landing on his hands and knees. The impact sprang the revolver out of his fist. It fell only inches away from him but he didn't grab for it. All of his concentration was on holding himself up on all fours, shaking with the enormous effort that required of him. His head was sagging and he was gasping for breath, the sound of it loud in the room.

"If you reach for that gun," Harp rasped, "I'll shoot your damn head off."

Slowly, Redpath lifted his head. His face seemed to have aged twenty years since Harp had last seen it. His tearing eyes were glazed as they looked at Harp. But they gradually registered the weapon aimed at him.

Harp finally made his finger touch the trigger, but unsure if he could make it squeeze that trigger fast enough if Redpath took the gamble and snatched up his own gun.

For almost a full minute the two men looked at each other without a word. Then Redpath sat back on his heels, raising his hands from the floor. But he didn't reach for his fallen revolver. Instead, grunting with the effort, he grasped the jamb of the opened door with both hands and hauled himself back up onto his feet.

He looked again at Harp, his face empty. "You got no reason to put disgrace on my family," he said in a voice that was thick and unsteady. "Don't let 'em know . . . about me. Don't tell. Please . . ."

With that, he turned and went out.

Harp sat and watched through the window as Redpath staggered away from the back of the house. Saw him keep going until he reached a snowdrift about fifty yards away. Saw him pause there, then slowly, deliberately begin to climb its side. Sinking to his ankles with the first steps; then to his knees, and higher. He almost made it to the top before he fell, face down in the soft snow.

Harp waited for him to try to get up. But Redpath did not move again; not even to raise his face out of the snow. Harp continued to watch for several minutes, then got up, limped to the door and closed it. He was panting when he sank back into his chair and looked through the window again. Redpath remained the way he had fallen: face down, legs buried, arms sprawled.

Feeling too feeble to move again, Harp continued to sit there gazing emptily through the window. His face and ears burned as the warmth of Redpath's house restored circulation to them. His lips felt cracked, and when he explored them with the tip of his tongue he tasted blood. His hands and feet throbbed, sending shooting pains through his arms and legs. After a time he fell asleep in the chair. . . .

When he awoke dusk was spreading over the bleak white landscape outside the window. But Redpath's dark figure was still visible out there, lying on his snowdrift.

The fireplace was giving off warmth but its flames had gone out. Harp got up and limped to it. His feet and hands continued to ache but they were at least functioning again. He rebuilt the fire, then went down into the cellar. The furnace had burning coals. He shoveled more coal on top of them: enough, he figured, to last the coming night. Back in the dining room he piled more logs on those blazing in the fireplace.

He needed food and a lot more sleep. There was nothing to eat in the kitchen and pantry. And nothing alcoholic to drink: something he wanted more than food just then. There wasn't even drinking water. He went outside to a tin bucket he had seen earlier under a rain spout. The water in it was frozen solid, but he carried it back inside. He did not look again toward Redpath's snowdrift, going or coming.

Leaving the bucket inside the fireplace, Harp got a cup from the pantry. When he returned with it the ice in the bucket was melting back to water. He dipped the cup into it and drank. After three more cupfuls he spread his greatcoat in front of the fire as a blanket and, using his hat for a pillow, stretched out and went back to sleep.

There were dreams. In one, Louise knelt beside her dead husband in the Wilderness, placing the tintype on his chest.

When he woke it was bright early morning and the wind outside had gentled. The clouds had broken and sunlight made the white landscape around the house shine and sparkle. The fire was almost out but the heat from it and the furnace had not yet abated.

Harp stretched himself slowly to get the stiffness out of him. His hands and feet no longer hurt much; and his face and ears not at all. But the swollen ankle had become more painful. After drinking three more cups of water from the bucket he spread kindling over the glowing embers in the fireplace. When they were blazing, he laid three slim logs on top, then limped upstairs to the master bedroom.

Alice Olcott's letter was where Redpath had said: deep inside the opening under the floorboards. Harp carried it and the nude painting downstairs, and burned them in the fireplace.

While they burned he got into his boots, the swollen ankle making getting into one of them a difficult and painful job. But once it was done, the boot's constriction gave the ankle support that strengthened it and dulled the ache. Harp put on his greatcoat and buttoned it up, stuck his revolver in one pocket and Redpath's inside the other.

After putting on his hat and gloves he looked at the fireplace. The fire was dwindling, and painting and letter were ashes. Harp used the tip of his hickory stick to spread the ashes apart on the smoldering embers before leaving the house the way he had come in. He closed the broken-locked door as best he could from the outside, then took one last look at the drift some fifty yards away.

Redpath's dark figure was barely visible, most of him covered by a dusting of powdery snow. Nobody was going to suspect suicide: not with Redpath. He wouldn't be the first person to go out into a snowstorm, lose all sense of direction and freeze to death.

And maybe it really wasn't what Redpath's church would call a suicide. He had probably kept walking as long as he could, and had fallen when he simply could go no further.

Harp limped to the road and started along it toward the Staten Island coast. He was anticipating a very long and painful hike when a farm couple came along in a sleigh on their way to Stapleton. They stopped and took him along with them, refusing his offer to pay. After gobbling down a big hot breakfast in a Stapleton lunchroom, he paid a reasonable sum for the short ride to the Old Quarantine ferry depot.

With the storm ended, all of the ferryboats were operating again and Harp boarded the next one for Manhattan. Halfway across, he dropped Redpath's revolver overboard.

Somehow he couldn't explain his reason for doing so. He was much more sure of why he had burned the painting of Alice Olcott and her letter. Redpath had murdered her—and Moe Saul. But Redpath had died for it, and that had to end it. Harp had no taste for extending vengence to Redpath's family.

Call it his offering to the gods. Did they ever return the favor? Some people thought so. Harp didn't—but cynicism as a defensive posture had its limits. He looked ahead, toward the city the ferryboat was approaching, and knew what he had to do next.

Remembering what Olivia Bixby Walburton had copied in her diary: *God does not love cowards.*

Forty-Five

Manhattan had not been hit as hard by the storm as Staten Island, but many telegraph lines were down and the snow had piled up there, too. The main avenues had already been cleared, however, and several of the more important cross streets were in the process of being cleared. There was a good number of hansom cabs gathered in waiting outside the Pier 1 ferry depot, their charges doubled this day. Harp snagged one and told the driver his destination.

On some of the better residential blocks the cab passed, groups of street boys were shoveling and sweeping the snow from stoops and sidewalks in front of houses. Harp remembered his gang doing the same after snowstorms during his childhood. Remembered, also, the exorbitant prices they had charged well-off families. And how they had thrown pebble-loaded snowballs at the windows of houses that refused to hire them. His cab passed a block where two gangs of boys had stopped clearing snow to battle each other for territorial rights to the block. Harp could remember that, too.

Most of the streets in Murray Hill, he noted, had been partially cleared. He got down from the cab and stood looking at Louise Vedder's house. Her garden was buried under deep mounds of snow but the front path had been shoveled. He limped along it to the entrance door, steeling himself against the pain that shot up his leg from his ankle with each alternate step.

The maid who responded to his knock let him into the entry hall and left him there while she went off to inform her mistress that he was there. Harp hung his hat and coat on the entry rack and leaned his stick against the wall. He did not intend to leave without seeing Louise.

The maid returned and told him Louise was waiting for him in the music room. He limped through the ground-floor hallway to the rear of the house. She stood there with her back to him, gazing through the music room's bow window past the bare, icicle-hung tree branches in her back garden, toward the spire of a church rising a block away.

He stopped a few steps from her. "It was the *war* that killed your husband, Louise. I didn't know him, and he didn't know me. We were just different uniforms to each other, both of us doing what we were sent to do. Without any kind of personal anger between us. You had friends, even brothers, shooting at each other. It was that kind of war."

"I understand that," Louise said, continuing to gaze out the window. "I think you and Simon would have liked each other if . . ." Without saying the rest of it she turned from the window and studied his face. "I'm sorry I left you the way I did two nights ago . . . I needed time by myself, to put what you told me behind us."

Harp registered her use of the word *us* instead of *me*—and looked at the piano, where Simon Vedder's photograph had been on his previous two visits. It wasn't there now.

"I've put it away," Louise told him. "Not for good, but for a while. Along with the picture you took from him. I've decided not to give that back to you."

"It's only a picture," Harp said.

"Yes," she said. "But I'm not. I'm not a picture."

"I know," Harp said, and closed the two steps separating them, reaching out at last for what he had desired for such a very long time. Closing his large hands around her slender arms, between shoulder and elbow. Delicately at first, and then more strongly as he drew her closer. He felt just a little resistance—and then none. When he kissed her, her lips were there, waiting. And after a moment she lowered her face against his chest, and her arms came around his waist and tightened with a hunger as strong as his own.